Insects

An illustrated survey of the
most successful animals on earth

Insects

An illustrated survey of the most successful animals on earth

Publishers · GROSSET & DUNLAP · New York

A FILMWAYS COMPANY

Contents

Published by The Hamlyn Publishing Group Limited
London · New York · Sydney · Toronto
Astronaut House, Feltham, Middlesex, England

THE ORDERS OF INSECTS
Dr Paul Whalley

Phototypeset by Tradespools Ltd, Frome, Somerset, England.
Jacket separations by Culver Graphics Ltd, Bucks, England.
Text colour separations by Vidicolour, Hemel Hempstead, Herts, England
Printed and bound by Group Poligrafici Calderara, Bologna, Italy

Contributors

Michael Chinery is a well-known natural history author and has published many books including *Field Guide to the Insects of Britain and Northern Europe, Animal Communities, Family Naturalist, Natural History of the Garden* and *Discovering Animals.*

Paul Freeman became Keeper of Entomology at the British Museum (Natural History) in 1968. He has been working at the Museum since 1947 and was responsible for the scientific direction of the new layout of the insect gallery. He has written numerous papers on the taxonomy of Hemiptera and Diptera and is particularly interested in midges and insects of medical importance.

Harold Oldroyd joined the British Museum (Natural History) in 1936 and returned after a break during the war when he served as a pilot in the RAF. His main research interest was the Diptera about which he published several books, among them *The Natural History of Flies* and *Collecting, Preserving and Studying Insects.* After retirement in 1973, he devoted much time to writing, translating (especially books on ergonomics) and photography, in particular microphotography. He had just completed work on this book when he died on 3 September 1978.

Dr Brian Selman is senior lecturer at the School of Agriculture, University of Newcastle-upon-Tyne. He has also worked extensively in the bush over much of Australia and published numerous scientific papers on insect taxonomy, systematics and

Ben Southgate is involved in pest infestation and control at the Scientific Civil Service laboratories in Slough.

Dr Paul Whalley is an entomologist at the British Museum (Natural History). Various entomological projects have taken him to worldwide locations. He is both a keen naturalist and a regular broadcaster on BBC wildlife programmes.

Artists

Line drawings by Richard Lewington
Illustration pages 10–11 by Eric Robson
Illustrations pages 15, 38, 44, 55, 46 by The Tudor Art Agency Ltd.

Foreword

Insects are quite incredible creatures. There are so many of them, they exist everywhere from the poles to the Equator, on land and in freshwater, though hardly at all in the sea. Their origins are hidden so far back in the mists of time that early fossils showing their evolution from worm-like animals are virtually undiscovered. When they appear in earnest in the Upper Carboniferous strata (about 300 million years ago) insects are fully formed and winged, and not dissimilar from present-day ones. Biologists are still undecided on the evolution of wings and flight and on the exact relationships of insects to all the other hard-shelled, jointed legged animals called Arthropoda, a group which includes Crustacea and spiders as well. In 'Evolution and Distribution' there is an in-depth discussion of these points which makes fascinating reading.

Flight is the one obvious characteristic that distinguishes insects from the other Arthropoda, and in fact from all other invertebrates. However, even this is not universal as some insects have lost their wings – particularly those parasitic on warm-blooded vertebrates and those that do not need them, such as cave dwellers. A few that are regarded as the remnants of the forerunners of winged insects, have never had wings at all. A universal definition of insects is difficult, though a simple one mentions the division of the body into three regions – head, thorax and abdomen, and the possession of three pairs of legs and two pairs of wings on the thorax. 'Basic Biology', which includes movement and flight, sets out clearly the various life processes.

One of the interesting features of insects is their conservatism: dragonflies in the Upper Carboniferous and Permian strata are not very different from present day ones, and the same applies to other groups such as cockroaches. It seems that successful lines evolved quite early and have remained with little change for millions of years. It is a sobering thought that insects were flying long before the flying reptiles evolved and still remain long after the latter have gone; birds and bats, of course, are quite recent in comparison. Fossil ants and termites with well-developed social life, occur as fossils in amber eighty-five million years old, showing how ancient is this way of life.

At present nearly a million species of insects have been described, but the final total may be twice or three times this number. Even now, more than three quarters of known animals are insects. Not only are insects numerous in species, they are also numerous in individuals – there may be 50 000 bees in a hive and a locust swarm covering hundreds of square miles may contain 40 000 million individuals, weighing perhaps 80 000 tonnes and eating their own weight in food in a day! Insects have also become adapted to innumerable different ways of life and often eat quite unusual food. Facts like these emerge time and time again while reading the different sections.

Being so numerous, insects have become involved in the lives of almost every land and freshwater plant and animal including man. Examples abound and will occur to anyone who cares to look around. The caterpillars of butterflies and moths feed on crops, so do the larvae of many beetles; locusts devastate vast tracts of land in warmer countries; grain stores can be badly infested with small grain beetles; clothes are damaged by the caterpillars of clothes moths. Perhaps, however, to man the most important of all insects are those that feed on his blood and transmit through their bites, parasites causing terrible diseases – malaria, yellow fever, sleeping sickness, typhus, plague, to name the better known ones. These diseases have been responsible not only for much death and human misery, but some have had much wider implications. Malaria is considered to have played a large role in the decline of the Roman Empire; sleeping sickness prevented the spread of civilization into Africa; typhus (jail fever) was until recently a scourge of armies, while plague decimated the populations of medieval cities.

In the preparation of this book, the authors chosen have been able to give good and readable accounts of different aspects of the evolution, distribution, biology, life styles and classification of this most successful group of animals. Each section makes compelling reading and all have plenty to offer to all readers however slight their knowledge of biology. It is hoped that the book as a whole will spark an interest in all who read it, for these little understood but all pervading animals.

Paul Freeman

Keeper of Entomology
British Museum (Natural History)

Evolution and Distribution

The early evolution of the insects

Insects are an incredibly ancient group. The story of their evolution can be found in the form of fossils in certain rocks scattered throughout the world. These are the remains of those insects which, by chance, were preserved in mud, sticky resin, volcanic ash or petrifying springs, often with other animal and plant remains. Fossil insects have been found at approximately 150 localities throughout the world. Over 90 per cent of these fossils have come from just twelve famous localities. Some of the less productive rocks are of great importance however, because they contain fossils found in no other rocks.

The evolutionary origins of the insects are difficult to discern and are the subject of much controversy. It is believed that their ancestors were very early aquatic segmented worms similar to the present-day annelids. These worms gave rise to forms with a limited number of segments, each with a pair of limbs, and a stiffened yet still flexible cuticle of chitin forming an external skeleton. It was forms like these which left the sea and colonized the land. The living animal nearest to these ancestral forms is the velvet worm, *Peripatus*, of the subphylum Onychophora. It is a terrestrial animal with jaws derived from leg appendages and it is found in plant detritus on the damp floor of tropical rainforests. The conditions in which it lives are presumably similar to those in which the first true insects evolved. Fossil Onychophora, very little different from the present-day forms, have been found in Cambrian rocks as old as 550 million years. However, it should be remembered that the transition from worms to true arthropods must have begun well back in the Pre-Cambrian at the time of the establishment of the first land plants. They were possibly the first land animals and had no competitors. These Pre-Cambrian

Velvet worm
(*Peripatus* spp).

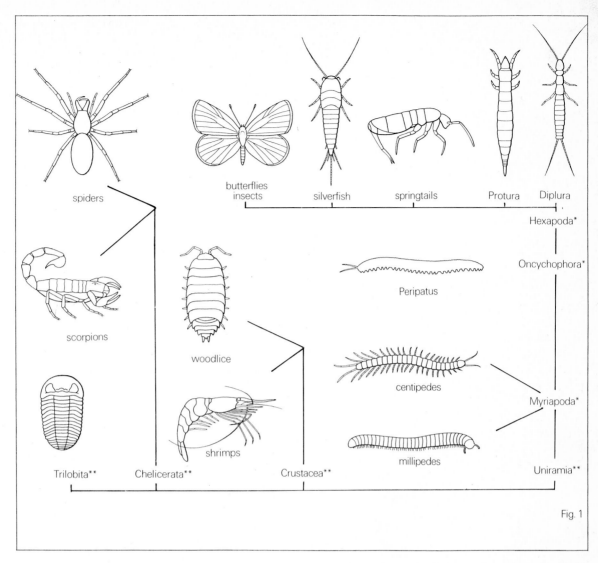

Fig. 1

Fig. 1 The classes of the superphylum Arthropoda. *sub-phyla, **phyla.

spiders

butterflies
insects

silverfish

springtails

Protura

Diplura

Hexapoda*

scorpions

Peripatus

Oncychophora*

woodlice

centipedes

Myriapoda*

Trilobita**

shrimps

Chelicerata**

Crustacea**

millipedes

Uniramia**

ancestors gave rise to the four great phyla of the arthropods (Fig. 1). The phyla include the Trilobita which is now extinct, and the very successful Crustacea which, although mainly an aquatic group, also includes the terrestrial woodlice. The other two phyla are essentially terrestrial. The Chelicerata includes the spiders and scorpions and also the marine sea spiders. The Uniramia includes the Onychophora, the Myriapoda (the centipedes and millipedes) and the Hexapoda (the insects and their allies). The widely accepted view is that the four phyla of the arthropods are polyphyletic: that is, they did not have a common ancestor. Further, it is also postulated that the presence of similar structures, such as compound eyes and biting jaws, in animals as different as crabs and insects is a case of parallel evolution. There are, however, alternative theories. (Also on this point see the 'Orders of Insects'.)

The hexapods are essentially terrestrial in their structure and physiology although some species have secondarily adapted to life under water. The development of walking on six legs seems to have been evolved on many occasions and is usually accompanied by a shortening of the body. Indeed, some crabs and spiders use only six of their legs for walking. The reduction in the number of legs to six seems to offer a distinct advantage for animals with long jointed legs, especially on land, allowing a long fast stride so that the body can travel quickly and maintain the maximum stability. Six legs and a short body have evolved in the true hexapods on five separate occasions and each of these groups is characterized by distinctive mechanisms for leg movement.

The first insect-like fossils were primitive springtails found in Devonian rocks over 350 million years old, before the evolution of the first amphibia and reptiles, and 150 million years before the first dinosaurs. The earliest of these fossils, *Rhyniella praecursor*, had a body divided into three parts: segmented antennae, a segmented abdomen and three pairs of thoracic legs. All these characteristics are also found in insects.

The first true primitive insects were wingless and almost certainly lived in, and fed on, moist rotting plant debris at the edges of the shallow lagoons in which the early plants lived. No fossils of these early wingless insects have been found, although the Thysanura (silverfish) give us some idea of what they might have looked like. However, the Thysanura and all the other classes of present-day wingless hexapods have followed separate evolutionary pathways.

The first true insect fossils all have large

Fig. 2   Reconstructed panoramic view of the appearance of insects in relation to the evolution of other animals and plants from the Carboniferous to the Jurassic Periods. 1   Blattodea – cockroach nymph; 2   Paleodictyoptera – *Lithomantis carbonaria;* 3   Protodonata – *Meganeura monyi;* 4   Megasecoptera – *Corydaloides seudderi;* 5   Paleodictyoptera – *Homaloneura ornata;* 6   Blattodea – *Phylloblatta carbonaria;* 7   *Dictyomylaeris poipaulti;* 8   Protorthoptera – *Gerarus danielsi;* 9   Plecoptera – stoneyfly nymph under water; 10   Protoelytroptera – *Protodytron permianum;* 11   Plecoptera – *Lemmatrophora typica;* 12   Eryops – one of the first amphibians; 13   Ephemeroptera (mayfly) – *Protereisma permianum;* 14   Orthoptera (grass-hopper) – *Metoedischia* spp; 15   Plectopera (stonefly) –

Permocapnia brevipes; **16** Protohemiptera (plant-sucking bugs) – *Eugereon böckingi;*
17 Odonata – Blue darner dragonfly; **18** Neuroptera (lacewings) – *Megapsychops illidgei;* **19** Hymenoptera (sawflies) – *Symphyta* spp;
20 the first Archosaurs – *Scleromochlus* spp; **21** Mecoptera – scorpion flies; **22** Odonata – dragonflies; **23** Leaf-hopper; **24** Hemiptera:
Homoptera – plant-feeding bugs; **25** Tricoptera – caddis flies; **26** Pterodactyls; **27** Hemiptera: Heteroptera (Pondskater) – *Chresmoda
obscura;* **28** Hymenoptera: Symphyta (woodwasp) – *Pseudosirex* spp; **29** The Magnoliaceae – early flowering plants; **30** Archaeopteryx;
31 Dermaptera (earwigs) – *Semenoviola* spp; **32** Stegosauria; **33** Neuroptera – *Mesopsychopsis hospes.*

Era	Period	Millions of Years	Animal Life	Plant Life	Development of Insect Habits
Palaeozoic	Cambrian	600	age of marine invertebrates		
	Ordovician	500	first marine vertebrates		
	Silurian	440	invasion of land by early arthropods		
	Devonian	400	age of primitive fishes, first amphibia and insects	plants with thick bark and short roots, first trees	scavengers of plant remains, climbing insects
	Carboniferous	350	age of amphibians, first reptiles, first radiation of insects	plants with thin bark and longer roots	flying insects, seed eaters, plant tissue suckers
	Permian	270	first endopterygote insects, second radiation of insects, development of reptiles, decline of amphibia	plants moving on to the drier land	leaf eaters
Mesozoic	Triassic	225	first dinosaurs		
	Jurassic	180	age of dinosaurs, first mammals and birds	rise of woody flowering plants, radiation of herbaceous flowering plants	leaf miners and pollinators olfactory attraction of pollinators
	Cretaceous	135	end of dinosaurs, flowering plants appear, second great radiaton of insects	beginning of age of flowering plants	visual attraction of pollinators, beginning of age of flowering plants, feeding insects
Tertiary	Palaeocene	70			
	Eocene	60			
	Oligocene	40			
	Miocene	25	the age of mammals, birds and insects		
	Pliocene	11			
Quaternary	Pleistocene	1	the rise of man		
	Recent	.015	the age of man		

well-developed wings and come from the Carboniferous Period some 300 million years ago. Carboniferous insect fossils are known from deposits scattered across Asia, Europe and North America, mostly as broken wing remains. We know nothing for sure of how insect wings evolved, but it is the evolution of wings that marks out the insects from all other invertebrate groups. It is the key to their staggering success as measured either by numbers and diversity of species, or by numbers of individuals. It is interesting to imagine what conditions may have led to the development of wings. True flight is likely to have been preceded by gliding and for this a vantage point such as a tree would be needed. We may conjecture that some of the early wingless insects were large, flattened species living in cracks in the thick cortex of the first trees in the late Devonian. By the Carboniferous, the trees were larger and more numerous and had smoother trunks. Vertebrates were more numerous, amphibia inhabited the edges of the water and the first reptiles were on the land. This must have made life much more dangerous for these early insects. The need for flattened bark-dwelling insects to get away from predators on the tree trunks may well have provided the selective pressure that led to the

Silverfish (*Lepisma saccharina*), an inhabitant of food cupboards and similar places where it feeds on scraps of paper, flour and so on.

evolution of wings. Many winged insects like *Stenodictya* from the Carboniferous had expanded lobes on the first segment of the thorax in addition to the longer functional wings (see Fig. 2). It is widely held that insect wings developed as expansions of the side of the body, which allowed them to glide down to earth from a tree although it has been suggested that wings evolved from respiratory gills in aquatic insects. The development of wings was followed by the acquisition of powered flight as a result of comparatively minor modifications of the body musculature. However, one point in the theory of the evolution of flight has worried entomologists. This was the difficulty in understanding how the beginnings of a small thoracic lobe could be so beneficial that individual insects with this character would have a selective advantage. Recently insect models have been tested in wind tunnels. These tests discovered that for insects of a body length of about 1 cm and a specific gravity of approximately 1, the airflow along the body was in a critically unstable state. The addition of even a tiny lobe increased the stability. The development of thoracic lobes would thus greatly increase the length of glide of an insect when it jumped to the ground. This size and specific gravity were optimal to give the insect a long glide path and not too fast a landing, so that it might land uninjured on its feet. Thus it was concluded that flight evolved in insects of about 1 cm long, initially as gliding, and that there was a very strong selective pressure towards the development of larger wings. This may account for the comparatively rapid transition from wingless to winged insects which has left no fossil record as far as we know. Insects with both pronotal and abdominal lobes persisted into the Permian, but eventually died out. Basically, all insects have two pairs of wings on the second and third thoracic segments although many have lost their wings secondarily and the Diptera have almost but not quite lost the second pair of wings. The basic uniformity of all insect wings is quite astonishing and leads to the conclusion that flight developed only once in the

insects and that all subsequent insects have evolved from that single ancestral group. Thus the insects are said to be monophyletic. Why insects should all have two pairs of wings and never three or more pairs is a mystery. Possibly the coordination of three pairs was too difficult and the resulting aerodynamics disadvantageous: or perhaps wings on the pronotum were too far forward and unbalanced the insect. However, lack of coordination seems to be an unlikely reason, since the dragonflies are among the swiftest of flying insects yet the wings are completely unsynchronized. When they fly, the wings clash together as they pass each other in opposite directions, causing a rustling noise.

The first known insects of the Upper Carboniferous already included scavengers, plant feeders and carnivores. It seems that in the Carboniferous Period, some groups of insects became dependent for the first time on living plants as opposed to plant debris. Already there were indiscriminate plant feeders chewing at the fronds and smaller stems, plant bugs sucking sap from the tissues and possibly even insects feeding on the reproductive structures of the plants leading to the first plant pollinators.

The Carboniferous insects were divided into two quite separate groups according to the position of the wings at rest. Insects of the Neoptera, which includes cockroaches, could fold their wings over their backs when at rest. By contrast, the more primitive insects of the Palaeoptera, which includes present-day dragonflies and mayflies could not do this. By the end of the Carboniferous Period eleven orders of insects were established. The dominant group was the litter-feeding Blattodea (cockroaches) which have survived the intervening 300 million years almost unchanged and are with us today. The most interesting of the extinct orders were the Palaeodictyoptera and the Protodonata, sometimes called the Meganisoptera. The Palaeodictyoptera comprised large broad insects resembling mayflies which were less specialized than any other known insects. The Palaeodictyoptera is the outstanding group demonstrating the development of pronotal and abdominal lateral lobes. The lobes often show a venation similar to the wings. The mouthparts of Palaeodictyoptera were of two quite different types. They were either biting with mandibles, or sucking with a long rostrum. The Protodonata were huge dragonfly-like insects with a wing span of 12–75 cm and a body length of up to 37 cm. They were the largest insects known on earth. They were carnivorous and presumably ruled the air from the late Carboniferous to the end of the Permian. Unfortunately, insect larvae with their comparatively delicate bodies seldom survive as fossils, with the notable exception of the numerous larval mayflies found in early Permian rocks. By analogy with the modern mayflies and dragonflies, it may be assumed that the larvae of all the ancient orders of the Palaeoptera were secondarily aquatic.

The beginning of the Permian, some fifty million years after the evolution of the first insects, was a time of major change. The forests which throughout the Carboniferous had developed in swampy deltas and shallow lagoons, began to move up on to the dry land as the taller and more deeply-rooted land plants, with their broad leaves and thinner bark began to evolve. Changes took place from a predominantly pteridophyte forest where the trees had scattered vascular bundles buried beneath a thick cortex, to a forest of gymnosperms where the trees had a continuous cylinder of vascular tissue below a thin layer of cortex on the surface. These changes produced many new niches which insects were not slow to use.

The Permian saw the development of ten new orders of insects, eight of which still survive today. Seven of the orders evolved in the Carboniferous became extinct. It would not be until the Quaternary, 225 million years later, that as many orders would be found again.

One of the groups of insects to evolve at this time was the Hemiptera (plant-sucking bugs). These are now specialist feeders on the vascular bundles of gymnosperms and angiosperms (flowering plants) and especially on the phloem cells carrying the sugar-rich products of photosynthesis away from the leaves. All Hemiptera have elongated plant-sucking mouthparts which could easily have pierced the cortex and reached the vascular bundles of the leaves and smaller stems of the gymnosperms of early Permian times. By the end of the Permian the forerunners of the froghoppers, leafhoppers, greenfly, whitefly and scale insects could all be found as fossils. Thus the ancestors of many of the most important pests of modern agricultural crops were present 225 million years ago. Two other orders closely associated with plants also appeared for the first time in the Permian. The Thysanoptera (thrips) is an order of plant-sucking insects feeding on the epidermal cells of the leaf surfaces: they are a modern pest. The Psocoptera (booklice) feed on plant remains including books and seeds, or on the microflora living on leaf surfaces.

It was in the Permian that the truly terrestrial reptiles were developing. Many of these were very active and probably fed on insects. Increased predation in addition to changes in the forest habitat may have caused the extinction of many of the larger, more primitive insects and promoted the evolution of many smaller insects living and feeding high up on the foliage of plants. Whatever the cause, insects of the size of many of those flying in the Carboniferous were never to be seen again.

Before the Permian all insects hatched from an egg into nymphs, which are larvae resembling an adult without wings. The nymphs gradually developed towards the adult form, the wings developing as outgrowths from the thorax. Insects with larvae of this kind are called exopterygotes. Accompanying the other changes in the Permian was a major innovation in the evolution of insects. Now insects were evolved which had complex life histories. They hatched from the egg into larvae which were often very different from the adults which they eventually became. These larvae developed wings inside their bodies and had a new stage, the pupa, during which the wings were evaginated to the outside of the body. Insects which develop in this way are called endopterygotes. They eventually gave rise to all the modern advanced insects such as beetles, wasps and flies. The development of a wingless larva, specialized as a growth and feeding stage, allowed the endopterygotes to exploit two very different habitats and food sources during one lifetime. The smooth streamlined body of the endopterygote larva was now free to burrow and thus insects could exploit almost any habitat including soil, dung, and plant and animal tissues. Wings allowed them to move on from exhausted feeding and breeding sites and even to make use of temporarily favourable areas.

The stage was now set for insects to become the most successful animals on earth.

Continental drift

Until Permian times, 250 million years ago, the fossil record is remarkably uniform throughout the world. Similar fossils tend to be found wherever there are suitable deposits whether they are in North America, Europe or Australia. By the late Cretaceous, eighty million years ago, each of the present-day continents was evolving its own peculiar flora and fauna independently of the others.

These facts had puzzled biologists ever since the classic work of Alfred Wallace (1876) in establishing the zoogeographical areas of the world, although scientific speculation about the distribution of animals and plants dates back at least to Francis Bacon in Elizabethan times.

In 1915 Alfred Wegener startled the world by publishing a little book entitled *Die Entstehung der Kontinente und Ozeane* or *The origins of the Continents and Oceans*. In this book Wegener suggested that the continents were not stationary but drifted like logs on a sea of molten rock. He believed that this must have occurred, for

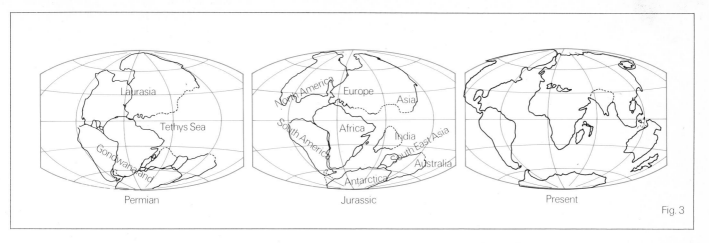

Permian   Jurassic   Present

Fig. 3

Fig. 3 The stages of continental drift from the single continent of the Permian Period to the seven continents of the Present. N.B. The maps show the edges of the continental shelf where the continents fit together, and not the shore lines.

Fig. 4 Section of the Earth showing how the convection currents in the Earth's mantle move the continents away from the mid-ocean ridges. This results in the formation of volcanoes which sink to give atolls in the ocean, and the lifting up of great mountain chains on the continents.

no other explanation could account for the pattern of glaciation, the distribution of similar rocks throughout the world and the uncanny fit of the continents (Fig. 3). Many biologists were attracted to the idea of continental drift because no other theory accounted so accurately for the present-day distribution of animals and plants across the world. Although Wegener was a meteorologist and geologist, most of his fellow geologists and physicists found his ideas far too revolutionary to believe. It was not until the mid-1960s that the theory became generally accepted by physical scientists, mainly as a result of the study of the physical characteristics of rocks and the unexpected movements of man-made satellites. These responded to variations in the earth's gravitational field resulting from differences in the density of the molten rocks beneath the earth's crust. They swung in towards the earth, over the great continental mountain chains where the rock was cool and dense, and out away from the earth, over the oceanic ridges where the rock was hot and less dense. This gave an indication of the pattern of the convection currents beneath the earth's crust.

The theory of continental drift states that, as the earth grows older, the convection currents in the molten rock beneath the earth's crust change (Fig. 4). These convection currents slowly move the lighter rocks of the continents across the globe. The continents move away from the upcurrents towards the downcurrents. The upcurrents occur in areas where the molten rock is hotter and less dense, and the earth's gravity thereby reduced. Most of the upcurrents are now in the middle of the oceans, with the notable exception of the Great Rift Valley of Africa, and are marked by volcanoes and young volcanic rocks. The downcurrents occur where the molten rock is cooler and denser, and the earth's gravity thereby increased. The continents tend to stop moving beside these areas and the resultant compression of the continental rocks tends to throw them up into great mountain chains as in the Andes and the Rockies, the Alps and the Himalayas.

There is evidence that changes have occurred in the distribution of the earth's surface on four occasions. The last great change started in the Permian and is still continuing today, Iceland becoming about 1 km wider every 20 000 years. During these movements the earth's crust frequently split and sometimes volcanoes erupted. As the molten rocks cooled, they preserved within their structure the direction of the earth's magnetic field at that place, in both horizontal and vertical axes. Wherever the rock is found today in the unbroken stratum, it still retains the magnetic axes in which it was laid down. This can be measured in three dimensions and collated with those other areas which

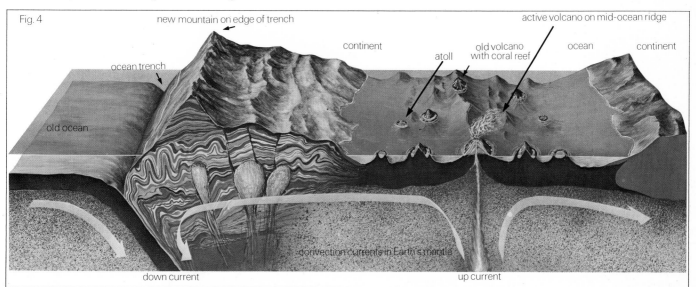

Fig. 4

new mountain on edge of trench

active volcano on mid-ocean ridge

continent   atoll   old volcano with coral reef   ocean   continent

ocean trench

old ocean

convection currents in Earth's mantle

down current   up current

exhibit the same characteristics. This then indicates where on the earth's globe the rock was formed. When correlated with the age of the rocks, the information indicates the drift of individual continents and also the movement of continents relative to one another. The palaeomagnetic data collected mainly during the last twenty years, have finally vindicated Wegener's ideas and have produced a plausible explanation for the distribution of the fauna throughout the world.

It is believed that in the Permian all the continents of the modern world formed a single giant universal continent, almost divided along the Equator by a great shallow sea, the Tethys. Wegener called the southern part Gondwanaland and the northern part Laurasia. This great universal continent began to break up in the Triassic and Jurassic until, by the Cretaceous, there were four main parts. These were Laurasia, India, Africa and a loosely-linked complex comprising South America, Antarctica, Australia and New Zealand. Later, the southern continent split up and dispersed to become Australia, South America, Malaya and Antarctica (initially joined to New Zealand). India drifted northwards and eventually collided with the underbelly of Asia, throwing up the mighty Himalayan mountains. Finally Laurasia split apart and North America began its westwards drift, eventually joining up again with South America. All that remained of the mighty Tethys Sea was Lake Baikal in Siberia with its curious marine fauna.

This drift of the continents was a fantastically slow, long-drawn-out process, spread over many millions of years. Nevertheless, the drift has meant that many of the continents like India and South America have moved through several different climatic zones and their faunas have been subjected to intense selective pressures.

Insect evolution after the break-up of the continent

It was the good fortune of the insects that they had evolved into highly mobile adaptable organisms, many of them plant feeders, by the time that the single universal continent began to break up and the flowering plants were evolving. This was a period of traumatic environmental change in which the climate and vegetation of some places changed dramatically. Besides the climatic changes resulting from the drift of the continents, the worldwide temperature of the earth reached a peak at the end of the Cretaceous Period, seventy million years ago. Tropical conditions moved far towards the poles. This was followed in the Tertiary by a steady cooling culminating in the Ice Ages of the Pleistocene. In the Tertiary Period, the flowering plants evolved the vast galaxy of species that we know today. The insects survived these changes and had the capacity to evolve with the flowering plants, until today they are by far the most numerous group of animals.

The Tertiary Period is a rich one for insect

A fly embedded in amber and thereby preserved for millions of years.

fossils, but the fossils we find today can give us only tantalizing glimpses of the early fauna: the record we have is fragmentary and often due to chance circumstances.

One exceptionally rich shale deposit is at Florissant in Colorado, USA, where there was a shallow lake dotted with wooded islets and surrounded by steep promontories and swampy inlets. All was buried under successive thick layers of volcanic sand and ash. The fossils there are beautifully preserved. The flora was varied. It included hardwoods and softwoods and abundant grasses and herbaceous plants. There were fish in the lake, but one of the most amazing features is the variety of insect life in its incredible state of preservation. These insect fossils show to perfection every appendage and wing vein, the patterns on the wings of the butterflies and scorpion flies, and even the bristles on the bodies of the flies. The shales have yielded lots of beetles including twenty-five species of Carabidae (ground beetles), 100 click beetles, 193 weevils as well as many Nitidulidae (pollinating beetles), Staphylinidae, woodboring and stem-mining beetles. Flies were common, especially Bibionidae (March-flies) and nectar-feeding hover-flies. Also found were Psocoptera, lacewings and thirty species of Aphididae. Some of the fossilized leaves showed the mines made by leaf miners. Eggs of *Sialis* (alder fly) have been found laid on leaves. Adult butterflies of the families Nymphalidae and

Pieridae, and a few moths including Tortricidae (leaf-rollers) and Pyralidae were also discovered. These are obviously highly-evolved families, so their origins must lie much earlier in geological time. The only earlier fossil Lepidoptera known are a few adults and the head of a single caterpillar found embedded in amber from the Cretaceous.

The best-known source of amber is the Baltic, famous for early Tertiary fossils. Amber is the resin exuded from the now-extinct pine *Pinites succinifera*, hardened with time. Often insects became embedded in the exuding resin to be perfectly preserved for thirty-five to forty million years. Ants are common in Baltic amber and are of great interest. Of the forty-three genera found, twenty-four still exist. Eight of the ant species are indistinguishable from living species and have the same castes and polymorphic forms of workers. It seems that some of these ants, then as now, milked aphids. So it appears that the ants were organized into structured societies long before man appeared. Bees are also found in Baltic amber, but almost all the genera extant at that time are now extinct. Some families have seemingly evolved much further than others since Tertiary times. Representatives of most modern insect orders and many modern genera are known from Baltic amber, especially flies, beetles, dragonflies and bugs. The remarkable thing about the Tertiary fauna is that so many of the insects are so

similar to those found today. The great difference is that the world was so much warmer. The range of many of the insects widespread in the Tertiary became much more restricted when the climate cooled down in the Quaternary. Many groups of insects found in Baltic amber are no longer found in Europe. Indeed, some are now restricted to places as far distant as Australia and South America.

The only insect groups absent from Tertiary rocks are those which are today dependent on mammals or birds as parasites, bloodsuckers or dung feeders. The orders Mallophaga (feather lice) and Siphunculata (sucking lice) evolved late in geological time and are unknown as fossils. Fleas, however, appeared in the fossil record as early as the Tertiary. So the Tertiary Period was a time which saw the development of innumerable species of insects especially those associated with flowering plants. Today the families which feed on flowering plants have more species than any other families. The weevils with 50 000 species and the leaf beetles with 45 000 species are the largest families of animals on earth.

Insect pollination and the rise of the flowering plants

The evolution of elaborate, colourful and scented flowers is intimately associated with the evolution of insects. Indeed, in the Tertiary,

Left
Insect pollination
on *Anthurium* spp.

the huge increase in the number of species of flowering plants was accompanied by a parallel increase in the number of species of insects. This continued until each became by far the largest group in their respective kingdoms. All over the world today the greatest diversity of insects accompanies the greatest diversity of flowering plants. Unfortunately, little is known of the early origins of either the flowering plants or their relationships with insects. It is still as Darwin described it, 'an abominable mystery'. There is strong evidence that beetles fed indiscriminately on the inflorescences of plants of many kinds in the early Mesozoic. This is also probably true of cockroaches, thrips, bugs and the more primitive flies. These groups were well represented in the Triassic and today they are indiscriminate visitors to a wide variety of flowers. These are the groups which even today form the majority of insects associated with the more primitive plants like cycads (the Biblical palms), conifers, palms and ferns.

It is usually agreed that the first flowering plants were probably trees, although all kinds of vegetation including herbaceous plants are represented among the first angiosperm fossils. These plants had hermaphrodite flowers, a prerequisite for pollination by pollen-feeding beetles. Even today, many of the more primitive flowering plants including waterlilies, magnolias and wintersweets, are beetle-pollinated and many primitive flowers temporarily trap the beetles on the reproductive organs.

Insect pollination confers certain advantages on flowering plants. When a plant relies on the wind for pollination, it has to produce large amounts of pollen. However, when a flower is insect pollinated there is very little wastage because the pollen is carried directly from one flower to another. Insect pollination almost ensures the fertilization of the plants even when they are living in complex communities where there may be large numbers of species, often with the individuals of each species widely separated from one another. An outstanding example of this may be seen in the Brazilian tropical rainforest. In $3\frac{1}{2}$ hectares there may be 1 482 individuals from as many as 179 different species of trees belonging to 48 different plant families. Insect pollination is especially advantageous in the very still air and moist atmosphere of these rainforests.

The development of flowers containing nectar in spurs made possible the evolution of the flower-feeding Hymenoptera, Lepidoptera and Diptera. Many of these higher insects have developed as precision mechanisms for transferring pollen from one flower to another, conferring on plants the advantages of cross-fertilization. Some 20 000 species of bees are entirely dependent on flowers for their food: the geographical and ecological distribution of the bees almost perfectly correlates with that of the angiosperms. Thus the distribution of the monkshoods (*Aconitum* spp) is determined by the distribution of bees of the genus *Bombus*.

Right
Fleabane (*Pulicaria dysenterica*) photographed in white light (above) and ultraviolet light (below).

Many bees will only visit one particular species of flower to collect pollen but will visit a much wider range of flowers to collect nectar. There are some bees that are confined to only one species of plant. These plants usually have certain specialized structures which make it easy for that particular species of bee to visit and pollinate it.

It is, however, rare for a flower to be restricted to a single species for pollination. Most have several visitors of varying importance as pollinators. This means that if there are very few individuals of a particular species of insect around in a certain year, still there will be other species which can pollinate the plant. Therefore in such a way the survival of the plant is ensured.

Although plants themselves cannot move, insect pollination gives each flower access to a wide range of characters. Flowering plants therefore have continuity of genetic material within an infinitely variable range of characters. As a result of the survival and subsequent breeding of the fittest individuals, the species can respond to nearly all forms of adversity.

In many flowers where the insects are attracted by nectar, the sexes have become secondarily separated. This is achieved in various ways. Sometimes individual plants are of a single sex or individual flowers are of different sexes. Sometimes the different sexual parts of each flower mature at different times. Primroses have two different kinds of hermaphrodite flowers on different plants (polymorphism). All the flowers on a primrose plant are either thrum-eyed with long anthers and stigmas on short styles; or pin-eyed with short anthers and long styles (Fig. 5). This mechanism ensures that insects cannot pollinate the flowers with pollen from the same flower or even with pollen from the same plant or any other plant of the same polymorphic form.

Insects can only pollinate flowers if they are first attracted to them. Most of the characteristics that we associate with flowers have evolved as insect attractants (Fig. 6). Shape, colour, scent and nectar all attract insects. Indeed, the evolution of flowers is almost certainly the direct product of insect pollination. Most flowers have stimuli which attract insects over long distances, and separate short-distance stimuli which attract the insect immediately before or after it reaches the flower. Both stimuli are usually scents or colours and often more than one signal must be present at the correct intensity to elicit a response. Colour is very important in attracting insects to flowers. Most insects have very good colour vision but few insects see red. This colour is apparently indistinguishable from black. However, they can see ultraviolet in addition to the visible spectrum. Many night-flying moths are strongly attracted to white and many moth-pollinated flowers have a large, easily-seen disc of white

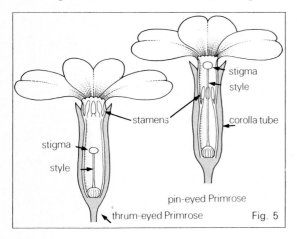

Fig. 5 Heterostyly: the thrum and pin-eyed flowers of Primroses (*Primula vulgaris*). The pin-eyed flowers are homozygous recessives and have the stamens half-way up the corolla tube while the style reaches the top. The thrum-eyed flowers are heterozygous and have the stamens at the top of the corolla tube while the style is short with its stigma only half-way up. Each plant has flowers of only one type. Pollination is normally between flowers of different types to give a Mendelian backcross producing progeny with equal numbers of each type of flower.

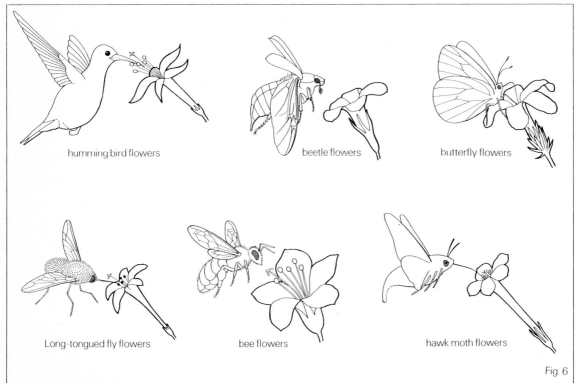

Fig. 6 The diversity of pollination mechanisms in flowers of the family Polemonaceae (the Phlox family) and their pollinators.

Flowers as a crop –
Freesia and bee.

petals. Often these flowers are strongly scented, attracting moths flying downwind of them from considerable distances. Summer jasmine, tobacco (*Nicotiana*) and honeysuckle are good examples of moth-pollinated flowers. Plants with brightly coloured tubular flowers are often pollinated by day-flying moths, butterflies or even by birds. Familiar examples include valerian and buddleia. The alpine flowers of New Zealand are particularly interesting because social bees and other members of the higher Hymenoptera were absent from the islands until they were introduced by man. Most of the flowers are white irrespective of their genera: even gentians and forget-me-nots are white and not a bee-attracting blue. These white flowers are pollinated mainly by beetles, flies or moths. *Ranunculus glacialis*, a very high European alpine, also has white flowers but these change to pink after pollination. This increases the chances of the unpollinated flowers being visited by an insect.

Insects are able to profit from past experience. They must benefit from their visits to a flower or they will quickly learn to stay away. Almost all insect visitors to flowers feed either on the nectar or on part of the pollen, though a few plants lure insects to their flowers by subterfuge and ensnare them in traps. Many flowers direct the insect towards the nectaries, past the stamens and stigmas, by means of special guide lines. Sometimes these are visible to the human eye although often they can be appreciated by man only as a result of taking a photograph on ultraviolet-sensitive film. The habit of flower feeding has evolved until some 165000 species including the whole of the Lepidoptera are primarily specialized nectar feeders. Their mouthparts are modified to form a long sucking proboscis. This is also true for a significant number of species belonging to the orders Hymenoptera and Diptera, and also occurs in some families of Coleoptera including some nectar-feeding species of Meloidae. Some of the Lepidoptera are secondarily adapted to feed on other insect foods such as moist dung and even blood. Several genera have developed sharp-toothed probosci, which normally pierce the skin of fruit, including oranges, and feed on the juice. One species in Malaya, *Calpe eustrigata*, has gone on to pierce the skin of mammals and feed on blood. Many female

21

Cup of Gold of the
Solanaceae family
showing honey
guides.

Eyebright (*Euph-rasia officinalis*)
showing honey
guides.

Pyrethrum – a plant heavily attacked by insects.

mosquitoes feed on blood before they can lay eggs whereas male mosquitoes are usually nectar or sap feeders. The origin of the sucking habit in mosquitoes is uncertain. It is thought that they originally sucked blood and it was at some later stage that they turned to feeding on plants.

Some very successful angiosperms evolved a type of pollen that was spread by wind, and as a result they no longer depended on being pollinated by insects. This has happened in the grasses, poplar trees and plantains of temperate regions. Nevertheless, when ribwort plantains were introduced to tropical Australia, many bees were seen to visit them. Various other genera are insect pollinated in the tropics, but are wind pollinated in temperate zones where it is often too cold for insects to fly.

The distribution of flowering plants with specialized insect-pollinated systems is limited by the distribution of the appropriate pollinators. Many unspecialized plants, when introduced into new territory, have turned into very successful cosmopolitan weeds, unrestricted by a lack of the right insects. In these cases, it is the very lack of specialized insect-pollinating systems which has led to their widespread success.

Nevertheless, insects have determined the flower structure of most angiosperms and continue to limit, in part, the distribution of plants by determining whether or not pollination can take place.

The plant feeding habit

In a walk round any garden or through any field, you will notice that some plants are heavily attacked by insects while other seemingly identical plants alongside are not attacked. This is because the plants vary and the insects have sharply-defined feeding preferences, though the range of plants which could satisfy their feeding requirements is much wider. Animals usually avoid certain plants because the leaves contain repellent substances or do not contain specific attractant substances. Indeed, it seems that plants may have evolved many of the repellent substances in response to the predation of insects. Because insects tended to feed on the most palatable plants, those containing noxious substances were left and could reproduce themselves. Thus the attack by insects exerted a selective effect.

During evolution, flowering plants developed noxious substances like alkaloids, terpenes and glycosides in self-defence against insects. Concurrently, insects produced detoxifying systems for dealing with these poisons. This has developed until many insects have come to rely on the presence of these poisons to attract them to the food plant and to initiate feeding. For example, the leaves of many brassicas contain the mustard oil glucoside, sinigrin, which quickly decays to release cyanide. Sinigrin deters many potential pests, but is an essential stimulus for egg-laying in cabbage white butterflies, whose larvae feed on the leaves. The larvae and adults incorporate into their tissues toxic substances derived from the host plant and this in turn gives the insects a high degree of immunity to many of their potential predators. This interplay between attractant and deterrent substances has evolved until most plants are hosts to a range of insects, which are often confined to that one host or its near relatives.

Part of the ability of insects to develop resistance to insecticides comes about because many plant-feeding insects possess recessive genes which control enzyme systems capable of detoxifying many plant defence substances. The commonly-used insecticides derris, nicotine and pyrethrum are all derived from plants, and derris root ground in water has been used by the Chinese to kill flies for several thousand years.

Often the relations between insects and their host plants are incredibly intricate. The plant may control the sex ratio, fecundity, size and longevity of the final adult stages of many hymenopterous plant parasites. Colorado beetles cannot reproduce on many species of wild potato because there are substances in the plants which prevent the development of the ovaries in the insect. Colorado beetles will, however, feed happily on these plants and the larvae will feed and grow.

In the complicated relations between insect and host plant, there is a delicate balance of ploy and counterploy; but ultimately it is the plant that determines what insects attack its leaves.

When a plant group like the eucalyptus trees of Australia is still rapidly evolving, one finds that its insect pests are rapidly evolving alongside. Both are in the early stages of adaptive radiation and therefore both are still difficult to differentiate from their close relatives. In tropical rainforests with their huge numbers of plant species, there is an extraordinary range of insect species, each feeding on its particular plant host. The high temperature and humidity make for faster growth and a shorter generation time, leading to a faster rate of evolution. It has been suggested that this, allied to the pressure of insect attack, has led to the development of the huge numbers of plant species. In the rainforest individuals of a species are scattered and mixed like a mosaic. The savannah on the edge of the rainforest follows the same pattern, since the pressure of insect attack is maintained even here, but the individual plants are much more widely spaced.

Farmland is the exact opposite. Here, there are great blocks of a single plant species, often of a single cultivar. Damage caused in these conditions, if a migratory pest should chance on such a paradise, could be crippling, far greater than if the same number of plants were scattered over a wide area mixed with other species as in natural conditions. Left alone to revert to nature, the selective pressure of insect attack would turn this land once more into a mixed mosaic.

European Drone-fly (*Eristalis tenax*) mimicking a hive bee.

Mimicry

Many insects advertise that they either are distasteful to would-be predators, or are well equipped to defend themselves. They do this by displaying bold, easily-seen colours, which predators can quickly associate with danger. Other harmless insects escape capture and death by having similar bold colour patterns. Some even evade attack by resembling flowers, dead leaves, lichens or the fruiting bodies of fungi. Mimicry is a term first used a hundred years ago by the famous British entomologist Henry Bates.

When a harmless insect mimics a commoner poisonous model by similarity of shape, colour, sound or smell, this is termed Batesian mimicry. The comparatively rare harmless species derives protection from the unfortunate experiences of the predators when attacking the obnoxious model. The European Drone-fly (*Eristalis tenax*) is a remarkably good mimic of the hive bee, so good that it was almost certainly this insect and not bees which came forth from Samson's dead lion (Judges *14*). The effect is enhanced by the position of the hindlegs which, in flight, are held out at an angle, the tibia folded tightly back against the femur simulating a bee's pollen basket. In addition, the wings of a drone-fly make a buzzing sound, especially when the fly is caught, at a pitch almost identical with that of a bee.

Many insects mimic ants. Often this gains them entry to ant communities and they may live for at least part of their lives in the ants' nest. The advantage gained is not always clear, although it must often give them protection, if only through force of numbers. Some leaf beetles are now so modified to resemble ants that the anterior part of the abdomen and elytra are narrowed to form an ant-like petiole or waist. Twelve separate groups of staphylinid beetles have come independently to mimic ants and in each case they have developed the narrow waist. This and other ant-like modifications can be so extensive that it is often extremely difficult to place the mimic in its correct family. Where ants 'milk' aphids, it seems that the shape of the rear end of the aphid is mistaken by the ant for the head of a fellow ant. When the ant taps the aphid with its antennae, the aphid responds by kicking out with its hindlegs, a natural defence reaction by the aphid. This is mistaken for a friendly response by the ant. At this stage, one ant normally produces a drop of sugary liquid to be consumed by the other. The aphid too, produces a drop of honeydew which reinforces the mistake. Ultimately the aphid produces far more honeydew for the ants than it would normally make and it is, in turn, protected from predators. In Batesian mimicry, the better the mimic, the greater is its chance of survival.

Müllerian mimicry, named after Fritz Müller the German zoologist, is different. This term is used when a number of different noxious species,

Seven-spot Lady-bird (*Coccinella septum-punctata*).

25

Left
The 'Ladybird mimic', *Endomychus coccineus.*

Right
Mantid (*Mantis religiosa*) mimicking a flower.

Below
Grasshopper (*Acanthacris* spp) mimicking a Canna flower. These large grasshoppers lash out with their spiny legs if molested.

often not very common, achieve the same colour pattern as each other. They therefore give the impression of a single species dangerous to predators. Since predators are assumed to learn by experience to avoid noxious food, they only need to learn once to avoid a series of different species if they all display the same colour signals. Thus the greater the number of species using the same warning coloration, the smaller the losses of individuals within each species. Most wasps and bees have a black and yellow striped body which predators learn to avoid. However, many Müllerian groups are mimicked in Batesian fashion by other harmless insects. Many wasp beetles (*Clytus* spp) and hover-flies (Syrphidae) look like wasps. Sometimes large numbers of species of insects in a district mimic one another in a single Batesian/Müllerian complex. Two famous examples are the Borneo and the Mashonaland mimicry rings. Lycid beetles, dung beetles, moths, wasps, longhorn beetles, bugs and many other insects are involved in the Mashonaland complex. In this case the lycids are the commonest and are very poisonous.

In the USA, the poisonous lycid *Lycus loripes* is mimicked in Batesian fashion by the longhorn beetle *Elytroleptus ignitus*. However, the long-horn can feed on the lycid without being poisoned and temporarily acquires the poisonous properties of the lycid. It thus gains the protection of Müllerian mimicry. Batesian and Müllerian mimicry are here alternating.

One common type of Batesian mimicry is warning coloration often allied with aggressive behaviour. Eye spots are often found on the

wings of moths and butterflies and even on caterpillars. The eye spots are nearly always in pairs with eccentric pupils resembling converging vertebrate eyes. Experiments show that eye spots are very effective deterrents against birds, especially when they are only briefly glimpsed. Nearly all eye spots are therefore on the hindwings of adult moths and are suddenly flashed out when threatened.

Instead of mimicking other animals, some insects mimic fungi or flowers. Praying mantids have developed two methods of using mimicry to capture their prey. In one, the mantid is coloured to blend in with the flowers in which it sits. The camouflaged mantid catches the insects coming to feed at the flowers. Other mantids have the front legs modified and conspicuously coloured to simulate a flower. In this case the insect mistakes the mantid for a flower and literally flies into the jaws of death.

Flatid bugs have polymorphic forms of different colours. One species, *Ityraea gregorii*, has a habit of arranging itself to look like a flowery inflorescence, with green bugs at the top and orange ones at the bottom. It is said that even experienced botanists have been known to pick such a 'bloom' in some excitement, only to have it fly away!

One remarkable case of mimicry is found in South America where *Fulgoria lucifera* mimics cayman crocodiles. Apparently many species of birds have myopic vision and they have great difficulty knowing whether they are looking at the small mimic close by (which could be good eating) or a real cayman further away (which

Above
Sawfly mimicking a wasp.

Right
Owl Moth (*Brahmea japonica*; below) and caterpillar of Elephant Hawkmoth (*Deilephila elpenor*; above) both showing flashing eyespots.

could not). Another type of confusion mimicry is found in both butterflies and fulgorids. In this case the insect carries a false head at its hind end and confuses predators by appearing to jump or fly backwards.

Probably the most famous case of mimicry occurs in the Swallowtail butterfly *Papilio dardanus*. It is highly variable and is found throughout Africa as a series of races. Each race has several different polymorphs which mimic a series of different unpalatable models feeding on the poisonous plants of the family Asclepiadaceae. The females in particular are polymorphic. There is no one female form which is common to all the races, but each particular mimetic pattern is found only in the area where the model also is present. Other species of African butterflies also mimic the same range of models. Sometimes only one sex is a mimic, but sometimes males and females mimic different models.

Entomologists have argued for years whether

The African Monarch Butterfly (*Danaus chrysippus;* above) resembling a Swallowtail Butterfly (*Papilio dardanus;* above right).

mimics have evolved by selective advantage or chance. Certainly any individual deviating from the normal in any animal population is usually at a disadvantage. Thus small changes towards the colour pattern of a model are usually disadvantageous. It seems that many butterfly mimics have resulted from a single large mutation and the resulting polymorphic patterns are therefore controlled by single genes. Many other mimetic insects, especially the more bizarre and specialized mimics, probably evolved with their models

over millions of years, and demonstrate parallel evolution. The abundance of a mimic is dependent on the abundance of its model. The model must be common, easily recognized and well protected from its predators. If a predator habitually picks up an insect which is unpleasant, it learns to leave alone insects of that type. If the noxious insect has several mimics which are not unpleasant, the predator's experiences with that type will be sometimes pleasant, sometimes unpleasant. When the number of mimics becomes

very great, the pleasant experiences outnumber the unpleasant ones and the predator is not repelled very often: the amount of protection will be less. The degree of protection is proportional to the number and strength of the unpleasant experiences. When several insect species mimic the same model, the abundance of all the mimics together is determined by the abundance of the model. Once a good mimetic form is established, provided that the selective pressure of the predators is great enough, there is a good chance that the quality of the mimicry will improve.

Although it is usually insects which mimic flowers, it is not unknown for plants to mimic insects. Orchids of the genus *Ophrys* have flowers which resemble the female of various species of Hymenoptera. When the male hymenopteran tries to copulate with the flower, it succeeds in pollinating the orchid.

Distribution of insects

Insects live almost everywhere in the world except at the extreme poles and in the depths of

A Brimstone Butterfly (*Gonepteryx rhamni*) hardly distinguishable from the surrounding foliage.

Orchid of the genus *Ophrys* with flowers resembling female bees.

the sea. The larvae of a few chrysomelid beetles feed on the marine plant *Zostera* (eel grass) just below the low tide mark, but this and the few intertidal beetles, bugs and flies are but a handful of exceptions. None penetrates far below the low tide mark. Some pond skaters may be found several hundred miles from land, but these live on the surface of the sea, feeding on surface plankton.

Collembola, breeding up to 6000m in the north-west Himalayas, hold the altitude record. Staphylinids and tenebrionids have been found

at 5600m and butterflies are known to have bred at 5800m, both above the permanent snow line. Butterflies have even been seen flying at 6000m. Many insects live below ground in caves. Some water beetles have penetrated so far along underground waterways that they are only known from bore holes in Japan sunk to tap artesian water. Other water beetles live in hot springs at temperatures as high as 60 °C.

The seas have always been a barrier to animal movements, though much less to winged animals like birds and insects. The famous American

migratory butterfly, the Milkweed, almost certainly occasionally flies unaided across the Atlantic Ocean to Britain if it is blown off course by westerly gales. Longhorn beetles have been recorded flying 230 miles off the coast of Africa and the Convolvulus Hawk Moth has landed on a ship 420 miles out to sea.

Many common insect pests of crops, domestic stock and stored products have been carried round the world by trading ships. Such insects are specially common in the tropics, where the same crops are now grown right round the world and are said to have a pan-tropical distribution. Prominent among these insects are the pests of cotton, maize and cucurbitous crops like melons. The American Bollworm (*Heliothis armigera*) is a good example. It is now found in all the areas where cotton, maize and tomatoes are grown. Temperate pests have also been distributed in this way. The Codlin Moth and Woolly Aphid, both pests of apples, have been spread round the temperate regions wherever apples are grown.

Despite the ability of some insects to fly great distances and of other small insects, like aphids, to be borne willy-nilly by the winds, the insect faunas of many parts of the world are highly distinctive. Alfred Wallace, in his great work *The Geographical Distribution of Animals* (1876), divided the continents into six zoogeographical regions (Fig. 7). Each region is an area with a distinctive fauna. These faunas developed after the break-up of the universal continent and each was strongly influenced by the climatic history of its own particular land mass. Large climatic changes favour adaptable insects with a wide tolerance of climatic change or those whose preferences lie in the direction of the change. Many specialized insects can tolerate only small changes in climate and their distribution is strictly limited by the temperature and humidity of the microclimate. The longer each region has been isolated, the greater the number of species and genera which are unique to that area.

There are two northern regions, the Palaearctic and Nearctic. The southern limits of the Palaearctic are defined by deserts, from the Sahara in the west to the Gobi in the east, which are barriers as effective as any sea. The Palaearctic and Nearctic are sometimes grouped together as the Holarctic, since they both have temperate faunas which are fundamentally alike. Approximately 500 species of beetles are common to North America, Europe and Asia, although some hundred of these are cosmopolitan pests of crops and stored products, or were introduced in ballast. The steady temperature gradient from north to south across these regions led to the development of belts of vegetation circling the globe. These are belts of arctic tundra, coniferous forest, deciduous forest and dry grassland and shrubs, each with its own distinctive insects. During the Ice Ages, tongues of ice broke up the belts of

Left
Milkweed Butterfly (*Danaus plexippus*), a famous migratory species.
Overleaf
Argus Butterfly (*Atricia artaxerxes*). This species is now found in Scotland.

35

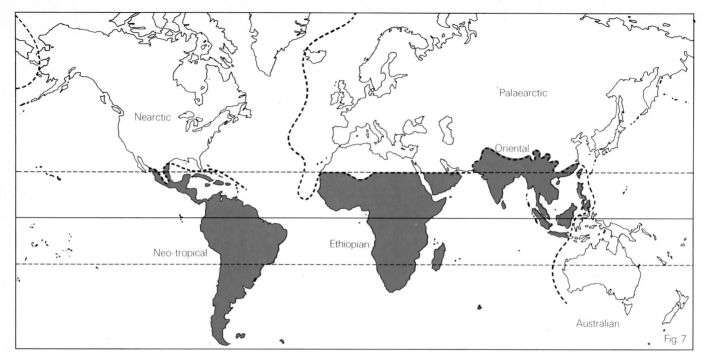

Fig. 7

Fig. 7 The zoo-
geographical
regions of the
world.

insects leaving isolated relict pockets where sub-species developed. For instance the Argus butterfly (*Aricia artaxerxes*) is now found in tiny isolated colonies in North Britain, Scandinavia and the Alps. Further south in the Nearctic and Palaearctic, the two regions have less in common. They have been invaded by species from the three distinct zoogeographical regions to the south, particularly at the wetter east and west edges of the Palaearctic. However, almost two-thirds of the rich Mediterranean fauna and much of the Chinese fauna are endemic. The resulting differences between insects in North America, Europe and Asia are most obvious in the newest orders; for example the only butterflies which they have in common are in the far north. The Nearctic region seems to have been much less affected by glaciation than the Palaearctic and to have received many comparatively recent immigrants from South America and north-east Asia.

The Ethiopian region, that is, Africa south of the Sahara desert and southern Arabia, is a very natural region. It has surprisingly little in common with the Palaearctic, but is clearly closely related to the Oriental region. There are many genera and even species which extend from India through Arabia to East Africa or the southern edges of the Sahara. These similarities have led some authors to combine the two regions into one Palaeotropical region. The Ethiopian region is very varied. At its centre lies the tropical rainforest of the Gulf of Guinea. This is surrounded by a great belt of tropical savannah eventually giving way to desert. Both the rainforest and the savannah are rich in insects. The rainforest is especially rich in Chrysomelidae (leaf beetles), weevils, wood-boring longhorn beetles and Cetoniinae (rose chafers). The forest is also rich in dragonflies and water beetles. The number of endemic species is huge. In the savannah and the edges of the forest, Meloidae (oil and blister beetles), Carabidae (ground beetles) and Lycaenidae (blue, copper and hair-streak butterflies) are found in large numbers.

High mountain tops of Africa such as Ruwenzori and Kilimanjaro have not only a strange endemic flora but also a unique fauna of endemic insects. Mount Nimbus in West Africa has an even stranger fauna. Some species of beetles belong to genera which are otherwise confined to the Drakensberg mountains of South Africa. These insects are related to others on the islands of the Indian Ocean and Austral-asia. They indicate that the old Gondwanaland fauna of Africa has been replaced by a new low-land Ethiopian fauna, leaving relict species on a few mountains and along the temperate coast of Cape Province and Natal.

Madagascar is often included in the Ethiopian zoogeographical region but has long been iso-lated from the mainland. Madagascar has very many endemic species sometimes belonging to genera showing more affinities with Sri Lankan and Australasian genera than with African insects.

The Oriental region can be divided into three parts: the mainland of India, Sri Lanka and South-East Asia. The fauna of India has strong affinities with the Ethiopian region but also con-tains elements from south-east Europe, the area east of the Caspian Sea, Tibet and South-East Asia.

The Himalayan foothills have sharply defined belts of vegetation and fauna with representative species from all the surrounding regions. The true lowland Oriental fauna has comparatively few endemic butterflies because India was isolated for a long time in the Mesozoic and Tertiary, a period when this group was evolving. Most of its butterflies are of African or Asian origin. One very important genus which prob-ably evolved in India, is the mosquito *Aedes*. Later it spread to Africa, and, with the help of man, to South and Central America. *Aedes* is the vector of yellow fever and dengue.

Sri Lanka has a rather different fauna. It has

many endemic species but also shows strong affinities with Madagascar and other islands in the Indian Ocean, with South-East Asia and with India. South-East Asia reaches to Bali. Initially it seems to have remained attached to Australia, but later during the break-up of the continents it joined India. The forests of Indo-China in particular, are rich in endemic species including Buprestidae (splendour beetles), Lucanidae (stag beetles), Elateridae (click beetles), Chrysomelidae (leaf beetles) and butterflies of many kinds.

The Australasian region is very varied indeed. Australia itself has a very high proportion of endemic genera and species indicating its isolation over a long period. This is particularly marked in insect species, such as moths with wood- and stem-boring caterpillars, and leaf beetles, which feed on large genera of plants peculiar to Australia, such as *Eucalyptus*. Scarabaeidae, Tenebrionidae and Isoptera (termites), inhabitants of grasslands and deserts, are also well represented and there is a small element of ancient Palaeozoic groups of worldwide distribution. Australia has a very large southern Gondwanaland element, particularly of freshwater insects from mayflies to beetles, and of Neuroptera (lacewings) and Megaloptera (alder flies). These include the more primitive genera of the orders which had already evolved in the Jurassic, and are also found in South Africa, New Zealand and South America. Australia must have remained in contact with South America and New Zealand long after the break with Africa. Thus many species of mayflies and stoneflies are extraordinarily similar in Chile, Australia and New Zealand. Then there are several groups including ledrine leafhoppers which are common to all the lands around the Indian Ocean. Many of these seem to have evolved in South-East Asia before it separated from Australia. New Zealand has affinities with Australia but has been isolated for even longer. It retains some very primitive groups and has much in common with Chile and Tasmania, but was not open to invasion by later insects in the same way as Australia. This has led to an unbalanced population where some insects, notably Coleoptera (beetles), Diptera (flies) especially Chironomidae (midges), and Coccoidea (scale insects) are extremely rich in species with many endemic genera.

The Neotropical region includes all South America, Central America and parts of Mexico. It can be divided into three distinct parts. One is Chile with an ancient temperate Gondwanaland fauna similar to Australia and New Zealand. To the north-east is a fauna centred on the Brazilian Highlands with similarities to the fauna of the Ethiopian region. This part of South America seems to have separated from Africa later than the southern part. Finally there is a fauna centred on the mountains of Venezuela. These three areas seem to have been separated by a great shallow sea which dried out in the late Tertiary as recently as one or two million years ago. This sea eventually formed the basins of the Amazon and the Paraguay rivers. The Amazon Basin with its very high temperature and rainfall was invaded by plants and insects from the surrounding areas which radiated explosively, producing large numbers of endemic genera. It is an area immensely rich in wonderful butterflies, bugs, wasps, bees, wood-boring beetles, weevils and leaf beetles. This is the richest and most recent flora and fauna in the world.

Islands and evolution

Besides the great continents there are innumerable islands scattered round the world. These are of two types. Many are fragments that broke off from the continents during the continental drift, e.g. the Seychelles. These are formed of old rocks, though some islands have later sunk leaving only the tops of the mountains or of old volcanoes projecting above the surface of the sea. The Galapagos Islands are thought to belong to this group. All have preserved a sample of the flora and fauna of their parent continent at the time of separation, although naturally this fauna has evolved since, along its own evolutionary path.

The other type of island is thrown up as a volcano from the seabed in the mid-ocean ridges. As the oceans widen, the volcanoes move down the sides of the mid-ocean ridges deeper and deeper into the sea, to be replaced by new volcanoes on the crest of the ridge. In the tropics, corals grow in the shallows surrounding the islands and where the volcanoes have sunk below the sea they form the atolls so characteristic of the Pacific Ocean. In this manner rows of volcanoes are formed, tailing off into atolls, each a little older than the next as in the Hawaiian Islands. Islands of this type provide superb laboratories for the field study of evolution. Each island starts as a barren lifeless waste and has to rely on chance migrants for its initial stock of organisms. This stock is then modified by evolution. Colonization is surprisingly quick. After the insects of some islands off Florida had been exterminated by methyl bromide, the islands regained their species, numbers and composition in 250 days. They were found to have a steady turnover, old species becoming extinct and new ones becoming established. Every island appears to have an optimum number of species when immigrants balance extinctions. In old, very isolated islands the rate of extinction balances the rate of evolution of new species. The larger the island and the greater the number of potential niches, the greater the optimum number of species. For many isolated islands, however, immigration is by chance and the fauna is usually unbalanced. Endemic speciation tends to correct this imbalance. On the island of Hawaii it has been calculated that over several million years the many thousands of endemic insect species have evolved from just 225 successful immigrant species. The Drosophilidae (fruit-flies) of Hawaii show a very great proliferation of species, typical of that found in island groups.

The classical study of speciation on islands is Charles Darwin's analysis of the finches of the Galapagos Islands, re-examined recently in greater detail by David Lack. These fourteen species of finch have clearly descended from a common ancestor. One may suppose that a pair or a few pairs of finches originally colonized one of the islands. Free from competitors and predators, with an initially large and seemingly infinite habitat, the population would grow rapidly. The lack of natural selection would mean that almost all combinations of inherited characters would survive and reproduce themselves. If the original finches differed in just fifty characters, a number that is very much less than would be found in almost any living animal, then within three generations there would be 3^{50} possible different combinations of characters. This is a huge number. Only a minute fraction of these possible combinations could ever be realized. It is highly unlikely that the most advantageous combination would ever arise. Eventually the birds would occupy all the island and selective pressure would quickly increase, leading to the establishment of a race of birds with stable characters. If a second pair of finches were to occupy an adjacent island, the chance combination of characters would inevitably produce a different race, even though the selective pressure might be the same. Eventually some of the birds might fly to neighbouring uninhabited islands and the whole process would start again. It is highly probable that each time this occurs the new race will be further away from the original stock. In time, new characters will arise by mutation on the separate islands. Thus a single species isolated on any island begins to evolve independently of its fellows on other islands, and begins to evolve into a new species. Often, after a long time, some manage to return to the island where they originated. Sometimes they will interbreed with the original stock. They will not interbreed if they have evolved further and especially if their niches have become different. The original stock has now evolved into two distinct species. Where different but similar species have evolved in different geographical areas they are called allopatric species. Where they have evolved in the same area they are known as sympatric species. When breeding takes place in a new habitat or island between individuals from two different habitats, it is found experimentally that a greater range of characters results than when the invasion is by individuals from a single habitat. The greatest variety of characters will result when a large new island is invaded by a very small number of individuals each coming from widely separated islands or geographical areas. This is because the smaller the number of immigrants, the greater the number of generations, and thus the greater the variety of characters, before the niche is full and selection becomes intense. Each island population may be likened to a new experiment.

Darwin's fourteen species of finches presumably evolved in this way and now feed on eight different sorts of food, one even using cactus spines to pull insects out of the cracks in the bark of trees. Eventually it may happen that a species that has evolved on a second island returns to breed on the island of its ancestors. This has resulted in as many as ten different species living on a single island, each species with its own niche. The commonest species of finch is found on sixteen of the islands, but is a slightly different colour on each one. On some islands as many as three very closely-related finches of the same genus now live side by side but are separated by comparatively small, yet very significant behavioural differences. Where the ranges of otherwise allopatric species overlap, it is often found that the species develop characters separating them. For example, two allopatric species of termites which swarm at the same time where their territories are separate, swarm at different times where their territories overlap. Although Darwin's finches have been used to illustrate island speciation, the principles apply equally to insect evolution and to evolution in habitats where the 'island' is a mountain on a continent, forests separated by farmland, or scattered fields of cabbages on farms. The difference between these three examples is solely in the degree of isolation of the habitats. Habitat 'islands', in contrast with islands surrounded by water, usually have a higher potential immigration rate. However, a complex habitat like climax forest has many species in many small niches. Its very complexity makes it a very stable community, where pest outbreaks are rare and where it is very difficult for an immigrant to establish itself. Annual farm crops are very simple young communities similar to nearly-isolated islands in the sea. Here natural variation is high in immigrant species and the rate of evolution is similarly high. Thus a sudden increase in selective pressure, as occurs when a new insecticide is used, will quickly select out the more resistant individuals present in the very variable population. The high rate of evolution resulting from the patchwork, unstable farm ecosystem, where selective pressures are fluctuating, has caused many common farm pests to develop a very high level of variation. This has now reached the stage when many agricultural pest insects are more like species complexes than clearly-defined single species.

Continents are but large islands. Single species may occupy a large area. Dobzhansky studied wild populations of *Drosophila* in the field in the USA. These insects have several generations in each year. He found that the proportion of some characters present in the population fluctuated with the seasons because the selective pressures varied with the seasons. He also found that the proportions of some of these characters changed steadily over the years. This happened because the selective pressures were slightly different in successive years, and they acted on characters which themselves were slightly different each year. Thus insect populations progress with time and few stay still. This is genetic drift. When an insect population is spread over a long distance, selection will vary from place to place and the species will tend to break up into a row of new species or subspecies. These are said to form a cline. It is often found that whereas adjacent subspecies can interbreed, specimens taken from further apart along the cline can not.

Speciation may be said to begin as soon as a population of interbreeding animals becomes separated into groups. This may be obvious in islands, but it is less obvious where the geographical separation is on different trees or even on different parts of the same tree. Therefore it is very difficult in practice to separate speciation into allopatric and sympatric speciation. Indeed, some authorities have claimed that sympatric speciation does not exist but that all speciation occurs as a result of geographical separation in the broadest sense. Some factors separating species are very subtle, especially differences in behaviour during courtship, such as the use of different light signals in fireflies, the use of sound signals by grasshoppers, or sex attractant chemicals and colour signals in butterflies. It is interesting to note that some forms of polymorphic butterflies tend to aggregate like with like, suggesting that mating is non-random. This could be a clear case of the beginning of sympatric speciation.

Modern fossils

Insect remains of the Quaternary Period, that is the last million years, are exceedingly common but usually consist of immense numbers of isolated fragments. The fragmentation of these remains discouraged most entomologists from working on insects of this period. Recently a brave few have begun this work with great success. It is a general rule that any deposit containing plant remains is likely to contain fossil insects. Thus they are found in peat beds and in organic silts left behind by slow-moving rivers and streams. Curiously, the insects in these deposits are not representative of their original faunas but include only beetles, fragmented flies, alder flies, the heads of ants, the larvae of caddis flies, the heads of larval midges and crane-flies, a few bugs and caterpillar heads. However, insect fossil beds are probably derived from one small segment of a habitat and the chances are that it will tend to contain only a few common species.

Almost all Quaternary fossils can be identified with species living today without the use of too much imagination. Some of the staphylinid beetles studied by G. R. Coope do not seem to have changed for at least a million generations. As far as is known, no fossil of this age has shown characters intermediate between closely-related living species. At first it seems somewhat surprising that such little change has occurred in these insects over so long a time, especially when many of the same species today have distinct geographical races and polymorphic forms. Just as surprising as the lack of evidence for speciation, is the almost total lack of species which later became extinct. Ancient fossil history indicates that major evolutionary changes, followed by the proliferation of genera and species, have always occurred in tropical climates. While there is almost no information on the rate of speciation in the tropics during the Quaternary, the indications are that it has been enormously greater than in the much more stable temperate regions.

What the recent fossil record shows is the changes occurring in some of the insect orders in Europe and North America especially in response to the ebb and flow of the Ice Ages. Many phytophagous species give a good indication of the changes in the distribution of their host plants. The Oak Weevil (*Rhynchaenus quercus*) has been used to plot the occurrence of oak forest in Britain and this has correlated with the distribution of oak pollen in the same deposits. Changes in the beetle fauna found in different fossil deposits can be correlated with the present-day niches and microclimatic requirements of their descendants. From this a detailed picture can be constructed of the changes in the climate and vegetation of Britain at intervals over the last few hundred thousand years. It seems from the fossil evidence that insects are much less tolerant to climatic change than are plants. Indeed insects can give us a better indication of small climatic changes over periods as short as a few years than can be obtained by almost any other method.

Insects and archaeology

The remains of insects are often found in old refuse pits, drains, grain stores and wells on the sites of archaeological excavations. Insects can tell us much about the food, habits, health and wealth of the people who lived on these sites. One excavation of a Bronze Age well in Wiltshire produced 138 species of beetles. Almost all of these species are found today in the district and have clearly-defined niches. Using this knowledge it has been possible to reconstruct from the list of beetle species, a picture of the surroundings of the well 3 000 years ago. The beetles indicated that the well had a wooden structure above full of woodworm, surrounded by open rough pastureland thick with thistles and almost devoid of trees. At least fourteen plant species growing in the vicinity can be identified from the plant-feeding beetles found in the well. From the large numbers of dung beetles it is inferred that many grazing animals congregated there. Unfortunately, the kind of dung beetle found can seldom tell one the kind of animal producing the dung, but only its habitat. Dermestid beetles indicated the presence of incompletely tanned hides or cured meat, possibly imported from the continent. Other beetles showed that hay had been stored nearby and had rotted down to compost. From a knowledge of the beetles alone one has a glimpse of agricultural life from a past age, a glimpse that could not be obtained using conventional archaeological techniques.

Roman grain stores usually contain the com-

mon pests of stored whole grain, *Oryzaephilus surinamensis* and *Sitophilus granarius*. Roman horse droppings may contain very large numbers of these beetles indicating that very badly infested grain was fed to the horses. Excavations at Vindolanda, close by Hadrian's Wall in Northumberland have produced many insects from rubbish heaps and floor levels including large numbers of Stableflies (*Stomoxys calcitrans*) which commonly breed in the bedding of stables and byres.

Ectoparasitic insects like lice have occasionally given us an insight into the cleanliness of past peoples and some indications of their possible diseases. Insects can even give us information on ancient trade routes. The discovery of the Mediterranean and south-east European wood-boring beetle *Hesperophanes fasciculatus* in large numbers in a Roman rubbish tip in Worcestershire is a clear indication that manufactured wooden articles were imported into Britain from at least 700 miles away.

Insects and man's history

Man and his domestic stock seem to have acquired most of their diseases in the last few thousand years, that is, since the coming of agriculture. Examination of man's bones indicates that, before he took to agriculture, he was remarkably free from many of the most crippling infectious diseases, including those caused by protozoa and viruses. After man became an agriculturalist new diseases arose in waves reaching a peak in the eighteenth century. Man's problems began with the development of agriculture. His numbers increased and he began to clear the forest to obtain good alluvial soil in which to grow his crops. Many of the mosquitoes and other insects which formerly lived high in the treetops now lived among his crops, a metre or two from the ground. Man had effectively brought down the forest roof to his own level and exposed himself to a new range of bloodsucking insects, some of which carried disease organisms which found him to their liking. These diseases were probably well adjusted in their former hosts, birds, primates and other animals. Man, with no immunity, must often have suffered terribly. When white men first encountered malignant tertian malaria in West Africa the death rate was often as high as 80 per cent and the area became known as 'The white man's grave'. Bubonic plague (the Black Death) was another such disease spreading into Europe with the black rat and being transmitted to man by the rat flea. The great Black Death pandemics reduced the population of Britain by one-third in the fourteenth century, a deficiency that was not made good for another 400 years. Similarly man acquired the virus of yellow fever from monkeys in the forests and established it in urban mosquito populations before carrying it round the tropical world. We can expect many new diseases to appear in this way and many of these will be viruses with insect vectors.

In moist temperate lands most diseases are spread by coughs and sneezes or by touch and most are comparatively benign. In the hotter tropical lands, conditions tend to be unsuitable for the spread of disease by aerial droplets. Most serious diseases in the tropics are spread by insect vectors. Good examples of diseases of this kind are malaria and yellow fever by mosquitoes, typhus by lice, bubonic plague by rat fleas, sleeping sickness by tsetse-flies, river blindness by *Simulium*, and Chaga's disease by reduviid bugs. Many of these diseases are extremely serious in man and the death rate is high. This is usually an indication that the disease is a comparatively recent one in man and neither has had sufficient time to adjust to the other by natural selection. With modern medicine man is never likely to adjust.

Many tropical diseases, including protozoan diseases like sleeping sickness, and virus diseases like yellow fever, almost certainly originated as insect diseases which spread to vertebrates with the development of the bloodsucking habit. Indeed it is widely held that the majority of both animal and plant virus diseases originated as insect diseases. Thus closely-related viruses are found in insects, higher plants and vertebrates. When insect-borne protozoan diseases have complex life cycles, the sexual stages of the life cycle take place in the insect and only asexual cycles in the vertebrate. It would be much more logical to consider man to be the intermediate host of many of the tropical diseases of insects rather than our more usual anthropocentric view of man as the primary host. Rickettsiae are also believed to have originated in insects, not as disease organisms but as symbionts.

It is therefore hardly surprising that man's recorded history seems to be a chronicle of new insect-borne diseases appearing at crucial moments. It appears that the great culture of ancient Greece declined after 400 BC with the introduction of malaria by the invading Persians. Writings of the time tell us that many people died and many families were childless, of how towns were abandoned and the fields left uncultivated. The Roman Empire declined similarly: agricultural production crashed as the incidence of malaria rose and the people became listless. Even today with worldwide malaria eradication schemes, it is estimated that 100 million people suffer from malaria every year. Today in Bangladesh, one can see every stage in the process: villages with a listless population unable to till the fields, suffering from malnutrition and famine; depopulated villages; abandoned villages swallowed up by the jungle. Of the ten plagues of Egypt, three were of insects, locusts, flies and lice and three were insect-borne diseases, probably bubonic plague, anthrax, and a form of boils. It was not without reason that the ancient Egyptians wore sacred flies and scarab beetles as jewellery and slept under mosquito nets. Nor was the god of the Philistines called for nothing Beelzebub, the 'Lord of the Flies'.

Basic Biology

Introduction

Insects with their comparatively small bodies have a large surface area compared to their volume. This means that they would rapidly dehydrate in dry surroundings. To combat this, the epidermis of insects is covered by a thick waterproof cuticle which protects them from desiccation. This allows insects to exploit arid as well as moist habitats. The thick cuticle is rigid and is also the skeleton of the insect, that is the structure to which the locomotory muscles are attached. In a small animal an external tubular skeleton is a much stronger structure than an internal structure of small bones.

Having a thick waterproof cuticle poses problems for an insect, for through that cuticle must pass the respiratory gases and all the external stimuli to the senses of sight, smell, taste and touch. Insects maintain their links with the outside world through a bewildering variety of specialized structures (Figs 8 and 9). Growth is achieved by changing or moulting their cuticle and replacing it with a bigger one. This affords insects the possibility of major changes in both the form and function of their surface. This has evolved until a single individual insect can have stages as different as a caterpillar and a butterfly,

one specialized for growth and feeding, the other for dispersion and reproduction. Each is beautifully adapted to a very different niche, feeding on different foods and receiving different sensory stimuli.

The cuticle

The insect epidermis is a single layer of cells which may have separate cell walls or may be a syncytium lacking cell walls. The epidermis is bounded on the inner side by the basement membrane and on the outer side by the cuticle, most of which it secretes (Fig. 10). The cuticle covers the whole of the outer surface of the insect and lines the trachea, the salivary glands, and the fore and hindguts. In the form of the peritrophic membrane it lines the midgut as well. Thus all parts of the insect exposed to the external environment in any way are protected by the cuticle.

The cuticle has three main layers. A thin outer epicuticle covers a thicker exocuticle which is lined with an even thicker endocuticle. The epicuticle itself has four layers. After apolysis (see page 80) tiny cytoplasmic papillae grow out from the epidermal cells. In the blow-fly there are 200 papillae in each epidermal cell, giving a density of 300000 per square millimetre. These papillae secrete around themselves a thin layer of the lipoprotein cuticulin, the first layer of the epicuticle to be formed. The next layer to be secreted is the exocuticle of chitin, a polymerized mucoprotein. Mucoproteins are compounds of sugar and proteins and can best be seen in the slime of slugs and snails. Polymerization is the linking of large numbers of molecules to form long chains of molecules often cross-linked to one another. This produces an immensely strong and resilient, yet light and chemically inert compound. It is the polymerized mucoprotein which gives the insect cuticle its characteristic strength and resilience. Polymerized compounds of this type are common in nature, forming wood, hair and horn. The exocuticle is formed around the cytoplasmic papillae, which continue to grow out from the epidermis as the cuticle is secreted, eventually becoming the pore canals. After the secretion of the exocuticle a layer of polyphenol is laid down over the cuticulin layer of the epicuticle

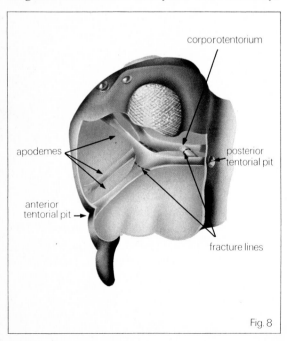

corporotentorium

apodemes

posterior tentorial pit

anterior tentorial pit

fracture lines

Fig. 8

Fig. 8 Section through an insect head, to show internal structures.

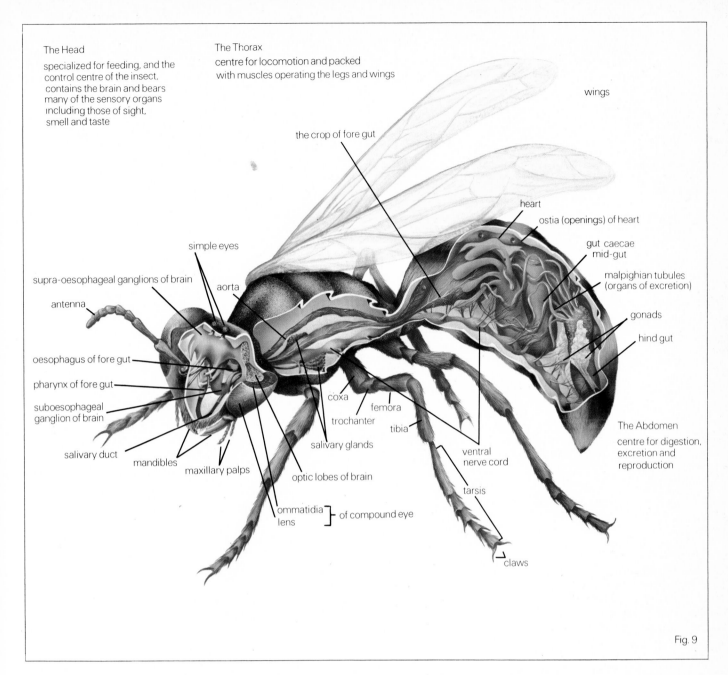

Fig. 9 The internal anatomy of a typical insect.

and this in turn is covered by a waterproofing waxy layer. Both these layers are secreted by the cytoplasmic papillae through the underlying epicuticle. Special glands in the epidermis (Verson's glands) secrete a cement layer of tanned protein which spreads over the surface of the epicuticle and hardens to give a tough scratch-resistant layer which protects the soft waxy layer beneath. The final epicuticle, though four-layered, is only 2–3 μ thick. Finally the endocuticle is secreted and additional layers may be added to the endocuticle at any time during the instar.

After secretion the cuticle is darkened and then hardened or sclerotized. Quinones, derived mainly from the blood, are incorporated into the cuticle and some are polymerized to form the dark brown or black pigments known collectively as melanin. Other quinones react with the protein chains associated with the chitin of the exocuticle to form sclerotin, a hard and immensely strong cross-linked lipoprotein. The chitin is

laid down as microfibrils which are often orientated in a particular plane. In the endocuticle this plane is always the same in cuticle laid down in the day. Cuticle formed at night is in a series of layers or lamellae. Successive lamellae have their planes arranged in sequence, each angled a few degrees on from the last so that in one night they turn through 180°. This daily alternation of layers in the cuticle enables one to determine the age of an insect larva by counting the layers just as one can tell the age of a tree. Sometimes layers of almost pure protein alternate with layers of chitin. One of these proteins is resilin, a highly resilient elastic compound. Exceptionally large amounts of resilin are found in the thorax where it gives much of the elasticity to the flight mechanism, and also to the flexible intersegmental membranes.

Insects are often brilliantly coloured. Sometimes this is because of pigments in the epidermis or fat cells underlying a transparent cuticle. The pigments are occasionally migratory, the colour

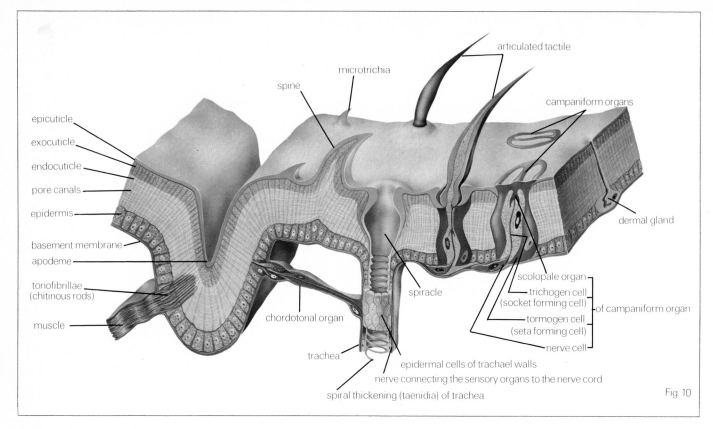

epicuticle
exocuticle
endocuticle
pore canals
epidermis
basement membrane
apodeme
tonofibrillae (chitinous rods)
muscle

spine
microtrichia
articulated tactile
campaniform organs
dermal gland

chordotonal organ
spiracle
trachea
scolopale organ
trichogen cell (socket forming cell)
tormogen cell (seta forming cell)
nerve cell
of campaniform organ

epidermal cells of trachael walls
nerve connecting the sensory organs to the nerve cord
spiral thickening (taenidia) of trachea

Fig. 10

Fig. 10 Section through the cuticle of an insect to show the layers composing it, three types of sensory organs, the attachment of a muscle, and a trachea opening through a spiracle.

of some grasshoppers and damselflies changing from black or dull purple to bright blue at high temperatures. This is thought to be an adaptation allowing the body to warm up by heat absorption when the weather is cool, and to keep cool by reflection when the weather is hot. Many other insects have brilliant iridescent colours, often changing with the angle of view. These are diffraction or interference colours produced by a variety of mechanisms. Diffraction gratings may be formed by rows of very closely set grooves on the surface of the cuticle. Alternating layers in the cuticle with different refractive indices produce interference colours. The colours of insects with diffraction gratings change with the angle of the light, whereas the colours of insects with interference patterns change much less with the angle of the light. The brilliant blue wings of the *Morpho* butterflies so often used for jewellery are outstanding examples of interference colours. Hinton found that the Hercules Beetle (*Dynastes hercules*) can change the colour of its elytra from black to greenish yellow and back again to black in a few minutes. It does this when it is threatened or annoyed, apparently by pumping liquid into or out of a sponge-like layer in the upper layers of the endocuticle of the elytra. When the spaces are filled with water, the cuticle is transparent, disclosing the black deeper layers of the endocuticle. When the spaces are empty the yellow matrix of the sponge-like layer masks the black, changing the overall colour of the elytra to greenish yellow. This beetle can absorb water through its cuticle from the outside environment. In the field, Hercules Beetles are black at high humidities of 80 per cent relative humidity at night, and are greenish yellow at low humidi-

ties in the day. The ability to absorb water through the cuticle is common to many insects but these apparently permeable cuticles are very much less permeable to water passing out of the insect.

It would be quite wrong to think that all insect colour patterns can be seen by man. Insects are sensitive to ultraviolet light and exhibit ultraviolet patterns produced by both pigments and interference mechanisms. Thus many Pieridae have distinctive and often sexually dimorphic ultraviolet patterns. To other insects their wings must flash in flight as the angle of the wing changes. Ultraviolet visual signals are often an essential feature of the courtship displays of many butterflies.

The skeleton

The tough cuticle of insects forms an exoskeleton enclosing the body tissues. Since insects are segmented animals, the exoskeleton is constructed like a suit of armour, each segment articulated with the next. This gives the maximum protection while allowing the maximum movement. The skeleton protects the soft organs, provides attachments for the muscles and protects the body from desiccation. The insect body is remarkably uniform in its basic structure indicating that the insects are almost certainly monophyletic in origin; that is, all insects are descended from a common ancestor. The body is formed of twenty segments divided into three separate regions. The first six segments form a head, the next three a thorax and the remaining eleven segments form an abdomen. Each of these regions is specialized for the efficient performance of particular functions. The head is special-

Scales on the wings of a moth of the Saturnidae family.

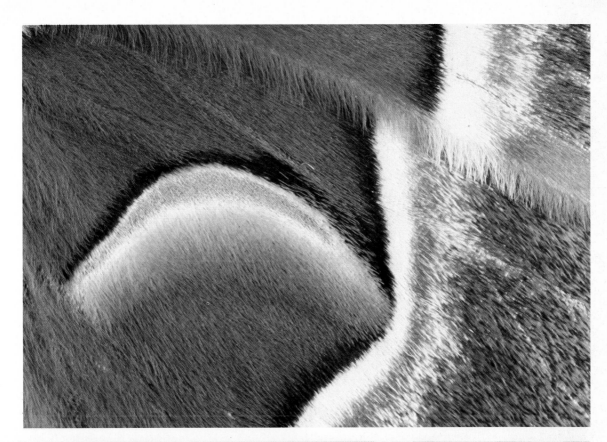

Scales from the wings of a moth (× 60).

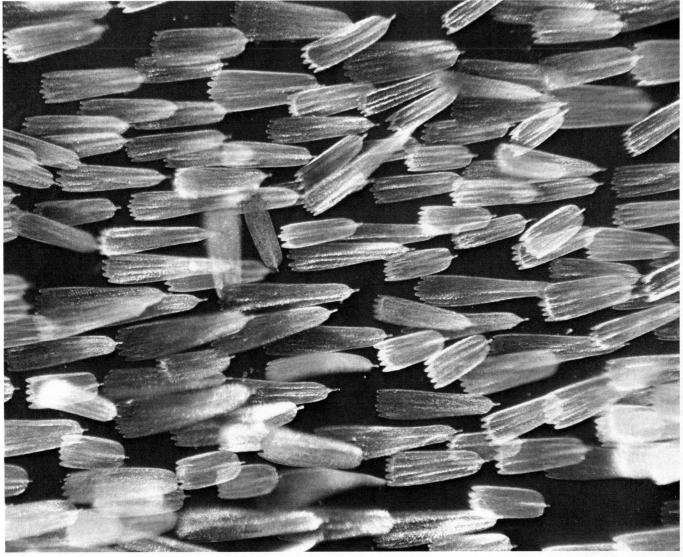

The Chrysomelid Beetle by its ability to absorb water through its cuticle is able to change to its bright colour.

ized for feeding and for gleaning information about the environment and it is the centre for the nervous initiation and coordination of many body functions. The thorax is specialized for locomotion and is packed with massive muscles which function as engines, consuming quantities of fuel and producing power for movement. In the abdomen the food is digested and surplus food products are stored in the fat body for future use. It is also specialized for excretion and reproduction.

Each segment of an insect has an exoskeleton formed from four basic plates of extra-thick chitin. These are the sclerites. The arrangement of these plates can best be seen in the thorax. There is a dorsal plate (tergum), a ventral plate (sternum) and two lateral plates (pleura) which are fused to make a solid box.

The head of all insects is a single fused capsule. The sclerites of all the segments are completely fused and little trace remains on the outside of the head of the original segmentation. Most of the head sutures are secondary structures. The epicranial suture with its typical Y-shaped end forms a line of weakness along which the cranium splits at ecdysis. Internally the head is braced by an endoskeleton or tentorium. This consists of four intuckings of the exoskeleton which can be seen on the surface of the head as tentorial pits. There are two intuckings from the front, one each side of the frontoclypeal suture, and two from the back at the base of the neck. This means that there is an intucking alongside each of the two articulations of each mandible. In many insects the intuckings from the front and back fuse to form a single rigid tube or apodeme. The posterior intucking usually continues upwards beyond the point of fusion and is attached to the top of the head near the antennal bases. This structure is finally locked into a solid structure by a transverse bar or corporo-tentorium which passes immediately beneath the foregut. The tentorium of the head gives the head great rigidity and strengthens the points of articulation of the mouthparts. It supports and protects the brain and foregut and provides origins for many of the head muscles.

Compound eyes are found in almost all adult insects and often occupy much of the top of the head. In addition, many insects also have simple eyes, or dorsal ocelli. Typically there are three of these arranged in a triangle. The median ocellus shows evidence of having arisen by the fusion of a pair of ocelli.

The original first head segment forms the upper lip or labrum which is hinged to the clypeus. On its inner surface is the setate epipharynx which carries a very large number of taste organs.

The second head segment bears a pair of antennae. The antennae are flexible and consist of any number of segments from one to more than a hundred. The muscles are invariably confined to the basal segment so that the antenna

moves as a whole. The antennae of some species bend and curl when moved. This curling is brought about by changes in blood pressure, differences in shape being determined by differences in the intersegmental articulations. The second antennal segment is filled with an important sensory organ called Johnston's organ. The rest of the antenna varies enormously from insect to insect. Even within the Diptera the antennae vary from the long filiform multisegmented antennae of some Tipulidae (craneflies), to the stout, horn-like multisegmented antennae of the Tabanidae (horse-flies) and the short, three-segmented antennae of house-flies. Other insects like weevils and ants have elbowed antennae with a long based segment or scape. Essentially the antennae act as the nose of the insect. Many of the smell receptors are borne on the surface of the antennae. Several of the modifications found in insect antennae are associated with increasing their surface area to accommodate more smell receptor organs. Thus the male Emperor Moth, which finds the female by scent, has magnificent pectinate antennae. Some male galerucid beetles have antennae notched to grip the female during copulation.

Head segments four, five and six bear respectively the mandibles, maxillae and labium, mouthparts which are derived from modified appendages. The mouthparts are very diverse. Primitive types are organized for biting and chewing with a massive pair of opposed jaws or mandibles. The power of the mandibles is such that many beetle larvae can bite through sheet lead, tin and copper. One American species is even known as the 'short-circuit beetle' because when it burrows to pupate, it sometimes cuts into power cables. The sharp mandibles of the soldiers of some African termites are used to 'stitch' open wounds. The termites are induced to bite and their bodies are then nipped off leaving the mandibles locked in position. All insect mandibles have a single segment, except the mandibles of some Thysanura which are two-segmented. They articulate on the head at two points, the anterior ginglymus and the posterior condyle, and are moved by massive muscles arising on the epicranium. Examination of almost any mandible tells a great deal about the feeding habits of the insect. For instance, some dung beetles have flexible mandibles, pollen feeders have setate mandibles (Fig. 11), snail-feeding beetles have sickle-like grooved mandibles to suck up the juices, and seed eaters have blunt mandibles with massive molar areas for crushing. The male Stag Beetle has huge antler-like mandibles used in courtship. In adult caddis flies and most adult Diptera and Lepidoptera, the mandibles have been lost.

The maxillae are the appendages of the fifth head segment and are richly endowed with

Maybug (*Melolontha melolontha*). The hard upper wing cases are kept elevated during flight to allow the lower pair of membranous flight wings to move freely. The legs are stretched out sideways and the fan-like antennae are spread.

taste receptors. Many biting insects use the maxillae to hold the food between the mandibles. Each maxilla has a two-segmented basal part which bears a one- to seven-segmented palp and a pair of lobes. One of these, the galea, has many setae and is sometimes two-segmented while the other, the lacinia, is toothed. Often only one of these is present, when it is called a mala. The galea of the pollen beetle *Malachius* bears many flexible trumpet-shaped setae. Each seta has a small suction pad at the tip, which enables the galea to transfer smooth-surfaced pollen such as that of grasses to the mouth. In the Lepidoptera it is the paired galeae which are elongated and pressed together to form the long, coiled, suctorial proboscis or haustellum. A lower lip, or labium, on the sixth head segment is derived from a second pair of maxillae which have been swung into the midline and fused together.

In addition to these paired mouthparts there is usually a median tongue or hypopharynx, formed by parts of the mandibles and maxillae. The hypopharynx projects forwards from the floor of the mouth and divides it into two. Dorsally there is a muscular cibarium which acts as a temporary food store, or a suction pump in sucking insects. Ventrally there is a salivarium into which the saliva is discharged. The salivarium may be modified into a silk press in caterpillars or a salivary syringe in Hemiptera. This leaves a small area beyond the hypopharynx still contained between the labrum and labium where the food is crushed by the mandibles. This is the food meatus.

Biting mouthparts similar to those described are found throughout the insects from dragonflies through grasshoppers to beetles and wasps. Sucking mouthparts have been evolved many times in many orders of insects including bugs, flies, fleas, butterflies, moths and beetles. Flies show a wide variety of sucking mouthparts. House-flies have a massive proboscis formed from all the head appendages. The original labium has been modified to form a sponge-like labellum covered in parallel food channels or pseudotracheae. Each channel is supported by

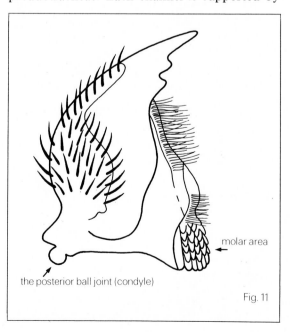

the posterior ball joint (condyle)

molar area

Fig. 11

Fig. 11 The setate mandible of *Meligethes* spp – a pollen-feeding beetle.

53

rows of slightly open split rings. Liquid food, often partially predigested by the salivary enzymes, is 'mopped up' by the capillary action of the food channels and sucked along them to the central mouth. The mouth is flanked by rows of small prestomal teeth. In wound and blood-sucking muscids, these teeth are highly developed for surface rasping. In the tsetse-fly the proboscis has been reduced to a series of sword-like stylets for piercing the skin. The labium is massive and encloses a sharp stylet-like labrum and hypopharynx. This whole structure is used as a single unit to pierce the thick skin of the host. Tsetse-flies, being relatives of the house-fly, have no mandibles or maxillae; only the sensory maxillary palps survive from these structures. Mosquitoes have all the head appendages and all are elongated. The host's skin is pierced by the maxillae and mandibles; the labrum and hypopharynx are then thrust into the wound for feeding.

The thorax is an extremely rigid box composed of only three segments and bears all the loco-motory appendages (Fig. 12). The thorax is further stiffened by intuckings of chitin from the sternum and the two pleurae. These intuckings form an internal skeleton or endoskeleton bracing the pleura so that they are quite rigid and form ideal fulcrums for the wings in flight. Many insects have each of their basic plates sub-divided into a number of sclerites. Subdivisions of the tergum are called tergites, of the sternum are sternites, and of the pleura are pleurites. Unfortunately these smaller plates are given differ-

ent names in different groups of insects; or are even given different names by different authorities writing of the same group! Each thoracic segment bears a pair of multisegmented legs which are articulated outgrowths from between the pleura and the sternum (Fig. 13). The last two

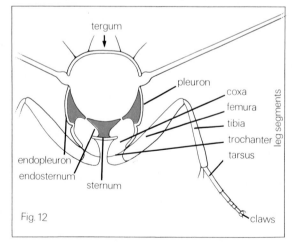

Fig. 12

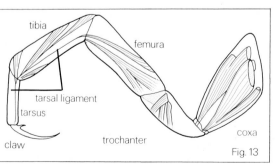

Fig. 13

Tiger Beetle (*Cicindella campestris*) showing biting mouthparts.

Fig. 12 Transverse section through a thoracic segment of an insect. The internal skeleton consists of inpushings from the external skeleton, cross-bracing the thorax and providing the origins for many muscles including the ventral longitudinal thoracic and upper leg muscles.

Fig. 13 The leg muscles of a typical insect.

54

Dark Green Fritillary (*Mesoacidalia aglaja*) showing close-up of head.

thoracic segments of adult insects, that is the mesothorax and the metathorax, usually carry a pair of wings apiece. Wings are formed as balloon-like outgrowths from between the pleura and the tergum. The two surfaces of the wing are pressed tightly together to form a very flat stiff sheet. This is stiffened by veins which are interconnecting channels between these two surfaces, allowing blood, nerves and tracheae to penetrate to all parts of the wing. Many of the veins are thickened, hardened and melanized to form those insect wing veins which can easily be seen with the naked eye or a low-power microscope. Occasionally wing veins have articulated joints along their length, especially those veins near the leading edge of the wing.

The abdomen is the least specialized part of the insect exoskeleton; however in adult insects most of the segments have lost their appendages. The sclerites of the abdomen are often limited to a tergum and sternum connected by a pliable pleural membrane. This means that the abdomen is much more flexible and distensible than any other part of the body. The final two or three segments are often partially fused and greatly modified to form the terminalia which retain some of the appendages. The appendages of segments eight, nine and ten form the genitalia in both males and females, facilitating internal fertilization, an essential attribute of a fully terrestrial animal. The appendages of the eleventh segment persist in many primitive insects as a pair of cerci.

Many insect larvae have an exoskeleton simi-lar to that of the adult. The larval exoskeleton of endopterygote insects may be very different from that of the adult. This is usually found in species where the larva is specialized to live in a habitat different from that of the adult. In the caterpillars of most Lepidoptera only the cuticle of the head capsule, pronotum and legs is rigid. The rest, except for small islands of cuticle around the main setae, is flexible, allowing the caterpillar to grow continuously between moults. The caterpillars of several orders have abdominal locomotory appendages in addition to the thoracic legs. Others lack legs altogether. All endopterygote larvae lack the adult's compound eyes. They usually have biting mouthparts though the mouthparts of the adults may be modified for other modes of feeding.

Locomotion

Insects are extraordinarily mobile creatures. Movement is a characteristic of some stage or other of all animals, but no other animals have mastered as many forms of locomotion as have insects. They excel in the air and many species are swift runners, swimmers, jumpers, skaters on the water surface, and tunnellers through soil and in plants. All this they do to establish new territories, to escape from danger, to seek food and mates, and to find a place to lay their eggs. True flight is confined to winged adult insects although small wingless larvae may be carried thousands of metres into the air. However, usually tunnelling tends to be restricted

Emperor Gum Moth (*Antheraea euca-lypti*) caterpillar.

to the more streamlined, wingless larvae.

In all but the simplest animals, locomotion depends on three basic body systems. There must be a sensory system telling the insect where it is, where each part of the body is relative to the rest, and the posture of the body as a whole. A central nervous system is needed to coordinate all this information and to initiate an appropriate sequence of movement. Finally there must be muscles which, in response to the commands of the nervous system, produce the power which moves the articulated lever systems of the skeleton. In soft-bodied insects the muscles act against the turgid, fluid-filled body which functions as a hydrostatic skeleton. This is most often found in insect larvae such as leather-jackets burrowing through the soil or caterpillars crawling over leaves, two forms which are fundamentally similar. In insects with a hard articulated exoskeleton of individual sclerites, there is a trellis of muscles passing from one sclerite to the next. Each muscle is attached to the cuticle by rows of chitinous rods, or tono-fibrillae, each embedded deep in the muscle at one end and into the endocuticle at the other. The tarsal retractor muscle in the leg of most adult insects, like some other important leg muscles, terminates in a flexible chitinized ligament. This muscle runs from the distal part of the tibia along the length of the tarsus to insert on the claw segment. It braces the legs, lifting the body off the ground while digging the claws into the ground. The body muscles are attached either directly to the sclerites of the exoskeleton, or to apodemes or other lever systems which act indirectly on the sclerites.

Crawling

When the muscles in one part of the body contract they force another part of the body forwards. This is crawling. Basically, it requires two sets of antagonistic muscles, longitudinal and transverse. In soil, this type of movement forces the animal through the soil and forms the tunnel by compacting the walls, a principle used by plant roots and modern pipe-laying machines. Legs are of little help to these insects. On flat surfaces, away from the constraint of the tunnel walls, feet are essential to grip the substrate. Butterfly caterpillars feeding on flat leaf surfaces have five extra pairs of abdominal legs or prolegs in addition to the normal three pairs of thoracic legs. These legs have a sucker which is surrounded by rows of hooks which bite into the leaf surface when the floor of the sucker is raised. Waves of contraction pass forwards along the body lifting each proleg in turn, which then takes a new grip a little further forward. This movement can be very swift and the beautiful rippling motion can be seen when the woolly bear caterpillars of drinker and tiger moths cross a road in search of a place to pupate. It is mainly the prolegs which are responsible for the crawling of caterpillars; the true legs serve as little more than props to support the head thrust along in front of the abdomen or to hold the leaf edges to the jaws during feeding. The looper caterpillars of geometrid moths have greatly

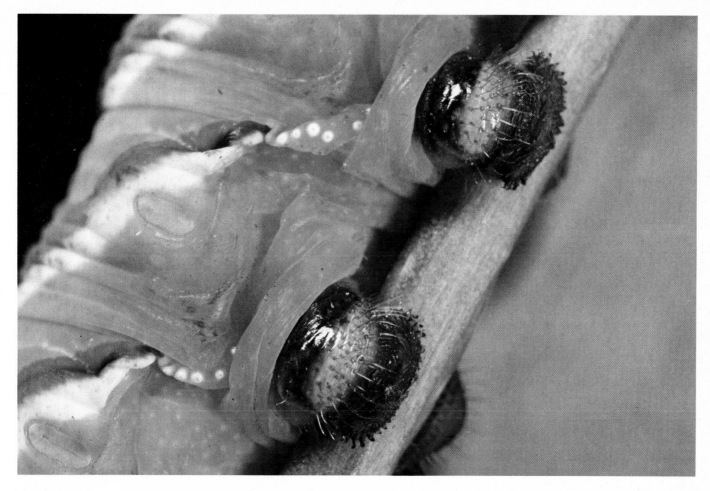

Privet Hawkmoth
(*Sphinx ligustri*)
larva showing hairy
adhesive prolegs.

elongated abdomens with the prolegs reduced to the two most posterior pairs. Movement is made by pushing the body as far forward as possible. The true legs grip the surface and the body is bent double until the posterior prolegs are brought up to the true legs. Then the process is repeated, giving a very rapid looping action, and each time this happens the body is bent into the shape of the Greek character Omega (Ω).

Walking

Walking is the typical mode of progression of long-legged insects on dry land. The configuration of six long legs, their bases close together under the thorax, fanning out to touch the substrate well clear of the sides of the body, is a very

Figs 14 and 15
The sequence of leg movements in a ground beetle. When moving slowly the beetle stands on a tripod of three legs while the remaining three legs move. At faster speeds the beetle changes to a swinging gait where all three legs on one side move, followed by all three legs on the other side.

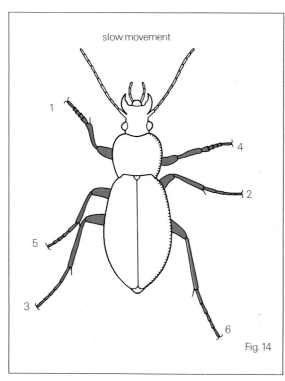

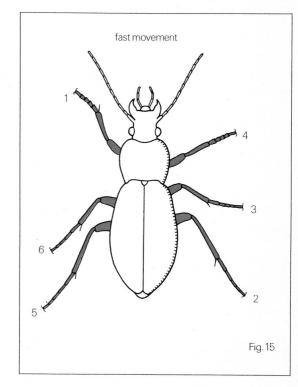

stable one. Insects, like all legged animals, change their gait with the speed of motion. This is well known in horses but is not quite so easily seen in insects except by looking at slowed down cinefilm. At very slow speeds the insect moves its legs in sequence, starting with the front leg on one side then the middle of the other side followed by the hindleg of the first side. This sequence of three is then repeated in mirror image on the other side of the insect (Fig. 14). Thus the insect always stands securely on a tripod while moving the other three legs forward in sequence. This movement rolls the body from side to side like a sailor on the quayside. As the speed of movement increases, the insect moves into a swinging gait, twisting the body alternately to each side of the direction of motion. The legs move in sequence, starting with the front on one side followed by the hind and then the middle leg of the other side (Fig. 15). The number of legs on the ground at any moment drops with increasing speed from five to four to three. This sequence is often modified and the loss of a limb immediately results in a change in the sequence of leg movements to compensate for the change in the balance of the body. So limb movement in insects is not a stereotyped sequence but is carefully monitored and coordinated by the nervous system in accordance with the needs of the time.

When walking, insects have the remarkable ability to grip a wide variety of surfaces. Many beetles can walk across wax-covered leaves or up a window pane whereas flies will walk upside down across the ceiling. The typical insect leg ends in a pair of grapnel-like claws which dig into the substrate when the leg is flexed. Insects also have a wide variety of adhesive organs which hold them firmly on smooth surfaces. They often consist of dense masses of glandular hairs on the underside of the tarsal segments. Each hair is hollow and secretes a tiny drop of moisture at the extreme tip which sticks the insect down by surface tension. Many insects, including houseflies, have an adhesive pad or arolium between the claws. The surface of the pad is covered with moist sloping ridges which readily slide over the surface in one direction but grip the surface tightly when pulled in the opposite direction. The size and form of the organs of attachment on the feet of insects vary with the way of life. Claws are best developed in insects living on wet, rough or hairy surfaces whereas adhesive hairs and pads are best developed in insects living on dry, smooth or shiny surfaces. There are several species of seaweed flies living on detached seaweed thrown up on the high tide line. The piles of weed dry out on top but remain moist and slippery underneath. Those species which live on the surface of the seaweed piles have well-developed adhesive organs and small claws; those living deeper down have well-developed claws and poorly-developed adhesive organs.

Leaping

The ability to jump is mainly confined to leaf-feeding insects and involves a wide variety of mechanisms. The explosive leaps of springtails, flea beetles and grasshoppers are of great value as mechanisms of escape from predators. Springtails have a forked tail which is bent under the body and held in place by a catch. Opening the catch releases the tail, springing the body into the air. Flea beetles have a special chitinous hook-like tendon in the femur. The tendon is hinged to the tibia and greatly increases the mechanical leverage applied to the tibia when the muscle attached to the outer edge of the tendon contracts. It transforms a small powerful movement into a much bigger movement, shooting the animal rapidly into the air. The flea leaps when it perceives the body heat, shadow or vibration of an animal which may prove to be its host.

Rat fleas, although weighing only approximately 0·3 mg, can jump as far as 31 cm, which would be equivalent in man to a leap of 250 m. This wingless insect uses its defunct wing mechanism to power its jump. Contracting the former longitudinal indirect flight muscles at the same time as raising the femora distorts the thorax, especially a small patch of exceptionally elastic protein called resilin, which forms the sclerite which, in a winged insect, would be the wing hinge. When distorted this sclerite locks into a 'cocked' position against the exoskeleton. Relaxing the femoral muscles allows the femora to push downwards. This is aided by the release of the cocking mechanism in the wing base, releasing the energy stored in the exoskeleton. This gives a further thrust to the legs, forcing the flea upwards. The mechanism allows the flea to respond immediately to the presence of its host, almost independently of the temperature at the time. Some maggots, like those of the Cheeseskipper, jump by holding their tails in their mouths and pulling hard until the body suddenly straightens and is thrown forwards. Click beetles jump without using their legs. When disturbed they fall to the ground where they usually lie upside down. Then the body is bent backwards at a sharp angle by locking the pronotum with the elytra, and braced by engaging the prosternal peg in a socket on the anterior face of the mesosternum like a set mousetrap. When this peg is released the beetle is thrown into the air with a distinct click. This action rights the insect and frightens off many predators. Grasshoppers jump into the air as a prelude to flight and the wings start to beat at the top of the leap.

Burrowing

Many insects burrow. This may be as larvae in search of food or shelter, or it may be as adults as part of their reproductive behaviour. The burrowing of legless larvae has already been described in the section on crawling. Other larvae dig their way through the soil with large shovel-like front legs. A few larvae like the antlions, use these legs to excavate large pits to ensnare their prey, whereas the larvae of tiger beetles excavate burrows in which they hide from their prey. Other larvae burrow through

Pond skater (*Gerris* spp) standing on water and feeding on a horse fly.

leaves, stems and wood. Usually these mining larvae eat their way through the plant, biting off and swallowing the tissues with their large forward-pointing jaws. Most leaf-mining larvae have reduced legs. The legs of wood-boring larvae are usually much better developed though some have the hind pair of legs modified to produce sounds. In the Stag Beetle these sounds enable the larvae to communicate with one another and thus to keep an even spacing in the log.

Some adult wasps excavate large chambers in the ground into which they pull the anaesthetized bodies of their prey on which they lay their eggs. Burying beetles excavate earth from under corpses and pile it on top until the body is buried. All these adults have front feet with flattened tarsi bearing rows of stout spines.

One specialized form of digging is found in the sawflies. The females of these insects have their ovipositors modified as large and often toothed drills or saws with which they cut through the tissue of leaves and stems and even the bark of trees to form a hole through which they lay their eggs.

Swimming

Swimming insects can be divided into those which 'walk' through the water using their normal walking movements; and those, like dytiscid water beetles and waterboatmen, which have fringed oar-like hindlegs which move in unison as in a jumping insect, sculling the insect along. A few insects like the whirligig beetle swim at the interface, half in and half out of the water. This is a highly specialized habitat involving many specialized adaptations, including a highly hydrophobic upper surface allowing the insect to break the surface film, and hind and middle legs which are expanded and oar-like. These beetles have their compound eyes divided; thus there is one pair specialized for seeing in air above the water and another pair specialized for seeing under water. Such specialization needs sophisticated nerve centres to correlate what is seen. A few very tiny parasitic Hymenoptera (family Mymaridae) actively seek their aquatic hosts by flying through the water using their wings for propulsion. Insect larvae show a wide range of swimming methods from the eel-like undulations of the elongated bodies of midge larvae to the rapid jet propulsion of dragonfly nymphs which force a jet of water out of their anuses.

Many adult insects skate across the surface films of water. Such insects as pond skaters have hydrophobic legs which support the body of the insect above the water, their weight causing depressions in the water surface. The insect moves swiftly across the pond surface by simultaneous rowing movements of the legs. One unusual

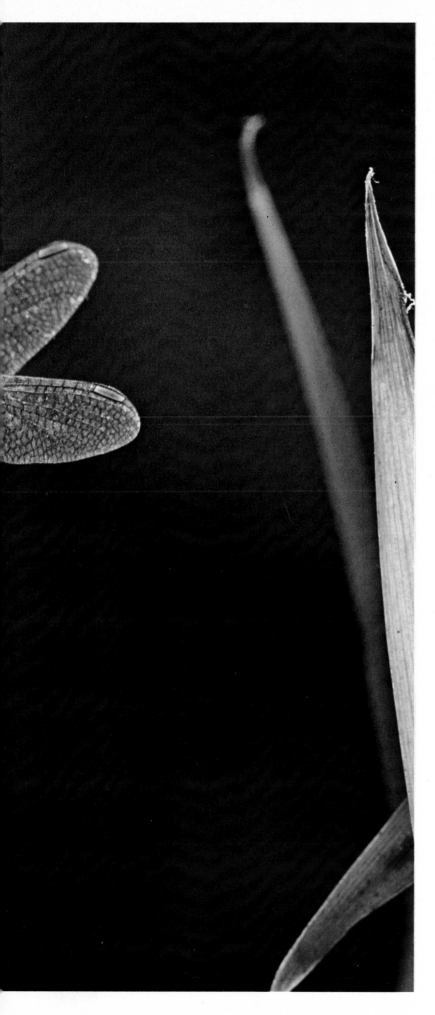

group of beetles which live on the banks of brooks and streams have a remarkable device to get them back to the land if they fall into the water. These are the camphor beetles which produce a small drop of liquid at the tip of the abdomen which greatly lowers the surface tension of the water behind them. The pull of the surface tension at the front of the beetle draws it forward like a child's camphor boat until it reaches dry land. Springtails are often found in great numbers on the surface of stagnant ponds, their hydrophobic bodies and feet above the water, their hydrophilic claws and ventral tubes on the abdomen anchoring them firmly to the water surface. The ventral tubes not only act as anchors, but are also able to take up water. These springtails drink with their tummies.

Flying

Although many insects spend most of their life on the ground, almost all fly at some time in their adult life. Wings are fundamental features of insects and, unlike the wings of bats and birds, insects' wings are special structures in their own right, not modified walking limbs. It is the power of flight that has made insects the dominant group of invertebrates and has given them an advantage over the spiders and their allies. It is flight that enables insects to find new habitats and to exploit temporary habitats for breeding, like pools of water in the rainy season or isolated patches of annual plants. Flight increases their ability to escape from predators, to find and catch food, and to find hosts. Above all else, flight increases the chances of new mutations spreading through the species and it maintains the continuity of the species. Primitively insects have four separate wings, each pair moving independently of the other, as in dragonflies and many scorpion flies. Most insects living today either have the hindwings hooked to the forewings so that the two together form a single aerofoil; or have only a single pair of wings for powered flight, the other pair being reduced in size or used for some other purpose. Butterflies and moths lock the wings of each side together, usually by some type of single hook. Bees and wasps have rows of tiny hooks which lock the wings tightly together like a zip fastener. Mayflies have greatly reduced hindwings, some species having lost them altogether, whereas the true flies have the hindwings reduced to small knobs or haltères which beat during flight. They act as complicated flight recorders giving the insect very detailed information about flight attitude and enabling it to make the precise adjustments associated with the swift, controlled flight of these insects. Grasshoppers have the forewings stiffened; in locusts the stiff forewings are used as aerofoils for long, effortless gliding flights. Beetles have rigid forewings or elytra which have lost their venation and serve mainly to protect the hindwings when the insects

Dragonfly (*Sympetrum striolatum*) to show head and uncoordinated wings.

61

Crane-fly (*Tipula lunata*)— better known as daddy-long-legs— showing hindwings reduced to small knobs (haltères).

are on or in the ground or under banks and other rough confined places. On the ground the soft hindwings of beetles are folded away under the elytra, which lock with one another and with the abdomen. The hindwings fold along predetermined folds as in origami. The whole wing often shuts like a fan; the tip then folds back over the basal two-thirds and is then tucked under the elytron, often with a helping push from the abdomen. In flight the elytra of beetles are usually held out motionless, clear of the rapidly beating hindwings, each of which beats through an angle as great as 180° from straight up to straight down. Rose chafers, some of which undertake long migrations, fly with their elytra closed. Their hindwings protrude through and are locked in position by notches in the bases of the elytra. It is in large insects, which rely on their own power for directional flight, that the most sophisticated flight adaptations are found; small insects, which rely mainly on the wind to carry them willy-nilly, often have small weak wings frequently fringed with hairs. These serve more as parachutes than wings, although the wing function is often important for take-off and landing.

A prerequisite for flight is the ability to stay aloft. There are three phenomena which may be used to achieve this. First, where there is a steady flow of air across a wing the resulting stable aerodynamics creates lift, a vertical force which counteracts the downward fall of the insect under gravity. Second, when the wings are moving unstable vortices are created along the wing edges again resulting in lift. Finally, where the insect wings are reduced to single rods fringed with setae, a screw-like twisting action of the wings causes the insect to 'swim' through the air, e.g. mymarid wasps and ptiliid beetles. Birds and insects power their flight by flapping their wings. In this case lift is obtained by using a combination of stable and unstable aerodynamics. During forward flight in large insects, e.g. locusts, most of the lift is derived from stable aerodynamics. This lift is greatest during the downstroke (80 per cent) but never becomes negative even during the upstroke because the wings twist during movement, altering their angle of attack. Forward movement is produced by the horizontal force known as thrust which must exceed the drag which restrains the insect's forward movement. Thrust is greatest in the middle of both up and down strokes. The insect uses very little energy to move forward compared with the energy required for lift. In the desert locust only 7 per cent of the energy consumed in flight is used to produce forward thrust, while 93 per cent produces lift. Many insects hover, or fly very slowly. These insects often clap their wings together at the end of the upstroke pressing the two dorsal surfaces tightly together. The wings are then flung open in a manner similar to the 'flinging open' of a book. This creates a vortex around each wing which gives the insect lift equal to its body weight, before the wings start their downstroke. At the end of the downstroke many insects twist their wings sharply in a flip, again creating vortices which give the animal lift. It is the 'fling' and 'flip' mechanisms which enable insects and pos-

Sub-imago of may-fly in which hind-wings are much reduced.

Figs 16 and 17 Flight muscle arrangement. The wings of dragon-flies are moved by direct flight muscles which insert on the base of the wing. The wings of a fly are moved by in-direct flight muscles which distort the thorax, causing the wings to 'click' up or down. The darker colour indicates which pair of muscles is contract-ing to produce each wing movement.

sibly birds to maintain hovering flight and are especially well developed in the hover-flies. The males of the Australian whistling moths *Heca-tesia* spp have ridged, scaleless, window-like areas on the upper surface of the forewings with a raised area immediately in front. These pro-duce a characteristic high pitched whistle when the wings are clapped together and flung open. The males apparently do this at will. The hind-wings of many insects are broader and more flexible than the forewings and produce most of the total lift. It is interesting to watch the Australian Swallowtail butterfly *Papilio aegeus*. This uses both pairs of wings for forward flight: while hovering at a flower, it holds the forewings almost stationary over the body while the smaller, more flexible hindwings beat rapidly.

The mechanisms responsible for moving the wings of insects are very simple in principle (Fig. 16). The muscles used are adapted from the nor-mal segmental muscles and are not special flight muscles. The power for flight was almost cer-tainly primitively derived from muscles at-tached directly to the wing bases. These are the direct flight muscles which even today in dragon-flies (Fig. 17) are solely responsible for the strong downbeat of the wing. The muscles insert on the wing outside the pivoting point of the wing and the leverage on the wing is very small. However, this apparently mechanically disadvantageous system does mean that a large wing movement is produced by only a very slight shortening of the muscle. As with car engines, a muscle with a short stroke can produce more power more quickly. However, in dragonflies the muscles

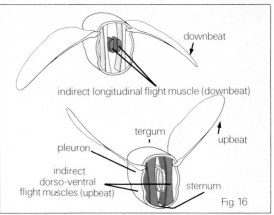

Fig. 16

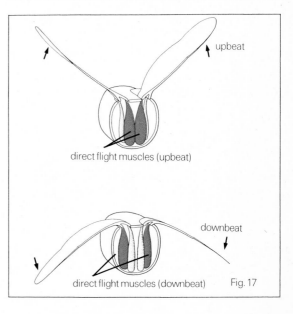

Fig. 17

responsible for the upbeat are indirect and insert on the tergal sclerites at the base of the wing. Similar arrangements are found in cockroaches, grasshoppers and beetles, all large insects with a comparatively slow wing beat of four to thirty strokes per second. These are speeds at which it is quite feasible for each group of muscles to be activated by a separate nerve stimulus. The smaller bees and house-flies have slimmer wings and are much more dextrous in the air. They move their wings at approximately 200 beats per second. But even these wing speeds seem low compared with the tiny midge's rate of up to 1 000 beats per second, speeds which give these insects their characteristic high-pitched whine. This rate of muscular contraction is far too fast to be initiated by nervous stimulation. In these insects the movement of the wings is brought about entirely by the indirect flight muscles acting on the exoskeleton of the thorax while the direct flight muscles act solely to fold and unfold the wings and to change the angle of incidence of the wing during each stroke. There are two sets of antagonistic indirect flight muscles which move the wings by deforming the elastic box of the thorax. These are the longitudinal and dorsoventral indirect flight muscles. The thoracic box is elastic because the chitinous exoskeleton contains the protein resilin which acts as an energy store. Contraction of the longitudinal muscles causes the tergum to bulge upwards, distorting the sclerites at the wing base. The stress at the wing base increases until the wing-bearing sclerite, which is composed of almost pure resilin, clicks over, forcing the wing downwards. This releases the pressure on the longitudinal muscles which therefore cease to contract. At the same time the upward bulge of the tergum jerks the dorsoventral muscles which therefore contract, pulling the roof of the tergum down and altering the stress on the wing-bearing sclerite which clicks back again, raising the wing. Again, the release of pressure causes the dorsoventral muscles to cease contracting while the downward movement of the tergal roof stretches the longitudinal muscles once more, and these again contract. This system of antagonistic muscles acting on a clicker mechanism produces rapid vibrations which move the wings with each stroke and which oscillate at a faster rate than could be achieved by nervous control. The system is kept going by a steady but much slower stream of nerve impulses. The very small movements of the muscles allow not only a rapid movement of the wings but also a powerful downbeat. Nearly 90 per cent of the energy expended for each wing beat is stored in the resilin of the thoracic sclerites and is therefore available for the next wing beat. Thus each cycle of muscular contraction only needs supply just over 10 per cent of the energy required each time to move the wings. Before this system can function for flight the thorax must be stressed. Stressing is produced by the contraction of the pleural-sternal muscles immediately before flight. In insects where the fast wing-beat is powered by the indirect muscles, the direct flight muscles control only the angle of the wings which changes throughout each stroke. They do this by flexing the main wing veins, causing the wing tip to twist through a figure-of-eight during each stroke. This produces a propeller-like thrust, pulling the insect upwards and forwards.

Most cold-blooded animals are very sensitive to low temperatures and insects are no exception. Most cannot fly until the weather is warm enough. Others, like night-flying moths, which have to fly when the temperature is comparatively low, warm up before take-off. They do this by contracting all their muscles simultaneously, producing an effect similar to shivering in mammals. They can then fly once the temperature of the muscles is high enough.

Flight requires large amounts of fuel, up to a hundred times what is needed when at rest. This fuel is 'burnt' to provide power for the muscles, and the process is called respiration. The fuel of most animals is sugar, especially glucose. Many flies will fly until all their glucose is used up, when they must stop until they have had a new feed of sugar. Some insects, including butterflies, respire sugars when walking or resting but switch over to fat as a fuel for flight. Locusts on migration burn up their sugars first before switching over to fat. The use of fat for fuel is found particularly in very active flying insects, especially those which migrate, because more energy can be obtained from fat than from the same weight of sugar. Thus the use of fat increases the insect's range and many insects have superbly-developed fat bodies ramifying throughout the body. Animals do not normally respire aminoacids or proteins except in conditions of extreme starvation. However, some bloodsucking insects, especially the tsetse-fly, can respire aminoacids derived from their victims. This effect is simulated by the insecticide DDT which causes disorganized hyperactivity of the muscles. These 'burn up' the aminoacid reserves of the insect in a manner similar to the respiration of aminoacids by tsetse-flies.

Feeding and digestion

Insects will feed on and digest a remarkable array of foods and their success as a group owes much to this. There are insects which feed on the bacteria in crude oil or the yeasts in fruit, on cotton wool, wax, wood, hair, horn, decaying corpses, faeces, the blood of living animals, and the nectar and pollen of flowers. Many of these insects are of great economic importance because they take our food, our clothes or even our blood, and by so doing spread many important diseases like malaria to man, or nagana fever to cattle. It is largely what an insect eats, and how much, that determines its ecological role and its economic importance.

Almost all insects have micro-organisms living inside them which break down at least part of the host's food and often provide the insect with vital nutrients and vitamins. The protozoa in the gut of a termite are totally re-

sponsible for digesting the wood on which it feeds almost exclusively. In return, the protozoa gain food and protection, and both partners benefit from the relationship. This is symbiosis and neither symbiont can live without the other. Sometimes we take advantage of the digestive processes of insects, as when we take from bees the partly-digested nectar of flowers and spread it on our bread as honey.

For a potential food to be acceptable to an insect it must fulfil three main requirements. It must contain all those substances necessary to enable the insect to live and grow. It must have the right texture to allow the insect to eat it. It must be attractive and contain substances which will stimulate the insect to feed. Many species of plants contain both attractant and repellent substances and it is the combination of these which determines whether a particular insect can feed on a particular plant. Insects which feed by sucking plant juices have to penetrate

deeply into the tough plant tissues. Numerous hemipterans feed on the nutrient-rich phloem cells which carry the products of photosynthesis away from the leaves. Insects like aphids do not attempt to penetrate the tough-walled epidermal and cortical cells on their way to the deeper-lying phloem cells. They push their mouthparts between the cells, dissolving away the substances which bond the cells together with special enzymes secreted by the salivary glands. Inevitably the route to the phloem cells is circuitous, usually turning steadily to one side or the other. The sides of the hole are strengthened by the secretion of a protein feeding sheath which guides the insect's stylets, thus aiding the penetration of the phloem cells by the tip. The way in which the proboscis seeks out and finds the phloem cells through the many other tissues is uncanny and misses are infrequent. This has important implications in pest control since systemic insecticides must penetrate to the phloem if they are to be effective.

The gut of an insect derives from inpushings of the epidermis from the mouth and the anus. These form the fore and hindgut and are lined with chitin like the outside of the insect. The fore and hindgut are joined by the midgut which is where the food is digested and absorbed. The foregut has a thick cuticle and acts as a food store or a gizzard, where coarse food is finely ground by strong teeth before it is digested in the midgut. Sometimes there is a little digestion in the foregut by enzymes in the saliva or by regurgitated midgut enzymes. Thus it is in the foregut of the bee that the nectar is converted into honey which is regurgitated after the bee enters the hive. Many plant-sucking, predatory or carrion-feeding insects have high concentrations of digestive enzymes in the salivary glands or regurgitate digestive enzymes from the midgut. These enzymes are pumped into their food, often along a proboscis or along specially-grooved mandibles. Flies predigest grains of sugar on a tablecloth and glow-worm larvae predigest to an easily-swallowed fluid the snails on which they feed. Blow-fly larvae condition the muscle of newly-dead corpses with their faeces, while feeding on the surrounding tissue. The faeces contain ammonia which neutralizes the acid in the fresh muscle, and proteolytic enzymes which reduce the intramuscular tissues to a soft pulp. Little absorption takes place in the foregut except for volatile fatty acids. The crushed and sometimes partially digested food passes through a valve into the midgut.

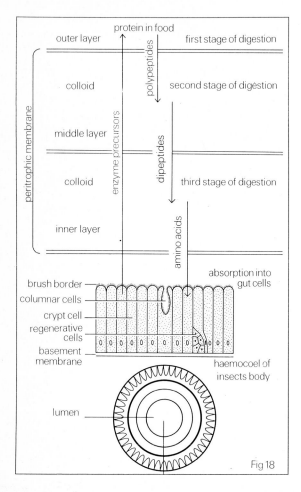

Fig 18

The delicate cells of the midgut of all insects are protected by a multilayered peritrophic membrane, even in those species with a liquid diet when the membrane is very thin (Fig. 18). The peritrophic membrane is usually secreted continuously by special cells at the anterior end of the midgut. In some insects a fresh layer of the membrane is secreted periodically by the whole midgut epithelium. Then the oldest layer of the membrane is shed. Seen under the electron microscope, the peritrophic membrane is reticulate with numerous minute pores piercing it. It seems that the peritrophic membrane usually has three chitinous layers separated by thin colloid layers of high osmotic pressure. There is an inner layer next to the gut epithelium, a middle layer and an outer layer next to the food in the gut lumen. In the Blowfly the entire multi-layered membrane functions as a complex bi-colloid dialyser which selectively passes various substances. It allows digestive enzyme precursors to pass from the cells to the food in the gut lumen but not in the reverse direction. The inactive enzyme precursors are activated in the gut lumen by food or substances released higher up the gut. The activation is a chemical process which results in a reduction of the molecular weight of the precursor. This process, whereby the digestive enzymes are released as inactive precursors is common to most animals and is why animals do not digest their own cells. In the gut lumen activated enzymes digest food and break it down to smaller, easily absorbed molecules. In the Blowfly it is believed that proteases break down protein to polypeptides which can pass through the outer layer only of the peritrophic membrane. The polypeptides are in turn broken down further to dipeptides which can pass through the middle but not the inner layer, and these are finally broken down to single amino-acid molecules which can pass through the final inner layer to the epithelial cells. Thus there is a series of reversible chemical reactions producing a series of ever smaller molecules. In a chemical reaction an equilibrium will be established, but if one of the end products is being removed, the equilibrium will be shifted to produce more of that product. Because the layers of the peritrophic membrane continuously remove the end products of each stage of digestion in turn, the rate of digestion is greatly speeded up. Food can take as little as 30 minutes to pass through the entire gut of many leaf-feeding caterpillars and leather-jackets. Starch is similarly broken down to smaller molecules able to pass through successive layers of the peritrophic membrane. Fatty acids and unchanged emulsified fat can pass straight through the peritrophic membrane to be absorbed by the epithelial cells. The peritrophic membrane protects the very delicate cells of the midgut from mechanical damage, high osmotic pressures and the digestive enzymes in the gut lumen. It insulates the midgut cells from infection by parasites while functioning as probably the most efficient and sophisticated digestive system in the animal kingdom.

Fig. 18 The mode of functioning of a multilayered peritrophic membrane when digesting proteins in the food.

The midgut cells are mostly columnar with a distinctive brush border. There are often many types of these cells, arranged to form distinctive patterns which differ in different zones of the midgut. They secrete the digestive enzymes and absorb the end products of digestion. Other cells lack a brush border, often have an internal cavity and are mainly concerned, not with digestion, but with the storage of waste products. In most insects these cells are regularly replaced by new cells developing from small groups of undifferentiated regenerative cells. This usually occurs at the moults and especially at the pupal-adult moult. Some insects have midgut caeca which increase the surface area of the gut and form sacs containig symbiotic organisms, especially in plant-feeding insects. Many plant-sucking bugs, including scale insects, have a looped midgut which allows most of the liquid in their food to pass directly from the fore to the hindgut through a membrane. The food to be digested is concentrated and only that part passes into the midgut. The rest passes out of the anus and dries on the leaves into the sticky honeydew which, in dry weather, so often forms an ideal medium for the growth of the black 'sooty fungus'. In the Sinai desert one species of coccid feeding on tamarisk bushes produces so much honeydew that it falls to the ground and builds up into the nutritious 'manna from heaven' used for food by desert nomads.

The hindgut is usually much shorter than the midgut and in most insects little absorption of foodstuffs takes place there. However, in termites, the hindgut houses the flagellate protozoa which break down the wood which forms most of their diet, and it also absorbs the end products of this digestion. The hindgut is a very important site of water and salt absorption, and the faeces of many insects living in arid environments are almost completely dry. The faeces are frequently wrapped in the remains of the peritrophic membrane like a disposable sac. The hindguts of many of these insects have a ring of sharp teeth which periodically cut the sac into suitable lengths. This is a very hygienic method of waste disposal.

Excretion

Like all animals, insects must excrete the toxic waste products of their bodies. Their chief excretory organs are the Malpighian tubules which are similar to the kidneys of mammals. The Malpighian tubules are blind ended and discharge into the posterior end of the midgut. A few muscle fibres wind along their length, their contractions causing the Malpighian tubules to undulate in the haemocoel. This helps to drive the urine along the lumen towards the opening.

Into the lumen pass almost all the substances found in the blood, including potassium which is actively secreted against the concentration gradient. The urine also contains the products of the breakdown of proteins. These nitrogenous compounds are converted initially to waste ammonia, but since ammonia is highly toxic, most terrestrial animals convert it into other less toxic compounds like urea or insoluble uric acid. Insects usually convert it into uric acid when water conservation is important.

Lower down the Malpighian tubules or even further down in the hindgut, the insect resorbs those substances which it needs, especially water, salts and sugars. Apparently animals find it easier to evolve mechanisms to select what they want, rather than to reject what they do not want. The final excrement often consists of little more than a dry powder of uric acid crystals dusting the outside of the faeces.

The secondarily aquatic larvae of many insects excrete waste nitrogen as ammonia diluted with lots of water. Terrestrial aphids, which have a copious supply of plant sap, likewise excrete ammonia, as also do blow-fly larvae living on decomposing corpses. These are both conditions where there is plenty of water to dilute the ammonia. Aphids are one of the very few insect families which lack Malpighian tubules, ammonia diffusing readily directly through the epidermis of the rectum. A few insects have nitrogen-fixing micro-organisms within their fat cells which remove the waste ammonia from the bloodstream and rebuild it into aminoacids which ultimately are incorporated once again into the insect's tissues. Springtails (Collembola) lack Malpighian tubules and waste products like uric acid build up in the fat body. These can become quite large just before the death of these short-lived animals, lining the heart and coating the brain. Thus in the autumn springtails are often found containing a crystalline structure resembling Malacca cane. This runs the length of the body and is expanded into a large star-shaped structure in the head. In these animals excretion only occurs as a result of death and the subsequent decomposition of the body. Many caterpillars and other larvae store much of their nitrogenous waste in the cells of the fat body and epidermis. This waste is transferred to the midgut cells of the pupa and is excreted when the cellular lining of the midgut is replaced at the pupal-adult moult. This is particularly noticeable in moths where soon after the adult has emerged from the chrysalis it empties its gut of the cellular remains of the pupal midgut together with a mass of bright yellow or orange nitrogenous waste. Many a young boy who has reared moths in his bedroom has incurred his mother's wrath when she discovered these brightly coloured stains on the wallpaper after the moths had emerged. Adult Lepidoptera are even known to store nitrogenous waste in their wing scales. Many insects absorb indigestible plant pigments from their food. Caterpillars often store these 'waste' substances in their body cells. This gives them some of their cryptic colours which naturally often perfectly match the colours of the plants they live and feed on. This is a valuable form of camouflage. Many substances very poisonous to mammals and birds are found in plants eaten by insects. Frequently these substances are stored safely away in the insect's body, often in a highly

concentrated form. This makes the insects very poisonous to predators which learn to avoid them when the insects are brightly coloured and easily recognized. Other waste substances are built into the cuticle and are excreted when the insect moults.

Respiration

The thick cuticle which is almost impermeable to water is also almost impermeable to oxygen. Insects need lots of oxygen to oxidize the sugar, fats and aminoacids to produce energy to power

their muscles, muscles with enough power to move the wings of a large beetle and to lift it into the air. Insects have evolved a special system of flexible tubes called tracheae which divide into tiny tracheoles to penetrate the organs and the muscles and even push into individual cells (Fig. 19). The tracheae have spirally thickened walls of chitin like fine springs which can be bent and stretched as the body moves but cannot collapse inwards. Air enters the tracheae through ten small openings on each side of the body. Some openings or spiracles have a device to open or close them while others have complicated covers

Lacewing larva camouflaged with cast-off skins.

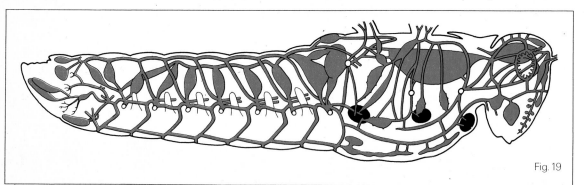

Fig. 19

Fig. 19   The trachael system of a locust showing the numerous thin-walled airsacs scattered throughout the body.

pierced by slits or small pores. Inside the body the tracheae from each spiracle join to form a single system of tubes running the length of the body. The tracheae are most numerous near tissues which have the greatest need for oxygen and more tracheae will develop in response to increased oxygen demand as occurs when a part of the body is injured. In adult insects the tracheal trunks are greatly expanded into large air sacs which increase the volume of oxygen available to the insect and also reduce the insect's specific gravity during flight.

The cells of the body use up the oxygen around themselves and this is replaced by oxygen diffusing through the walls of the tracheae from the air inside the lumen. This in turn is replaced by further oxygen diffusing in through the spiracles. At the same time carbon dioxide and water from the tissues diffuse into the tracheae and out through the spiracles. Unfortunately the amount of oxygen which can diffuse in through the spiracles is only just sufficient to supply the basic needs of most insects at rest. Also while insects need to get rid of the carbon dioxide, many living in dry places need to conserve their water. Many insects release carbon dioxide in bursts and then almost close their spiracles leaving only a narrow slit. The carbon dioxide content of the tracheae between bursts is low. No one has suggested a respiratory advantage in releasing carbon dioxide in bursts. The advantage seems to lie in the reduction in water loss and is a phenomenon least developed in insects living in moist places and best developed in those living in dry ones. When the spiracles are almost closed oxygen enters twenty times as fast as carbon dioxide leaves. Oxygen is often absorbed faster from the tracheae than it can diffuse in, and a partial vacuum develops inside the tracheae and air is sucked in. One might expect the nitrogen in the air to accumulate and impede breathing. Fortunately the rate of nitrogen diffusion out balances the rate of nitrogen inflow, oxygen entry is accelerated, and water and carbon dioxide escape are retarded.

Watching insects will show that insect spiracles are either wide open or almost shut. Insects do not adjust the opening of their spiracles to suit their precise oxygen needs. Indeed two botanists, Brown and Escombe, working on plant stomata showed that 88 per cent of the area of the opening could be closed before the rate of diffusion through it was reduced. The rate of diffusion through a spiracle of this size is approximately proportional to its circumference and not to its area. Up to eight times as much gas will diffuse through a large number of small holes as would diffuse through a single opening of the same area. This is why so many insect larvae have spiracles blocked by covers pierced by slits or by many smaller holes. Air also goes in and out of the spiracles every time a larva moves, because as the body flexes, its volume changes, changing the length of the tracheae.

Rapidly flying adult insects need large quantities of oxygen and they obtain this either by breathing in and out or by taking air in through one spiracle and passing it out of other spiracles further down the body. The breathing movements of insects can easily be seen if one watches a wasp or a large beetle, in which the abdomen constantly rises and falls. Most flying insects have a mixture of both types of breathing. The desert locust at rest takes air in through the first thoracic spiracle and breathes it out of the abdominal spiracles. At the same time air is pumped tidally in and out of the second and third thoracic spiracles. These two spiracles lead to an almost separate system of small tracheal sacs attached to and supplying oxygen to the

Bush Cricket (*Ephippiger ephippiger*), often known as 'tizi' because of the sound it emits. Note the spiracle on the thorax.

flight muscles in the thorax. The faster the insect flies, the larger the volume of air breathed in.

The aquatic larvae of many insects have an almost fully permeable cuticle and their spiracles are blocked. Oxygen dissolved in the surrounding water diffuses through the thin cuticle and into the tracheal system while carbon dioxide diffuses in the opposite direction. Many of these larvae have gills which are outgrowths of the body and which greatly increase the surface area across which the gases can diffuse. They are copiously supplied with tracheae. Many larvae with gills either live in fast-flowing streams or create their own water current over their gill surfaces by constant movements of their body. Some like the alder-fly larva, construct burrows or tubes through which they can pass a constant stream of water and adjust the rate of flow to the oxygen concentration of the water. A few insects like the larvae of midges living in mud low in oxygen, have haemoglobin in their blood. This red respiratory pigment acts as an oxygen store enabling the insects to pentrate deep into the mud in search of their food. Other aquatic larvae and adult insects living in water breathe in air through open spiracles. Many have their spiracles reduced to a single pair protected by whorls of water-repellent hairs which support the insect from the surface film by surface tension and close the spiracle under water. Some larvae, like those of the remarkable leaf beetle *Donacia*, obtain their oxygen by thrusting their sharp pointed spiracles into the air spaces of submerged water plants. Many larvae take a bubble of air down with them to increase the length of time they can remain under water. These bubbles are always attached to the spiracles. As the oxygen in the tracheae is used up, it is replaced by oxygen diffusing in from the bubble, this in turn is replaced by further oxygen diffusing in from the surrounding water. Four-fifths of the gas in air is nitrogen and while it is much less soluble in water than is oxygen, it will slowly dissolve. The bubble therefore slowly decreases in size until the insect has to surface to get a new bigger

bubble. The bubble is a temporary physical gill. Many beetles like the Giant Water Beetle (*Dytiscus marginalis*) are able to carry a larger volume of air by containing it beneath their elytra. Many other insects like *Notonecta*, the 'water boatman', carry an air store held in a mass of close-set water repellent bent hairs or basket-like extensions of their spiracles. The surface tension of the water across these struc-

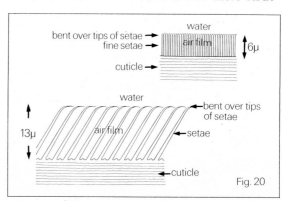

tures maintains a constant volume. These are permanent physical gills or plastrons (Fig. 20). When the oxygen tension of the water is high, the air in the plastron seldom needs replacement. Many eggs laid in places liable to flooding have superbly developed plastrons as part of their eggshells. The pupae of some wasps which parasitize aquatic insects have a long air-filled silk tube into which their spiracles open. The principle of plastrons has been used for centuries in the famous Indian coffin trick, where a man is placed in an open-ended coffin which is tightly bound with fine linen cloth and lowered into a river. This is left there for several days before the man is hauled up, none the worse for his rest on the river bottom in a permanent bubble of air.

The blood and circulatory system

The blood forms the environment in which the organs of the insect's body live. It brings food, salts and oxygen to the organs and also hormones to control their functions. It carries away carbon

Damselfly nymph clearly showing gills at the hind end.

Fig. 20   The permanent plaston of the aquatic bug *Aphelocheirus* (above). The short very close-set hairs, almost two million to the square millimetre, preserve a thin permanent film of air even at considerable depths. This is the insects aqualung from which it withdraws oxygen. This is replaced by oxygen diffusing in from the surrounding water.

The temporary plastron of the aquatic leaf beetle *Haemonia* (below). The coarse hairs with their bent over tips preserve a film of air for several hours. This slowly diminishes and eventually has to be replaced with more air. Some insects collect air from the surface but *Haemonia* collects air from underwater plants with the help of its antennae.

Silver Water Beetle (*Acilius sulcatus*) carrying an air bubble.

dioxide and other waste products. The blood cells clot in wounds, engulf microbes when the insect is diseased and form capsules around parasite eggs, especially when they are laid in the wrong host.

Most animals have a single heart to pump the blood round the body. This is sufficient for an animal like a cow or a dog with a compact body and only four comparatively fat legs. Insects have the problem of pumping blood in and out of long thin appendages like the antennae and wings, appendages often packed with sense organs needing an excellent circulation of blood to function properly. Insects have solved this problem by having many small accessory hearts in addition to the big main heart. These accessory hearts are found at the base of each long appendage and pump the blood through blood vessels and valves like those in man. The shorter, broader appendages like the maxillary palps and the legs of some adult insects have blood vessels and valves to direct the flow, but lack accessory hearts. The blood is pumped round whenever the appendages move, as a result of small changes in their volume. Unlike in mammals, the blood vessels seldom connect up, but empty into the body cavity, the blood flowing around the organs. The abdominal cavity is divided horizontally by two sheets of muscular tissue into three compartments or sinuses. The main heart is a long tube with many valves running the length of the upper compartment. It pumps the blood forward through the aorta in the thorax, to the head. The blood flows back down the body and along the ventral sinus of the abdomen. Waves of contraction in the muscular sheet drive the blood through the sinus to the tip of the abdomen.

It would be wrong to think that the flow of blood in an adult insect is sluggish. It is very quick and flows along definite pathways even in the body cavity. In the alder-fly larva it takes just 64 seconds for all the blood in the body to go round once. A circulatory system such as an insect's, where the blood flows around the organs, is called an open system to distinguish it from a closed system, as in mammals, where it flows right round the body confined in blood vessels. In insects, however, most of the tissues are prevented from coming into direct contact with the blood by a cellular membrane which only allows certain substances to pass through. This means that the body cells are insulated from the small changes which frequently occur in the blood, and which would be sufficient to kill most other animals. Where changes in the internal environment would be large, these are limited by compensatory mechanisms. For instance, small changes in the pH of the blood are not transmitted to the cells because of the cellular membrane. Large changes in pH are avoided by a system of buffers which becomes more efficient the greater the potential change. Some changes are seasonal. In the autumn glycerol builds up in the blood of many insects. It acts as an antifreeze, preventing the blood from freezing. This is extremely important where a small,

cold-blooded animal is to survive the winter. Such systems make insects extremely adaptable and resistant to adverse conditions.

Sense organs

When trying to catch insects, one quickly realizes that they are acutely aware of their surroundings by touch, sight, hearing, smell and taste. Some even have specialized receptors for humidity, temperature or depth.

The surface of most insects bears many articulated hairs or setae. These setae are sensitive to touch and will also record sound and wind speed. Indeed, insects sometimes have difficulty distinguishing between these senses. The setae are therefore generalized mechanoreceptors. Each has a nerve cell attached to its base within which lies the scolopale, a bell-shaped chitinous structure. Movement of the seta distorts the scolopale and stimulates the nerve. Sometimes the seta is reduced to a thin circular or semicircular dome of cuticle, often thickened along one side. These are chordotonal organs which respond to the stresses in the insect's surface, giving it information on body posture during movement. Thus the haltères of flies have some 418 chordotonal organs arranged along different axes, giving the insect essential flight information. They are the 'black boxes' or flight recorders of insects.

Nerve cells containing scolopales are also found stretched across the haemocoel between the organs and give the insect essential information on internal body functions and movement. Thus the bloodsucking bug *Rhodnius*, which has only a single meal before each moult, has a chordotonal organ between the body wall and the gut. After a blood meal the chordotonal organ is stretched and sends a series of impulses to the brain. This causes the brain to initiate the release of the hormones which cause moulting. (See also page 8.)

The setae of caterpillars respond to low-pitched sounds. However, many insects have well-developed ears similar to those of man, with a tympanum and countertympanum. The tympana are again modified setae with scolopales attached to their centres. Noctuid moths have a pair of ears, one on each side of the abdomen. The ears are very sensitive and are able to detect the ultrasonic sounds produced by hunting bats in time for the moths to dive for cover. Crickets and grasshoppers have well-developed ears either on their legs or on the abdomen. They rely on these to recognize the calls of their mates during courtship. Indeed it is often easier to recognize a grasshopper from its call than by looking at it.

There are many different structures which detect chemicals in the external environment. Chemicals may be tasted or smelt though there is no real difference between these two senses. The receptor organs are usually specific for sweet, sour, salt, sex attractants, etc. and vary in their structure accordingly. Taste and smell receptors are very common on the heads of insects, especially on the antennae, and there are large numbers of taste receptors on the labial palps. Sometimes the antennae are greatly expanded to carry the receptors as in male silk moths which find their mates by following the smell produced by special sex attractant glands from as far as a mile away. Other smells called pheromones are produced by one insect and act on other individuals of the same species, slowing down or speeding up specific parts of their metabolism. In locusts pheromones like this synchronize the development of the swarms so that all individuals are ready to mate at the same time. Bees recognize their own hives by smell and leave smell signposts to guide their hive mates to good feeding sites. Obviously in insects the sense of smell is highly developed as a means of communication, probably more so than in any other group of animals.

Most animal cells are light sensitive although the animal itself may not realize it. So it is not surprising to find that insects do not need eyes to respond to light. Blow-fly maggots have no eyes on the surface of the body but have special light-sensitive cells deep in the head. The larvae of many water beetles have cells particularly sensitive to light around the terminal spiracles of the abdomen. These assist the insect to orientate the terminal spiracles towards the surface of the water when it comes up to breathe. Most insect larvae have groups of simple eyes on the head (Fig. 21). Each has a transparent area of cuticle which is often lens-shaped with a retina of pigmented, light-sensitive cells below. No one knows if these simple eyes can form an image but many predacious larvae can see the size and estimate the distance and speed of their prey with remarkable precision.

The larvae of ant-lions and the caterpillars of butterflies and moths have more complicated eyes similar to the simple eyes or ocelli of adult wasps and bugs (Fig. 22). These have an outer lens with a second lens below, focusing the light on to seven retinal cells grouped in a ring around a common light-sensitive core or rhabdome. These simple eyes and ocelli are certainly capable of discerning shapes and some may be able to recognize colours.

Adult insects have compound eyes composed of large numbers of separate light-sensitive units or ommatidia. These act like large numbers of ocelli grouped tightly together yet separated by pigment cells. Each focuses light from a narrow segment of the outside world on to the light-sensitive rhabdome, light from adjacent segments being absorbed by the pigment cells. As each ommatidium is at a slightly different angle to the rest, each records the average light intensity from a different patch and the insect brain builds up a mosaic picture of the whole field of view. It is assumed that the greater the number of ommatidia the greater the amount of detail that can be seen. Thus the number of ommatidia in a compound eye can vary from a few, to 28 000 in the larger dragonflies. In nocturnal insects the ommatidia are elongated and the pigment can be withdrawn at night allowing light to be focused by seven, nineteen or thirty-seven adjacent lenses across the eye on to a single rhabdome. These eyes collect much more light, giving a brighter but less sharp image. Many noctuid moths have eyes like a cat which glow in the light of a torch. These have a mirror-like back to the eye which reflects the light back on to the rhabdome, again increasing the brightness of the image.

The size and shape of the ommatidia vary greatly even within the same eye. Each of the compound eyes of the whirligig water beetle *Gyrinus* is split into two. One half of the eye is on top of the head and surveys the aerial world; the other half is under the head and sees the aquatic world. Experiments indicate that insects are not very good at recognizing static shapes but are very sensitive to movement. This causes a flicker effect as light from a single moving object is focused on one rhabdome after another. It also enables insects to measure their flight speed as the ground passes by.

Most adult insects have colour vision but the colours that they see are only blue, yellow and ultraviolet. Few insects other than butterflies can see red. Thus most species of gentians are blue and are pollinated by insects, but there are also some gentians which are red and these

Fig. 21 Cross-section of a simple eye.

Fig. 22 The structure of compound eyes. Each eye is composed of many separate light-sensitive units or ommatidia. Some insects have apposition eyes where each retinal rod receives light only through its own lens. Many nocturnal insects have superposition eyes where the retinal rods are set well below the crystalline cones and in the dark adapted state receive light entering many ommatidia. In the dark adapted state the pigment moves downwards to form a screen and the eye acts as an apposition eye.

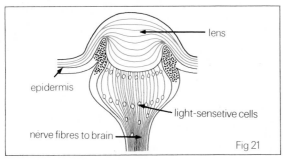

lens

epidermis

light-sensetive cells

nerve fibres to brain

Fig 21

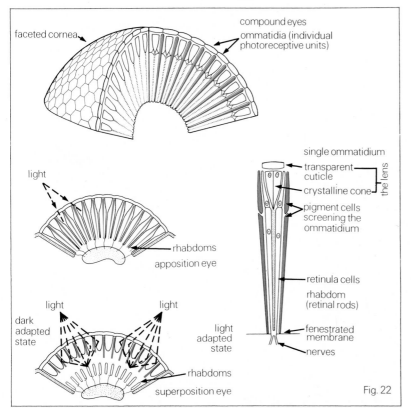

faceted cornea

compound eyes

ommatidia (individual photoreceptive units)

light

rhabdoms

apposition eye

single ommatidium

transparent cuticle

crystalline cone

the lens

pigment cells screening the ommatidium

retinula cells

rhabdom (retinal rods)

light adapted state

fenestrated membrane

nerves

dark adapted state

light   light

rhabdoms

superposition eye

Fig. 22

are pollinated by birds. Ultraviolet photographs of many flowers show patterns invisible to man which guide insects to the nectaries.

Many insects use their eyes to measure the angle of the sun or moon. They then use this information to navigate when flying. This can be unfortunate for insects flying past man's artificial lights. Moths will fly at a constant angle to a light and thus circle round the light until they collide with it. Bees and ants use the angle of the sun for navigation even when the sun is obscured by cloud. They can do this because the light waves coming from the sun are polarized in one plane and it is the plane of polarization that the bees measure. Thus they can use any small patch of blue sky for navigation.

Some insects have sense organs associated with specialized habits. Body lice, which live on the moister areas of the bodies of warm-blooded animals, have humidity receptors. Many blood-sucking or desert-living insects have temperature receptors and water insects which dive have depth receptors.

Central nervous system

Sensory organs are only of use to an animal if the information obtained is passed on to a centre which sorts out the information and initiates the appropriate response. This is the central nervous system. The nervous system of all animals is composed of a large number of similar simple cellular units or neurones. How these are put together determines the form and function of the different parts of the nervous system. The axons (fibres) of the sensory neurones of insects run from the cell bodies in the sensory cells to the nerve cord. Here they connect to motor neurones with their cell bodies in the nerve cord or with collateral neurones which connect with motor neurones somewhere else in the central nervous system. The motor axons run out to the muscles and produce a muscular response to the original sensory stimulus. The whole sequence from the stimulation of the sense organ to the final muscular response constitutes a reflex arc.

The cell bodies of the neurones of the central nervous system are grouped together in each segment of the body to form a pair of fused rounded ganglia. The ganglia of each body segment are connected to those of the adjacent segments by the longitudinal connectives thus forming a double nerve cord running the length of the body. The ganglia of the first three segments of the head are fused to form the brain above the oesophagus. The ganglia of the last three head segments are also fused and form the suboesophageal ganglion below the oesophagus. The brain receives information from the antennae, the compound and simple eyes and the labrum. Thus it is the correlating centre for these very important sense organs which play such a vital role in locomotion, host selection, feeding and mate finding. Unlike vertebrates, the brain of insects inhibits locomotion, while maintaining the tonus of the muscles. If an insect's brain is cut out, the animal will walk steadily forwards, but cannot climb or go backwards, and it will be almost oblivious of its surroundings. The body is held low because of the loss of muscle tonus. The suboesophageal ganglion receives information and initiates movement in the mandibles, maxillae and labium. Thus it is the correlating centre for feeding. In addition it produces the diapause hormone. Each segmental ganglion of the thorax and abdomen controls the functions of its own body segment. Thus a male praying mantis will continue to copulate while its mate eats first its head and then its thorax and most of its abdomen. A silk moth will lay eggs when its head, thorax and first third of the abdomen are removed, although without a head the eggs are laid on any surface for it is the head that selects the correct host plant. Without a thorax the eggs are no longer laid in their characteristic patterns for this is controlled by rhythmic movements of the legs. Thus in insects much of the behaviour is locally organized and coordinated by the segmental ganglia. The brain acts as the centre for the sensory organs of the head and as an inhibitory centre controlling the release of the segmental and intersegmental systems.

In addition to the central nervous system insects have a sympathetic nervous system intimately connected to the brain and lying mainly along the foregut. As in vertebrates, this system enervates the visceral organs and the nerve endings secrete many hormones.

Nerve impulses travel quite slowly down the nerves of insects. Their speed is directly proportional to the diameter of the fibre. The important life and death reflex arcs, which enable insects to detect an enemy and to escape, have very thick fibres while the other nerve fibres are much thinner. The hind jumping legs of grasshoppers have a giant 'fast' nerve fibre which divides into a large number of nerve endings which simultaneously stimulate the whole of the femoral jumping muscle, and a few thin 'slow' fibres which insert at one end of the muscle. The giant fibre stimulates the muscle to give one great galvanic twitch, making the animal jump, while the thin fibres cause a slow wave of contraction to pass along the muscle, resulting in delicate precise movements of the limb as when walking or feeding. Impulses pass chemically from one nerve ending to another as a result of the transitory production of acetylcholine by the end of the axon. All neurones are therefore secretory. Some neurones have greatly developed secretory functions and produce neurohormones when they are stimulated. These neurosecretory cells are scattered in groups throughout the nervous system, but are especially common in the sympathetic nervous system. The sympathetic system includes the corpora cardiaca which release the hormone controlling the secretory cycles of the prothoracic glands which in turn initiate moulting. In the blood-sucking bug *Rhodnius* a blood meal swelling the crop stretches a chordotonal sensory organ which responds by sending a stream of impulses to the brain. The result is that the neurosecretory cells of the roof of the brain produce their secretions which move down the nerve fibres to the corpora cardiaca where the secretion is released as a result of nervous stimulation. Thus the nervous and hormonal control of the body is integrated, the brain controlling many long-term metabolic and developmental changes in the body by means of nervous control of hormone secretion both by neuro-secretory cells and by glandular tissue. The responses of insects are, therefore, characteristically predictable and, when danger threatens, characteristically quick.

Reproduction

Insects reproduce in a prodigious number of different ways. Most have two sexes and mate, the sperm fertilizing the eggs to begin the development of the embryo. Sexual reproduction produces eggs often able to resist adverse conditions and which hatch into variable offspring on which selection acts, only the fittest individuals surviving. Very few insects are hermaphrodites. They include Cottony Cushion Scale (*Icerya purchasi*), a pest of citrus orchards. In this species, the outer cells of the gonads move inward to fertilize the eggs. In the bisexual bees and wasps most of the eggs are fertilized and all these develop into females. The unfertilized eggs nevertheless develop, but grow up into males. It may not be a matter of chance whether or not the eggs are fertilized. It seems that there may be two polymorphic forms of eggs, only one of which can be fertilized. One species of spider beetle no longer has a male of its own, but the female still has to mate with the male of a related species because though her eggs are never fertilized they cannot begin to develop until they have come into contact with sperm. Many parasitic wasps have no males, the eggs developing parthenogenetically (virgin birth). In a few species each egg divides asexually after it has been laid in the host and produces several hundred separate larvae. This is a valuable adaptation when hosts are hard to find.

After fertilization, or the initiation of development, the eggs are usually laid and develop and hatch in the outside world. However, chrysomelid beetles sometimes delay laying their eggs in the north of Britain until shortly before hatching or they may even produce live young. These are species which lay their eggs at the normal time in warmer regions. Tsetse-flies living in the African bush produce viviparously a single full-grown larva which is so well developed that it immediately pupates. The mother feeds on the blood of mammals and is responsible for the feeding of the larva through a 'milk' gland in her uterus. Viviparity is often associated with parthenogenesis especially in plant-feeding species like aphids. Both these adaptations increase the speed of population growth. It is even known for insect larvae to become precociously mature as in the beetle *Micromalthus* and to produce further larvae parthenogenetically. Aphids have combined the advantages of the sexual production of eggs with the advantages of asexual viviparity. Often aphids migrate between a perennial host on which their eggs are laid and an annual host which they rapidly exploit asexually. In the spring the sexually-produced eggs hatch into a great variety of aphids which differ in genetic constitution. Natural selection quickly kills off most of these until only the few fittest kinds survive. These rapidly reproduce asexually to give large numbers of uniform copies. This inevitably means that this year's aphids will not be quite the same as last year's, for natural selection and therefore the characters it selects, differ from year to year.

In insects which reproduce sexually, the eggs and sperm are produced by the paired gonads in the abdomen. The ovaries contain numbers of tubes or ovarioles. The mother cells are formed at one end and slowly move down the tube dividing a number of times. This results in an egg with the reduced chromosome number and several nurse cells which produce the yolk which is passed into the egg. Other cells break away from the wall of the mother's ovariole and envelop the egg. It is these cells which secrete the eggshell. Later all the cells surrounding the egg including the yolk cells, break down leaving the fully developed egg in its shell. The egg passes on down the oviduct to the uterus where fertilization occurs, the sperm entering through small holes at one end of the egg. These are the micropyles. Sperm is stored by the female after copulation and a little is released each time an egg arrives in the uterus. Finally the eggs are laid and glued down, covered up, or enclosed in a purse-like container formed by the accessory glands.

The testes are similar in structure to the ovaries, the gametes repeatedly dividing as they pass down the tube, to be stored as bundles of sperm with the reduced chromosome number. These bundles are then either incorporated into a proteinaceous capsule or spermatophore or are injected directly into the female during copulation. Some spermatophores like those of crickets are very complicated structures with pressure bodies which slowly swell forcing the sperm down a narrow tube which the male firmly cements into the female's copulatory opening. These spermatophores act as hypodermic needles, inseminating the female by remote control. Many moths are remarkable in that the female has two genital openings, one for copulation and one for egg-laying. The moth spermatophore is a simple capsule formed by the male within the females bursa copulatrix during copulation. Afterwards the male seals the female's copulatory opening with a plug preventing further matings. The spermatophore is then punctured by the chitinous spikes lining the bursa copulatrix which are driven into it by muscular contraction. The released sperm migrates across the uterus to the spermatheca where it is stored and fed until it is required for fertilization. Thus the sperm actively swims, probably in response to chemical stimuli, on four distinct occasions, twice in the male and

Variety in eggs of
Lepidoptera: egg
cluster of a moth
(left) and Fritillary
Butterfly egg (right).

twice in the female, each separated by a period of quiescence.

Most of the higher insect orders do not produce spermatophores but pass the sperm directly as a fluid suspension through a penis or aedeagus. This is a tubular structure often bent in the middle into an L-shape which allows the male to make contact with the female after mounting. Many insects have a long tubular filament within the aedeagus which is extruded during copulation and it is often only this filament and not the aedeagus itself which enters the female. Whereas most insects inject the sperm into the copulatory opening, the bedbug *Cimex* inseminates the female by forcing its aedeagus anywhere through the body wall of the abdomen and injects the sperm into the haemocoel. The sperm then swims through the blood and reaches the eggs through the wall of the ovary. One can tell how many times a bedbug has mated by counting the number of wounds in the body wall. This insect frequently inseminates other males instead of a female, especially in the autumn, a clear example of homosexuality. Many of the sperm of bedbugs are engulfed by blood cells and it has been suggested that the recipient insects derive a significant boost to their nutrition, enabling more eggs to be laid or more individuals of both sexes to survive the winter at the expense of many of the males.

Insects eggs are laid in a very wide variety of places and the structure and adaptations of the eggshell are correspondingly varied. Many eggs are ovate, but some are stalked and others have flanges, respiratory horns or complex caps. Eggs laid in flowing water may have anchors or suction pads to attach them to the substrate. Hatching from a tough eggshell is a difficult process for a small insect larva. Some larvae have sharp blade-like spines on their backs or on the back of the embryonic cuticle to split the shell, or spikes on the head to break open the egg cap. Other larvae bite their way out of the shell or press hard on it causing it to fracture along preformed lines of weakness. Lacewings have highly cannibalistic larvae and many species have eggs supported on long filamentous stalks. It seems that by isolating each egg these stalks prevent cannibalism immediately after hatching. Ladybirds lay groups of eggs, many of which are infertile. After hatching the young larvae eat their own eggshells and also any nearby unhatched eggs. The infertile eggs give the newly-hatched larvae enough nutrition to keep them going until they can find and consume their normal prey, which may be scattered and difficult to find for a small newly-hatched larva.

Insect development

Insects hatch from their eggs as larvae which vary enormously in their structure (Figs 23 and 24). It was once believed that all the nymphal stages of the exopterygotes were the equivalent of the endopterygote pupa and that the endopterygote larvae were equivalent to the later embryonic stages found in the exopterygote egg. This was the Berlese-Imms theory of the origin of the pupa. All insect embryos develop vestigial abdominal appendages at the so-called polypod stage, but these are always resorbed. It was at one time thought that in the caterpillars of butterflies and moths, these primitive embryonic abdominal legs persisted as the prolegs. However, the prolegs of caterpillars are new specialized structures not homodynamous with the thoracic legs and are formed just before hatching. The difference between endopterygote larvae and exopterygote nymphs is more imaginary than real and is a measure of the extent to which the larva is specialized as a streamlined feeding stage living in soil, vegtation, dung, etc. All embryos develop in the same way and hatch from the egg at the same stage of development, secondary specialized structures like the prolegs of caterpillars developing just before hatching. Later workers accepted that there was no real difference between larvae and nymphs and thought that the pupal stage was an additional adult stage required in endopterygote insects because the muscles could only be attached to the cuticle by the tonofibrillae at a moult. One moult was required to form the new adult shape and the new muscles to go with it, and an additional moult to attach those muscles to the cuticle. Thus two adult stages were required when the larva was very different in

structure from the adult. These two stages are the pupa and the imago. This was the Poyarkoff–Hinton theory and was very attractive because many exopterygote insects like scale insects and whitefly, which have specialized larvae very different from the adults, also have pupae.

It is now known that muscles can attach to the cuticle at any time during an instar and that all the new adult muscles are already present as a few primordial strands long before the formation of the pupa. It is now accepted that the pupae of endopterygote insects are specialized final instar larvae equivalent to the final instar nymphs of exopterygotes, and are retained as a stage when the wings which have been developed inside the body of endopterygote larvae are evaginated and continue to grow outside the body. The pupa bridges the difference between the specialized wingless larva and the winged adult, and the greater the difference between larva and adult, the greater the changes that occur in the pupa and the less mobile it is. There is therefore no significant difference between the pupae of exopterygote and endopterygote insects, nor between larvae and nymphs.

Heteromorphosis

A few insects belonging to a wide variety of orders have more than one kind of larva. This is called heteromorphosis and is found particularly among parasitic insects where the eggs are laid a long way from the final host. Oil beetles lay huge numbers of eggs in the soil, up to 10 000 per female. They hatch into active triungulin larvae, many of which climb up the vegetation and into the flowers. If they are in the right flower and it is then visited by the right hymenopterous insect, the larvae jump or crawl on to the host and are carried back to its nest, where they feed as parasites on the larvae of the host. The next instar is a resting pseudopupal stage during which the larvae metamorphose into the subsequent very different, grub-like instars which feed on honey or scavenge in the nest. The life history of the oil beetle is one of the more extreme examples of heteromorphosis. Many other insects show it to a lesser extent, especially

Pupal case of a Swallowtail Butterfly with wings showing through.

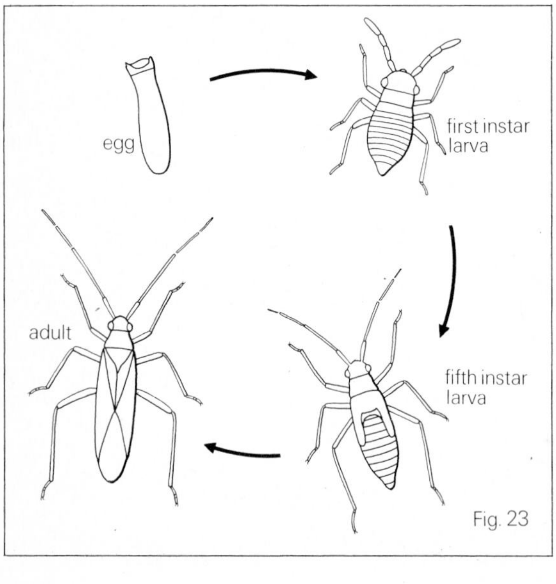

Fig. 23 The life-cycle of Hemiptera showing the development of a typical hemimetabolous insect, where the larva or nymph gradually develops into an adult without an intervening pupal stage. These insects are also exopterygotes – the embryonic wings develop outside the body of the larva.

Fig. 24 The life-cycle of Lepidoptera showing the development of a typical holometabolous insect, where the larva metamorphoses into a pupa and finally into an adult. These insects are also exopterygotes – the embryonic wings develop inside the body of the larva.

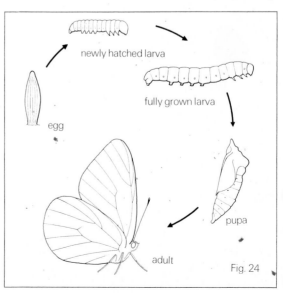

first instar larva

egg

fifth instar larva

adult

Fig. 23

newly hatched larva

egg

fully grown larva

pupa

adult

Fig. 24

those Lepidoptera whose early instars are flattened leaf miners or resemble bird droppings or where the later instars live in ant nests; and also Hymenoptera parasitic in animals.

Puparium

Many pupae are protected by a puparium. This is formed in many ways, from a wide variety of materials. The puparia of many beetles and some horse-flies are made of mud whereas those of some Hymenoptera and Lepidoptera are of silk spun just before the larval–pupal ecdysis. It is the silk of these puparia which man unwinds to produce silk thread for textiles. In the Lepidoptera, Trichoptera, Hymenoptera and Psocoptera the larvae produce silk from the salivary glands of the labium, the salivary function being taken over by the mandibular glands. This contrasts with the Coleoptera and Neuroptera where silk is produced by one of the pairs of Malpighian tubules.

The insects may break out of the puparium either before or after the pupal–adult ecdysis but always after the pupal–adult apolysis. It has been shown that the chief structural differences between pupae are related to the way in which the adult escapes. In most primitive endopterygote orders the cuticle is used to escape from the puparium and therefore the appendages are free (exarate) and the mandibles are movable (decticous). In these insects the pharate adult uses the pupal mandibles to bite open the puparium and this may be followed by burrowing through the soil, or, as in most caddis flies, swimming to the surface before ecdysis can occur. Other pupae are adecticous. They do not have movable mandibles, although their appendages may be free (exarate) as in many beetles and wasps or glued down to the body (obtect) as in most fly pupae. Butterflies and moths are obtect, although they lack mandibles. Adecticous pupae break out of the puparium using either spines on the abdomen or similar structures on the head. The adults of most beetles and wasps emerge before leaving the puparium and it is the adult which bites its way out. Other insects without biting mouthparts build escape mechanisms into the puparium as shown by the funnel-shaped exit from the silk cocoon of the Emperor Moth. Muscid flies have a large sac, called a ptilinum, on the head between the antennae. This inflates like a balloon when the adult is emerging, forcing off the cap-like end of the puparium.

Insect life histories are very complex and diverse. This enables them to exploit successfully a very wide range of habitats and an even wider range of niches within these habitats.

Moulting

Many insect larvae have a hard external skeleton which allows very little room for growth. Others have a soft external skeleton which can expand with growth, but only to a limited extent. Further growth can only occur by secreting a new bigger cuticle and shedding the old one. This potentially dangerous process is called moulting and is common to all arthropods. Moulting is initiated by the secretion of the hormone ecdysone by the prothoracic glands. The result is a burst of active cell division, followed by reorganization of the cells and accompanied by varying degrees of change of body form. The period from one moult to the next is an instar. The number of instars is greatest in the more primitive insects and least in the more advanced orders. Thysanura continue to moult throughout their lives. Mayflies have twenty or more larval instars and two winged instars, the subimago and the adult. Muscid flies have three larval instars, a pupal instar and an adult instar.

The first physical sign of moulting is the separation of the epidermis from the old cuticle and the production of moulting fluid, a substance which dissolves the inner layers of the cuticle. The separation of the epidermis from the cuticle is called apolysis and marks the time when an insect changes from one instar to the next. The insect epidermis is naked, without a cuticle immediately after apolysis, a condition which is often transitory but may continue for days or even weeks. This period of nakedness is the exuvial phase and allows the cells of the epidermis to divide and rearrange themselves to form the structures of the new instar. The length of the exuvial phase tends to be proportional to the extent to which the epidermis is remodelled. Then the epidermis begins to secrete the new cuticle through tiny cytoplasmic papillae which grow out from the surface of the cells. The papillae eventually form the pore canals through which the protective outer layers of the cuticle are secreted. Throughout this time the new instar is protected by the cuticle of the previous instar and is therefore hidden or pharate. In many insects the scolopales of the sensory setae of the old cuticle still pass through the moulting fluid and the new cuticle to the original sensory cells. In this way the pharate instar maintains its sensory connections with the old cuticle and remains aware of what is happening in the world outside. Sometimes tonofibrillae of the muscles also pass through the new cuticle to the old so that the new instar can use its muscles to operate the cuticular structures of the previous instar. Indeed many adult insects operate the cuticular mandibles of the pupa to bite their way out of the pupal cell or chrysalis. The moulting fluid, after it has dissolved the inner layers of the old cuticle, is resorbed by the epidermis and replaced by air. Much of the material from the old cuticle is rebuilt back into the new, a nice example of recycling. Eventually, days, weeks, or even months after apolysis, the insect swallows air or water, the old cuticle splits along special lines of weakness and the new instar crawls out. This is ecdysis. The newly-emerged insect swallows more air and stretches its much-folded and creased new cuticle until it assumes its new shape and size. The inner layers of the cuticle are then secreted and the previously-formed layers of the cuticle hardened. The exoskeleton of the new instar is now fully formed, although additional layers may be added to the inside of the inner layers of the cuticle throughout the instar. The caterpillars of butterflies and moths have a soft, much-folded cuticle and continue to increase in size between moults, the cuticle losing its wrinkles and becoming smooth and stretched.

The pharate stage is often brief and usually ends with ecdysis, but it may be prolonged as in the first instar larvae of many exopterygotes and the pupae and adults of many endopterygotes. There is no free pupal stage in muscid flies, but the final instar larval cuticle is preserved and hardened to form the characteristic puparium after the larval–pupal apolysis. The pupal–adult apolysis follows to produce a pharate adult still enclosed in the cuticles of both the pupa and the final instar larva. The pharate stage gives the new instar time to undergo the changes associated with moulting, especially when those changes are very large as at the larval–pupal and pupal–adult moults of endopterygote insects.

Moulting is controlled by neurohormones secreted by special nerve cells in the roof of the brain. The neurohormones flow down the axons to the corpora allata of the insect's sympathetic nervous system and are released into the bloodstream as a result of nervous stimulation. This so-called brain hormone stimulates the prothoracic glands to secrete their hormone. This is the unfortunately named ecdysone which initiates apolysis and not ecdysis. Ecdysis is controlled by recently-discovered ecdysial hormones. Each stage of moulting including the deposition of endocuticle, the retraction of the posterior abdominal segments and the tanning of the cuticle of pupae, is controlled by separate hormones secreted by special cells, usually in the central nervous system. While the insect is a larva the corpora allata of the sympathetic system secrete a hormone which ensures that, during moulting, the body cells form only larval structures. This is the juvenile hormone which, at high concentrations, keeps larvae as larvae. If the apolysis hormone ecdysone is secreted in the presence of a low level of juvenile hormone, then pupal characters result at the moult. The secretion of ecdysone in the pupa in the absence of juvenile hormone results in the production of adult characters. The relative proportions of juvenile hormone and ecdysone at each moult therefore control the rate of metamorphosis and therefore control whether metamorphosis is gradual throughout larval life as in most exopterygotes, or sudden and 'complete' as in those insects with a pupa, e.g. the endopterygotes. Even in the endopterygotes when the first instar larva hatches from the egg it already contains small groups of cells or imaginal discs which will later develop into adult structures. Little development of these structures occurs until the pupal stage. In the more advanced endopterygote orders, almost all the larval structures are broken down in the pupa and replaced with new adult structures developing from the imaginal discs. The pupal stage is almost a second embryonic stage during which the adult structures develop.

Diapause

The pupa is a stage which reverts biochemically to an embryonic condition. Sometimes in either the egg or pupa there is a delay in the start of the next developmental stage due to a failure of the cell nuclei to produce the necessary coenzymes. Developmental delays of this type commonly occur in insects immediately before and during times of adverse environmental conditions, especially the winter in temperate climates and the dry season in tropical and subtropical climates. Such developmental delays, which are long lasting and, once initiated, can only be broken by a trend of change in the environment, are called diapause.

Diapause is either inherited and therefore obligatory, or is facultative and initiated by particular environmental stimuli including day length, humidity and temperature, or by combinations of several stimuli. The time of stimulation may be long before the onset of diapause, even during the previous generation of the species. In the Silk Moth (*Bombyx mori*) the day length and temperature experienced by the eggs determine whether females hatching from those eggs will themselves lay eggs which will or will not diapause. The environmental stimuli act on the brain which stimulates the suboesophageal gland to secrete the diapause hormone. In temperate regions the diapause hormone is broken down by temperatures just above freezing; breakdown is most rapid at 6–10 °C. Thus the diapause hormone breaks down mainly in the autumn and the spring until a point is reached when ecdysone begins to be secreted. Once secreted, ecdysone seems to actively break down the remains of the diapause hormone and moulting follows. Diapause is vital to the survival of many insects enabling them to survive unfavourable conditions and especially times of food shortage. In temperate climates it often prevents insects from emerging in the warm days of autumn and keeps them quiescent until winter is reached when temperatures are too low for development or activity. In the early spring diapause has often ceased some time before the temperature is high enough for development to resume and moulting to occur. Diapause in the egg and pupal stages is inevitably quiescent diapause, the maintenance of the embryonic cytochromes resulting in the cessation of protein synthesis and the adoption of mainly anaerobic respiration. Diapause also occurs during larval and adult stages when it is seldom quiescent and respiration does not become anaerobic. Indeed, diapause in these stages is often restricted to only a part of the body. Thus adverse conditions can cause a developmental delay or diapause in the maturation of the ovaries of locusts. This type of diapause is common in the hotter parts of the world and is often controlled by day length or humidity.

Diapause acts as a delaying mechanism synchronizing the insect's development with favourable times. This enables it to exploit its environment efficiently without too high a mortality.

Insect Habitats

With something like a million species known already, and many more undoubtedly still to be discovered, the insects far outnumber all the other kinds of animals put together. If we search for the reasons for this abundance of species we find two major factors: the relatively small size of most insects, and their amazing adaptability. These two factors combine to enable the insects to make use of a vast number of habitats and food materials that are denied to other animals. There are very few parts of the world that are completely devoid of at least some insects, and there can be few, if any, plant or animal materials that are not eaten by some kind of insect. Some idea of the adaptability of insects with respect to their feeding habits and equipment has already been given. Other factors which have been involved in the success of the insects include their tough, waterproof coverings and their ability to fly. Flight has allowed many insects to spread themselves into environments which they might otherwise never have reached, although some have since lost the power of flight. Less obviously, perhaps, the dramatic change or metamorphosis which most insects undergo during their development has also contributed to their success. Many young insects have eating habits which are quite different from those of the adults, and this means that a given area can support many more insects than it could if both young and adults had the same diet. This increase in individual insects can also affect the number of species eventually, because a greater number of offspring means a greater chance of mutations – the spontaneous variations in genetic make-up which can lead to the development of new species. A relatively short life cycle is yet another factor coming into play here, for an animal having two generations in a year is clearly more likely to produce new species by evolution in a given time than an animal that breeds only once a year or even less frequently. Given the habitats, the insects are thus supremely suited to invading and occupying them all. Most insects live in unremarkable habitats. In this chapter we will concentrate on some of the more exceptional insect environments.

Insects over the world

Only the sea has proved a major barrier to the insects, and we don't really know why they have not yet managed to conquer it. It has been suggested that competition with the crustaceans already in residence is one factor, but there are certainly chemical and physical problems for the insects to solve as well. Nevertheless, there are some marine insects, and the sea may yet succumb to the insect legion. Several hundred insect species – admittedly very few compared with the total number of insects – live in coastal salt marshes and in the intertidal zones of the shore, and it seems that these insects may be in the process of moving from a terrestrial life to a marine existence, just as some periwinkles are moving up the shore and becoming terrestrial animals. The insects are already pre-adapted for life in the sea in that their outer coverings are impermeable to salt, but salty diets pose problems for many insects, although these problems are not insuperable. (To be pre-adapted does not mean that the insect can anticipate future conditions and prepare for them. It merely means that the insect happened to find new conditions to its liking, because of some device such as diapause which it already possessed.) Some shore-dwelling rove beetles of the genus *Bledius* have solved their salt problem by a very neat piece of behavioural adaptation: they collect their food only after rain, when much of the salt has been washed away. Other insects have solved the problems biochemically within their bodies. Moving and breathing in the water present no real problems, as can be seen from the large numbers of insects living in freshwater, but the turbulent nature of coastal waters may complicate things for some.

No insect is known to spend the whole of its life beneath the waves, and the majority of those that do actually live in the water are young insects. The nearest approach to a full-time submarine existence is seen in the lice that infest seals. Those that live on the true seals, as opposed to the fur seals, attach themselves to the flippers and other naked areas and they are freely exposed to the water. Specially adapted spiracles prevent water from entering the tracheae under pressure when the seal dives. The lice are rather inactive for most of the time, but their life cycle has been beautifully adapted to tie in with that of the seals. The latter come ashore for just a few weeks each year to breed, and there is frenzied activity at this time among both hosts and parasites. The lice produce a new generation within three weeks, and a good few of the young lice transfer to the seal pups. Another generation of lice is produced before the seals go back to the sea. Low

temperatures in the water ensure minimal activity, and the low oxygen concentration is therefore of little significance.

Insects on the seashore

The most familiar of the seashore insects are probably the clouds of small flies that swarm over the piles of rotting seaweed. They belong to two families – the Ephydridae (shore-flies) and the Coelopidae (kelp-flies or seaweed-flies) – and they are all unwettable, so they come to no harm if they are swamped by breaking waves. The kelp-flies are greasy and they simply float to the surface and fly away. The shore-flies are covered with water-repellent hairs. Shore-fly larvae have a high salt tolerance and most live carnivorously in the sea water itself. Kelp-fly larvae feed in the rotting seaweed, but they are unaffected by immersion in sea water and they can be swept in and out by the tides without harm. Several shore bugs of the family Saldidae live in the intertidal zones, relying largely on physiological and behavioural adaptations to cope with the ever-changing environment. Most of them are flightless, as are most marine insects apart from the flies, and some are clothed with very fine hairs which form a physical gill (see page 00) and enable the insects to breathe happily under the water. Some bugs survive submersion by crawling into small air pockets, while others simply run away from the advancing tide. Some salt marsh species climb up the grass stems when the tide comes in.

With their tough elytra, the beetles are pre-adapted for life in the water, because the spaces under the elytra act as air reservoirs. The lack of wings in most marine species increases the capacity of these reservoirs, but no marine beetle goes up to the surface to renew its air supply in in the way that freshwater species do. Most of the intertidal beetles simply go into burrows or air pockets when the tide comes in. They can thus survive in the intertidal habitat with virtually no anatomical modifications.

Sea skaters

Apart from the seal lice, the only insects which are truly pelagic are five species of *Halobates*, which are bugs allied to the familiar pond skaters. They live far out in the tropical and subtropical seas and have no contact with land at all. They have lost their wings and they spend their time 'skating' on the surface. If they are upended by a wave they float to the surface again because they are completely clothed with fine hairs which trap a layer of air all round the body. *Halobates* bugs feed on floating dead animals and lay their eggs on floating seaweed and other debris. Despite its pelagic habits, however, *Halobates* has not solved the problems of living *in* the water: it is essentially an air-dwelling insect.

Forest beginnings

On land, the greatest numbers of insect species are found in the tropical forests. The physical conditions here are ideal for rapid growth and reproduction, and the competition within and

The Peppered Moth (*Biston betularia*). The light form is shown here against a pale background.

between species is intense. The insects have thus been under constant pressure to explore all possible avenues of food supply, and with perhaps 100 tree species per hectare and vast numbers of epiphytic plants as well they have had plenty of food sources from which to choose. The abundance and variety of plant life in the forests is thus responsible for the variety of insect life, but competition keeps down the numbers of individuals in each species. Competition has also been responsible for the evolution of some really remarkable examples of camouflage among the tropical insects, and for the establishment of some truly bizarre forms. Camouflage is, of course, well developed in many other parts of the world, but the adaptations are never as abundant and bizarre as they are in the tropical forests.

Although insects must have arisen much earlier, the earliest flying insects are found in the tropical forests. The swampy forests of coal-measure times, for example, were full of large dragonflies and other insects, many of which were highly specialized with sucking mouth-parts, ovipositors and complicated wing patterns. Later, insects spread into less favourable environments as the forests shrank. The physical environment inside a tropical forest is fairly constant throughout the year, and one of the first hurdles for the exploring insects to overcome was the seasonal fluctuation in other habitats. This was probably quite an easy hurdle, for many of today's tropical insects pass through a resting stage called a diapause, and we can imagine that earlier insects had similar pauses in their life histories. The insects were thus pre-adapted for the seasonal changes outside the forest. It is not difficult to imagine a species whose diapause coincided with the unfavourable season just outside the forest being able to survive quite happily in the new environment. Migration might well have played a part in the conquest of habitats outside the forest. Many insects, notably some butterflies and moths, migrate today. They fly to the cooler regions during the summer

and a subsequent generation will go back to warmer climates for the winter. Insects may well have migrated out from the ancient forests and found they could survive without going back. With the problem of the unfavourable season solved, the insects were free to spread right through the temperate regions, and further adaptations then evolved and allowed the insects to expand into some of the most hostile environments on earth. Present day migration patterns may well have been established in the Pleistocene Ice Age, but there may have been earlier migration patterns too.

Insects of the desert

The fundamental feature of the desert is its dryness, and efficient water conservation measures are clearly essential for all animals living in deserts. The insects' waterproof outer coverings pre-adapted them for desert life in this respect, and many insects have been able to conquer the desert with only small changes in their behaviour. Apart from those groups which grow up in the water, we can find representatives of all the major insect groups in the desert. There are not large numbers of species, and the low productivity of the desert cannot support vast numbers of individuals, but those that do live there are extremely well adapted. Most of them live in the rocky parts of the desert, where stones provide shelter from the fierce heat of the sun, but some beetles manage to survive and make a living on the shifting, plantless sand dunes.

Many of the plant-feeding insects are distinctly seasonal in their appearance, for their lives are geared to the annual rains and to the plants which spring up in their wake. Grasshoppers and sap-sucking bugs come out with the plants, and so do swarms of nectar-drinking butterflies and bees. These insects have few, if any anatomical specializations and their secret lies in their life cycles. The butterflies, for example, lay their eggs on the plants and the caterpillars feed very quickly and reach the

Above
A well-camouflaged Bush cricket of the family Tettigonidae. This species (*Pyc-nopalpa bicordata*) is found in the West Indies.

Right
The Leaf Mimic Mantid, displays well the camouflage mechanism found among forest insects.

pupal state before the leaves wither and die. Other insects may pass the long dry season as eggs.

The insects which do not feed directly on plants can be found at most times of the year. They are predators or scavengers and their food or energy chains are based very largely on the hordes of bristle-tails which scuttle about in the wind-blown debris. The ability of this group of wingless insects to survive in dry and dusty places, although they prefer moist places, is well shown by the little silverfish which lives in our household cupboards. The best adapted of all desert insects are undoubtedly the beetles, especially the members of the families Tenebrionidae and Dermestidae. Many of these scavenging beetles can live on dry food without any water at all. Tenebrionid beetles exceed all the other insects on the sand dunes of the Namib Desert, where they exist entirely on the seeds and dried grass that blow about on the sand. Both of these groups of beetles have, not surprisingly, contributed several important domestic and stored-product pests. The hard wing cases or elytra of the beetles are clearly an advantage, and this is increased by the fact that many of the beetles are wingless, thus leaving an insulating space between the elytra and the body. This helps to keep the body cool and also greatly reduces the amount of water lost by evaporation from the spiracles – the major site of water loss in any insect. One interesting anatomical adaptation that has evolved in several groups of desert beetles is the lengthening of the

Camouflage among desert dwellers. Dune cricket (*Comicus* spp) from the sand dunes of the Namib Desert, S.W. Africa. Note modified hindlegs to provide traction of the sand.

legs. *Stenocara phalangium*, which lives in the Namib desert, has extremely long legs which lift its body clear of the hot sand just as if it were walking on stilts. Some beetles always rest with some of their legs raised from the ground. They change legs periodically to prevent their feet from getting burned. These anatomical and behavioural adaptations enable the insects to move about in the desert by day: the majority of ground-dwelling species are nocturnal.

Ants are very common in the desert, and many of them are clothed with silvery hairs which reflect the sun's rays and keep the insects relatively cool. Most of the desert ants are predators or seed eaters, but there are some species which feed on nectar and on the honeydew exuded by aphids and scale insects. This food is of seasonal occurrence, but the ants make sure of supplies in the dry season by stocking up in times of plenty. The 'honey' is stored in the swollen bodies of large workers called repletes, and the other ants tap the barrels when necessary. These honey-storing species are generally known as honey-pot ants.

Winds are often quite strong in the desert, but they do not seriously hamper the desert insects, many of which are flightless in any case. Several species of small blue butterflies have the remarkable habit of flying inside the confines of desert shrubs, where they are protected from the worst of the wind. The insects can remain on the wing for hours, just flitting from branch to branch, and they may never leave the home shrub at all. Some hairy caterpillars actually turn the wind to their own advantage: they roll up and let the wind bowl them along on the desert floor. Many undoubtedly perish, but others reach new feeding grounds and the species as a whole must benefit from this behaviour.

Mountain insects

The main problem facing insects at high altitude is the extreme cold, but once an insect has acquired tolerance to the cold, the low temperatures themselves help it to overcome the other problems of mountain life. Low temperatures restrict growth, directly and also by shortening the growing period, and this reduces oxygen consumption and makes it easier for the insects to tolerate the thin atmosphere, although experimental work has shown that insects can withstand remarkably low pressures even at ordinary temperatures. The cold also restricts flight, because the insects must have warm muscles before they can take off, and so even those species which can fly are not exposed to the strong winds. In addition, the low temperatures of the mountain tops retard evaporation and encourage rainfall (or snow), two factors which counteract the drying effect of the wind and protect the insects from desiccation. As a result of these interacting factors, a surprisingly large number of insect species can be found in what is known as the nival zone—a region of rock, snow and ice, together with a few scattered plants, high above the tree line on the mountains. The winter snow cover is very important, for it forms a protective

blanket against the worst of the weather: the nival insects exist largely because of the snow and not in spite of it. Many species can survive for up to three years under snow and ice—a very important attribute for insects living in places where, in a bad year, the snow might not melt at all. The nival insects are active at temperatures between −10°C and +10°C, which means that they are active only during the summer. During the winter the insects go into hibernation, when they survive temperatures down to −25°C. They hibernate in various stages of the life cycle and they do not wake up until the snow melts and moistens the ground. Development is then very rapid, especially in the upper zones where there is only a short time between the melting of one winter's snow and the arrival of the next. At lower levels, nearer the tree line, the snow-free period may be long enough for some species to rear two generations each year.

The rocky terrain of the nival zone is very important during the summer because it provides calm pockets in what is usually a very windswept environment. The small size of most mountain insects comes into play here, allowing them to take advantage of the smallest crevices. These sheltered nooks are often very crowded during the summer. Relatively few species have managed to adapt to the cold conditions on the high mountains, but most major groups are represented in the nival community. Stoneflies, caddis flies, beetles, grasshoppers and bush crickets, true flies (Diptera), and butterflies and moths are all numerous at high altitudes, while springtails are especially abundant at the highest levels.

Although the number of nival species is not high, the number of individual insects is sometimes enormous, especially along the edges of the receding snow where there is plenty of moisture. There are plenty of plants in the lower parts of the nival zone, and perhaps 50 per cent of insect species are plant feeders in this region, but plant life is more sparse at higher levels and the number of plant-feeding insect species falls rapidly. Only about 10 per cent of the insects living above 4000 m in the Himalayas feed on plants. The majority of these nival insects are scavengers or predators, whose food chains rest very largely on the debris-feeding springtails. Many of these scavengers move right out on to the snow to forage on pollen grains and other plant debris and on the surprising number of insects which are blown up from lower levels and deposited as corpses on the snow. It has been estimated that each square metre of snow in the Himalayas receives one dead insect every 30 seconds. Further proof of the abundance of food in this Aeolian zone is provided by the famous 'grasshopper glacier' of Montana. Huge swarms of grasshoppers were once blown on to this glacier, and an almost constant stream of bodies now pours out from its melting snout. Similar concentrations of food are deposited by the receding snows, and this, together with the moisture, attracts large numbers of mountain insects. Even butterflies, which normally prefer the sweet juices of flowers, are eager to imbibe the organically rich fluids surrounding the defrosted debris. Blue butterflies are especially fond of these liquids.

The thin atmosphere of the high mountains allows a large amount of ultraviolet light through to the ground. This can be dangerous to life, but it is counteracted by the generally heavy pigmentation of most nival insects. The proportion of darkly coloured species increases noticeably as the altitude increases, and the high-level springtails are so dark that they darken the snow as they swarm over it to feed. The heavy pigmentation protects the insects from the ultraviolet rays, but it absorbs heat rays more readily and so helps the insects to warm up more readily in the sun.

Many insect groups, such as the crickets and grasshoppers, have wingless and short-winged, flightless species in all kinds of habitats, but the proportion of wingless or short-winged species is very much higher in the mountains. About 50 per cent of the insects living in the nival zone of the Himalayas are completely wingless, and a good many more rarely take to the air. About 95 per cent of the Orthoptera of this region are completely flightless, and similarly high figures apply to the ground beetles and some other groups. It is not clear what factors bring about the flightless condition, but flightlessness is certainly an advantage in a habitat swept by violent winds for most of the time. Even those species which do fly keep very close to the ground and fly only in good weather. This prevents them from being swept away.

The nival zone in any mountainous region is clearly a fragmented zone because it occurs only above a certain level on the peaks. Dense forest may fill the hollows between the mountain tops and effectively isolate each nival area from its neighbour. With the majority of nival insects unable or unwilling to fly, there is little chance of genetic exchange between populations, and this inevitably leads to divergence and the evolution of new species. This is particularly well seen among butterflies of the genus *Erebia* in the Alps. About fifty species can be found on these mountains, and many of those living at the higher altitudes have very restricted distributions, often being limited to just a few neighbouring peaks. The species are all basically very similar and it seems that they have all evolved from a common stock since being isolated on their lofty peaks.

A place to live

Within the broad habitats of forest, desert, or mountain each species of animal has its preferred ecological niche—a little slot in the complex fabric of life to which that species has become particularly well adapted. This might not be so obvious in the desert or on the mountains, where the numbers of available microhabitats and food sources are small, but it is very obvious in the tropical forest. Competition there has forced each species to adapt or perish, and all existing species have therefore been moulded according to their niches. Ecological separation of this kind is also well marked in the grasslands and in the

deciduous and evergreen forests of the temperate regions. These habitats are not so rich in species as the tropical forests, but the climatic conditions are favourable for insect life for much of the year and the microhabitats and food materials are much the same as those that we find in the tropical forests. The species that fill these microhabitats are often very different from those occupying similar places in the tropics, but their adaptations are usually very similar. After all, apart from the temperature, there is very little difference between living inside a tree trunk in the tropics and living inside a tree trunk on the Arctic Circle—even the temperature difference will not be great in such a sheltered situation.

The concept of the ecological niche is perhaps more easily understood in relation to the young stages of insects than to the adults, because the young stages are all earthbound and, being the main feeding stage in the life history, they are much more closely tied to specific food sources. Many are confined to just one kind of plant, or even to just one part of that plant. Most adults can fly, and therefore have much more freedom to move from one habitat to another, but because they grow up in a particular microhabitat and have to lay their eggs in a similar place, they do tend to stay in a fairly well-defined environment. Some dragonflies even maintain territories, which they defend against other members of the same species. Many adult insects are much more earthbound, however, or even completely flightless, and these are much more tightly bound to a particular microhabitat. We can now go on to look at some of these microhabitats in more detail, and to see how the insects have become adapted for life in these places.

Insect life in freshwater

A very large number of insects have taken to living in freshwater, either for just their early stages or for the whole of their lives. Freshwater is not just one microhabitat, however: it contains a range of microhabitats almost as varied as those found on the land. Insects can live on top of the surface film, hang from the surface, swim freely in the water, crawl over the bottom or on the plants, and burrow in the mud of the bottom. Most species are specialized or adapted for life in just one of these zones, but they are generally nomadic within their own zones and they rarely have any distinct homes.

The surface dwellers, such as the pond skaters and the whirligig beetles, can remain on top of the water because water behaves as if it has a very thin elastic skin over it. The familiar pond skater (*Gerris*) balances on its middle and hindlegs, whose ends are clothed with fine, water-repellent hairs. The feet make little depressions in the surface, but they do not break through and the insect can move along at high speed by 'rowing' with its long middle legs. The hindlegs act as rudders.

Whirligig beetles of the family Gyrinidae and a water boatman of the family Corixidae.

Pond skater (*Gerris* spp) using its long middle and hind-legs for balance. Note also long rostrum.

Water Scorpion (*Nepa cinerea*). Note forelegs used to catch prey and the siphon which is pushed through the water surface in order to conduct air to the abdominal spiracles.

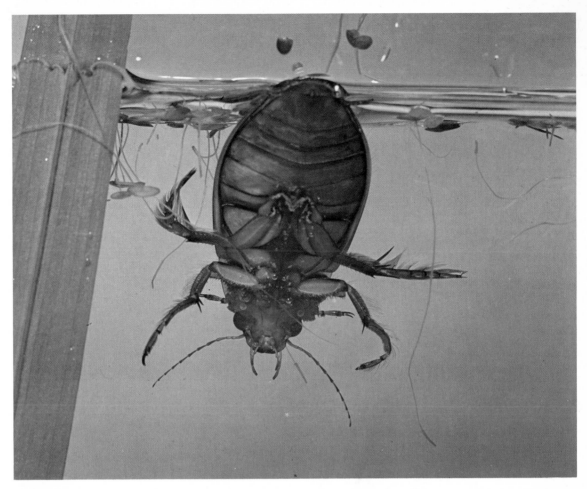

Great Diving Beetle (*Dytiscus* spp) taking in air at the water surface.

Whirligig beetles look like tiny bullets as they speed round and round on the surface. Their shiny elytra repel the water, but the lower half of the body is submerged and the broad, hair-fringed second and third pairs of legs act as powerful paddles. The whirligig eye is beautifully adapted for life on the surface: it is divided into two halves, one looking out across the surface, and the other looking down into the water. The beetles can dive when they want to, carrying an air bubble attached to the hind end of the body and another reservoir under the elytra, and they also fly well. Both pond skaters and whirligigs rely on the surface film to provide them with food in the form of small insects that fall on to the water. They detect the vibrations of the struggling insects with their legs or antennae and then skate over to collect their dinners! (see also 'Basic Biology', page 44).

One other group of surface dwellers deserving mention are some of the rove beetles belonging to the genus *Stenus*. These live mainly in the damp waterside vegetation, but they often go skating and they do it in a very unusual way (see 'Basic Biology', page 44).

Surface-dwelling insects have no respiratory problems, but those that actually live in the water need modified breathing apparatus. The majority of adult aquatic insects still retain their air-breathing habits and they come to the surface periodically to renew the air in their tracheae or in their reservoirs. Oily secretions and water-repellent hairs play an important role here by holding back the water and allowing the res-

piratory openings free access to the air. Many water bugs and water beetles carry air supplies under their elytra or trapped by a layer of hairs on their bodies, but one of the most fascinating breathing systems is that employed by the rat-tailed maggots – the larvae of the Drone-fly (*Eristalis tenax*) and related hover-flies (Fig. 25). These creatures can live on the mud at various depths and maintain contact with the surface by means of their telescopic tails (which may reach a maximum length of 55 mm or five times body length). A number of young insects, including various mosquito larvae, obtain air by tapping the air channels in the roots and stems of aquatic plants. Some mosquito larvae, for example, have some tiny saw-like teeth on the breathing siphons and they use them to cut holes in the plants. They then hook themselves up to the air supply and they can stay there for long periods. Some of the other important respiratory modifications, involving both air-breathing and water-breathing (gilled) insects, are described in 'Basic Biology'.

Locomotion under the water may be by swimming, by crawling or walking, or by jet propulsion. The swimmers generally have broad, hair-fringed legs which act as paddles or oars, and the wings, if present are tucked neatly away under the elytra, but one tiny creature called *Caraphractus cinctus* actually swims with its wings. It is one of the minute fairy flies and it parasitizes the eggs of various water beetles. The female can remain under the water for several days while searching for suitable eggs and she swims by beating her tiny wings up and down.

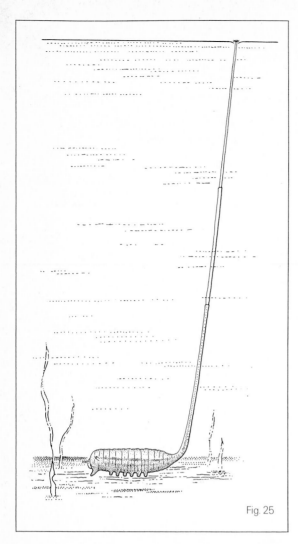

Fig. 25

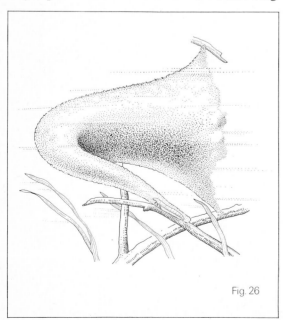

Fig. 26

This produces a very jerky movement not unlike that of a water flea, which swims by beating its antennae.

Crawling aquatic insects tend to have strong claws for gripping the water plants or the bottom. Those that live on the bottom of fast-flowing streams generally have flattened bodies which cause little hindrance to the flow and can thus stay in place without too much effort. Burrowing forms tend to have more cylindrical bodies.

Feeding methods in the water do not differ significantly from those employed by terrestrial insects, but the water does allow one extra method to be employed, and this is filter feeding. This has been exploited by several kinds of mosquito larvae, which use 'mouth brushes' like overgrown moustaches to sweep water currents and suspended material into the mouth. Anopheline and culicine mosquito larvae can live quite happily together because the anophelines feed right at the surface and the culicines, which hang almost vertically from the surface, gather their food from a slightly lower layer. The net-spinning caddis flies also employ a form of filter feeding, although they do not use their own bodies to do the work. They spin silken nets among the submerged vegetation and wait for the current to bring the food (Fig. 26). This is one of the very few examples of traps constructed by animals. Other examples include the spider webs, the ant-lion pits, and the luminous snares of the New Zealand glow-worm.

Winter poses no serious problems for aquatic insects, even when the water surface freezes over. Gill-breathing insects can carry on normally, although activity may be reduced by the low temperatures, while most of the air-breathing species overwinter in a dormant state in the mud. Their oxygen requirements are low under these conditions and they can absorb sufficient direct from the water. Some pond skaters and other surface dwellers leave the water altogether in the autumn and spend the winter buried in the waterside vegetation.

We cannot leave the aquatic habitat without mentioning the Petroleum–fly (*Psilopa petrolei*), which is a relative of the shore-flies. The larvae of this little fly live in a liquid environment, but instead of water they have colonized the pools of crude petroleum oil that dot the ground in California. They do not actually feed on the oil, but on the other insects that become trapped in it. This food is abundant and we should not really be surprised that an insect has managed to take advantage of it, but to live in a pool of oil, which is used as an effective insecticide against many species, is surely an amazing achievement. The larva relies on an impermeable coat and specially modified spiracles to keep the oil out, while a special lining to the food canal prevents it from being poisoned from the inside. Pupation takes place among the surrounding vegetation, away from the oil, but the adult fly can walk on the oil surface as long as only the tips of its feet touch the oil. If the body dips on to the surface the fly is trapped and doomed to be eaten – perhaps by its own off-spring. It is interesting to note in this respect that the female, who has to walk over the oil to lay her eggs, has hairier feet than the male.

Nomads and settlers

Turning now to the truly terrestrial habitats, we find that the majority of insects, especially in the adult state, live freely exposed in their chosen environments. Many caterpillars, for example,

Fig. 25   Rat-tailed maggot showing its heliscopic breathing siphon.

Fig. 26   Caddis net made by the larva of *Neureclipsis* spp.

Fig. 27 Frog-
hopper home inside
which there is a
nymph sucking sap
from the plant.

feed openly on the leaves, butterflies and moths fly freely in the air, and beetles crawl on the ground and the vegetation. Some of these free-living insects, such as the dragonflies, have distinct territories, but the majority are nomads. Home is wherever they happen to be, although they do not normally move far from their food supplies. These insects rely very heavily on camouflage to protect them from their enemies, and there are some truly amazing examples of insects that resemble leaves, twigs and other objects. This form of camouflage is known as protective resemblance and, like all other features, it has evolved through the agency of natural selection. Birds and other enemies have always weeded out the least fit insects, which in the present context means the most conspicuous, in each generation, and so there has been gradual improvement in the camouflage because only the best examples are left to breed (Fig. 27).

Many other insects have much more distinct homes, ranging from simple feeding tunnels in the ground or in plant tissues to the elaborate nests of bees and other social insects. There are obviously great advantages in having a home, even if it is occupied for only a part of the time, for a home gives protection against many enemies – not all of them – and if the home is shared with other insects of the same kind, as it is among the social insects, it can become a veritable fortress.

Under the ground

Mole cricket
(*Gryllotalpa* spp).

Subterranean insects are mostly young stages and the bulk of them feed on plant roots. They

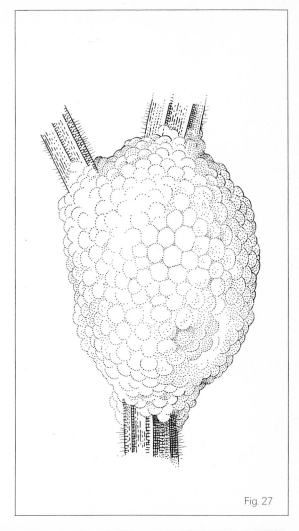

Fig. 27

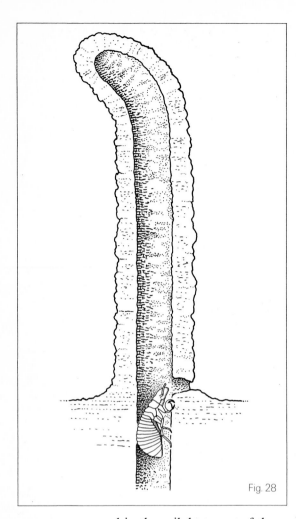

Fig. 28

wonderful example of convergent evolution producing similar adaptations in unrelated animals with similar habits. Mole crickets dig networks of narrow tunnels just under the surface and they live there on both plant roots and other insects. Young and adult mole crickets all live under the ground, although the adults often come out to fly. The males attract the females with a soft churring song and they normally construct special singing burrows which are designed to amplify the sounds. The mouth of the tunnel opens out as it reaches the surface and resembles a megaphone, with the insect sitting in the bottom. One French species builds two such 'amplifiers' in his song burrow and broadcasts his song over a wide area.

Many dung beetles excavate tunnels and bury animal dung in them to form larders for themselves and for their offspring. The best known are the scarabs or tumblebugs, which roll balls of dung about until they find suitable places in which to bury it. Others, less spectacular but no less important as scavengers, simply undermine cow-pats and other dung and drag quantities down into their tunnels. Most of these beetles have the broad front legs which one would expect in digging and burrowing insects.

The larvae of certain ant-lions also burrow in the soil and they have developed a clever way of catching their food. They live in areas of sandy soil and each digs a conical pit by using its head and jaws as a shovel. The larva then snuggles down into the sand and leaves just its large jaws showing at the bottom of the pit – waiting to snap up the ants and other small insects that tumble down the unstable sides of the pit (Fig. 29). The ant-lion risks getting cooked on a hot day, but it avoids this fate by moving round during the day so that its body is always under the shadier side of the pit.

Insects in caves

Caves and the dens of various large animals provide fairly constant and protected environments for a wide range of insects. The absence of green plants means that, apart from a few fungus-eating species, the insects are all predators, scavengers, or parasites. Many of the more specialized troglodytes are wingless and blind but, in contrast to many aquatic cave dwellers, the insects do not lose their pigmentation as well. Large numbers of crickets inhabit caves, usually fairly near the entrances, and feed on a variety of plant and animal debris. They have probably lived in such places for a very long time, but some of them find our houses just as acceptable today, for a house is not really much more than a cave with furniture and windows. The more specialized cave crickets of the family Rhaphidophoridae can be found much deeper in the caves. They are all wingless and they have enormously long antennae. They do have eyes, but these are useless in the depths of the caves and the antennae take over the job of finding the way about. Cave crickets feed mainly on living or dead animals, including hibernating butterflies.

may move around in the soil, but most of them make no distinct tunnels and, although confined to the soil, they are to some extent nomadic. Many are legless or else have very small legs and they simply wriggle through the soil. Examples include the notorious leather-jackets, which are the larvae of various species of crane-flies, and the wireworms, which are the larvae of various species of click beetles. Other well-known root feeders include the fat, C-shaped grubs of the cockchafer and its relatives. Several of these, together with the wireworms, have tough, flattened shields on their heads which protect them as they wriggle through the soil. Another group of burrowers, typified by the cicada nymphs (Fig. 28) and the mole cricket, possess greatly enlarged front legs and actually dig their way through the soil. The mole cricket's 'paw' is incredibly similar to that of a mole, providing a

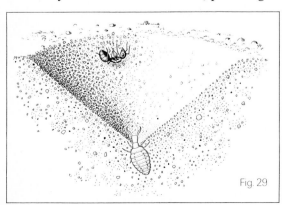

Fig. 29

Fig. 29 The ant-lion larva with jaws agape waiting to receive an unfortunate ant.

Dung beetle of the Scarabaeidae family rolling a dungball.

94

Quite a number of dung-feeding flies live in caves, where they exist largely on the droppings of bats. The Common House-fly (*Musca domestica*) may well have lived in such situations originally and then tagged on to human society when our ancestors began to use caves. The most famous cave-dwelling insect is probably the New Zealand glow-worm, which is actually the larva of a small fly. The larvae hang from the ceilings of caves and tunnels, surrounded by webs of sticky threads, and they glow quite brightly. The light is reflected by the numerous sticky droplets on the threads and it produces an effect so dramatic that some of the caves are real tourist attractions. But tourists are not the only creatures attracted by the lights: swarms of chironomids and other midges fly up to them and become trapped in the webs to provide food for the glow-worms.

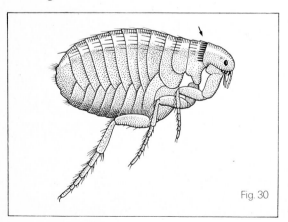

Fig. 30

Parasitic insects

The bodies of other animals provide food and shelter for a wide variety of parasitic insects. Some of these insects live on the outsides of their hosts' bodies and are called ectoparasites. Others live inside their hosts and are called endoparasites. Apart from some ichneumon larvae (see below), the ectoparasites are all adult insects or the nymphs of exopterygote species. Some eat fur, feathers and skin, but the majority are bloodsuckers and they have specialized piercing mouthparts. Many are blind and many are wingless or unable to fly, and they usually stay put on their hosts. Strong claws, combined with rows of spines (combs) and flattened bodies, help them to resist the hosts' cleaning and grooming activities. The lice and fleas are among the best known of the ectoparasites (Fig 30). These and several others which attack us and our domestic animals are described in 'The Lives of Insects' and 'Insects and Man'; some can spread dangerous diseases, but they rarely do much harm in themselves.

The endoparasites are all larvae of endopterygote insects – those with complete metamorphosis – and they are sometimes called protelean parasites. Most are the grubs of Hymenoptera and Diptera, and their hosts are normally other insects, although some flies, such as the warble-flies and bot-flies, attack mammals. The most famous of the protelean parasites are the ichneumons, which mainly attack the caterpillars of butterflies and moths. The female ichneumon uses her sensitive

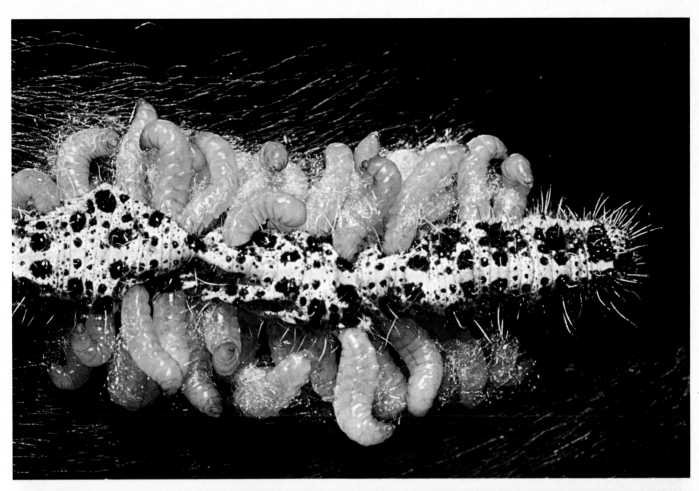

antennae to locate a suitable host and then, using what is often a very long ovipositor, she lays one or more eggs inside the caterpillar. The ichneumon grubs grow up inside the doomed host, but they are careful not to damage any vital organs at first and the host is not killed until they have finished feeding. The parasitic grubs then pupate either inside or outside the shrivelled skin of the host. The little yellow cocoons that are so commonly seen clustered around the skins of the Large White caterpillar belong to a close relative of the ichneumons called *Apanteles glomeratus*. Some ichneumons actually lay their eggs on the surface of the host larva, and the ichneumon grubs feed on it from the outside. This happens mainly when the host lives in a concealed apartment inside a plant.

Many tiny hymenopterans called chalcids have life histories similar to those of the ichneumons and their relatives. Because all these insects kill their hosts in the end, they are called parasitoids, to distinguish them from the normally non-lethal parasites, such as the strepsipterans. The latter insects merely soak up food from their hosts and do not inflict the kind of damage done by the ichneumons, even though the adult female strepsipteran remains inside her host throughout her life.

Wood borers

Many insects find board and lodging by burrowing into tree trunks and other timber, both living and dead. Wood consists very largely of cellulose, which few animals are able to digest. Unless they have some way of dealing with the cellulose, the wood-boring insects have to consume vast amounts of wood in order to obtain sufficient nourishment. Their strong jaws have to work overtime to crush the cellulose cells and release the meagre supplies of sugars and pro-

teins. Many of the species thus take a long time to grow up, but the length of life does depend on the nature of the wood: moist timber with some fungal decay is much more nourishing, and the insects can mature more quickly.

The most notorious of the wood borers are the Common Furniture Beetle or Woodworm and the Death Watch Beetle, which are described in 'Insects and Man', but many other beetles spend their larval lives in timber. The Stag Beetle is one well-known species whose grubs tunnel in old tree stumps and other damp and decaying timber. The larvae of longhorn beetles often invade living trees, and they may continue their activities after the trees have been felled and turned into timber (see 'Insects and Man', page 184). Some longhorn larvae appear to be able to convert cellulose into sugars, but the majority are still long-lived in the larval state.

The bark beetles are another well-known group of wood borers, although their larvae do not bore deeply into the wood. They stay in the nutritious, living region of the inner bark, where each chews out a tunnel for itself. The larvae gradually spread out from the egg site and they make a pattern of tunnels which is more or less constant for each species. The fan-like pattern is only seen when bark falls from the dead trunk or branch, when a very clear pattern is seen on the bark but a much fainter one on the wood itself. The notorious elm-bark beetles, which are responsible for the spread of Dutch elm disease, produce an attractive fan-like pattern radiating out from each side of a vertical egg gallery excavated by the parent female.

Other insects with wood-boring larvae include the Goat Moth, which attacks various living trees and often damages fruit, and the large wood wasps or horntails. Various hover-fly larvae developing on rotten wood include *Caliprobola*

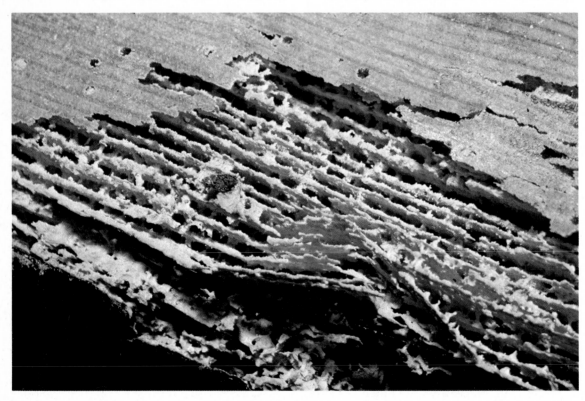

Furniture Beetle (*Anobium punctatum*). Damage caused to a floor board.

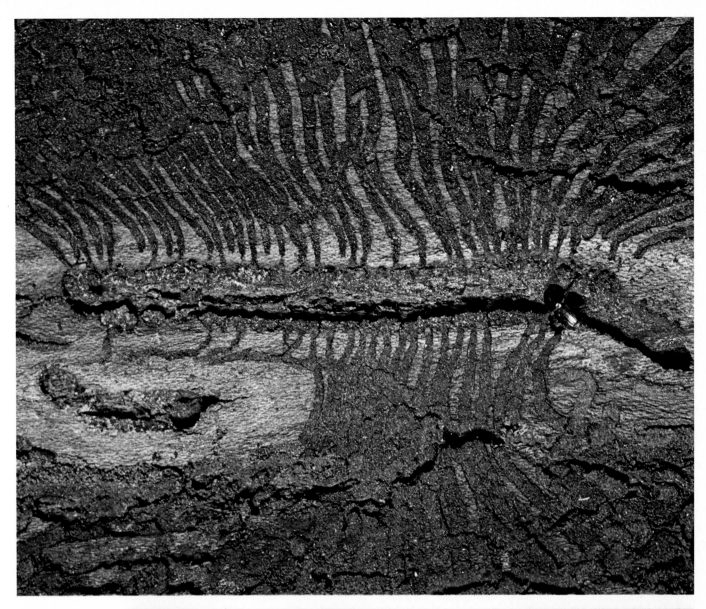

Galleries excavated by bark beetles in elm bark.

Damage caused by termites to a pile of books.

99

speciosa. Snipe-fly larvae (Rhagionidae) such as *Xylophagus* spp also live in rotten wood but feed on insects there. Most of these insects lay their eggs on the surface, but the female horntail drills into the wood with her fearsome-looking ovipositor and lays her eggs singly as much as 2 cm below the surface. Each egg gives rise to a tough-jawed grub which chews its way through the wood. It might be thought that the grubs are safe in the wood, but they are not: *Rhyssa persuasoria*, an ichneumon with an even longer and more slender ovipositor than the horntail, can detect the tunnelling grubs and drill down to lay her own eggs on them. The ichneumon grubs then attach themselves to their hosts and feed on them.

The most famous of all the wood feeders are probably the termites, although only a few of them actually make their homes in timber. These are the more primitive species, known as dry-wood termites, and they live in quite small colonies which eat out irregular galleries in the wood. These insects employ armies of flagellate protozoans to break down the cellulose in their intestines, and they can therefore breed and grow rapidly with only wood to eat. Many of the more advanced termites feed on non-woody materials and have no symbiotic protozoans in their guts.

Fruit borers and leaf miners

It will come as no surprise to learn that many insects live inside fruits and seeds, for these bodies are full of nourishing food, provided primarily for the embryo plants in the seeds and for the birds and other animals that scatter them. The housewife knows only too well that apples and peas regularly contain 'maggots', which may be the larvae of moths, flies, or beetles. The eggs of these insects are laid on the very young fruits or even on the flowers, and the grubs work their way inside at an early stage. Many weevils attack cereal grains in the fields, and several have adapted themselves to carry on

A leaf attacked by a leaf mining larva.

their lives throughout the year in grain stores (see page 186).

The space between the upper and lower surfaces of a leaf is extremely small, but this has not prevented a number of insect larvae from making their homes there. These larvae are called leaf miners and they are mostly the larvae of moths, flies and beetles. They have flattened bodies and wedge-shaped heads, making it easier for them to push their way between the leaf surfaces. They eat the nutritious leaf cells as they go, and the hollows they produce are called mines. The mines show up as pale patches on the leaves. Some of them are irregular blotches, produced when the larvae remain more or less stationary and nibble in all directions, while others are delicately twisting galleries called serpentine mines. These are formed by those larvae which gradually move through the leaf. They are extremely thin at first, when the larvae are young, but they get wider as the larvae grow. The leaf epidermis is not damaged until the miners are fully grown and ready to leave. Some grubs break out of the leaves and pupate elsewhere, while others pupate in their mines. There are grubs which mine in stems, fruits and flowers, as well as those which mine in leaves, but they all tunnel just under the epidermis and this distinguishes them from the borers.

Gall dwellers

Apart from the song burrows of the mole crickets, none of the homes so far described involves any construction work. The hollowing out of feeding chambers and burrows is destructive, and the hollows are merely by-products of the feeding activity. But if we now turn to the numerous gall-dwelling insects, we find that their homes really are built – although not by the insects themselves: the galls are actually built by the plants, under chemical 'orders' issued by the insects. The galls are, in fact, abnormal growths on the plants, produced specifically to shelter and nurture the invading insects (Fig. 31). They

Neuroterus quercus-baccarum, a member of the Cynipidae family is responsible for the reddish galls which are abundant on oak leaves in late summer.

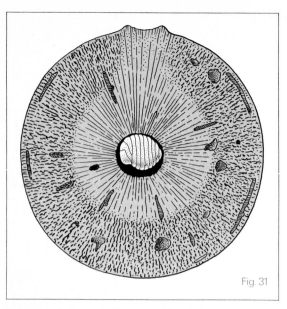

are produced from unspecialized tissues which multiply and provide the nutritious cells on which the insects feed. The first stimulus is sometimes given when an insect lays her eggs in the plant tissues, but more usually it is the presence of the young insect that triggers off the growth of the gall. Each kind of gall insect has its own special kind of gall, which develops on a particular part of a particular plant. Many sawflies, aphids, and midges induce gall formation, and so do many non-insects, but the best-known gall insects are perhaps the gall wasps—tiny hymenopterans of the family Cynipidae which live mainly on oaks. The galls of aphids and sawflies are partly open to the air, but those of the gall wasps are completely closed. They may contain one or many insects.

It is thought that the gall-causers were originally miners which gradually evolved ways of inducing the plants to produce additional

Fig. 31 An oak marble gall cut open to show the grub of *Andricus kollari* in the centre. The grub feeds on the mass of nutritious tissue around it.

Acorn gall induced by *Cynips quercuscalicis.*

102

Galls caused by a
species of *Apocrita*.

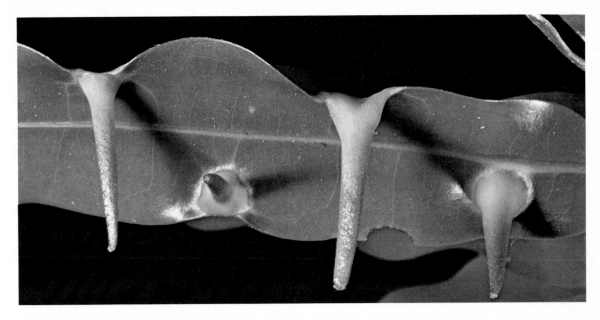

nutritive tissues. This idea is supported by the structure of the mine produced on holly leaves by the larva of the little fly *Phytomyza ilicis*. The grub eats its way through the tissues in the normal way, but the uninjured cells in the lower part of the leaf respond by multiplying rapidly and refilling much of the mine with new tissue. Although galls often exist in huge numbers – a single oak leaf may carry more than 100 little spangle galls – they do not seem to do the plants any harm.

Insect builders

We can now move on to look at those insects which actually construct their own homes (Fig. 32), as opposed to those which merely hollow out living quarters in the soil or in plant tissues. The materials used include silk, leaves, resin, wax, wood pulp (paper), clay and soil, often in conjunction with the insects' droppings and saliva which are used as cement. Except for the social insects, building operations are concerned almost entirely with constructing nests to receive the eggs and to house the young. Most construction is therefore carried out by the adults, although some young insects do make homes for themselves – usually making them largely or entirely with silk.

Tents of silk
Many caterpillars cover the leaves of their food-plants with strands of silk, and some actually spin tents into which they retire when not feeding. These tent-dwelling larvae usually live in family colonies consisting of all the youngsters from one batch of eggs, and each caterpillar contributes silk to the tent. The most famous of these tent-dwelling species are the processionary caterpillars, so called because they periodically leave their tents and march off in long lines, each animal nudging the tail of the one in front as they walk. The pine processionary caterpillars of southern Europe spin tents as big as footballs among the pine needles, and when they finally leave them to pupate the tents are absolutely full

of the caterpillars' droppings.

Several caterpillars are known as leaf-rollers because they roll leaves or parts of leaves over to make living rooms. They generally use silk strands to hold the leaves in position, and they may eat these leaves or else go out to dine on neighbouring leaves. Weaver ants also make nests by 'sewing' leaves together with silk threads, but they go about it in a remarkable way. The adult insects cannot make silk, and so they use their own larvae as shuttles. One group of worker ants use their feet and jaws to draw the edges of the leaves together, while another group wield the larvae. They squeeze them gently to make them exude the sticky silk, and then they dab them on both sides of the junction to join the leaves together.

The only adult insects which use silk for building purposes are the web-spinners, rarely-seen little insects which live under logs and stones in the warmer parts of the world. The silk is produced in glands in the swollen front legs and it is used to make slender tunnels under the stones and among the neighbouring grass roots. The insects live in these tunnels in small family groups, although the males are usually winged and they can fly away to mate with females in other tunnels.

Fig. 32   Portable homes: (a – d) cases of caddis larvae (a) *Limnothilus flaviornis* (b) *Odontocerus albicorne* (c) *L. rhombicus* (d) *Halesus radiatus* (e) A bagworm case.

Overleaf
Caterpillar tent.

Potters and masons

Many solitary bees and wasps, known as miners and diggers respectively, make simple nest burrows in the ground. Some of the species actually fashion clay cells in their burrows, but the most striking pottery nests are those made by the little potter wasps. The Heath Potter Wasp (*Eumenes coarctata*) scoops up little pellets of clay with her front legs and her jaws and she uses these lumps of clay to build a neat, vase-shaped nest with a little neck. If the clay is too dry, the wasp will fly quite a distance to bring back a stomachful of water with which to moisten it. Having completed the vase to her satisfaction, the wasp collects a number of small caterpillars or other grubs and paralyses them with her sting. She then pushes them into the vase, lays an egg in it, and seals it up. The paralysed grubs remain

Weaver Ants (*Decophylla smaragdina*). The workers use larva as a silk weaving shuttle to build the nest.

106

in good condition for the young wasp to eat as it grows during the succeeding months. Mud wasps or mason wasps also go in for some kind of pottery or stonework. Some of them excavate nesting tunnels in the ground, but they usually choose steep banks or walls and the excavated soil or sand is often used to make a 'chimney' over the tunnel entrance. This chimney usually curves downwards at the end and its main function seems to be to keep out the rain, but it may also deter some of the cuckoo wasps and other parasites from entering the nest burrow.

Plasterers and tailors

Quite a number of solitary bees and wasps merit the title of plasterers from the way in which they construct their nests. Some of the mason wasps, for example, build clay cells in narrow crevices in

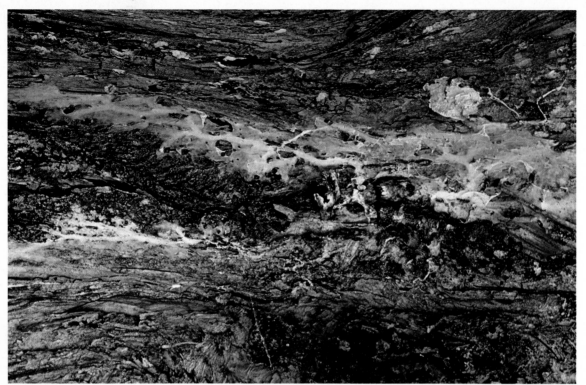

Web spinners (*Clothoda urichi*) of the order Embioptera showing silken webs on the tree bark.

Lackey Moth (*Malacosoma neustria*) larvae. These larvae often cover fruit trees with the silken tents.

cliffs and walls and then plaster mud or clay neatly over the cracks so that you would not know they were there. All kinds of tubular spaces are of interest to solitary wasps and bees, and many species make their homes in hollow stems. Having selected a suitable stem, the insect sets to work to convert the empty space into a block of flats, each divided from its neighbour by a neatly plastered partition. Mud, grass, spider silk, resin and saliva may all be used to make these walls (Fig. 33).

Pride of place among the tailors goes to the leaf-cutter bees, whose activities are well known to most rose growers. Using their sharp jaws, the bees cut neat semicircles from the leaves of roses and other plants and they use these leaf sections to make little sausage-shaped cells in their chosen nest cavities, which may be hollow stems or any other suitable crevices. The leaf sections are lightly glued together, with a good overlap, to make the sides of the cells, and perfectly circular pieces are cut from the leaves to make the caps. The cells are so well made that they hold a semi-liquid mixture of pollen and nectar without any trace of leakage.

Fig. 33

Paper architects

Some of the most elaborate of all insect homes are made by the social wasps or yellow-jackets, and they are made almost entirely from paper. The wasps make the paper themselves from wood which they scrape from trees, fence posts and other objects with their powerful jaws. You can sometimes hear the scraping going on, and you can then track down the source of the sound and watch the wasp at work. It always works in the direction of the grain and rolls up the stripped

wood in its jaws before flying back to the nest. The wood is then thoroughly chewed until it is pulp, when the wasp adds it to the appropriate part of the nest. It is one of the many wonders of the insect world that the wasps know just where to add their paper loads when building their nests. Some wasps build their nests under the ground or in hollow trees, while some merely hang their nests from the branches of trees. The following paragraphs give a brief account of the construction of the nest of the Common Wasp (*Paravespula vulgaris*).

With a few rare exceptions, the colony of the Common Wasp lasts for just one year, and new colonies are started each spring by the over-wintered females or queens. Waking from her long sleep, the female begins to look around for a suitable nest site. This will usually be under the ground – perhaps in an abandoned mouse hole – but the queen is equally happy with some other kind of cavity, such as a hollow tree or your roof space. Having selected her site, she begins to collect wood pulp and then she begins to make her nest. She starts from the top, which might seem surprising, and she makes all her 'rooms' without floors, but she is following her instincts and all turns out well in the end. The nest actually hangs in its cavity, and the first

Digger Wasp (*Mellinus arvensis*) taking a fly to its nest.

Nest of leaf-cutter bee showing open cocoon.

building operation is to construct a strong stalk from which to hang it. Several loads of wood pulp are applied to the chosen spot, and then later loads are used to make a stalk about 12mm long. When this is complete the queen begins to make the first cells, like two tiny upturned wine glasses sharing a single stalk. She then begins to make the nest covering, which starts out as a little 'umbrella' over the first few cells. More cells are built and eggs are laid in them right away, and the 'umbrella' is enlarged to make a spherical covering right round the cells. The queen goes on building cells until there are twenty or thirty in a layer spreading out from the bottom of the

original stalk. The cells all open downwards, but the larvae manage to remain inside them. Further layers of paper are added round the outside, and the first batch of young workers soon begin to help with building operations. Within a few weeks the nest may have six or seven layers of cells, each suspended from the one above by narrow paper stalks and each consisting of several hundred cells.

In late summer there may be as many as nine tiers of cells and upwards of 12 000 cells, almost all built by the workers while the queen devoted herself to egg-laying. The workers also have to extend the underground cavities in most in-

stances, usually keeping a gap of 1–2 cm between the soil and the outer nest envelope. The soil is excavated by moistening it, possibly with excess saliva collected from the larvae, and forming it into little pellets which can be carried away in the jaws. Stones have to be left behind and they accumulate on the floor of the cavity. As the tiers or plates of cells grow, the original nest envelopes become too small, so they are chewed up and the paper re-used for new cells or for larger envelopes on the outside. Extra supports have to be built to hold the larger nest to its support. When complete, the nest is like a large football, with a single entrance at the bottom. The whole thing is covered with the most exquisite scalloped pattern consisting of thousands of overlapping 'shells' of paper. Each 'shell' is made up of

several bands of varying colours, each band being the product of one load of wood pulp from one worker. A certain amount of work is also carried on outside the nest. Grass which grows up and obstructs the nest entrance, for example, is regularly 'mown' by the workers so that a free flight path is maintained at all times.

Some ants also make their nests from a tough form of paper which is generally called carton. The chewed wood fibres are glued together with a strong sugar solution composed largely of honeydew, and a fungus invades the material and actually strengthens the walls with its interwoven hyphae. These nests, which are frequently somewhat conical or pyramidal in shape, can often be seen clinging to the trunks and branches of tropical trees. Although they are made of

Paper Wasp (*Polistes smithii*). Females shown on their nest chewing pieces of caterpillar.

112

Interior of wasp's nest to show adults feeding larvae.

Fig. 34 A bumble bee queen sits on her first batch of cocoons from which the first workers will soon emerge. The open honey-pot, on her right, provides her with food in bad weather.

paper, that is the only similarity between these nests and those of the wasps, for the ants make none of the neat, hexagonal cells produced by the wasps. The chambers in their nests are very irregular and the individual grubs get no privacy.

Houses of wax

The solitary bees, as we have already seen, use a variety of building materials, but the social bees – the bumble bees (*Bombus*) and the honey bees (*Apis*) – rely largely on wax produced in their own bodies. The most elaborate wax nests are built by the honey bees (Fig. 34). Although we always tend to think of them living only in the hives that we provide, their natural homes are in hollow trees and rock crevices where, unlike the common wasps, they build vertical sheets of

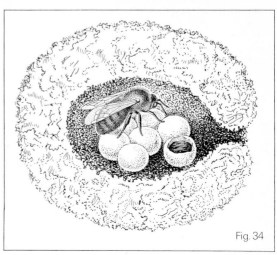

Fig. 34

113

cells. Each sheet is called a comb and, again unlike the wasps, it has cells on both sides. The cells are of two sizes, but they are all perfect hexagons and they are built with amazing precision. The smaller cells, known as worker cells, are all exactly 5·2 mm from one wall to the opposite wall, while the drone cells are exactly 6·2 mm across. The hexagonal shape has clearly evolved, as in the wasps, because it gives the maximum number of cells in the comb with the least amount of building material. The worker bees do all the building, for the queen is unable to make wax or even to collect food. She does nothing but lay eggs in the cells, and she uses her front feet as calipers to tell her whether she is entering a drone cell or a worker cell. She needs to know this so that she can lay the right kind of egg in the cell: drone-producing eggs are not fertilized. The drone cells tend to be built mainly in the outer parts of the combs, which are not used for egg-laying until well into the summer, and few drones are therefore produced in the spring. The cells are not used only for rearing grubs, however: most of the outer cells are used as warehouses for pollen and honey. The cells are accurately sloped on the combs at an angle of about 13° from the horizontal – just enough to prevent the honey from running out before the cells are capped with wax.

Recent work has shown that the honey bees can also detect the direction of the earth's magnetic field. This is a fascinating ability, and a most important one when the bees are building a new home. Imagine what a mess they could make if the thousands of bees from a swarm started to build in a different direction in a hollow tree. But they do not make a mess of it at all: they remember the direction of their old combs in relation to the direction of the earth's field and they all buckle down to build their new combs in the same direction. The earth's magnetic field acts as their invisible foreman. Nevertheless, when the bee-keeper provides a new home with comb frames already in position the bees are perfectly happy to build on these frames whatever their orientation.

Although wax is the main building material used by the honey bees, they do use other products, notably resin or propolis. They collect this sticky material from the buds and other parts of trees, usually in the autumn, and they use it to plug draughty gaps around the nest. In warmer climates the industrious bees have another even more amazing use for propolis: they mix it with the wax they use for comb building and thus raise the melting point of the wax – a very clever way of preventing their home from melting away on a hot day.

Castles and catacombs

Although no other insects approach the honey bees and the social wasps in their ability to construct neat tiers of cells, the master builders of the insect world are surely some of the ants and termites. These are all social insects living in colonies with anything up to perhaps ten million

individuals. The nests of some of the smaller colonies have already been mentioned, and here we can deal with the more spectacular edifices built by these little insects. Among the largest of the ant nests are those built by the large, red wood ants in many European woodlands. The nest mounds may be a metre or more high, and the nest complex will go just as far down into the

Above
Ant's nest made from carton on a Jonka bean tree in Trinidad.
Right
Honey and pollen storage cells of the Honey Bee (*Apis mellifera*).

ground as well. The subterranean part of the nest is always the first part to be constructed by the embryo colony, but before long the ants begin to pile pine needles, moss, grass and other materials over their nest openings. It is quite a striking sight to see the ants dragging and carrying needles much longer than their own bodies. Both the mound and the earth beneath it are riddled with irregular chambers and passages whose walls are strengthened with 'mortar' made from the soil and the ants' own saliva (Fig. 35). The mound clearly enables the colony to absorb more of the sun's warmth, and the uppermost chambers are generally used as incubators for the pupae so that they hatch as quickly as possible. The pine needles and other vegetable materials that constitute the bulk of the mound are continually being re-worked by the ants and the nest entrances are continually being changed. Needles from deep in the nest are always being brought up to the surface, and by spraying the surface with various dyes entomologists have found that it takes about a month for pine needles to sink down into the centre of the nest and then be brought back to the surface. This re-working of the nest material clearly prevents mould growth. It is also interesting that when pine needles are used they are always placed running up and down the slope, just like thatch. This helps to shed rainwater. Many other ants, including the familiar yellow meadow ants, make mounds, but these are generally much smaller than the wood ants' nests and they are made entirely of soil particles, so they do not need re-working.

Many tropical termite mounds are very similar to ant hills, but the largest ant hill is virtually nothing compared with the largest termite mounds. Some of these 'castles' tower more than 7 m into the air and, as with the ants, the ground beneath may be honeycombed with chambers and passages (Fig. 36). A colony may develop underground for many years before starting to build the characteristic mound. It is very often possible to determine the termite species just by looking at the mounds, for each species tends to build to a fixed pattern. This is

Termite mounds.

particularly striking in species of *Cubitermes*, which live mainly in the African rainforests. The outer part of a termite mound is always fairly resistant to rain, but the *Cubitermes* species build mushroom-shaped nests which shed the water just like umbrellas. Long-established nests usually have several umbrella-like roofs on them, making them look like small pagodas. Even more spectacular are the great wall-like mounds of the compass termites of Australia, which reach

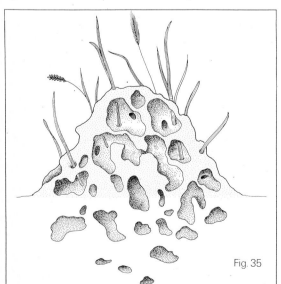

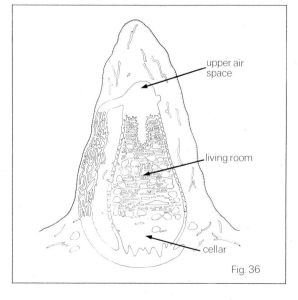

Fig. 35 Diagrammatic section through the nest of the meadow ant showing the irregular chambers in which young are reared and food is stored.

Fig. 36 The structure of the nest of macrotermes showing the channels of the 'air-conditioning' system.

heights of 5m and lengths of more than 3m although they are usually much less than 1m thick. Built in the arid heart of the continent, the mounds are exposed to the full force of the sun, but the termites cleverly build them with their long axes running due north–south, so that the broad faces face east and west and never receive the full power of the midday sun to become unbearably hot. In cooler weather the insects can keep warm by spending the morning on the east face and the afternoon on the west face.

The largest mounds are built by termites of the genus *Macrotermes*, which actually grow their own food in the form of fungi within their colonies. It is worth looking at the architecture of these mounds in some detail because they are built to a much more rigid plan than most other termite nests, and also because of their amazing central-heating and air-conditioning systems. The insects really do create their own habitat within their mounds. *Macrotermes bellicosus* lives in various parts of Africa and builds somewhat conical mounds up to about 4m high. The walls of the mounds are composed of soil particles cemented together with the insects' saliva and droppings and, although they are porous, they are extremely hard. Several flange-like buttresses run from top to bottom of the mound. The living quarters with the all-important royal chamber and the numerous other chambers and passages are in the centre of the mound, together with the fungus gardens. The whole complex is supported over a large air space called the cellar, and there are other air spaces around and above the living quarters.

The growth of the fungi and the activities of the termites create a great deal of heat and use up a great deal of oxygen, which could soon lead to the suffocation of the termites, but the construction of the mound ensures that the living complex receives a constant stream of fresh air. The heat generated causes the stale air to rise into the upper air space, from where it passes along thick ducts into the mound buttresses. Here, the ducts break up into narrow channels and the stale air is forced down through them. Because of the porous nature of the walls, oxygen from the outside can diffuse into the air stream, and excess carbon dioxide can diffuse out. The air is thus purified, and it is also cooled during its journey through the buttresses. It flows along some more ducts into the cellar, and then rises up through the living complex to keep the termites happy. Many other nest designs can be found among the termites, and the insects also modify their habitats a good deal by carrying out other building operations in the surroundings. Most of them dislike light, for example, and they nearly all make covered ways or tunnels leading from their nests to their feeding grounds.

The Lives of Insects

Preceding chapters have shown how the insects of the present day have evolved, and have described the various habitats in which they live. The chapter on basic biology has explained the mechanisms by which insects function. The aim of the present chapter is to try to draw all this together into an overall account of the living world of insects.

We must try to look at insects impartially, without thinking of them as being 'good' or 'bad', or unpleasant in their habits. These are human judgments, and out of the million or so species that we know, only the tiniest fraction ever comes into contact with man. Of course these few are immensely important to human well-being, and they are discussed in Chapter 5. Yet even these insects are not dependent on man, and could live just as successfully, or not, as the case may be, if there were no human beings in existence. After all, they had been evolving for hundreds of millions of years before man appeared on the earth, and nearly all the existing species of insects are older than the human species.

The insects of today are the survivors of a long evolutionary history. They are the successful insects, and the present chapter tries to analyse this success. Some insects have succeeded by becoming highly adapted to one particular way of life which is all very well as long as conditions remain the same, but vulnerable if conditions change. An example is the fig-insects, whose existence depends on the peculiar life history of the fig-tree. Most insects feed either on decaying materials, or by catching and eating other insects and small organisms. This way of life is much less precarious, for if one source of food fails it is not too difficult to find another. A third way of ensuring the future of the species is that of the social insects (bees, wasps, ants, termites) which live in huge colonies, and have a highly organized social life. Individuals may perish, but the colony goes on. Let us look at the life histories from this point of view, dividing them roughly and arbitrarily into the following groups according to their apparent degree of success.

The Least Successful Insects
few in species
limited in distribution
restricted to a narrow habitat
less numerous than formerly

The Successful Insects which may be subdivided as follows:

The Moderately Successful Insects
reasonable number of species
fairly widespread
limited in habitat, but not uncommon there
seem to be holding their own

Highly Successful Insects
many species
widespread occurrence
great diversity of habitats
numbers have increased in recent periods
signs of continuing evolution today

At the outset we must remember that evolution is not uniform throughout large groups. Within the highly successful orders, such as the Lepidoptera, there are some families that have been only moderately successful, and some that even seem to be on the decline.

Let us look at the insect world from this point of view, starting with those groups that seem to be the least successful in the present age.

The least successful insects

Our very first group is a doubtful one. When you switch on the light in a larder or a storeroom you will quite often see a quick, silvery gleam as a tiny insect on the floor runs for shelter, or 'freezes' into immobility. This is a silverfish, a member of the order Thysanura (bristle-tails). In warm places, such as near hot pipes, or in boiler-houses and bakeries you may see the bigger firebrat (*Thermobia*), and on the seashore you will find *Machilis* and *Petrobius*. All these are furtive, wingless insects, which feed on small scraps of organic materials. They hatch from the egg in a form just like the adult, and live long lives, sometimes up to seven years, moulting frequently, but never changing their appearance.

Can we call these insects successful or not? It is hard to say. They are certainly not a progressive group. They are known as fossils back to Permian times, 200 million years ago. If we think of the luxuriant variety of other insects that have evolved since then it makes Thysanura seem very stagnant, yet they have survived all the vicissitudes of life for 200 million years. They still find abundant food, and a secure niche in which to live their long, if uneventful lives. Their very changelessness suits this way of life. Only one thing breaks the monotony: at each moult the females lose the lining of the spermatheca, and so have to be fertilized again to ensure a steady supply of eggs.

Similar questions can be asked about two of the other orders of primitively wingless insects. Diplura are slightly more versatile than Thysanura, being divided into three families: the vegetable-feeding Campodeidae, the carnivorous Japygidae, and the rare and primitive Projapygidae. Some of the Japygidae show a simple form of maternal care of the eggs and young nymphs, so that their evolution has led them further, in this direction at least, than most groups of insects have achieved. They, too, like the Thysanura, live concealed lives under stones, dead wood, leaf litter and the like.

Protura are even less well known. Very few entomologists have seen one, and they are still exhibited as rarities at entomological meetings. This is largely because they are very small – less than 2 mm – but other equally tiny insects, such as the fairy flies (Mymaridae, page 230) are familiar to all students. Protura also live in soil, peat, woodland litter, and beneath bark. They are unique among insects in having no antennae, using their first pair of legs as feelers instead. This is practical confirmation of the theoretical assumption that antennae, mouthparts and genitalia are modified limbs. It also shows that Protura have evolved into an entomological backwater.

Only one group of primitively wingless insects is outstandingly successful. This is the order Collembola, or springtails, which have become an abundant and important constituent of the soil fauna. We shall have to consider Collembola later, among the most successful groups of insects.

Winged insects

We should expect winged insects to have been more successful in evolution. The ability to fly must surely have enabled them to spread over a wide range of territory, and to seek out a wide variety of habitats. This is generally true, but a surprising number of the descendants of winged ancestors have either lost their wings, or allowed them to fall into disuse. Loss of flight is not necessarily a bar to success – the fleas are an outstandingly successful group – but some flightless orders have suffered a serious decline.

Here is how Imms (1957, page 319) describes the biology of *Grylloblatta campodeiformis*. 'The insects are found beneath stones etc., at altitudes of 1 500–6 500 ft. They are apparently omnivorous and nocturnal, with a low temperature preference (about 4 °C). The black eggs are deposited singly in the soil or among moss when the adult female is about a year old. There is an incubation period of about a year, and eight nymphal instars, which together occupy about five years.' This is the very picture of a cramped, shrinking existence. Here are insects, apparently descended from ancestors that had wings and eyes, which have lost the former and reduced the latter. Even though they have limited themselves to a furtive existence they are still able to live only in remote, high places. Notice how their whole existence has been slowed down, with a year to reach maturity, and a further year of incubation, a total life of about five years. How reminiscent this is of such archaic vertebrate groups as the crocodiles and tortoises. Slow, sluggish animals seem often to be archaic survivals: the rapid evolution and high adaptability that go with success require a short life cycle together with a quick succession of generations.

The order Embioptera shows distinctly more enterprise. Females are still wingless, but many of the males have two pairs of wings, with winged and wingless males occurring within the same species. Although they are furtive and avoid daylight, males sometimes come to a light at night. This does not mean, of course, that they find the light attractive, but merely that its presence confuses their navigation, and they blunder into it.

Members of Embioptera are not severely restricted in range, but occur throughout the tropics and into warmer temperate regions. Although they are uncommon and rarely seen, they seem to be holding their own in a quiet way. That they have been doing so for a long time is shown by the fact that they have one very specialized activity. Males, females and nymphs all have silk-spinning glands in the forefeet, and use them to construct silken tunnels or galleries, in which they live. Perhaps it is unfair to dismiss Embioptera as unsuccessful, but they seem to be in another entomological backwater. No one knows how many species exist: numbers from 200–2000 have been suggested. The females have retreated into their gallery life both literally and metaphorically. They spend their whole lives there feeding on lichen and other vegetable materials. They are gregarious insects, often found in colonies of galleries close together, and the females show a certain maternal care of their eggs. This is another retreating existence, which seems to afford no stimulus or incentive to evolutionary experiment.

A similar history of evolutionary obscurity applies to the Zoraptera, an order of which scarcely two-dozen species are known, all belonging to one genus, *Zorotypus*. These, again, are tiny, even minute insects, which hide under bark and among vegetable debris. Within one species there are usually both winged and wingless forms, each of which includes both sexes. The dark, winged forms possess eyes and ocelli, which have been lost in the pale, wingless forms. This is a development that occurs throughout the animal kingdom, whenever animals spend their lives in darkness, and so we might expect there to be a corresponding difference in habitat between the two forms of *Zorotypus*. They seem to be gregarious, but without any social life:

that is, although they congregate together they do not share maternal duties as do the bees and other true social insects.

The fact that all Zoraptera belong to one genus, and that the few species are scattered throughout the world, suggests that they may be merely an aberrant member of one of the bigger orders, which has adopted a very narrow view of life and in consequence has found itself in an evolutionary blind alley. It is perhaps significant that *Zorotypus* is not known from Australia. Archaic groups of animals usually abound in Australia, protected by the long isolation of that continent from the rest of the world.

There are two other orders of insects that are well established in the world today, yet nevertheless cannot be called even moderately successful. One such group is that of the earwigs, the order Dermaptera. With more than 1000 living species, and a fossil history of about 150 million years, back to the Jurassic, earwigs are familiar to people all over the world. They eat almost any animal or plant food that they can chew, and can sometimes be a practical nuisance when they nibble the foliage or fruits of cultivated plants. They are nocturnal and furtive, and show a well-developed level of maternal care for their eggs and nymphs. Though they have complicated wings they seldom fly. Their only bizarre ventures have been *Arixenina*, living in association with bats in Indonesia and *Hemimerus*, living in association with rats in Africa. Both genera are apterous and viviparous.

The insects that we have so far considered, and judged to be relatively unsuccessful in the modern world, all have several factors in common. They are elusive, hiding away in daylight, and shunning the light; they have tended to lose their wings, or at least to fly little; and they are omnivorous, feeding on small scraps of anything they can pick up. They have stuck to a monotonous, unadventurous way of life. Yet a moment's thought shows that most of these things could be said about ants, except the last: far from being unadventurous, ants are probably the most successful of all insects. Their secret is social life, as we shall see.

The successful insects

Now that we have looked at a few examples of comparative failure, we can understand better why most insects have flourished. Expansion is the clue: expansion into a wider distribution, and a more varied range of habitats. Of course there are specialist insects, which have become supremely efficient at exploiting the possibilities of a narrow habitat, but, like specialist animals and plants in all epochs, they may at any time fall victim to changing conditions, and especially so in the present period, when man is changing the physical environment more rapidly than it has ever changed before.

Insects owe their increased powers of expansion and adaptability in particular to two evolutionary 'inventions': flight and metamorphosis. A third aid to flexibility has been the number of ways in which the primitive biting and chewing mouthparts can be modified into organs for piercing and sucking.

The adventure of flight

Undoubtedly the most important landmark in the evolution of insects came when they acquired the power of flight. The groups that we have just considered, and judged unsuccessful, have either never had wings, or have not exploited them effectively. The advantages of being able to fly are many, and include escape from enemies, active pursuit of prey, dispersal to wider habitats, migration to alternative host plants, or in search of more suitable climatic conditions, finding a mate, and the ability to live in one habitat when young and a different habitat when mature. All these activities enrich life, and make for a flourishing insect group. When highly successful groups such as fleas and ants have wholly or partly abandoned flight, we shall expect to find that they have found compensating advantages elsewhere.

When we speak about the ability to fly, we think first of *active flight*, that is of launching into the air and flying purposefully in a chosen direction, but we must not overlook the importance of *passive flight*, of being carried along by the wind. Of course all flight, except in still air, is a mixture of the two. Watch a butterfly on a gusty day: during the lulls it flits from one flower to another, but when a gust comes the butterfly either clings tightly, or sails away downwind.

The number of insects that fly actively is small compared with the very many that are carried high in the air, and transported passively over long distances, by wind and by convection currents. At any time of day or night the air supports a huge 'aerial plankton', the extent of which is still only incompletely known (Fig 37). There are enough of them in the summer for swallows, swifts and martins to spend all the hours of daylight catching them. Obviously a high proportion of these airborne insects must fall victim to birds, or die of starvation before they reach land again, but it seems certain that

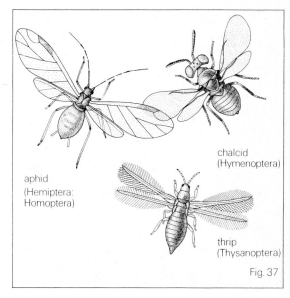

aphid
(Hemiptera:
Homoptera)

chalcid
(Hymenoptera)

thrip
(Thysanoptera)

Fig. 37

Fig. 37 Some examples of aerial plankton.

121

passive flight is a major factor in distributing insects to remote islands, as well as across continental masses. The known distribution of many insects seems to support the belief that the smallest insects are most affected by passive flight through the air. Bigger, more powerful flyers are better able to resist being carried away. Thus among an island group such as the Canaries, powerful robber-flies of the genus *Promachus* belong to different species in the various islands, and passive flight has never been able to mix them all up.

Passive flight involves wingless insects as well as small and weak flyers. Indeed it has been suggested that insect flight may have begun among small insects, from which the more powerful active flyers evolved, though the palaeontological evidence, especially that of huge dragonflies in the Carboniferous Era, rather conflicts with this theory.

Metamorphosis

Metamorphosis means changing from one shape to another, and in living creatures this term is applied to changes that take place during the lifetime of one individual. The insects that we have talked about so far have had little or no metamorphosis. Apart from the weak powers of flight of adult earwigs and male Embioptera, all these insects have been compelled to spend their whole lives in the same environment. 'Basic Biology' has already explained that metamorphosis may be *gradual,* leading by slight bodily changes up to the final moult into a fully winged individual, or *complete,* with an adult that is totally different from the preceding stages. The caterpillar and the butterfly are the proverbial example of this latter.

Complete metamorphosis has the great advantage that the larva and the adult can live in completely different habitats, feeding on different foods. In fact it is as if these insects could live their lives twice over, with twice as many opportunities to exploit the possibilities of their environment. It is not surprising, therefore, that many highly successful insects have a complete metamorphosis. Insects with gradual metamorphosis have fewer evolutionary opportunities, unless they choose to pass their immature stages in water. Life under water presents problems of breathing and movement (swimming or crawling), in response to which highly efficient organs have been evolved for these purposes. Insects which have an aquatic nymph and an aerial adult (e.g. dragonflies) have what amounts to a third kind of metamorphosis, but we shall see later that this is not true of all aquatic insects.

One of the most important advantages of metamorphosis is that feeding can be redistributed during the lifetime of the individual. Each insect needs a certain total amount of food during its lifetime: for growth, for movement, and to lay down yolk in the eggs that the female will lay. The insect may feed throughout its life, keeping pace with demand, or it may concentrate its feeding during only part of its life.

Most insects do the bulk of their feeding during their immature, growing stages, reserving the adult phase for courtship, mating and dispersal. In extreme cases, notably the non-biting midges (Chironomidae), the adults do not feed at all, living entirely on reserves built up by the larvae. At the other extreme, tsetse-flies (*Glossina*) feed only as adults, and the females nourish their larvae internally.

It seems to be easier for vegetable-feeding insects to stock up when they are young, and so to release the adult for other activities, whereas carnivorous larvae usually have carnivorous adults, as if animal food was an uncertain source from which to build up reserves.

Feeding habits

A third development during the evolution of insects has been a changeover from biting and chewing their food to sucking up liquids. The mouthparts of insects evolved originally from three pairs of segmental limbs, or at least leg-like appendages near the front of the body. These were fairly easily adapted as instruments for seizing, biting and chewing: the mandibles, maxillae and labium, with their attached feelers, or palpi. All primitive insects chew, but it is not true that all advanced insects suck. Beetles are

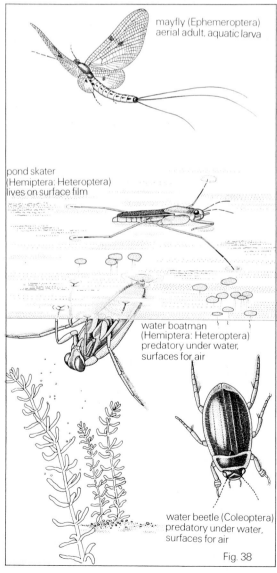

mayfly (Ephemeroptera)
aerial adult, aquatic larva

pond skater
(Hemiptera: Heteroptera)
lives on surface film

water boatman
(Hemiptera: Heteroptera)
predatory under water,
surfaces for air

water beetle (Coleoptera)
predatory under water,
surfaces for air

Fig. 38

Fig. 38 Insect adaptations to life in water.

Dragonfly nymph.

an example of a most successful group that have retained the primitive chewing habit. In contrast, flies (Diptera) have gone over completely to sucking, whereas Hymenoptera (bees, wasps, ants, etc.) use one method or the other, as it suits the way of life of different sections of this diverse and eminently successful order.

Thus mouthpart structure and feeding methods of an insect group are more clues to their present way of life than their evolutionary history.

With these three criteria in mind – powers of flight, type of metamorphosis, feeding habits – we can examine the rest of the insects, and assess their evolutionary success.

The moderately successful insects

We might start with those insects that live in water when they are young, and leave it when they mature (Fig. 38). We start here because these insects include two ancient groups, which trace back to the early days of insect flight, before there was any mechanism for folding the wings. In those days the wings were either held out flat when they were not in use, or at most raised vertically, back-to-back. These two ways of holding the resting wings can be seen today in the dragonflies (Odonata), the first method in the true dragonflies, with their broad, powerful wings, and the second method in the fragile damselflies. Here we have an order of insects that goes back in the fossil record to Permian times and with close ancestors in the preceding coal measures or Carboniferous times. They were one of the earliest groups of flying insects, and grew to the huge size of over half a metre wingspan. By all the rules they should have exhausted themselves long ago, and disappeared

into fossil history. Instead, today there are over 5 000 species throughout the world. What is the secret of their toughness?

Perhaps their carnivorous habit has helped. With rare exceptions, dragonfly nymphs live under water, breathing by specially designed gills, and stalking their prey by walking about on underwater vegetation, or just lying in wait for it to pass within reach. Their mouthparts are unique among insects in having the labial palps carried at the end of the 'mask', a hinged plate which can be projected forwards to seize prey and carry it back to the waiting mandibles and maxillae. This is a highly efficient development from the primitive biting jaws: just how effective it is can be seen by putting a dragonfly nymph into a dish of water and giving it a tadpole to catch. The quick snatch, followed by leisurely mastication, look like something out of science fiction, as in a way they are, when we remember how many millions of years dragonflies have been doing this. The macabre aspect of dragonfly nymphs is enhanced by their readiness to devour anything living that they can catch and hold: insect larvae (including other dragonfly nymphs), tadpoles, even small fish. Nymphs of damselflies are replete within a year, but the big nymphs of true dragonflies feed for two to five years before they are ready to leave the water and continue their predatory career in the air.

Dragonflies of both kinds leave the water for good when they become adult. The nymph crawls up the stem of a plant standing in the water, or at least lies barely submerged on a flat stone, and from a split in its back the soft-skinned adult slowly and painfully squeezes out into the air. Hardening off takes a surprisingly long time – often one or two hours – and it seems

A male Dragonfly
(*Sympetrum strio-latum*) showing
mites on its wings.

Dragonfly nymph
devouring a tadpole.

Common Red Damselfly (*Pyrrhosoma nymphula*) eating a mayfly.

that dragonflies must be most vulnerable to their enemies at this time. Yet they survive in large numbers, perhaps because their drab colouring at this time merges into the mixed background of the water vegetation.

The adult dragonfly is a highly efficient machine for capturing prey. Damselflies, with their fragile wings, flit about among waterside vegetation, catching small, soft-bodied insects such as little moths and leafhoppers. The big dragonflies fly much more purposefully, ranging far out over the water, and far inland, often hunting over a territory that is remote from any body of water. Each individual tends to establish a 'beat' for itself, coming back time and again to the same series of perches, from which it can see all around. Like other powerful predators, dragonflies will eat anything that they can catch and hold. If they cannot make their meal satisfactorily while still flying they will settle on vegetation and munch away there until all the succulent body fluids of the prey have been extracted.

The bodies of dragonflies are admirably suited to this life. Unlike the wings of more advanced insects, those of dragonflies can still move independently, an arrangement that makes for a highly manoeuvrable flying machine. It is very suitable for a relatively slow wing-beat, and flapping flight, which the big wings and powerful muscles of the biggest dragonflies convert into a rare turn of speed. When one swoops past, you can hear the click of the wings, and feel the

rush of air. A curious arrangement of the thorax of dragonflies pushes the legs forward, which helps in grasping prey, and the wings backwards, keeping them clear of the legs when flying. True dragonflies have huge eyes, with strong binocular vision; damselflies achieve this result with smaller eyes by having them widely separated on a broad head.

Here we have one of the most ancient orders of insects still living in the old way after 200–300 million years, yet no one can call them stagnant or unenterprising. The constant search for living prey has kept them on the alert, and has stimulated both nymphs and adults to exploit the insects of their day. They have therefore remained adaptable in detail, while preserving the general pattern of their way of life.

The striking posture they adopt while pairing is a unique feature of dragonfly life. Pairs are often seen flying together, with the tip of the male abdomen gripping the neck of the female, and the female abdomen curved round to reach the undersurface of his abdomen. Although the male genital opening is in its usual place on the ninth segment, the copulatory organs are not there, but in a pocket on the second/third segment, the genital fossa. Before pairing, the male transfers sperm to this pocket, from which the female collects it during the mating flight.

It seems strange that evolutionary pressures should have been strong enough to perfect such a complicated device, when other insects pair, even in flight, without any special devices.

125

Crane-flies (daddy-long-legs) are often seen paired end to end, with male and female facing opposite ways. The more powerful female does the flying, while the more slender male dangles behind. There seems no obvious reason why dragonflies should not do the same, but this is a frequent comment that one can make on evolutionary trends, particularly in regard to courtship and mating. A possible advantage of the dragonflies' method of clasping is that it may be continued even while the female is laying eggs in the water.

Only one other surviving order still has the primitive, non-folding wings which characterize the Palaeoptera. These are the mayflies (Ephemeroptera), and they have so many old-fashioned features, while living in a waterside world that has been invaded by so many more modern groups, that it is strange that mayflies did not become extinct long ago. Although they lack the flamboyance of dragonflies, mayflies must be considered at least a moderately successful group. Huge clouds of fragile insects flying over water have been known as ephemerids since classical times, getting their name – which means 'living for a day' – from the fantastically short life of the adults.

The life cycle of mayflies has been organized with extreme economy. The underwater nymphs feed steadily on vegetable food, algae and perhaps tiny animals as well, for up to three years, and from this food they accumulate reserves that will be enough for the whole life of the adults, which need not feed at all. The sole function of the adult stage is to mate, and for the female to lay eggs. The adults range over water in countless numbers at a time, so that it is easy and quick for the males and females to meet. The eggs are already well matured, and need only to be fertilized before they are dropped into the water. After this short burst of activity the adults are exhausted; not surprisingly, since they cannot feed themselves to replenish their store of energy. Many are snapped up by predators, birds, bats, dragonflies. The rest fall into the water and fish rise to take them. This usually happens in the evening or early night, and accounts for the 'evening rise' of many fish.

Perhaps mayflies have succeeded because they have always maintained a close relationship with fish. Their nymphs are a most important part of the staple underwater diet of fish, while the chance to snap up an ovipositing female, and the mass of males and females falling on to the

Stoneflies (*Isoperla grammatica*) mating. Note the wings laid flat over the body.

water surface are additional bonuses. The lives of mayflies and fish are perhaps more closely geared together than those of any other waterside insects.

Mayflies have the further distinction of being the only insects which moult after their wings have fully extended. This is not a throwback to a primitive condition, but a special adaptation to the lives of these particular insects. Nymphs of mayflies do not crawl out of the water before the adult emerges, but this emergence takes place at the water surface, or even just below. Surface tension is a most powerful and dangerous force at that time, and if the insect were wetted it would not be able to break away. The first winged form is covered with fine hairs which prevent wetting, and is called a 'dun' by fishermen, and a 'subimago' by entomologists. Having safely escaped from the grip of the water surface, the dun moults again, revealing the full colour and pattern of the adult mayfly, which is now called a 'spinner'. All is now ready for the mating flight.

What mayflies lack in number of species – about 1500 known, but probably others still to be recognized – they more than make up in numbers of individuals. They remain so essential a

part of waterside ecology that they must surely be accepted as a moderately successful group.

While we are by the waterside it is convenient to look at one or two other groups of insects that are to be found there. Stoneflies, alder flies and caddis flies are all familiar to fishermen as models for fishing flies. They are not very closely related entomologically, and any resemblances between them must be looked on as the result of convergent evolution.

Take stoneflies (Plecoptera). They are so-called because the adults do not fly much, particularly in the daytime, spending their lives among the stones beside streams. Some species are about at night, and their males sometimes come to a light. Having the more advanced wing attachments of the Neoptera, stoneflies are able to fold their wings over the abdomen, flat, like a pair of scissors, though the wings are often curled at the edges, giving the insect a characteristically 'rolled' appearance.

The adult life of stoneflies is in striking contrast to the strenuous life of mayflies. They mate sluggishly on the ground, or on stones, and eat little or nothing, sometimes taking a little pollen from flowers, or scraping algae from stones. They live for a week or two, and are attractive

127

to watch, easy to observe because they do so little, and are not easily disturbed while they are doing it. Their young are 'perlid nymphs', and by chance this expression (which comes from the generic name *Perla*, and strictly applies only to nymphs of the family Perlidae) suggests the kind of clear, pellucid water in which they occur. They need water that is well oxygenated, and so their typical habitats are brooks and rushing streams with a bed of stones. Since such waters occur mostly in the upper reaches of streams, stoneflies are at home in hilly districts, mountainous country, and in cold water. Consequently they must be tolerant of low temperatures, and may be seen at most times of the year in temperate countries. Large bodies of still or slow-moving water do not suit them, and as they are very sensitive to pollution, they tend to be even less frequent in lowland waters nowadays than they used to be. Stonefly nymphs are mainly vegetable feeders, but nymphs of the family Perlidae feed on other aquatic animals, including the nymphs and larvae of other water insects.

In view of the sluggish habits of adult stoneflies it is surprising that they are often copied in fishing flies. The adult females do approach the surface to deposit their eggs, either crawling in from the margin, or flying over the water to dip the tip of the abdomen below the surface. It is then that they may be snatched by a fish.

Other insects that we might notice at the waterside include caddis flies of the order Trichoptera and alder flies (Megaloptera). These are more advanced insects, which have a complete metamorphosis, that is not a nymph, changing shape gradually, but a larva totally unlike its parent, and a pupal stage to make the transformation to the winged adult. As soon as we look among the stones underwater we are sure to see many caddis larvae in their silken cases. The cases are really tubes, open at both ends, and made from silk spun by the labial glands of the larva inside (the 'caddis worm'). The silken tube is encrusted with small stones, particles of grit, and even small fragments of vegetation, all of which help to camouflage the tube and make it difficult to see against the stony background: at least until the larva moves, which it does by extending its head and thorax out of the tube and dragging the case along with it. For breathing purposes a current of water is drawn through the tube from front to rear. Many caddis larvae do not make cases, though they may spin a silken net to entrap prey. These more mobile (campodeioid) larvae are less easily seen unless they are netted in a general collection of underwater insects. All caddis larvae have biting jaws. The case-bearing species are omnivorous, that is they will eat anything they can get. However, the more mobile, non-case-

Caddis fly (*Limne-philus* spp) – an insect of the water-side.

bearing species are on the whole carnivorous.

This is the first group of insects we have met so far that have a pupal stage to bridge the gap between larva and adult. Unlike some aquatic insects which pupate on dry land, caddis flies form their pupa under water. Case-bearing larvae fix their cases to a stone or underwater twig, and use them as ready-made cocoons. Caseless larvae have to spin a cocoon. The adult is formed beneath the pupal skin (called a 'pharate adult') and operates a pair of large crossed mandibles to cut its way out and reach the surface, where the adult caddis fly emerges into the air.

Adult caddis flies look like small moths, mostly drab in colour and brown-speckled. Looked at more closely they are seen to have their wings covered, not with scales like moths and butterflies, but with very fine hairs: hence the name Trichoptera, which means 'hairy wings'. Except when they are newly emerged, and making mating flights over the water, caddis flies are very quiet insects, and easy to overlook as they sit immobile on a twig or a stone near a stream. On the other hand their case-bearing larvae are very common, once one has penetrated their camouflage by happening to see one of them move. There is a wide variety of designs for cases, which are often diagnostic of the particular species.

Among the caddis flies resting on waterside vegetation you will see a number of brown insects with clear wings, on which the pattern of the veins is particularly obvious. These are alder flies, Sialoidea, or dobson flies, Corydaloidea, if they are much bigger, with long, curved mandibles. They belong to an order of insects (Megaloptera) that is essentially terrestrial, although members of the superfamilies Sialoidea and Corydaloidea have rediscovered the water as a larval habitat: a step that, as we shall see, has been taken by many insects in a wide variety of orders. Hatching from eggs that are laid on dry land, the larvae move immediately into the water, where they are fully at home, because they are equipped with gill filaments for underwater breathing. They also have powerful jaws, and can eat larvae, small worms, in fact all the food that the voracious dragonfly nymphs also enjoy. The big larva of the dobson fly (*Corydalus cornutus*) is known to American fisherman as the 'hellgrammite'.

After spending the winter feeding in the water, alder fly larvae come back to the soil to pupate, and emerge into the air. Their close relatives, the snake flies, Raphidioidea, are completely terrestrial, with active, voracious larvae living under loose bark, and adults which are usually only to be found high up in the trees. The sub-order megaloptera includes the alder flies and

129

the dobson flies as well as the snake flies.

It will be noticed that all the winged insects with gradual metamorphosis that we have studied so far seem to have been committed to a life in water from their remote ancestry, but as soon as we come to insects with a complete metamorphosis we seem to be dealing with land insects which have migrated back into the water for a part of their lives. So let us leave them at this point, and go back to look at the land-living insects that have only a gradual metamorphosis: that is, remember, those which hatch from the egg into a nymph, which is like an adult without wings, and which changes gradually at each moult, until at its final moult it spreads its wings, as well as becoming sexually mature.

The groups of insects that we will now consider have had few advantages in the evolutionary struggle. They do have wings, and wings of the 'new' neopterous type, with an adequate folding mechanism. They do not have the advantages of complete metamorphosis, and some of them retain the primitive mouthparts of a biting and chewing type. Cockroaches are a good example. They are among the oldest insects, having a fossil history that goes back 400 million years. Back in the coal measures of the Carboniferous, cockroaches were both abundant and big. Today fewer than 4000 species are known, but these are distributed throughout the world, and no doubt there are many others still unknown. For these are essentially furtive insects, hiding away in the daytime and coming out at night. They are lovers of warmth, and so away from the tropics they flourish best in artificial environments in warm buildings.

It is interesting to compare cockroaches with the unsuccessful primitive insects that we considered earlier. Whereas cockroaches have stuck to a relatively simple life plan, they have not allowed themselves to be forced into a narrow declining backwater of life. Their simple chewing mouthparts are demonstrated to students as illustrating the basic type from which all the more complex types of mouthparts have been derived. The domestic species can be captured and kept alive on scraps of almost anything edible. The wild ones are assumed to be similarly omnivorous, perhaps with a partiality for dead animal matter. Attempts to rear wild species in captivity have not been very successful, and it seems as if the early nymphs will feed only under some special conditions that are not reproduced in the laboratory. (This is often a major obstacle to the artificial breeding of wild-caught insects. Presumably 'domestic' insects, that is those that breed readily in man-made habitats, are free of any such limitations.) Some wild cockroaches seem to be capable of digesting rotting wood, and the domestic species can sometimes infest old wood: in my own experience, kitchen cockroaches were discovered in a museum specimen of a section from a 'big tree' (giant redwood).

The long history of cockroaches is remarkable for its lack of variety. They all look very much alike, and as they have always looked: broad, rather flattened bodies, with long antennae and spiny legs, and simple, little used wings. Contrast this with the enormous range of size and shape among beetles. Only in sexual matters do cockroaches show enterprise. Sperm is transferred in a package called a spermatophore, and the fertilized eggs are glued together in bundles, each of which forms an ootheca. In some, perhaps most, of the species, the ootheca is dropped, and lies until the eggs hatch (oviparous species), but other species retain the ootheca within the body of the female cockroach for a shorter or longer period of time. The young nymphs may be merely protected by this device, but those species in which the nymph receives nourishment from its mother are therefore viviparous.

Looking back at the earliest groups we studied, the silverfish and their allies, is there any significant difference between their level of success and that of the cockroaches? Or is it merely that cockroaches are bigger, and better known because of their domestic species? They would certainly be a very obscure group if we only knew their wild species.

One item in the cockroaches' favour is that they have a carnivorous offshoot, the mantids. Most non-entomologists have at least seen pictures of the 'praying' mantis, and anyone who has lived in the tropics or subtropics will know the insect well. To the human mind there is something macabre in its coldly deliberate behaviour, as it seizes and devours its prey, compared with the brisk struggle when a wasp or a robber-fly tackles prey as big as itself.

At first glance cockroaches and mantids seem quite dissimilar, and only a detailed comparison of structure establishes their close relationship. The conspicuous differences are obviously related to the very different modes of life. So here we have an evolutionary line that has existed a very long time, preserving one conservative branch, but throwing off an effective predatory sideline. We can hardly call the line 'highly' successful, but we must allow it a moderate rating.

Rather similar things can be said about the Phasmida (or Phasmatodea) the stick and leaf insects. Stick insects are fairly familiar animals these days, because some species are easily kept in captivity, but in nature they are scattered, and usually few in number, though sometimes more numerous. They change colour according to how much they are crowded together, as well as in response to such factors as light intensity and humidity. This reminds us of the phase changes of locusts, between their solitary and gregarious phases, and in fact for a long time Phasmida were classified along with the locusts and grasshoppers. These last, of course, are one of the most successful of all insect groups, and we shall talk about them later.

Phasmida contains leaf-feeding insects of a highly sedentary habit. They spend almost their whole lifetime, which lasts several months, motionless on the vegetation. Stick insects have an extremely elongate body and legs – that is, even in small individuals these parts are long and narrow – and are easily mistaken for twigs, a resemblance that is enhanced by the elaborate detail of shape and pattern, which camouflage the insect very effectively. Leaf insects rely for their camouflage upon broad, flattened areas of the abdomen, legs and forewings, which look like leaves, not only in shape, but in precise detail of colour and pattern.

Phasmida have two pairs of wings, the fore pair acting as covers for the others. The hind-wings are broad, and open out like a fan. Males can use them effectively to fly to another plant in search of a female, but mostly the wings are used as gliding planes. It might be expected that such scattered insects would find it difficult to pair off, and in fact many Phasmida are parthenogenetic, only females being known for many successive generations. This is one reason why stick insects have become popular as 'pets', because they can be kept in captivity without the problem of inducing them to mate.

The remaining insects with incomplete, or gradual metamorphosis are undoubtedly successful, though they can hardly be called 'highly' so. These include the lice, which have established their success by adopting a parasitic life. Everyone has heard of lice, though few have had the misfortune to see any. The two kinds used to be lumped together, but nowadays the biting, or bird lice form the order Mallophaga, and the sucking lice of mammals are Siphunculata. Taken together, they illustrate the principle already mentioned, the evolutionary tendency to replace the primitive biting mouthparts with equipment for piercing and sucking.

Both groups of lice have the characteristics of parasitic insects. Their bodies are flattened, stripped of all projections that might impede their movements, but equipped with strong legs and backwardly projecting bristles which act as a sort of ratchet device, and propel the insects forward between the feathers or hairs of its host animal. Since vision is of little use in such situations, they have reduced or lost the eyes, and have no ocelli. Some groups of parasitic insects retain the wings for mating purposes, either the males alone, or both sexes just for the duration of a mating flight. Both groups of lice, however, have abandoned flight altogether, and are completely wingless.

Of course the loss of wings is secondary: that is, the lice are certainly descended from winged ancestors, and have lost their wings as a direct adaptation to parasitic life. By this means they remove a possible encumbrance, but impose serious limitations upon their powers of dispersal as a species. Lice can no longer move from one host animal to another – even to another individual of the same species – except when their hosts are in contact, or in close proximity. Neither chewing nor biting lice can live for more than a short time away from the warmth of their host, so they can parasitize only animals that herd together, or birds that huddle together in nests or on perches.

There is an interesting contrast here between lice and fleas, which suffer from the same limitation of dispersal. Fleas are insects with a complete metamorphosis, that is a larva that is quite different from the adult flea. This larva is able to move away from the body of the host, and live in crevices round the host's sleeping quarters. Lice, having only a nymph that is very similar to the parents, and which lives on the same host, must pass their entire lives in the fur or feathers of their warm-blooded host. As a consequence, each species of lice is closely bound to one species of host, or at most one or two closely allied species. Host and parasite have evolved closely together, so that the more closely related the host animals, the more similar are the lice found on them. Resemblances and differences between the one group are often quoted as evidence of the degree of relationship of the other.

So much for similarities between the two kinds of lice. What about their differences? Mallophaga (biting lice) are the older, more conservative group. They are mainly scavengers, munching among the bases of the feathers, where there is a debris of dead feathers and skin. Mallophaga are among the tiny minority of insects – or indeed of any animals – that can digest keratin, the very stable chemical compound that is the strengthening constituent of feathers, hair and wool. Other insects with this ability are the larvae of clothes moths, and dermestid beetles. There is evidence that some bird lice nibble at the sockets of the feathers to get blood and other body fluids from their host, but this is only a minor source of food.

Mallophaga are principally known as bird lice, but they also occur on a few mammals. Australia and South America each has a family of Mallophaga that is parasitic upon their marsupial mammals, evidently a long-standing relationship. All over the world domesticated animals – dogs, horses and donkeys, cattle, guinea-pigs – may be infested with certain species of biting lice.

On the other hand Siphunculata are exclusively parasites of mammals, and have far fewer species than the bird lice: fewer than 300 species of sucking lice compared with more than ten times that number of biting lice. Yet sucking lice make up in importance what they lack in number of species. The Body Louse of man, alone, is responsible for serious outbreaks of typhus and of relapsing fever. 'Insects and Man', emphasizes the medical importance of sucking lice, but from a biological point of view a deciding factor in their life history is their need for a constant environment of warmth and high humidity, which can be maintained only close to the body of the host. Since so much of the human body is almost hairless, and man no longer has a fur or pelt in which the lice can live, the necessary climate can be attained only under clothing. The lice are easily killed by removing the clothing and letting it cool. Hence lousiness (or 'pediculosis', to give it a more polite term) flourishes only when clothing is worn for long periods without changing.

131

Should we rate lice as successful insects or not? They have contrived a way of life that is stable, that is, it does not depend on conditions that are liable to change suddenly. The Human Body Louse might conceivably become extinct if everybody in the world changed his clothes every day, but this is so unlikely to happen that the Human Body Louse can be considered safe for the foreseeable future. The Human Crab Louse, which lives in the few areas where hairs remain, particularly in the pubic region, is in an even stronger position, and all other lice of fur and feather would find a congenial habitat as long as there are mammals and birds in existence. So lice are certainly successful as an evolutionary experiment. The only reason for not rating them as being highly successful is their lack of mobility, which fleas have achieved through their complete metamorphosis. So fleas get a place in the top group.

Remaining among the insects with gradual metamorphosis are one small group and one large. The small group is that of the booklice (Psocoptera), tiny insects which live on dry scraps, and like silverfish, attract unfavourable attention by gnawing the pastes and glues of books, sometimes causing serious damage. Being winged, they are more mobile than silverfish, and probably flourish well in wild conditions, but in a comfortable obscurity. They are only moderately successful.

The last group, and the apogee of the insects with gradual metamorphosis is the sucking bugs of the old order Hemiptera (see 'The Orders of Insects', page 206). Note that these have all taken the decisive step of converting to sucking their food. Hemiptera split rather obviously into two groups, sometimes considered as separate orders: Heteroptera and Homoptera, with a marked difference in degrees of success. Heteroptera are varied, but hardly a dominant group, whereas Homoptera which include the devastating aphids and many others of a like kind, must come into the highly successful group on any assessment. I think it will simplify matters if we consider the two groups quite separately, so anything further applies only to Heteroptera.

Here is an order of insects that is completely committed to feeding by piercing and sucking, and thereby obtaining a fluid diet, either the sap of plants or the body fluids of animals, warm-blooded or cold. Which did they do first, feed on plants or on animals? No one really knows, though there are many more opportunities to feed on plants than on animals, and plants are there to be eaten, whereas animals are elusive. On the face of it, therefore, we might expect the plant feeders to come first. Today most Heteroptera suck the juices of plants, but some take body fluids from other insects, and a whole section of aquatic families is entirely carnivorous. It is convenient to divide Heteroptera into land bugs (or Gymnocerata, that is with the antennae exposed to view) and the water bugs (or Cryptocerata with the antennae concealed, or at least short).

In total there are some 25 000 species of Heteroptera, so this evolutionary line has certainly achieved a reasonable success, yet the only heteropteran that is well known is the Bed Bug (*Cimex lectularius*) and this is a very exceptional species. It is one of the minority of bugs that have come to use their piercing proboscis to take blood from warm-blooded animals. It belongs to a small family, the other members of which feed principally on birds and bats, and less commonly on man, whereas *Cimex lectularius* has adapted itself closely to man's ways. In particular it has exploited man's habit of using regular sleeping quarters, which provide crevices in which the Bed Bug can hide during the daytime. Unlike the Human Louse, the Bed Bug is not conditioned to requiring steady warmth and humidity; on the contrary, its life cycle is highly adaptable, from a few weeks under favourable conditions in the laboratory to six months or more in unheated buildings in cool climates. This adaptability gives the Bed Bug the ability to follow man all round the world, and indeed to become primarily dependent on him, though when opportunity occurs it will also bite other mammals, including birds and bats.

The link with bats is interesting, because there is a closely related family of bugs, Polyctenidae, that is exclusively parasitic in the fur of bats, and has become flightless and blind, as parasites often do. (Compare with Nycteribiidae, a family of flies to be discussed later.) One way in which bed bugs may have begun their association with man might have been when early man slept in caves where bats roosted.

The other major family of man-biting bugs are the cone-nosed bugs (Reduviidae), which form an interesting contrast to the bed bugs. There are many more species – more than 3 000, in twenty subfamilies – and most of them either suck the juices of plants or the body fluids of insects (assassin bugs). Even these species can usually bite man, painfully. The European Fly-bug or Masked Bug (*Reduvius personatus*) hunts small insects under the bark of trees, and often in crevices indoors, but if it is interfered with it can give a nasty bite. One subfamily, Triatominae, with about eighty American species and a few in the East, transmits the human blood parasite *Trypanosoma cruzi*, causing Chaga's disease, though the natural hosts of most of the species are ground-living rodents and other mammals, as well as large iguana lizards.

Whereas bed bugs have abandoned flight, and keep close to their host's habitations all the time, reduviid bugs make the most of their flying abilities. Some are in the air by day, others are nocturnal. Although Triatominae are completely dependent on blood for food they have remained more mobile than have the bed bugs, and consequently have the choice of a wider range of food sources.

The habits of the rest of the land bugs (Gymnocerata) show that the piercing proboscis evolved by the Heteroptera is a versatile organ, equally suitable for sucking the sap of plants,

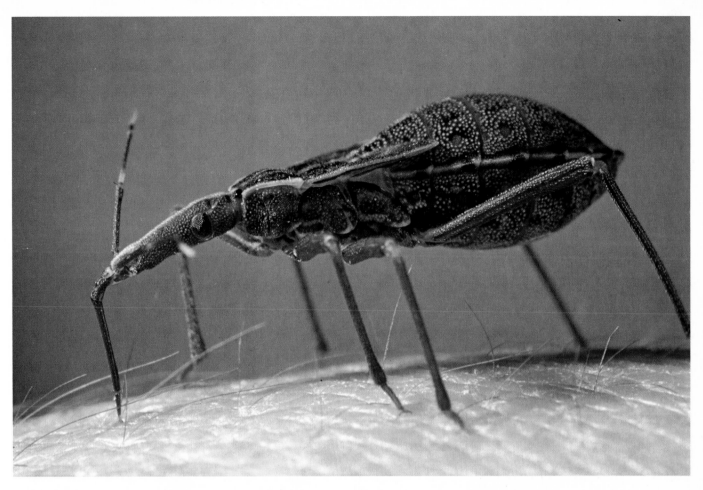

Reduvid or assassin bug from the family Reduviidae. Note the long proboscis sucking blood.

the body fluids of insects and the blood of vertebrates. Very few families of this group are exclusively plant feeders, though some of these are serious pests of cultivated plants. Thus the family Pyrrhocoridae, the firebugs, includes some predacious members, but the most notorious members are the 'cotton stainers' of the genus *Dysdercus*. Their habit of piercing the bolls of cotton plants transmits a fungus which stains the fibres.

Other plant bugs are not so obviously spectacular, though some of them are major pests in various parts of the world, particularly in North America, where the Chinch Bug (*Blissus leucopterus*) damages cereal crops and grasses, including cultivated grasses on lawns and golf courses, and the Squash Bug (*Anasa tristis*) damages cucurbitaceous plants (pumpkins, squashes, gourds, etc.). A heavily infested plant suffers such a serious loss of sap that growth is retarded, and in extreme cases wilting and blackening occur. Here for the first time we come across insect pests as a man-made problem. It is the planting of large areas of a single crop which enables any insect that feeds upon this plant to build up a huge population. When this huge population has fed, little of the crop is left for harvesting. Under natural conditions such an outbreak would be followed by starvation among the insects, and slow recovery of the crop, until insects and crop reached an equilibrium. This does not suit the commercial grower, who not unnaturally sees the insect as an enemy, but it is important to realize that, biologically speaking,

the insect is reacting to its environment as it has always done.

In this chapter we are not concerned with insects and man, but are trying to look at the lives of insects in perspective. Seen as a whole, the Heteroptera are probably a carnivorous group, with a few plant-feeding members. We shall see later that their 'twin' group, Homoptera, are pre-eminently plant feeders, and are so good at this that they rank among the most successful groups of insects. We shall talk about them in due course, but for the present it is enough to note that Homoptera, the plant feeders, are relatively uniform in appearance, with a monotony of structure, compared with the diversity and even bizarre appearance of the Heteroptera. There is little doubt that this diversity was generated by a diversity of feeding habits.

This structural diversity extends even to the plant-feeding members of the Heteroptera, the most bizarre of which are the lace bugs of the family Tingidae. These get their English name – and their German names of Gitterwanzen or Netzwanzen – from the elaborate reticulate pattern of the flattened forewings, sometimes matched by similar extensions on the thorax. This lace-like pattern is impressive in an enlarged drawing, which could be exhibited as a work of art, but it is less obvious in the living insects, at least to the human eye, and its biological significance is obscure. Only the winged adults have this appearance, the nymphs being ordinary-looking. Odd members of other fam-

133

ilies have somewhat similar outgrowths from the body or legs: for example *Phyllomorpha* of the family Coreidae has spiny, flattened areas, which in this case are used as 'nurseries' for keeping the eggs safe when they hatch.

These plant-feeding bugs are related to the large and important family Miridae (formerly well-known as Capsidae), some species of which do extensive damage to commercial plants. A particularly destructive genus is *Helopeltis*, which includes species attacking cotton, tea and coffee plants. Once again we have to realize that the commercial importance of a species is only rarely an index of its biological importance. Its status as a pest species arises from the accident that we present it with a great deal of suitable food, under favourable conditions, and then complain that the insect makes the most of it.

The commercial importance of Miridae as plant feeders obscures the fact that some species prey on other small creatures, including mites. When this prey includes the tiresome Red Spider Mite that attacks all kinds of fruit and greenhouse plants the predator is admitted to the Official List of Beneficial Insects as the 'Black-kneed Capsid', an easier name to remember than its scientific name of *Blepharidopterus angulatus*.

One other family of mainly plant-feeding bugs is that of the shield bugs (Pentatomidae), conspicuous because the scutellum of the thorax is enormously enlarged to form a triangular shield, which may cover most of the abdomen. Being highly coloured as well as rather sluggish, shield bugs are more often noticed than the more active, predatory bugs. They are best watched without handling them, because the smell they emit from their scent glands is even more unpleasant than that of most land bugs. But even this family includes some predaceous members which attack caterpillars.

We come back, therefore, to a picture of the land bugs as essentially animal feeders, though a small minority of plant feeders attract more attention than the rest because they attack commercial crops. When we consider water bugs, animal food predominates even more. By custom, certain bugs that find their food among the small creatures trapped on the surface film of water are usually included among 'land bugs' (Gymnocerata). The reasons for this are partly structural—they have the long antennae of this group—and partly ecological, because they show all the intermediate stages between living around the margins of water-courses and moving out over the surface. This habit is foreshadowed in the shore bugs family (Saldidae), where one or

Common Pond
Skater (*Gerris
lacustris*) feeding
on a damselfly.

two species live in entirely dry places, while the
majority seek the water more or less closely,
including moving into the intertidal zone and
being submerged every high tide. The tropical
genus *Omania* has committed itself fully to
intertidal life by becoming flightless, and seeking
protection at high tide by retreating into small
crevices, especially where there are coral reefs.

The real surface bugs belong to the superfamily Gerroidea, sometimes set apart as Am-
phibicorisae, in contrast to the Geocorisae, or
fully terrestrial bugs. Some are scarcely modified at all for this way of life: Hebridae and
Mesoveliidae families simply haunt the surface
of quiet waters, among moss and floating vegetation. Gerridae are more venturesome, and
include the well-known pond skaters, or water
striders, which can literally 'walk on the water',
without the tips of their legs penetrating the
surface film. Their feet are quite complicated,
each with a pad of water-repellent hairs to support the weight of the insect – you can easily see
the six hollows in the water surface where the
feet rest – and a claw which is wetted and so gets
a grip on the water for propulsion. The middle
pair of legs is used to row along, making swift,
decisive strokes which send the insect skimming
over the surface at very high speeds.

Life is simple for pond skaters. Eggs are laid
among floating vegetation, or plants emerging
from the water, and stick to these so as not to be
washed away. The nymphs are tiny replicas of
the adults, except of course that they have no
wings. They live in the same way as their parents,
seizing and sucking any small creature that they
find on the surface. The short front legs are
efficient in holding prey, and there is an abundance of food among the insects that have fallen
into the water, or have failed to escape from the
grip of surface tension when they are emerging
from pupae. Gerridae often have wings, and use
them mainly at night to fly to new waters, but
many short-winged and flightless individuals
abound. This inclination towards winglessness
is a negative adaptation to the life, compared
with the positive adaptations that have made the
feet so effective in supporting the insect on the
water surface.

Water measurers (Hydrometridae) have taken
up a contrasting kind of surface life, sluggish
instead of active, living among vegetation instead of skating out on to the open water. They
look for their food under the surface rather than
on it, and use their elongate head and strong
proboscis to spear mosquito larvae and other
prey which approaches the surface from below.

135

In fact a way of life that neatly complements that of the pond skaters, and reminds one, on a miniature scale of the hunting habits of herons! Water crickets (Veliidae) are a less specialized family, of rather intermediate habits, spearing their prey like Hydrometridae, but feeding on the surface like Gerridae.

The impression one gets from these few families is how neatly each of the possible habitats and ways of living has been exploited by a different family of bugs. This impression becomes greater when we look at the true water bugs (Cryptocerata; Hydrocorisae), that is those which search for their prey beneath the surface of the water. Their two major problems are breathing and locomotion. The toad-bugs (Ochteroidea) are squat, ugly creatures, which make short excursions under water from the edge, and need little or no adaptation. The water scorpions (*Nepa* and *Ranatra*) are underwater predators, crawling about after their prey as if they were on dry land, but reaching to the surface with a long posterior siphon, a sort of rear-end snorkel. Although the tube can be fully submerged without asphyxiation, the air contained in the tracheal system cannot be renewed under water, and so the insect must remain within easy reach of the surface, and conserve oxygen by not being unnecessarily active. The active underwater bugs carry a bubble of air trapped close to the body, and covering the spiracles. This is not merely a limited supply, but has some powers of replenishing its oxygen content under water. As oxygen is used from the bubble, more diffuses out of the water to take its place. Unfortunately this cannot go on indefinitely, because the inert nitrogen is diffusing away all the time, and so the bubble continually shrinks.

This system is improved if the bubble is spread out as a thin layer, exposing a much bigger area to diffusion, but, more important, being held by a covering of minute, water-repellent hairs, which set up an enormous surface tension, and stop the bubble from collapsing. This type of 'lung' is called a plastron, because the layer of air shines brightly under water, and resembles the breastplate of a suit of armour. It has been extensively studied in the naucorid bug *Aphelocheirus*, which can stay below water indefinitely with its help, provided the water is pure and well oxygenated. The bubble breathers, which include water boatmen or backswimmers, must come to the surface to renew their air-supply, but this apparent disadvantage is offset by the fact that they can live in more stagnant water than the plastron breathers, since their oxygen comes directly from the atmosphere. Corixidae, the true water boatmen are unusual in that most of them feed on fine plant debris, diatoms, algae etc., though they can still give one a powerful 'bite' with their piercing proboscis. The other underwater bugs are carnivorous, and include the giant water bugs (Belostomatidae), which can be as long as 100 mm or more. The adults come out of the water at night and fly about, sometimes coming to lights in warm countries. As part of their formidable character, some of the females lay their eggs on the back of the male, where they can be protected very efficiently. Giant water bugs can tackle much larger prey than most water bugs, including tadpoles and small fish.

A fascinating order, but are Heteroptera 'successful'? They have filled a number of ecological niches, particularly in aquatic habitats. From terrestrial beginnings they have evolved surface feeders and underwater feeders, each group excellently adapted to its own way of life, its own means of locomotion, and its own food supply. They have skilfully modified their wings and powers of flight, remaining fully equipped when dispersal was an advantage, and reducing the wings, or being entirely flightless, when this was not so. The land Heteroptera are perhaps less successful as a group, though certain members have become well established. They are hardly a dominant group today, compared with what they may have been in the past.

The rest of the moderately successful insects are groups which have developed a more or less complete metamorphosis, but have not exploited this device very well. What we might call an 'experiment' in this direction has been made by the 'thrips' of the order Thysanoptera (not to be confused with Thysanura, the bristle-tails with which we started this chapter). Thysanoptera are tiny insects, never more than 12 mm long, and sometimes as small as 0·5 mm, with a sucking proboscis, and possibly an offshoot of the Heteroptera we have just been discussing. They are most commonly seen on flower heads, particularly Compositae: those narrow, black, seemingly wingless insects crawling about on a dandelion head are thrips. Populations of thrips can vary very widely, mostly as a result of weather conditions; in thundery weather they may be so numerous that the flower head is covered with them. Although their proboscis is short, and they cannot suck as efficiently as the sucking bugs, their numbers make them serious pests at times, both to glasshouse crops and to fruit blossom in the open.

Hatching from the egg as a nymph, the thrips (this word is both singular and plural, and is also the scientific name of the typical genus of the order) changes significantly in its later instars, particularly in the development of wing-pads, and internally, so that thrips are said to have a 'prepupa' and a 'pupa'. These are not the equivalent of the true pupa of more advanced insects, but rather a tentative evolution towards a form of complete metamorphosis. It is fair to call this an 'evolutionary experiment'.

Another 'experiment' made by thrips is in the wings and method of flight. Instead of the flat membrane that is otherwise normal in insect wings, thrips have a narrow rib supporting a double row of stiff, long hairs (Fig. 39). The wings of thrips are so tiny that the usual laws of aerodynamic lift do not apply. Instead, the insect 'rows' itself along through the air, much as a water bug rows itself under water. This type of wing is a simple modification made necessary by small size: the fairy flies (Mymaridae) of the order Hymenoptera similarly 'row' themselves under water, using their wings as oars.

Thrips are a good example of a middle-of-the-road group. No one can call them either a failure or a huge success. Their size, structure and life history are well suited to their ecological niche. A tendency to fluctuate widely in numbers is perhaps a sign of dependence on meteorological factors (a common name for them is 'thunder flies'), but on the whole they show an ability to recover well from setbacks. In some ways these things could be said about the locusts, which everyone would rate as highly successful insects. Can it be that locusts seem successful to us merely because they are big, and because they cause more trouble to man?

There remain three orders that I would rate as only moderately successful, for different reasons. Firstly Neuroptera which are the counterpart of the mostly aquatic Megaloptera. The best-known Neuroptera are the green lacewings of the family Chrysopidae, beautiful insects, with golden eyes and filmy, pale green wings held roof-like over the soft abdomen. In spite of their fragile appearance they are fierce

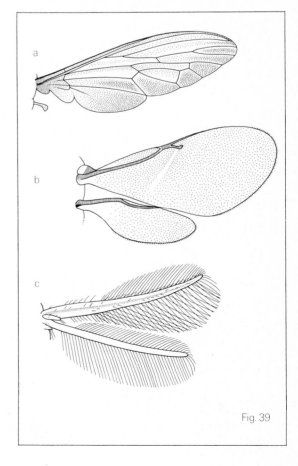

Fig. 39

Fig. 39 Varieties in wing structure: (a) fly (Diptera) – membranous wing with many veins (forewing only), hindwing reduced to halteres (balancing organ); (b) parasitic wasp (Hymenoptera) – membranous fore and hindwing with reduced veins; (c) thrip (Thysanoptera) – hairy wing with reduced membrane, but the surface area needed for flight is increased by long hairs.

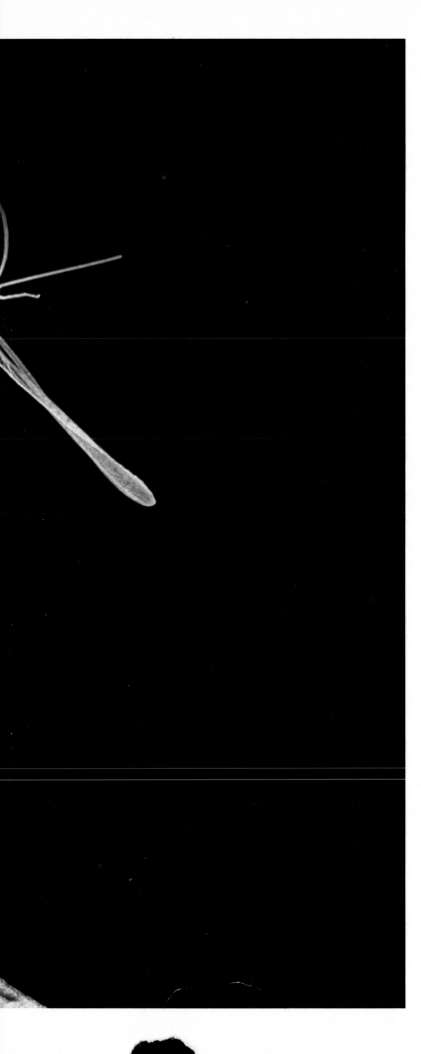

predators all their lives, eating great quantities of aphids and other insects. Adult lacewings have biting mouthparts, but those of the larvae are peculiarly modified into piercing and sucking equipment, though retaining enough of the mandibulate form to be able to grasp as well as suck. A characteristic habit of lacewings in temperate countries is to hibernate as adults, thus getting an early start in spring.

The rest of the Neuroptera include such diverse forms as the brown lacewings of the Hemerobiidae family; the waxy Coniopterygidae, which feed on scale insects and jumping plant lice (Psyllidae); Mantispidae, which are like a miniature praying mantis, and seize their prey in the same way, with specially developed forelegs; and Osmylidae, which lurk near water. Spectacular and fully terrestrial groups of Neuroptera are the Nemopteridae with peculiarly attenuated hindwings, and the Ascalaphidae and Myrmeleontidae which look like dragonflies, and hunt their prey in a somewhat similar way. The larvae of these groups have very powerful mandibles, which they use to seize and devour ants and other prey. The 'ant-lions' trap their victims by digging conical pits in sand or fine dust, and lying in wait at the bottom, only their mandibles visible, open and ready to seize any unfortunate creature that may fall into the pit. When an ant begins to slide down the steep sides, the ant-lion may hasten its fall by bombarding it with fine grains.

The order Mecoptera is unimportant in itself, but highly significant in the evolution of insects, because it is believed to be at the centre of a 'Panorpoid Complex', named after *Panorpa*, the scorpion fly, the best-known member of the order Mecoptera. This complex includes the orders Mecoptera (scorpion flies), Trichoptera (caddis flies), Lepidoptera (butterflies and moths), Diptera (true flies), and, surprisingly, Siphonaptera (fleas).

The habits of Mecoptera reflect several curious echoes of life in the bigger orders that are thought to have arisen from it. The common scorpion flies of the genus *Panorpa* have their heads drawn out into a snout like that of many crane-flies (daddy-long-legs, Tipulidae), and members of the family Bittacidae look very much like crane-flies, but with four wings instead of two. On the other hand, the larvae of most Mecoptera are like caterpillars, and so suggest a link with butterflies and moths. The family Boreidae ('winter scorpion flies') live in moss, and come out on the snow in winter, and it seems possible that all Diptera arose from moss-living ancestors among archaic Mecoptera.

So no one can deny the importance of Mecoptera in the evolution of the higher insects, yet the status of this order at the present day is a modest one. At some time in the past they must have been a young, plastic, fast-growing group,

Lacewing (*Chrysopa* spp). The insect is shown doing a backwards somersault after leaping into the air from its perch. Note how the four wings move independently of each other.

from which two large and vigorous orders (Lepidoptera and Diptera) evolved. These went along at a great pace, leaving a residue of Mecoptera to plod along in their own limited niche. Fewer than 400 species of Mecoptera survive today.

Except for the Boreidae, which are partly herbivorous, and partly carnivorous, preying on springtails etc. in the moss in which they live, most Mecoptera are believed to be scavengers, feeding on dead or disabled insects rather than pursuing active prey. In this they are equivalent to the surface-feeding bugs that we have just seen, and to the surface-feeding beetles we shall meet later. There is a regular supply of this sort of food. All the many insects we see about have to die sometime, of old age, fungus infection, or wounding by a predator that loses its prey before being able to suck it dry. If a predatory wasp drops its prey it does not pick it up again. The sequence of reflexes is broken, and, finding itself without prey, the wasp goes off to find another victim.

Incidentally, the name 'scorpion fly' does not mean that this insect has any sting. It refers merely to the appearance of the male, where the tip of the abdomen often curls up and over in the manner of a scorpion.

The appearance of a caterpillar-like larva, totally different in structure from the adult, makes a pupal stage essential (as we have already seen in Megaloptera and Neuroptera and the flies, Trichoptera, which we discussed earlier, among the waterside insects, though their logical place is here, among the Panorpoid Complex). Note that the larvae of Mecoptera, in spite of their different appearance, eat much the same food as the adults. Even today Mecoptera have not learned to exploit what is the principal advantage of a complete metamorphosis, the ability to feed quite differently as a larva and when adult. Perhaps this is one reason why the surviving Mecoptera have changed so little, whereas Lepidoptera and Diptera have made the fullest use of this 'double life' to evolve into highly diverse and successful ways of life.

One final group needs to be looked at here, a tiny group of parasites with no common name, the Strepsiptera. About 300 species have been described, most of them from the Northern Hemisphere, but there are probably many more to be discovered. Until recently only nine were known from Australia, but this number is now put at nearly sixty. Members of probably the oldest family, the Mengeidae, show primitive characters, and appropriately feed on Thysanura,

Scorpion fly (*Panorpa communis*) feeding. Note the beak and upturned tail characteristic of the male.

the bristle-tails that are the most primitive living insects. After feeding inside its host the larva pupates under stones, and both males and females are free-living, that is they move about looking for a mate, and then the females seek a victim. Only the male has wings, and these are most peculiar, and characteristic of Strepsiptera. The forewings are reduced to drumsticks, but the hindwings are broad and relatively very large, with a simple, fan-like arrangement of veins. In all other Strepsiptera the female never leaves its host, and the male flies about looking for a sedentary female with which to mate.

The life history of Strepsiptera is very strange. The larvae hatch within the body of the female, and the first stage larvae are an active form called 'triungulins'. This is the name given to any first stage larva that is unusually active, and equipped to seek out a new habitat from that in which the egg was laid. The triungulins of Strepsiptera emerge in enormous numbers – hundreds, or even thousands – and disperse to look for new hosts. They need to be numerous, because nearly all of them perish on the way, but those that do find a new host penetrate into its body and begin to feed. The host insect is attacked at its nymph or larval stage as the case may be, and the strepsipteran larva changes into a legless, inactive form which feeds on the surrounding body fluid of the host. Each type of larva, the active triungulin and the inactive legless larva is perfectly suited to that stage of the larval life, and the change of larval form is called hyper-metamorphosis. When feeding is complete a pupa is formed between the abdominal plates of the host insect, which by now has transformed into an adult. If the pupa contains a male, this breaks out and flies away, but females remain within the pupal skin and are fertilized *in situ* by visiting males.

The list of hosts of Strepsiptera is large and varied. Besides the Thysanura attacked by Mengeidae, victims include Blattodea, Mantodea, Homoptera, Orthoptera, Diptera and parasitic Hymenoptera (bees, wasps, ants). The loss of nutrients and other chemical constituents of the body fluids of a nymph or a larva disturbs the metabolism of the host, and upsets its regular development, especially in the balance between male and female characteristics. The process is known as 'stylopization', and a stylopized bee or wasp often develops into a confusing intersex. Note that stylopization affects the whole body, by chemical means, and so the result is an intersex; localized disturbances which affect only the cells of certain areas produce a genetic mosaic or gynandromorph.

The order Strepsiptera is one of the best examples of close and complex adaptation to one particular way of life. This is undoubtedly success, as far as it goes.

The highly successful insects

Coming now to the highly successful insects, we note at once that there are fewer orders, only nine of them against the twenty or so orders we have dismissed as having achieved only a limited success. Here are the nine orders:

1 Collembola – springtails
2 Orthoptera – locusts and grasshoppers
3 Homoptera – aphids and other plant-lice
4 Lepidoptera – butterflies and moths
5 Diptera – true flies
6 Siphonaptera – fleas
7 Hymenoptera – sawflies, bees, wasps, ants, parasitic wasps
8 Isoptera – termites
9 Coleoptera – beetles

This list includes all the big orders, those from which we get our general impression of insects as a successful, indeed a dominant group of animals. The list also includes two very small orders: Collembola and Siphonaptera.

Four of the nine orders (nos. 1, 2, 3, 8) have only a gradual metamorphosis, so that the nymphs live essentially the same lives, and eat the same food, as their parents. We have seen that this can be a handicap to a group of insects, limiting their powers of diversification. How, then, have insects of these four orders overcome this handicap, to become highly successful. Order Isoptera, the termites, have developed a highly complex social life, which gives them diversity within the species as well as outside it: the members of different castes look different, and perform different functions in the colony. We shall discuss these later, when they can be compared with the other social insects, all of which belong to the very advanced order Hymenoptera. That is why Isoptera are listed as number 8, instead of number 3, where they might be placed on a more systematic arrangement.

The success of the first three orders is a success of numbers rather than of diversity, a maximum exploitation of a rather limited way of life, but one that relies upon a source of food that is unfailing. The first order, Collembola, has never had the advantage of wings at any time in its history. With Collembola we go right back to the start of the insect line. In fact some entomologists argue that Collembola members are not insects, but the arguments for and against including them are outside the scope of this chapter. Accept them provisionally as insects, with several peculiarities which place them out on a limb by themselves, and which suggest that they must have branched off from the main line of insect evolution at a very early stage. The oldest of all fossil insects, *Rhyniella*, from the Devonian, over 300 million years ago, appears to belong to Collembola. On the other hand, Collembola members probably hold the record for being the most numerous insects living today, since it has been estimated that there may be 100 million per hectare in the soil of an English meadow, and up to 60 000 of one species have been counted in one square metre in Australia. A group of insects that has persisted for so long, and is still so abundant today cannot be denied a place among the highly successful orders, even if the average person has never noticed them.

One reason why Collembola representatives

are so little known is their small size, 10 mm or less, and more usually only 1–2 mm long. If we turn over moist soil or leaf mould they can be seen as tiny white specks, which sometimes leap suddenly, using the apparatus under the abdomen from which they get their name of springtails. Throughout the world there are about 4000 species, with differences that are interesting to the student, and to agriculturists and horticulturists who have to control them, but not indicating any real diversity within the order. The order divides into Symphylopleona, with a rounded body and Arthropleona with a more elongate body, and clearer segmentation. The former tend to live on foliage and the latter in soil or leaf mould. Most Collembola feed on decaying plant material, but the Sminthuridae (one of the families of foliage feeders) will attack growing plants, and can become a commercial pest. A root crop such as mangolds may be attacked both above and below ground level by different species from the two main groups. In certain circumstances Collembola members can become carnivorous, and eat dead or even living insects, and when crowded they become cannibals, that is, eat other members of the same species. A carnivorous diet is particularly characteristic of shore-living species, such as the large, dark grey *Anurida maritima* which occurs in rock pools round the British coast. A few feed in the nests of ants and termites.

This diet therefore is that of a scavenger, obeying no precise rules, but eating whatever is available. Probably the varying diet of different species is less a matter of preference than an accident of habitat: the microhabitat in which each species lives is dictated by its metabolic requirements in the way of moisture, oxygen and perhaps certain chemical elements. Thus Collembola long ago settled for a food supply that was always available, and a series of microhabitats that could be found all over the world, and in all geological periods. In spite of having no wings, Collembola members seem to occur everywhere, and to be able to disperse freely. They are well-recognized members of the 'aerial plankton', where they are carried to great heights, and over long distances, by passive flight. This is rather remarkable for a wingless insect that can survive only in moist conditions, and most often in the soil. It suggests that the major sources of Collembola in the air are areas where the soil has dried, and is being blown into the air in the course of soil erosion.

Collembola members have retained one primitive flexibility in the large and variable number of moults that each individual undergoes during its life. It becomes sexually mature after about five moults, and reaches maximum size after six or eight, but goes on moulting all its life, and may have as many as fifty moults without change, or further growth. Laying over 100 eggs, and with five generations a year, a single pair could increase to 100^5 or 10 000 million, so that even with heavy casualties the huge populations of springtails are easily accounted for.

Orthoptera, the grasshoppers, locusts, crickets and their allies, are one of the basic groups of insects, and the grasshoppers themselves are examples of the basic way of life. The common field grasshopper has large chewing mouthparts; two pairs of substantial wings, well supported by veins, but not elaborately developed, nor coupled together, the front pair being rather leathery and acting as covers for the hind pair; a soft, bag-like abdomen as suits a chewer of plant fragments (all herbivores have to eat a great quantity to extract enough nourishment). The most obvious specialization is in the hindlegs, which are long and powerful, looking like a jumping organ, and functioning as one. The most typical reaction of a grasshopper to any disturbance is to jump, click and away. Not, apparently, in any particular direction, so that jumping is not a purposive movement, but a negative avoiding reaction. Since field grasshoppers feed in the open, in daylight, and are exposed to every kind of predatory insect, reptile, bird or mammal, their long survival since Carboniferous times (about 250 million years) must owe a great deal to this easy method of escape. Grasshoppers often open their wings briefly as they fly, partly to extend the jump by gliding, in the manner of a flying-fish, and partly to expose a pair of hindwings, which may be brightly coloured, and at rest are completely hidden beneath the drab forewings. A sudden flash of bright red or blue is startling enough to the human eye, and must be completely distracting to an animal predator.

The family Acrididae, short-horned grasshoppers and locusts, may be taken as the key group of the Orthoptera, especially in a discussion of success in insects, because they are the most obviously successful members of this order. The 5000 known species are divided into seventeen subfamilies, but this apparent diversity is only relative: that is, it consists of variations round a single pattern, with different proportions of head, thorax, abdomen and legs to suit living and feeding in varied terrain. Yet the family remains a group of herbivores chewing and swallowing a large quantity of foliage, mainly from grass and low herbage. Some of the bigger species feed on the leaves of trees and shrubs, and under pressure of numbers, as in a locust swarm, any green plant is devoured.

All Orthoptera have a gradual metamorphosis, hatching from the egg as a nymph which becomes gradually more like the adult at each moult, until finally the wing-buds open into functional wings. There is no external ovipositor in acridids, which use the tip of the abdomen to excavate a hole in the ground, and then proceed to lay a clutch of eggs at the end of it. There may be as many as 100 eggs in the clutch, which is covered with a sticky secretion to form a sort of ootheca. Up to ten clutches may be laid in a season, and each is left in its hole in the ground until the nymphs emerge in three or four weeks' time. (In temperate climates most species overwinter as eggs.) The nymphs feed on the surrounding vegetation. Since they cannot fly they have to reach for their food by crawling, with a peculiar hopping motion because the hindlegs

Meadow Grass-
hopper (*Chorthip-
pus parallelus*).

are so much longer than the others. Hence nymphal grasshoppers are called just 'hoppers'.

The great majority of grasshoppers are solitary, that is each individual, nymph or adult feeds alone, and moves about independently of the others. A huge population that is spread over an area of grassland may be noticed only by the leaping of those disturbed as one walks along, and by the sound of their 'song'. This song is produced by stridulation, or scraping, rubbing the hind femora against a ridge of the closed forewings (tegmina), and it is mainly, though not quite exclusively, produced by males. This 'song' is not, in fact a musical note, but a rapid succession of impulses, and it is the rhythm and not their pitch, that is meaningful to others.

Solitary grasshoppers do not fly much, and then usually for short distances. Locusts, which are famous for their long flights, are not a distinct group, even within the order Orthoptera, but just a few species which under certain conditions become 'gregarious', and migrate in search of feeding and breeding grounds. Uvarov's Phase Theory explains this as a change of 'phase'. Under conditions of overcrowding, nymphs of these species change not only their coloration but their behaviour, massing together in huge bands, and becoming more and more excited in the hot sun, until they 'march' away

in an apparently purposeful manner, devouring all the vegetation that they crawl and hop over. This feverish activity is passed on to the adults into which the nymphs transform, and which are fully winged. These form the devastating swarms of flying locusts that are so much feared in countries that are liable to them.

The occurrence of locust swarms is much better understood now than it has been in the past, at least to the point of being able to predict the probable outbreak of a swarm, and to monitor its progress, though it is still not known why only certain species react in this way. This behaviour enables them to burst out of an overcrowded breeding area, where the population has been growing steadily for many years of innocuous life. Although individual locusts fly at an average speed of 15 km per hour, they do not all point in the same direction, so the flight of the adults is not like the purposive 'march' of the hoppers. The adults instinctively keep together in a swarm, which is carried steadily downwind. The Desert Locust (*Schistocerca gregaria*) is carried in this way across the arid areas of the Sahara and countries to the east of this, right across to India and Pakistan. The swarms start initially from permanent breeding grounds in swamps, and they can only breed again where the soil moisture is higher than that

143

in the arid areas they cross. Skilled detective work by the Anti-Locust Research Centre has shown that a passive migration downwind will take the swarms into what is called the Inter-tropical Convergence Zone, a low-pressure area where rain is likely to fall before long. Thus the special behaviour of the gregarious phase of the Desert Locust is precisely calculated to take the locusts out of an overcrowded breeding area, and to direct them to a new area where there is, or soon will be, enough soil moisture for the survival of the egg-pods in the ground and emergence of the hoppers. The new generation of hoppers will develop into gregarious or solitary adults according to the degree of local crowding, passing through a third phase 'transiens' on the way. Thus swarms which started out in the area of the Central Niger River in West Africa may migrate, over a period of years, throughout Africa even down to the western Cape Province. The life of an individual Desert Locust is thought to be about six months in the wild state, though they can be kept alive for over two years under controlled laboratory conditions.

The importance of locusts as a pest will be more fully dealt with in 'Insects and Man', where some mention is made of their staggering numbers and ravenous appetites. In the present chapter we are concerned only with the question whether Orthoptera in general, and locusts in particular, may be classed as highly successful insects, in a biological sense; or do we get this impression merely because they are big, numerous and destructive? The Desert Locust certainly deserves full marks for having utilized the winds and clouds to enable it to break out of its overcrowded breeding grounds, and to move to areas that are not only more suitable for breeding, but which allow the insects to become less crowded and to revert to the solitary phase.

Phase change in itself is a remarkable adaptation, but it is not confined to locusts. A few other insects have 'kentromorphic phases', triggered off by overcrowding, the insect existing in a low-density solitary phase and a high-density gregarious phase: in particular Phasmida and the larvae of some Lepidoptera. Phasmida merely change their appearance as they become more crowded, and they have not developed the gregarious and migratory behaviour that is the real advantage of phase change. That is why they remain only moderately successful.

About ten species of Acrididae rank as locusts, because they undergo phase change, and a few others are known as 'swarming grasshoppers', because they produce troublesome swarms by a rapid increase in numbers, but do not have a gregarious phase, nor follow a clear path of migration. Yet even the common meadow grasshoppers are a highly successful group of insects, feeding, as they do, on a wide range of grasses, among which they are effectively concealed by their cryptic coloration, and moving by sudden leaps which take them out of danger and into concealment among the broken grassy background as soon as they alight.

Acrididae and several related, but less successful families form one of three great groups of the Orthoptera, the Caelifera, or short-horned grasshoppers. The second group, the long-horned grasshoppers, bush crickets or katydids are in strong contrast to these. The first two of their common names draw attention to this contrast. The antennae are very long and thread-like ('long-horned'); the body is shorter and deeper, emphasized by the long hindlegs, and is more in the proportions of the crickets of the third group; and although a few are ground living, the majority are found in trees and shrubs, and among low herbage. There they feed mostly on foliage, though some are predacious, and others will accept either vegetable or animal food. A conspicuous ovipositor in the shape of a scimitar or sickle, is used to push the eggs into plant tissues or into the ground.

Again there is one typical family, Tettigoniidae, the bush crickets proper, and a number of less successful relatives. More closely allied to these than to the field grasshoppers are the true crickets or Grylloidea. They have equally long antennae, long hindlegs, and share the same method of stridulation which–in contrast to the leg/wing stridulation of Acrididae–operates by rubbing the two forewings together. Each wing has areas specialized for this function, and wings may be retained for stridulatory purposes even in some species that no longer fly. Female crickets, however, have an awl-shaped ovipositor, flanked by two long needle-like cerci. Crickets may live on the ground, under debris, in holes, in ants' nests, and of course indoors in houses and other warm buildings. They are omnivorous, that is they will eat anything that is available. There is one group of tree crickets, however, the Oecanthinae. Note that we have to call them 'tree crickets' to distinguish them from the 'bush crickets' which are not true crickets, but long-horned grasshoppers (Tettigoniidae).

One further group of particular interest is the small family of mole crickets, Gryllotalpidae, which are beautifully modified for tunnelling underground like a mole. The forelegs are short and very broad, and tibia and tarsus have strong fixed teeth or spines which are used in conjunction with the big claws to excavate a hole, while the broad femur and tibia act as scoops, throwing the earth sideways and back. The thoracic plate, which is always big in Orthoptera, is unusually broad in mole crickets, and turns over at the side to form a digging shield analogous to the shield used for the same purpose in excavating machinery.

Mole crickets make a nest underground, where they lay up to 300 eggs. The nymphs have a two-year life cycle. There are about fifty species, all in one genus, and scattered all over the world. This kind of distribution is not easy to explain, because these are large insects (35 mm or bigger), and although fully winged species can fly, some species have reduced wings or none at all. In flight, the heavy body is allowed to hang down vertically, like that of the Stag Beetle (*Lucanus cervus*). This is not a group of insects that can

Oak Bush Cricket (*Meconema thalassinum*) on a scabious.

Wood Cricket
(*Nemobius sylves-
tris*) a native of
southern England.

have been distributed about the earth by passive flight, or, so one would think, by long, active migrations. It can have spread only slowly, over long periods of time, thus indicating that mole crickets must have an ancient history. In spite of the large number of eggs laid, mole crickets are not common insects, even allowing for the fact that their subterranean habits keep them out of sight. They are vulnerable to moles and, surprisingly, to some birds, for example the Hoopoe (*Upupa epops*), perhaps when they sit at the mouth of their burrow and stridulate, or during their slow, lumbering flight.

A curiously parallel evolution has occurred in an Australian group of 'pigmy mole crickets' (*Tridactylus*), but these still have the Gond-wanaland distribution, often an indication of an archaic group (see 'Evolution and Distribution').

With Homoptera we come to the first group of insects that is an unqualified success, including as it does a number of families of plant lice that are some of the most vigorous and flourishing insects of the present day. As we recall, Hom-optera can be looked upon either as forming with Heteroptera the two halves of the order Hemip-tera, or as a related, but separate, order them-selves. From our present point of view it is more convenient to treat them separately, and we have already relegated Heteroptera to the category of only moderate success.

Homoptera are a uniform group in the sense that they are all plant bugs, terrestrial, herbivor-ous, and many are weak fliers, if not wingless, but easily transported through the air in passive flight. They lack the diversity of structure seen in other successful groups, for example Hymen-optera, yet if one looks through the illustrations of Homoptera in a textbook – the easiest way of comparing these small insects from all over the world – they show an astonishing variety of fine detail. In fact the diversity of structure far ex-ceeds the diversity of life history, and it is not obvious why – in an evolutionary sense – such a lot of different shapes should be needed to carry out what is an essentially similar life cycle.

Leaving aside, for the moment, the aphids, which are notorious because of the damage they do to crops, the Homoptera that are most familiar as adults are the cicadas, at least in all the warmer countries. They are more familiar to the ear than to the eye, through their loud and persistent 'song'. This is a more musical note than that of stridulating grasshoppers, in the sense that it has a fairly clearly defined frequency. The sound is produced by a *tymbal*, or diaphragm, vibrated by variations in tension in an attached muscle, like the earpiece of a telephone is vibrated by the fluctuating pull of an electromagnet. Adults cicadas sit tight on the branches of trees and shrubs, and in spite of their relatively large size (up to 40 mm or more) they are extremely diffi-cult to find, even when one is directed by the song.

Many other Homoptera, and some insects

146

from other orders, can produce sound by means of tymbals, but among Homoptera only cicadas have evolved effective organs for hearing the sound they produce. So we see once again that the primary object of sound production in insects is to frighten off enemies, when of course other individuals of the same species do not need to hear the sound. Only later when hearing organs have been added could sounds be used for species recognition.

Cicadas are untypical of Homoptera in general, in that their nymphs spend their lives underground. The eggs are laid in slits cut in the twigs of trees, a method of concealment that is practised by insects of other orders as well as Homoptera. It gives the eggs good protection from enemies and from drought, and must have been a successful device because it can be effective only after the insect has evolved an ovipositor that can make the necessary slit in plant tissue. The nymphs of cicadas burrow down into the soil and feed on plant roots, sometimes for long periods. The North American 'seventeen year cicada' is accurately named, since it is seventeen years, at least in the north, before the nymphs are fully fed and ready to become adult. The emergence of a new generation can be predicted. This holds the record for the longest known life history of an insect, as a regular cycle, and even this is shortened further south, to thirteen years. The nymphs are well shaped for subterranean life, with the forelegs shortened and flattened in much the same way as those of mole crickets (see above).

Cicadas apart, the rest of Homoptera are plant-feeding bugs of varied shape, but relatively monotonous habits. Perhaps the most decorative family are the lantern flies (Fulgoridae) and their relatives, which have a curious, inflated extension to the head, curving forwards and upwards at the tip. 'Alligator Bug' is the fitting name given to the American species *Fulgora lanternaria*. Lantern flies often have an elaborate pattern of many colours, green, black, red, blue, perhaps a disruptive coloration, and this may be the function of the swollen head, which in some South American species is grossly inflated, like a groundnut. No other function has been discovered for the characteristic fulgorid head.

A close second for striking appearance is the tree hopper family, Membracidae, in which the thoracic shield, the pronotum, is drawn out into a variety of shapes which gives these bugs a grotesque appearance. This seems all the more strange to the human eye, since Membracidae are quite small insects, the largest not exceeding 20 mm long, and usually much smaller. Of course the entomologist is familiar with the perfection of detail in tiny insects, but usually this perfection is directly functional, and we can readily understand that even (or perhaps 'even more') a micromechanism must be constructed to fine limits of tolerance. What is odd about Membracidae is to wonder what adversaries these structures are meant to frighten.

Apart from these extravagances, which appear less prominently in other families, Homoptera in general are small, pale (greenish, yellowish or blackish) insects with a broad head, eyes wide apart, a large, triangular thorax, and clearish wings with prominent veins and cross-veins, held together roof-like over the abdomen. Some, like the Flatidae, may have beautifully marked wings, but the general appearance is drab.

Their lifestyle, too, is a series of changes rung on a central theme. They suck the juices of plants, some generally, some specialized to one type of plant (grasses, trees, shrubs, herbaceous plants). They often protect themselves and/or their nymphs by producing wax, in long filaments, in a tangled mass, or just as a general dusting as in the whiteflies (Aleyrodidae). Though wax may make them unpalatable to predators, its main advantage is that it repels water. The greatest single hazard for small insects exposed on the vegetation is that of being trapped in droplets of rain or dew. If the insect is wetted, surface tension will prevent it from breaking free, and the adhering film of water will seal down the wings and legs and block the spiracles. The skin, or integument of all insects is water-repellent, but not sufficiently so to overcome the surface tension of a very small water droplet, with its relatively enormous surface area. So a waxy covering is a further defence which serves the double purpose of keeping water out, and keeping it in, that is of protecting the insect against desiccation.

Some Homoptera go further, and actually enclose themselves in a protective covering for part of their life cycle. The froghoppers (Cercopidae) are so-called because many of the adults not only have a frog-like head (on a tiny scale!), but also have enormous leaping powers. Nymphs of Cercopidae spend their lives enclosed in a mass of 'cuckoo spit', a white froth that we have all seen on grasses in a country meadow, as well as on plants in the garden. This froth is generated by the nymph, which has a special channel underneath the abdomen, and blows air through a film of liquid expelled from the anus. The frothy mass can scarcely be said to conceal the nymph, but rather advertises its presence, though it may deter small predators by its clinging nature. Undoubtedly the main function is to keep the nymph in a saturated environment, and so to protect it against drying up. Such a thin-skinned, soft insect would easily dry up if exposed to the air.

A similar form of protection, this time for the female throughout the whole of her life, is the scale of scale insects of the superfamily Coccoidea. This group of insects, of which almost 6000 species are known, has taken what we might call the 'logical' step, in response to a food supply that is always there, waiting to be tapped. Why waste energy on moving about? The problem is how to strike a balance between sufficient mobility to ensure a wide distribution, and complete immobility under a protective cover. Coccoidea have opted for the latter. Eggs, older nymphs and wingless females are all pro-

tected under a waxy covering ('mealy bugs'). The cast skins of the nymphs, mixed with wax, form a soft or hard 'scale' which completely covers the female. So the living plant becomes encrusted with a scaly covering, underneath which a whole population of insects is sucking away at its sap. Little wonder that scale insects do very serious damage to many commercial crops. Fortunately these sedentary insects attract many natural enemies, and so there is a fair amount of biological control, but vigorous spraying with chemicals is needed when heavy infestations appear on commercial crops.

The males of scale insects are feeble creatures, often wingless, and not always necessary, since many species can reproduce parthenogenetically. Males have reduced mouthparts and do not feed, so obviously they cannot help to distribute the species more widely. The main active stage is the first instar nymph, and the range of this is clearly limited to nearby plants. Yet scale insects occur throughout the world, so their distribution must have been gradual, over a long period. Almost the only conceivable method is by floating plants already infested with scales, which would, of course, give adequate protection to the insects within them during their travels.

Throughout most of their evolution, therefore, scale insects must have experienced a great degree of isolation in small areas, and it is not surprising that they have divided up into about a dozen families. Because their classification must be based almost entirely upon the females, and these are degenerate, taxonomy

of the groups is very difficult, but there is no doubt about the variety of habitats and host plants throughout the world. The growth of worldwide travel has introduced a new factor into the distribution of scale insects, and in spite of stringent quarantine regulations it seems certain that some species will spread even more widely in future.

The 'jumping plant lice' of the family Psyllidae have chosen to compromise between an active and a sessile way of life. Some of them construct a kind of scale, or 'lerp', while the saliva of others causes the plant cells to multiply, and form a gall (see 'Insect Habitats', page 82) in which the nymph shelters. These shelters do not house the adults, which are free-living and winged in both sexes. Although adult Psyllidae are very active they do not make long flights, but use their wings and legs together to move in a series of flying leaps – hence their name of 'jumping plant lice'.

This is activity rather than mobility, and perhaps because of this, Psyllidae tend to be associated with one kind of plant rather than being general feeders. For instance, one group of Psyllidae (Spondyliaspinae) attack eucalyptus trees in Australia, and can be numerous enough to kill them. In the Northern Hemisphere Psyllidae are generally less damaging, though two well-known species attack fruit trees. The Apple Sucker (*Psylla mali*) has only one generation a year, passing the winter in the egg, and the first nymphs emerging in April, when the juicy buds of apple trees present them with

148

plenty of sap. In return they cause the buds to shrivel and die. In contrast, the Pear Sucker (*Psylla pyricola*), which attacks only pear trees, has four generations a year in the United States. It is a species of European origin, first found in Connecticut in 1832, and has since spread widely. It may be that the increased number of generations a year in North America is a response to the different annual climatic cycle that it found there. Nymphs of the first (spring) generation are yellow when they hatch, becoming green and then black as they grow older. The nymphs of later generations during the year are smaller and paler, and used to be thought a different species. Here we have the beginnings of a differentiation into seasonal forms, which has been carried further by the aphids.

Three remaining groups of Homoptera include the most serious plant pests and, by the same token, groups that are vigorously successful, and which readily make new evolutionary experiments. The whiteflies (Aleyrodidae) are the least active of the three, and it has been suggested that they might be a degenerate offshoot of the Psyllidae. Their common name, which is very apt, refers to the coating of mealy wax with which the adults cover themselves, excreting it from large glands underneath the body, and spreading it all over themselves, including their wings, by using the hindlegs, the tibiae of which have special combs for this purpose.

The nymphs of whiteflies are flattened and inactive creatures. They have legs and antennae at first, but lose these after the first moult. The last nymphal instar is a non-feeding stage, covered with the cast skins of previous nymphs and has some of the features of the pupal stage of more advanced insects.

The inactive life of whiteflies is accompanied by a strong tendency to parthenogenesis. They are found mostly on the undersurfaces of leaves of flowering plants, where the sap they extract is not the principal harm they do to the plant. They have a more serious effect on the breathing of the plant through its leaves. Apart from the incrustation of wax-covered insects, the sugary honeydew that they excrete in great quantities encourages the growth of fungi known as 'Sooty Moulds' which block the stomata of the leaf.

A more active group are the leafhoppers (Cicadellidae, formerly Jassidae). These rather plain, yellow or greenish insects can be stirred up from any grassland or herbage, when they take leaps of considerable distance in relation to their own length. There is nothing particularly remarkable about either their appearance or their life history, but they make an impact on plants by their sheer numbers. They are an example of what one might call the 'sparrow pattern', that is, like the common house-sparrow, Cicadellidae, and many other insects, succeed in existing in very great numbers, in a wide range of habitats, and on a variety of foods, without the help of any of the complicated structural or behavioural devices that others have evolved.

Which brings us finally to the most successful of Homoptera, and one of the dominant groups of insects: the aphids. Aphids are notorious as pests of cultivated plants, but in this chapter we are concerned not with their importance to man, but with their status in the insect world. How successful are they, and why? Briefly, it can be said that they are successful because they make full use of all the devices that we have already noted in other groups of Homoptera: structural variety; seasonal forms; alternation of generations; asexual reproduction (with parthenogenesis and viviparity) for rapid build-up of populations; sexual reproduction to revitalize the species and provide mutations upon which natural selection can work; wingless generations when food is plentiful, winged forms for migration to a new host or a new area; wax and honeydew freely produced. Finally, a short life cycle of two to eight weeks according to temperature, ensures a rapid replacement of generations, and allows all the above factors to be exploited to the full. All this can be summed up in one word – flexibility.

The various forms (polymorphs) of aphids have been given pseudo-Latin names, and it is perhaps best to accept these, as follows:

1 *Eggs* during winter.
2 *Fundatrices* emerge from overwintering eggs: wingless, parthenogenetic, viviparous.
3 *Fundatrigeniae* second generation: also wingless, parthenogenetic and viviparous. Feed on primary host plant.
4 *Migrantes* winged females developing among otherwise wingless generations: parthenogenetic, viviparous. Fly to secondary host.
5 *Alienicolae* means 'living abroad'. Offspring of *migrantes*, living on secondary host plant. Reproduce there, with several generations of both winged and wingless individuals.
6 *Sexuparae* (*Gynoparae*) parthenogenetic, viviparous females with wings; also winged males. Fly back to primary host at end of summer.
7 *Sexuales* (*Oviparae*) reproductive, egg-laying females, mated with winged males which fly from secondary host. Lay the overwintering eggs with which the cycle begins again (see 1, above).

This cycle varies somewhat in different species of aphid, and there is considerable overlap between stages. The changeover from one stage to another is progressive, not instantaneous as it might appear from the above table. Although aphids are to be found on most groups of flowering plants they are not general feeders, and each species has only a limited range of primary and secondary hosts. The primary hosts are usually more closely related to each other than they are to the secondary hosts, and vice versa, so that migration from one to the other is a movement to a new environment. This provides some of the flexibility that insects with a complete metamorphosis get from having a larval habitat and a completely different habitat as an adult. In fact the alternation of hosts can be seen as making

up, to some extent, for the fact that the nymphs and adults of all generations of aphids normally live together, and feed on the same food.

This is a much simplified picture of the lives of aphids, and is subject to almost unlimited variation. Apparently no aphids feed on conifers (gymnosperms). This is the special province of the related family Adelgidae (Chermesidae), which has a life cycle that is broadly similar, alternating between two hosts, but taking two years to complete. Another family, Phylloxeridae has a few species living on oak trees, but is famous for its addiction to the grapevine. *Viteus* (*Phylloxera*) *vitifolii* is the notorious 'phylloxera' that has attacked European vines so disastrously in the past. It is an American species, which lives on wild grapevines, where it forms galls on the leaves and roots. American vines have evolved a rootstock that is resistant to the *Phylloxera*, and grafting on to an American rootstock was the only way of saving the European vines, once the *Phylloxera* had been introduced to Europe.

One further way in which aphids have exploited every factor is in the production of 'honeydew'. This is a sugar solution, which is passed out of the anus and is the undigested portion of the sap that the insect is continuously swallowing. It is necessary for the aphid to pass a large volume of sap through its intestine because only a small proportion of the sap is utilized by the insect, mostly nitrogenous compounds and trace elements, with a little of the carbohydrate content. Although each insect is tiny, the cumulative effect of continuous excretion and a very large number of individuals produces so much honeydew that the plant is covered in a sticky solution, and at the height of summer this may be so abundant that it drips down from the leaves. Lime trees are particularly noted for their 'rain' of honeydew. Aphids, psyllids and aleyrodids are particularly productive of honeydew. We shall see later in this chapter how ants have developed a fondness for this easy source of carbohydrates, and learned to 'keep' aphids and 'milk' them by stroking to stimulate the flow of honeydew.

We now come to the big orders of insects, that are familiar to everyone: butterflies and moths, flies, bees, wasps, ants and beetles. The very fact that they are familiar to the ordinary person in any country of the world is a measure of their success in becoming part of the everyday scene. It is not so much that they are abundant—insects in very large numbers tend to be looked on as a disastrous visitation, like a plague of locusts—but that they are seen to follow a cycle of birth, life and death, and to be part of the permanent community.

Lepidoptera, the butterflies and moths, can be described in a few words, or whole libraries of books can be written about them. As an example of the former, here is the definition of the order given in Imms's *Textbook of Entomology* (1957 edn., page 511):

Insect with two pairs of membranous wings; cross-veins few in number. The body, wings and appendages clothed with broad scales. Mandibles almost always vestigial or absent, and the principal mouthparts generally represented by a suctorial proboscis formed by the maxillae. Larvae eruciform, caterpillar-shaped, peripneustic [with spiracles opening all along the abdomen], frequently with eight pairs of limbs. Pupae usually more or less obtect, and generally enclosed in a cocoon or an earthen cell: wing tracheation complete.

The key points are: body covered with scales; sucking proboscis; larva is a caterpillar, chewing plant food; pupa like a mummy, often enclosed in a cocoon.

Yet within this simple formula Lepidoptera have evolved about 165000 species that are still living today, and countless others that have lived in the past and become extinct. A recent revision of the *Moths and Butterflies of Great Britain and Ireland*, about 2000 species, is planned to be completed in eleven volumes, totalling something approaching 3000 pages. The need for a library of books to deal with the Lepidoptera of the world is obviously not an overstatement.

In the world of music, there is no limit to the number of compositions that can be created from the eighty-eight notes of the piano. Similarly, the range of Lepidoptera is one of endless variations upon one simple theme, and is full of paradoxes. The order includes some of the biggest of all insects, nearly 30 cm in wingspan, and some of the smallest (3 mm), though not the very tiniest. Many butterflies are spectacularly beautiful, yet most members of the order are drab and dull, and we dismiss them as 'just moths'. . . . A few have a striking shape, but this is usually the effect of quite superficial 'tails' and other irregularities of wing outline in the adults, or hairs and other bodily processes in the larvae. There is nothing to match the variety of structure and function that is to be seen in Hymenoptera, Diptera or even beetles.

In fact Lepidoptera is an order of insects that has evolved for one purpose only, to exploit the flowering plants, and which first arose in the Cretaceous, about 100 million years ago. The eruciform larva, or caterpillar, uses its chewing mouthparts to fill its bag-like abdomen with plant fragments, then hangs motionless in its pupa, with or without a protective cocoon. The adult that emerges flies to flowers, and extracts nectar from them by means of a sucking proboscis. With the exception of one small, archaic group, Micropterigidae, modern Lepidoptera no longer chew pollen, but take such nourishment as they may need in the adult stage, entirely in liquid form. There is nothing in their life cycle that calls for great elaboration of structure, only for endless modifications of size and shape.

The main adaptation of Lepidoptera is chemical. Every species of plant is chemically unique, so that its tissues contain a unique assortment of substances upon which caterpillars feed. The contents of one plant cell are incredibly complex, packed within its cell walls, and the electron microscope is revealing more and more complexities every day. In millions of years of evolution, the digestive processes of caterpillars have become highly specialized machines for processing the cell contents of a small range of plants, sometimes of one species only. How do they find this species in the first place? Usually they don't have to, because the female has located a suitable plant, and laid eggs on it attaching them firmly in a neat arrangement, so that when the larvae emerge they will find suitable food immediately.

To do this butterflies and moths have to be equipped with sense organs, more particularly organs of sight and smell. With few exceptions, the eyes are well developed, but not conspicuously so, when compared with the huge eyes of dragonflies, or the males of many flies. Experiments on the vision of butterflies indicate that they can distinguish the two ends of the spectrum (blue to violet and yellow to red) better than the blue-green section in the middle. They can also see ultraviolet, which is invisible to us, although we are sometimes subconsciously aware of it as a troublesome 'glare'. Anyone who takes colour photographs of flowers will know that blue is the most difficult colour to reproduce well, and that a mysterious overexposure often kills the delicate blue colour that is so attractive to the eye. The flower is reflecting ultraviolet light, which the eye cannot see, but which records itself on the film. In the same way, butterflies and day-flying moths can see differences between colours that are confusingly similar to us.

In fact the vision of butterflies is subject to the same limitations as that of insects in general. Their eyes see a mosaic of coloured spots, and colour is undoubtedly the main attraction. There is some perception of shape, but only in a crude way, rather a recognition of a pattern than of a shape in the round. Some flowers have exploited this fact by developing 'guide-marks' which direct the butterfly (or any other nectar-seeking insect, such as a bee) to the nectaries. Many, perhaps most flowers have some sort of a guide-mark, familiar examples being pansies and violets, and conspicuous examples among the irises. Response to a pattern is a characteristic of the insect eye.

Whereas sight is the most important sense when a butterfly is feeding, smell and taste predominate when the female is seeking a host plant on which to lay its eggs. Vision being poor in the green range, it is likely that food plants are seen almost in monochrome, perhaps in shades of grey, while each plant species has a distinctive odour. At a distance, and in flight, the response is to smell, that is to the detection of chemical substances in the air. The antennae are held out in front, in the airstream, and carry many organs of smell. Organs of taste are essentially similar, but respond more to direct contact with the chemical concerned. Butterflies carry organs of taste on their feet, and 'taste' a plant by settling on it. Other organs of taste are in the maxillary palpi, which, together with the antennae, are used to 'palpate', or beat upon the surface they are tasting.

Peacock Butterfly (*Inachis io*) larva feeding.

Lepidopterous larvae (caterpillars) have eyes, called lateral ocelli, which can be seen as six dark spots on each side of the head. Collectively, these act as a rudimentary kind of compound eye, giving a crude visual pattern. Most caterpillars move their head up and down and from side to side, and thereby extend their field of vision. It is unlikely that they can see with any precision, even approaching that of the adults, but this is apparently enough for them to find their way slowly about the stem and leaves of their food plant. Surface-living caterpillars have three pairs of well-developed thoracic legs, and the abdomen is supported by up to five pairs of fleshy 'prolegs', each with a ring of tiny hooks, or crochets. These prolegs support the weight of the bulky abdomen when it is full of vegetable fragments, which the caterpillar has chewed

from a leaf. The crochets also grasp the rough surface of the leaf or stem, and allow the caterpillar to detach its thorax and turn the front end of the body in search of another place to feed, without at once falling off the plant.

The typical butterfly lives an exposed life, both as caterpillar and as adult, and attracts the attention of enemies. Hence the bright colour and disruptive coloration of most species, both adults and caterpillars, which serve the dual purpose of cryptic coloration (camouflage) and frightening or warning off enemies. A collection of pinned and mounted butterflies is a display of wings, with the rest of the body inconspicuous, and even in life the wings of butterflies are their dominant feature. The name Lepidoptera means 'scaly wings', and each scale is a most elaborate structure. Yet the scales are not new

153

structures 'invented' by Lepidoptera. They are an extreme development from the hairs which occur all over the bodies of insects. A few butterfly scales (androconia) are associated with scent glands, present in the males, and producing a powerful attractant to the females, but scales in general are a superficial covering of the wings and body. They are obviously not necessary for protection, since most insects manage without them, though scales occur sporadically, for example in mosquitoes. Evolution in butterflies has produced scales as a result of selection pressures towards a variety of coloured patterns. Some of the colour is produced by optical interference, set up by the very fine ridges and grooves with which the scales are marked, and varying according to the angle at which the light is scattered by them. This phenomenon is re-

sponsible for the shifting colours of some of the most beautiful butterflies. Other colours are pigmentary, including most of the clear, bright colours from which a fixed pattern is produced. Much has been written about the source and chemical composition of the various pigments, but as a general summary it is enough to say that: (a) they are waste-products of body processes (metabolism) during the larval and pupal stages; and (b) they are of immense importance to the butterfly because its very survival depends on its defensive coloration.

Defensive coloration in adult butterflies lies almost entirely in the wings, whereas in caterpillars it affects the whole body. Besides colour, structural features play a big part. Many caterpillars are hairy, and even bristly, and some have long filaments, or whip-like appendages, and a

Brimstone Butterfly (*Gonepteryx rhamni*) feeding.

Comma Butterfly (*Polygonia c-album*). Note the small white mark resembling the letter 'C' on the underside of the hindwings.

grotesque appearance at either the head or the tail end – which brings us to the subject of *mimicry*. Even with the immense range of variation that is possible, it is perhaps inevitable that coincidences should occur, so that insects that are not closely related should come to look superficially alike. Unfortunately too much has been made of this in the past, with the result that the whole subject of mimicry has fallen into disrepute. In spite of some far-fetched theories, it seems certain that some species are distasteful to eat – because they have evolved chemical waste-products that are unpleasant to a predator – and that other species that happen to resemble them may escape being eaten as a result. It should be remembered, too, that the resemblance does not have to be perfect enough to deceive a student examining the two speci-

mens at leisure, under magnification. A split-second's confusion or doubt in the mind of the attacker may be enough for the intended victim to escape. A similar result may be produced by the sudden uncovering of the 'eyespots' which many butterflies bear on their hindwings, and which are normally hidden under the forewings.

In the opposite sense, patterns are variable for recognition purposes. Here again it is not likely that the pattern of the vision of, say, a fritillary butterfly is precise enough for it to be able to distinguish between the High Brown (*Argynnis adippe*) and the Dark Green (*Argynnis aglaja*) fritillaries by pattern alone. Movement is an even more important recognition feature, and the combination of pattern and movement can be very characteristic, as any collector knows.

So butterflies are a group that have made the fullest use of colour and pattern for concealment, for defence, and for recognition. They have found their ecological niches in the varied food supply of their larvae, on different parts of different plants, in different ecological habitats, and at different times of the year. What about the moths? They are far more numerous than the butterflies, and they have exploited smell and taste more than colour and pattern. A moth specialist may say that this is not so, and point to the immense variation in pattern among the wings of moths, as well as to defence mechanisms such as the bright yellow or orange hindwings of some members of the Noctuidae family. Allowing this to be so, and not forgetting such spectacular examples as the Malagasy Silk Moth (*Argema mittrei*), it is still true that moths in general have opted for drab, inconspicuous coloration. Obviously this is appropriate when they fly at night, but, contrary to the general impression, many moths are about in daylight. In fact the pattern of day-flying moths is just as important to them as pattern is to butterflies, especially that of the forewings. At rest these cover the hindwings, and their cryptic pattern is very difficult to detect against the usually lichen-covered surfaces on which they rest.

The diversity of moths is much greater than that of butterflies, but it is expressed in chemical rather than structural terms. Moth larvae (also caterpillars, like those of butterflies) are unusually versatile, and have learned to exploit almost every source of food. The commercial pests among larvae of Lepidoptera (apart from a few butterflies) are those of moths. Some structural modification occurs, particularly in reduction of the number of abdominal prolegs, as in the 'looper caterpillars' of the family Geometridae. Here the reduction of prolegs to two pairs, widely separated on the sixth and tenth segments of the abdomen, increases the deceptive resemblance of these caterpillars to the twigs on which they rest, as well as enabling them to move more quickly by arching the body upwards. Loss of prolegs, as well as of thoracic legs, goes to an extreme in leaf-mining larvae of some families.

Physiological adaptation, to eat and digest the variety of different chemical substances that occur in different plant tissues, accounts for the great diversity of moths. Not only do some species of moths feed on every group of the flowering plants, chewing the leaves, or mining in the tissues, but moth larvae have also adapted themselves to feeding on woolly fibres (clothes moths) and wax (*Galleria mellonella*, the Wax Moth).

For the first time in this chapter, we can have no hesitation in declaring that here is an order of insects that is highly successful by any criterion. They are the newest of the big orders. Flowering plants are known from the Lower Cretaceous, as are fossil Lepidoptera. Since then their evol-

The upperside of the Comma Butterfly (*Polygonia c-album*).

Left
Cinnabar Moth
(*Callimorpha jaco-
baeae*) larvae.

Right
Pepper Moth (*Bis-
ton betularia*) larva.
This 'looper' cater-
pillar is named after
the way in which it
moves.

Below
Vapourer Moth
(*Orgyia antiqua*)
larva.

ution has been rapid, and it is not surprising that it has been expressed in chemical rather than in structural diversity. If we compare Lepidoptera with Hymenoptera, another order that has exploited the flowering plants, we shall see that Hymenoptera have evolved much more structural diversity, over a longer period of time. On the other hand the higher Diptera, like the Lepidoptera, show signs of a rapid physiological (chemical) evolution, while remaining relatively conservative structurally.

Let us take the Diptera next. These are the two-winged, or 'true', flies, to distinguish them from all those other insects that include 'fly' in their common English name: dragonflies, scorpion flies, etc.* Diptera are much older than Lepidoptera, making their first appearance as fossils in the lias formations of the Lower Jurassic, about 170 million years ago. Even at this remote date they were closely similar to modern flies, and so they must have been evolving long before that. Certain fossils back to the Permian have been claimed as ancestral Diptera, some of them with four wings.

Adult Diptera living today never have more than one pair of functional wings. We have seen that dragonflies, in particular, are able to fly fast and far with two pairs of wings beating independently, though at a relatively slow rate of beat. More recently evolved groups of insects have adopted a more rapid rate of wing-beat, for which independent action is too cumbersome. This difficulty has been overcome in one of two ways: either by coupling the two pairs of wings together, so that they beat as one; or by using only one pair for active flight, and relegating the other pair to a subsidiary function. Lepidoptera and Hymenoptera have adopted the former solution; Coleoptera, Diptera and to a lesser extent Orthoptera and Hemiptera the latter. All except Diptera use the forewings mainly as covers for the hind pair, which are the active organs of flight. Diptera fly with the forewings, having reduced the hindwings to haltères or 'balancers', pin-like organs which act as gyroscopic stabilizers during flight.

All adult Diptera have mouthparts of a sucking type, with mandibles, maxillae and labium combining to form a sucking proboscis. In the females of certain families the mandibles may be retained as piercing instruments, to bring about a flow of blood from vertebrates (mosquitoes, black-flies) or, less commonly from insects (some biting midges).

Diptera have a complete metamorphosis, and their larvae are totally unlike the adult flies, living a completely different life. The non-biting midges (Chironomidae) have gone to one extreme, compressing their whole feeding into their larval life, so that the adult midges need not feed at all. Their life cycle is a latter-day echo of that of the much more primitive, and older order Ephemeroptera. The water-living larvae feed for a very long time, then transform into short-lived adults, which gather over water in huge mating swarms, mate, lay eggs, and die. It is a commentary on the strange ways of evolution that mayflies have preserved this ancient way of life from the distant past, while Chironomidae have arrived at the same result by a tortuous course of evolution lasting millions of years. It also seems that the Chironomidae have 'wasted' their great advantage of a complete metamorphosis by not exploiting the adult stage more fully. They seem to be descended from ancestors which had blood-sucking females, so that their subsequent loss of the necessary piercing mouthparts is a positive evolutionary step. Presumably the larvae have become such efficient feeders that it is no longer necessary for the adults to spend time and effort searching for a blood meal.

The opposite extreme, of concentrating all active life into the adult stage, has been taken by the tsetse-flies (*Glossina*), and by flies of the three families Hippoboscidae, Nycteribiidae and Streblidae. All these flies live entirely upon vertebrate blood, which both sexes of the flies obtain by piercing with a stiff proboscis developed from the labium–a new evolution, quite unrelated to the piercing mandibles and maxillae of female mosquitoes, etc. The females of these more recent flies no longer lay eggs, but retain the larvae–one larva at a time–within themselves, and feed it in a kind of 'womb', until it is ready to turn into a pupa, which happens as soon as it is expelled. For this reason the last three families mentioned are often referred to as the Diptera–Pupipara, though this grouping is objected to by specialists who consider that the three families are convergent rather than closely related.

Here again the advantage of complete metamorphosis has been sacrificed, this time to allow the adults to concentrate on a single source of very rich food. Nycteribiidae and some Streblidae have even abandoned their wings to concentrate more closely on their hosts, which are bats, and conveniently roost in colonies, where it is easy for a wingless insect to crawl from one to another. Tsetse-flies, and most Hippoboscidae retain active flight, and so are able to seek hosts among a variety of mammals and birds, though even here they tend to keep to hosts living in one habitat: for example *Ornithomyia avicularia* on woodland birds, and *Ornithomyia fringillina* on birds living in hedgerows.

In between these two extremes, the lives of Diptera are a balance between larval feeding and adult mobility. Larvae feed in order to grow, and also to build up surplus stores of nutrients which they can pass on, through the pupa, to the emergent adult. Any feeding by the adult merely supplements this, providing energy for the male and female to fly about, and for the female to lay eggs with an adequate supply of yolk. Many, perhaps most flies take nectar from flowers: we usually think of bees and butterflies as the flower-feeding insects, but a few minutes' observation will often show that flies are more numerous than bees and butterflies on the flowers. A few Diptera are known to be able to eat pollen. This is true of some Syrphidae (hover-flies), which crush the pollen grains be-

161

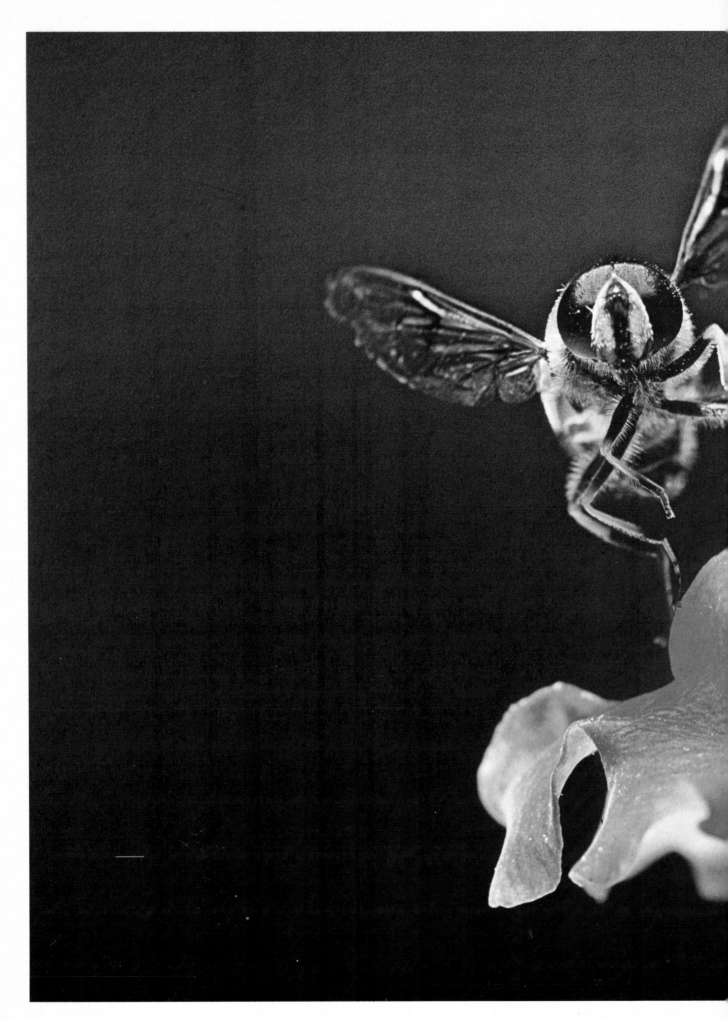

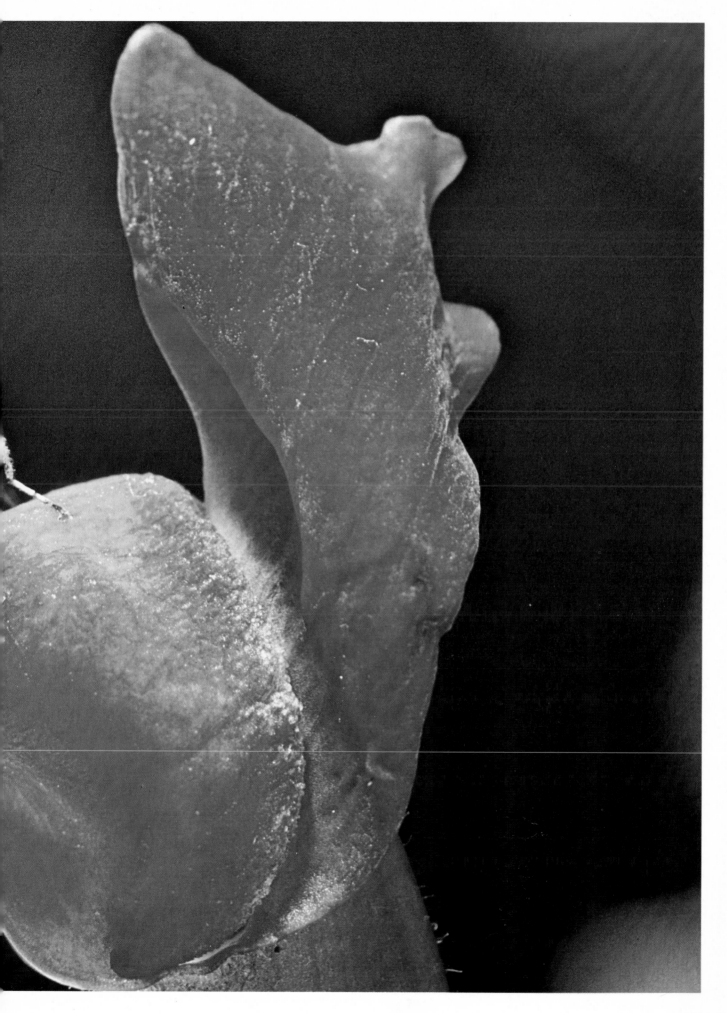

Bee-fly (*Bombylius major*) feeding on Bugle (*Ajuga reptans*). Note the superficial resemblance to bumble bees.

tween the prestomal teeth until they are small enough to be ingested through the sucking proboscis. The tiny *Desmometopa* has been observed to lick pollen from the leg of a worker bumble bee. The group of diminutive flies to which *Desmometopa* belongs (Milichiidae and Carnidae) will attach themselves to any predatory insect or to a spider, in order to mop up oozing fluids, and they have been called 'jackals of the insect world'.

Some families of flies evidently find it difficult to accumulate enough food reserves during larval life to satisfy the wants of the adult, which then must seek some source of food for itself. Early Diptera appear to have lived among moss, or in rotting vegetable materials, such as those

in the rot holes of trees. The adults had enough food for active flight, and could supplement this with nectar from flowers (when these had evolved!), but this was not enough protein to supply the eggs with yolk. So the females of some of the oldest families of Diptera adapted their mandibles and maxillae to suck blood from the vertebrate animals that were available to them. Female mosquitoes are the standard example of this type of nutrition, which also survives in biting midges (Ceratopogonidae), black-flies (Simuliidae), and sand-flies (Phlebotomidae). It seems likely that originally all this group of flies had bloodsucking females, but that later on the larvae became more efficient feeders in their watery habitats, and bloodsucking declined,

Robber-fly (*Asilus*
spp) with prey.

with consequent loss of mandibles in females, to match those of males. The end of this evolutionary trend is seen in the Chironomidae already mentioned.

This bloodsucking habit arose early in the evolution of Diptera, at a time when mammals were few, and the most readily available sources of blood were reptiles and birds. It seems to be associated with a change of larval habitat from the ancestral moss to wetter, more fully aquatic media, where there was a richer diet, including not only rich growths of algae and fungi, but also bacteria and protozoa. One of the first evolutionary experiments seems to have been the family Psychodidae (moth-flies). The larvae of some *Psychoda* species are an essential ingredient

in the operation of sewage filters, where they clear up the incrustation of sludge that forms over the gravel of the filter-beds. So effective is this larval diet that the adult moth-flies do not need to feed. Their close relatives the sand-flies (Phlebotomidae) have colonized much drier areas, including deserts, where open water is non-existent. The larvae of sand-flies still require a saturated atmosphere in which to live, otherwise they dry up and die. They find this moisture in tiny crevices between the stones and grains of sand, where condensation occurs even in the most arid regions, as a result of the sharp drop of temperature during the clear desert nights. These larvae survive, but are scarcely well fed, so the adult females have become effective bloodsuckers. They have followed this way of life long enough to have become vectors of human diseases: sand-fly fever, kala-azar, and Oriental sore.

The biting midges (Ceratopogonidae) also live their larval lives in very damp places. Their larvae have no open spiracles, so that they can breathe only by absorbing oxygen through the skin, and this requires the skin to be kept continuously moist, otherwise water would evaporate quickly, and the larvae would soon dry up and die. Many of them live in wet soil, and the adult females are a great pest in swampy areas, usually coming out to feed around dusk and dawn, when the atmosphere is moist. *Culicoides* is the most notorious genus, tiny flies with speckled wings, and with a powerful bite out of all proportion to their minute size. They are difficult to see even when they are felt to be biting, and have earned the name of 'no-see-ums'. Yet the members of this family that bite human beings are very much in the minority. Most Ceratopogonidae pierce and suck the wings of insects, a remote and seemingly arid source of nourishment.

The move to a fully aquatic larval life has gone further still in mosquitoes (Culicidae), and in black-flies (Simuliidae). We all know about mosquito larvae, the 'wrigglers' that appear in our ponds and water-butts. Most of their time they are not wriggling much, but lie close to the surface, reaching out to the air with their breathing siphon. In fact the larvae of mosquitoes are not fully aquatic, but surface dwellers. The old-fashioned method of dealing with a mosquito outbreak was to pour a little oil on to the water, where it spread out into a thin film, and effectively cut off the mosquito larvae from access to air.

Black-flies have gone into water more fully, with larvae that cling to underwater surfaces, stones, stems and leaves of growing or floating plants, even to underwater animals, such as crabs, and the larvae of dragonflies and mayflies. Whatever they are attached to, black-fly larvae need plenty of oxygen in the water, since they have no means of collecting it from the outside air. So these flies are found only in well-aerated water, in streams where the flow is rapid and turbulent over waterfalls and rapids, and in slow-moving water provided that there is enough green vegetation to supply bubbles of oxygen as a result of photosynthesis.

The addiction to an aquatic larval life persists in other families, notably Tabanidae (horseflies) and Rhagionidae (snipe-flies). The latter family has almost lost the habit of bloodsucking by females, more particularly in those members of the family that have moved to drier land and have terrestrial larvae. The same trend has occurred in the family Tabanidae, except in the more recently evolved genera: *Tabanus*, *Haematopota*, *Chrysops* and *Pangonius*. These genera seem to have proliferated during Miocene and Pliocene times, when the great herds of grazing animals roamed the plains, and probably are in decline today, along with their host animals. *Pangonius* has a second line of feeding, having evolved a very long proboscis, with which both sexes can probe into deep-belled flowers to feed on nectar, though of course this does not give them the proteins that blood provides. The females can still suck blood by bending the long proboscis aside.

As the feeding of the larva has become more efficient, an intermediate step before the disappearance of female mandibles comes when the larva has accumulated enough food for the female to lay one batch of eggs only. If the female can then obtain a blood-meal it can go on to lay a second and even a third batch. This explains how the Arctic tundra can support huge populations

Conopid-fly (*Conops* spp) mimicking a wasp.

Horse-fly of the family Tabanidae showing large head and bulging eyes.

of biting flies (mosquitoes, black-flies, biting midges, horse-flies), which descend in insufferable clouds on any person who goes there. What do they find to feed on when he is not there? The answer is that they make do with what eggs they are able to lay on larval reserves, but are only too eager to add to these if they have the opportunity.

Outside these aquatic flies, with bloodsucking females, the rest of the Diptera are essentially terrestrial, though some of them – for example many hover-flies (Syrphidae), marsh-flies (Tetanoceridae) and shore-flies (Ephydridae) – have moved their larvae back into the water under later evolutionary pressures. The larvae that live in the soil can be vegetarian or carnivorous; growing plants provide a very wide range of sources of plant food; but the biggest source of larval food that has been exploited by flies is that of organic fluids, either in decaying plant or animal tissues, in wounds, pus, or even in healthy flesh (like the warble-fly of cattle). This versatility in larval feeding is a key to the great success of Diptera as an order.

Another key to their success is that they manage to exploit such a range of larval foods without needing to have a complicated larval structure, which might have confined them to one sort of food and so restricted their evolution. No fly larva has any true legs, and even the false legs that are seen in many of the aquatic larvae (and redeveloped in those larvae that have returned to the water) are lost in terrestrial larvae. The gall midges (Cecidomyiidae) are an extreme example. The larvae live a completely sheltered life inside a plant-gall, and have lost all external structures, even mouthparts. They obtain their food by sucking, and modern electronic equipment has made it possible actually to hear them doing so!

The logical progression from structural to physiological adaptation has led all the higher Diptera – the larger part of the order – to adopt a type of larvae that will serve for all purposes: the maggot. This is familiar as the maggots of the blow-fly, the 'gentles' of the fisherman. The front end is pointed, with no distinct head, but with a pair of strong mouthhooks which scratch and scrape at food materials. Saliva is often poured out, and helps to soften up the food, reducing it to a liquid form in which it can be

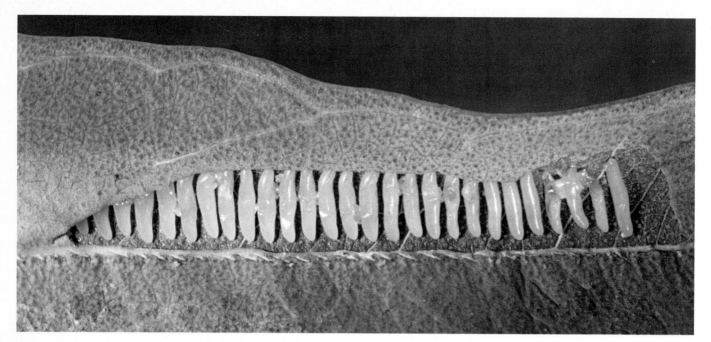

sucked up. The rest of the body of the maggot becomes broader posteriorly, ending in a pair of large spiracles, or breathing apertures. These can remain open to the air while the rest of the maggot is plunged into its food. There are no legs, 'real' or 'false', but round the abdominal segments are fleshy swellings which help the maggot to push its way through soft materials, and into narrow spaces.

The great evolutionary advantage of this type of larva is that it can quickly accustom itself to a new kind of food, if one source dwindles. The adaptation is not a structural one, requiring new organs which take a long time to evolve, but a chemical adjustment in the digestive fluids. Even this is probably not great, since maggots feed mostly on organic matter that is already breaking down into simpler compounds, and the end products are much the same whatever their origin. The supreme example of this adaptability is the House-fly (*Musca domestica*), which has followed man all over the world, finding its larval food among the waste products that he creates everywhere.

The pupae of Diptera show a similar progression from the externally complex to the apparently simple. The complex pupae have antennae, wings and legs visible in external sheaths, and are often furnished with bristles, spines or strong teeth which help to push the pupa out of the soil or other material in which it lies, allowing the adult to emerge into clear air. There is argument whether the pupa itself is capable of this activity, or whether it is the adult fly still imprisoned in the pupal skin (the 'pharate adult'), but this is a point of theoretical interest only. The end result is the same. More than half of the families of Diptera belong to the suborder Cyclorrhapha, in which the pupa remains within the last larval skin, smoothed off and hardened into an ovoid or barrel-shaped puparium. Such a puparium is quite immobile, and often lies below the surface of the soil or other material into which the larva crawled

when it was about to pupate. The adult emerges by pushing off a circular cap (to which the name 'Cyclorrhapha' refers), and then must make its own way up to the surface. Both these actions call for a physical effort that is difficult for a fly at this stage, before its skin has hardened. Most Cyclorrhapha (the group known as Schizophora) have evolved a very complex organ for this purpose. The forehead splits, and a huge bag, called a ptilinum, is inflated again and again until the insect is free.

This poses an interesting evolutionary problem. It is not obvious why the puparium should be so superior to the earlier types of pupa, that it has been worthwhile to evolve the ptilinum to make up for its deficiencies.

This is the point at which to mention the fleas (order Siphonaptera), which are unusual among parasitic insects in making full use of a complete metamorphosis, with a larval life distinct from that of the adult. This is a difficult problem for a parasitic insect, and fleas have solved it in an ingenious way. Adult fleas are always wingless, flattened from side to side, and with exceptional powers of leaping: up to fifty times their own length upwards, and seventy-five times forwards. This is a hit-or-miss way of finding a host, made necessary by the fact that larvae and pupae are not on the host animal, but on the ground, so that the newly emerged flea has to find its first host for itself. Flea larvae live on organic debris, especially on the faeces of the adult fleas, which contain undigested blood – that is how fleas make brown spots on the bed-linen! So fleas breed only in association with mammals or birds that have a den, or a nest, or regular sleeping quarters. They lay eggs in the fur or feathers, the eggs fall off, the larvae feed, and the adult flea, sensitive to warmth and vibration, is able to recognize when a host is nearby, and to jump blindly in its direction.

Larval fleas have biting and chewing mouth-parts, and are tiny, worm-like creatures, rather like the larvae of some primitive flies. Adult fleas have sucking mouthparts and live exclusively on blood. They will pierce and suck from any warm-blooded animal whenever they have a chance, but their full breeding cycle is adapted to the nesting or sleeping habits of one host, or a group of hosts with similar habits. We can speak of the 'cat flea', or the 'squirrel flea' in this sense.

Hymenoptera is probably the most varied order of insects, both in adult structure and in larval life. The larval habits divide into two distinct suborders: sawflies (Symphyta) have plant-feeding larvae with structures appropriate to an active life, searching for their own food; the rest (Apocrita) have legless, helpless larvae, dependent upon finding a supply of suitable food around them when they hatch from the egg.

Sawflies get their English name from the ovipositor of the female, with its serrated edge for cutting into plant tissues to insert the eggs. The larvae of the commonest species are like caterpillars, with a well-developed head, strong mandibles, and the fleshy abdomen supported by false legs, which are even more numerous than those of lepidopterous caterpillars. The way of life is similar: the way in which the larvae of the Solomon's Seal Sawfly (*Phymatocera aterrima*) demolish the leaves of that graceful plant can hardly be beaten by any true caterpillar. The laying of eggs under plant tissue is a protection in the first place, but not all sawfly larvae emerge to feed on the outside of the plant. Those of the stem sawflies (Cephidae) bore into growing stems, a notorious example being the Wheat Stem Sawfly (*Cephus pygmaeus*), which can cause the stems of wheat to break off just below the ear. The biggest and most striking sawflies are the wood wasps, which use their saw as a boring instrument, so that they can lay their eggs under the bark, in the new wood of trees. When the larvae hatch they bore into the heart-wood, and may live there for up to two years. The Great Wood Wasp or Horntail is known throughout the Northern Hemisphere as a pest of coniferous trees. This conspicuous black and yellow insect is often mistaken for a hornet.

As an offshoot of this wood-boring group the small family Orussidae has legless larvae living as internal parasites of wood-boring insects. These juicy beetle larvae must be succulent to predacious and even normally herbivorous insects which meet them in their burrows. A parallel occurs in Diptera, where a large subfamily of Asilidae (robber-flies) has taken to a larval life in beetle burrows instead of the more usual habitat in the soil. These genera (Laphriinae) apparently just eat their way through a beetle larva if they happen to meet it.

The rest of Hymenoptera, within the suborder Apocrita, with their helpless, concealed larvae, are customarily divided into Parasitica and Aculeata, the parasitic and the stinging forms respectively. The Parasitica use their complex ovipositor, not for cutting into plants, like the sawflies, but for piercing living insects, to lay eggs. The Aculeata or stinging group, have changed the function of the ovipositor from that of an egg-laying tube to a sting, which can be used for either attack or defence.

In fact the two groups are not as sharply distinct as their names suggest. Gall wasps (superfamily Cynipoidea) which are technically Parasitica, push their eggs into plant tissues, where the irritation set up by the presence of the subsequent larvae causes the plant to form a swelling or gall. The shape and colour of the gall depend as much on the idiosyncrasies of the plant as those of the insect, and are often very distinctive. Two examples familiar in Europe are the 'marble gall' of the oak, produced by *Andricus kollari*, and the pincushion gall of roses, produced by *Diplolepis rosae*.

Parasitic Hymenoptera are of necessity small, the biggest being the ichneumon flies (Ichneumonidae and Braconidae), graceful, elongate insects, often seen on foliage, moving about delicately on their long legs, and palpating with their long, often white-tipped, antennae. Their favourite hosts are the caterpillars of Lepidoptera, and less frequently the larvae of Hymenoptera, Coleoptera or Diptera. The parasitic larva at first avoids the vital tissues of the host, eating its reserves of non-essential materials, and so causing symptoms of malnutrition, including sexual malfunction, or 'parasitic castration'. Eventually the parasite kills its host and pupates inside or outside the empty skin. If you split open the stems of dead reeds during the winter you will often find empty larval and pupal skins of Lepidoptera with pupae of Hymenoptera inside them.

Most parasitic Hymenoptera are even smaller, often minute, only 1–2 mm long, but what they lack in size they make up in diversity and adaptability to different hosts. The group seem to attract superlatives: they practise hyperparasitism, and exhibit hypermetamorphosis and polyembryony – not all of them, but often, when it suits their lifestyle or that of their host. Hyperparasites are parasitic on another parasite, either another member of the Hymenoptera or of some other order of insects: for example Diapriidae mainly parasitize larvae of flies (Diptera), including flies of the family Tachinidae, which are themselves parasites of Lepidoptera and other orders. Hypermetamorphosis we have met before: insects with a complete metamorphosis usually have a single type of larva, which changes little except in size when it moults, but exceptionally the larva may change its appearance and behaviour during larval life. In such a case the first stage larva is usually an active, highly mobile form called a triungulin, which migrates from where the egg hatched to a more suitable place for feeding. Arrived there, the larva loses its limbs at the next moult, and becomes a static, feeding machine.

Polyembryony means that a single egg can produce not one, but a multitude of embryos, each of which develops into a separate larva. This is a particularly frequent occurrence in the proctotrupid family Platygasteridae, whose members attack gall wasps, and the chalcid family Encyrtidae, parasites of Lepidoptera.

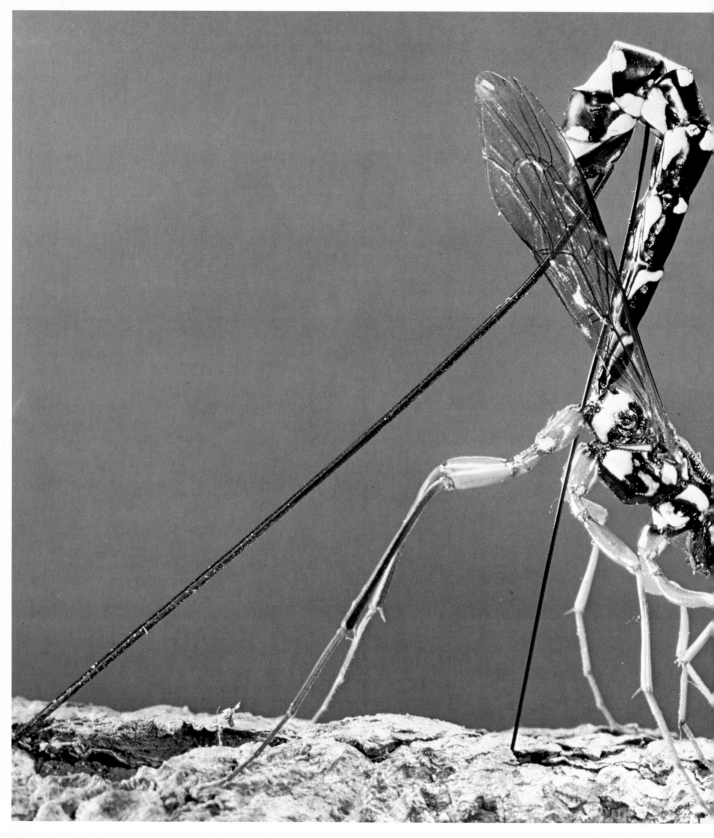

Note that this is not a matter of the parasite laying a number of eggs in the same host. The starting point is one egg, which divides as usual into a number of daughter cells, but instead of these grouping themselves into the tissues of one embryo, each one becomes a complete embryo in itself. About 1 000 larvae from one egg have been recorded in *Litomastix truncatellus*.

These tiny parasitic insects have become adapted to their life not only by their small size,

but in other ways too. They retain wings, which are large in relation to the size of the insect, and paddle-shaped so that they have a large, flat surface. The usual pattern of wing veins in Hymenoptera includes a number of closed 'cells', with a network of veins. In most parasitic families nearly all these veins have been lost, except for a single strong rib near the leading edge. Their place is taken by large hairs, or macrotrichiae.

Ichneumon Fly (*Rhyssa persuasoria*) parasitizing a Wood Wasp (*Urocerus gigas*). The ichneumon is laying eggs in the larva – note the length of the ovipositor.

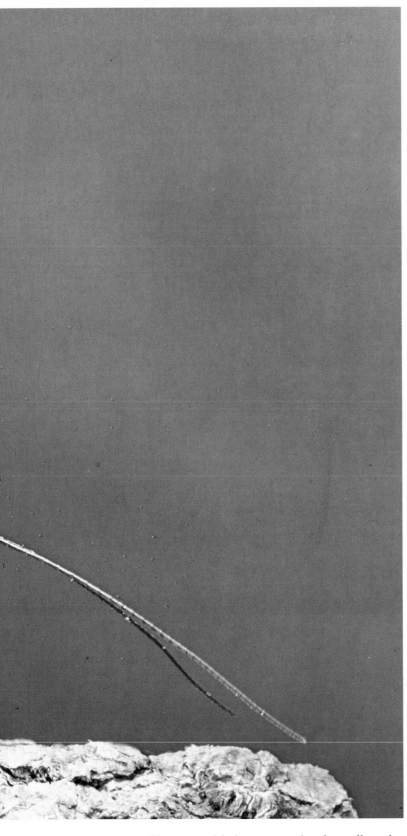

Since parasitic insects need to be well equipped to locate a suitable host, they have large heads with well-developed eyes, ocelli and long, sensitive antennae. It is fascinating to watch *Trichogramma evanescens*, an egg-parasite, smell out the egg of a butterfly, and then crawl over it, testing it with the antennae before deciding to lay an egg in it. The size of the insect can be judged from the fact that it can stand on a butterfly's egg!

The importance of parasitic Hymenoptera in the balance of the insect world cannot be overestimated. Their larval food – and that is virtually the whole food of their lives though some adults are known to suck at the hole in which they have laid an egg – is derived entirely from the tissues of a host animal, which is eventually killed. They are sometimes known as 'parasitoids', because true parasites, such as fleas or lice, live at the expense of another animal without killing it. Parasitic Hymenoptera keep down the numbers of moths and flies, which uncontrolled would reach plague proportions, though of course some other ecological factor would intervene to limit their numbers, and restore a balance. The long-term effect of parasitic Hymenoptera is to force their host insects to be very prolific in order to offset the losses through parasitism. This means that a very large number of mutations become available for natural selection to act upon, so that parasitism is a stimulus to the evolution of its victims.

The aculeate, or stinging Hymenoptera, comprising the wasps, the bees and the ants, have made the latest of the big steps forward in insect evolution, that of *social life*. This step has been taken by only two orders, and those totally different, and only remotely related: Hymenoptera and Isoptera (termites). For the purposes of this section, discussion of the termites has been held over until after Hymenoptera have been considered, when it will be easier to make comparisons between the rival forms of social life.

Only a small minority of aculeate Hymenoptera are social insects, but these include all the ants, whereas both bees and wasps are predominantly solitary. Even they have helpless larvae, which cannot seek their own food, and so have to be provisioned by their parents, either once in a lifetime, or progressively throughout larval life. A few of these so-called aculeate Hymenoptera still use their ovipositor for its original purpose, as an egg-laying tube, and lay their eggs wherever instinct leads them. Sapygidae and Chrysididae (cuckoo wasps) are intruders into bees' nests, where their larvae either feed on the bees' larvae, or steal the food that the foraging bees have collected. Dryinidae are internal parasites in plant bugs of the order Homoptera.

The path towards social life starts with the solitary wasps. These have already progressed a good deal further than most insects, which either scatter their eggs at random, or lay them in some natural situation where they will find protection and food. A female spider-hunting wasp (Pompilidae) looks for a spider, catches and stings it, and lays it aside while digging a hole or burrow in the ground. Then she puts the spider into the burrow and lays an egg on it. She may add one or two more spiders for good measure, before sealing up the burrow. The mother does not return again to see how her offspring is getting on, since she has provided it with enough food for all its larval life. Although paralysed, the spiders are not dead, and remain fresh until required.

171

Even this is advanced behaviour in several respects. Finding and stinging a spider may be instinctive, but the wasp lays it aside, and remembers where to find it again, and uses some kind of judgment of the number of spiders needed to provision the cell. Moreover, the conversion of her ovipositor into a sting, complete with poison gland, and a venom of the right toxicity to paralyse without killing, are all evolutionary changes that must have taken place before the provisioning behaviour was possible.

Sand wasps make the nest first, then find their prey – which is often a caterpillar bigger than themselves, which they drag along the ground between their six feet, like three workmen dragging a large pipe. Once again, the cell may be closed, leaving the larva to feed itself without any further attention, but some of the more advanced sand wasps leave the cell open, or reopen it at intervals, to give the larva some more food. This is a significant step towards complete care of the young.

Social life

We tend to think of bees as social insects, but in fact the great majority of bees, too, are solitary. They make nests in burrows, like those of the solitary wasps, the important difference being that while adult wasps visit flowers, they feed their young on animal food, chewing insects and feeding the fragments to the larvae; bees, on the other hand, feed both themselves and their larvae on pollen, nectar and honey. Honey is a product made by predigesting the nectar in the bee's crop, or 'honey stomach'. Bees are more furry than wasps, and this is functional as well as giving bees a characteristic appearance: their furriness comes from having branched hairs to which pollen grains stick, and a pad of special hairs on each hindleg acts as a 'pollen basket'. These two pollen stores can often be seen as yellow patches on the hindlegs of bees as they forage from flowers. Like wasps, solitary bees may either provision the cell once only, or repeatedly.

Solitary wasps and bees are often *gregarious*, that is, a large number of the same species may make their nests close together. A sandy bank may be riddled with their burrows, but each female looks after her own brood only. True social life begins when females look after broods that are not their own, thus opening the way to division of labour, with some members of the colony foraging, some feeding the brood, some cleaning out the nest, and so on. The next step is a *caste system*, in which individuals are physically different according to their role in the colony.

The mechanism of sex determination in Hymenoptera is particularly well suited to the caste system. In most insects only fertilized eggs hatch into larvae, which are male or female according to their sex chromosomes. Hymenoptera are unusual in that fertilized eggs, with two sets of chromosomes, are always female, while unfertilized eggs with only one set are male. To exploit this device fully for social life, it is necessary that the founding female, the 'queen', should be able to store the sperm she receives at her mating, and release it as required to produce male or female eggs. Both wasps and bees can do this, and the life of the colony throughout the year is regulated by the queen's control of the sex of her offspring.

Wasps and bumble bees have annual colonies, and may be considered together, though remembering that wasps feed their young on animal food, and bees on nectar, pollen and honey. Only fertilized females survive the winter, hibernating in some sheltered spot. Emerging again in spring, the 'queens' found colonies, making about a dozen cells from chewed wood (wasps), or wax (bees), laying an egg in each, and progressively feeding the larvae until they pupate. These eggs are fertilized, and so produce females, but a deficient diet results in their being smaller than the queen, and sexually sterile. These are the worker caste, which take over cell construction, maintenance, repair and cleaning of the nest, food gathering, larval feeding and defence. In fact the workers are the only members of the colony that are seen outside the nest. From now on the queens remain inside, being fed by the workers, and having no duties outside. Towards autumn the queen lays some unfertilized eggs, which produce males, or 'drones', whose only duty is, to fertilize young queens: hence the use of 'drone' for an idle fellow. The fertile females for them to mate with are produced from larvae which receive extra food, owing to a reduction in the number of eggs being laid by the queen.

Once fertilized, these young queens are the only members of the colony to survive the winter, and will be the founders of all next year's colonies. Wasps do not store food, presumably because the animal food they supply for their larvae would not keep indefinitely; bumble bees make small stores of pollen and honey, but not enough to keep the colony supplied during the season (whether cold or dry) during which flowers are not about for visiting. So drones and workers die of starvation.

At some stage in their evolution, honey bees or hive bees (Apidae) have been able to accumulate enough food in the nest to feed the colony over the bad season, and in this way they achieved perpetual colonies. Mere numbers are a big factor here, and bee hives may contain as many as 80 000 workers. Colonies on this scale become literally 'a hive of industry', with enough workers to dispose of waste products, and to ventilate the hive, so that the atmosphere inside it remains as they like it whatever the weather outside. When the hive becomes overcrowded, pressure is released by 'swarming'. The old queen leaves the hive, accompanied by a swarm of workers, which protect her until their scouts have found a place to establish a new colony. Bee-keepers do their best to recapture such swarms and induce them to take over an empty hive. In the old nest a young queen takes over, thus rejuvenating the original colony.

A most remarkable ingredient in the daily life

Above
Honey Bees (*Apis mellifera*) feeding on spilt honey.

of honey bees is the way in which a successful forager is able to tell the others in the hive where to go and look for food. There is no need to recount here 'The Dance of the Bees', which has been discussed at both scientific and popular levels. Those who work with honey bees confirm that dances such as those described by von Frisch do actually take place, and that bees then go out and find the flowers in bloom. The trouble is that the complicated code that they are supposed to use requires powers of comprehension and abstraction that would seem to be beyond the capabilities of an insect's small 'brain'.

Probably more has been written about the honey bee (*Apis mellifera*) than about any other insect, yet it is scarcely known in the wild state. Like other domestic animals, it is kept going in areas of the world where it could not otherwise live, and in return man takes away its produce, in this case honey, for his own use. There are a few species of wild honey bees, and it seems likely that the domesticated race came from the tropics, where social life, as in human societies, made it possible to support much larger populations

than had previously been possible. The ability to create an optimum atmosphere inside the hive may be the factor that enables the bees to spread into savannah areas, where there is a long dry season, with no flowers to provide a continuous supply of food. Although these same factors allowed hive bees to cope with the winter of temperate climates, *Apis mellifera* did not spread naturally into these areas, but had to be introduced there by man. The simpler annual colonies of bumble bees and wasps have been more advantageous to them, allowing them to to put all their resources into hibernating females, and to start the colonies again each spring. So they occur naturally in temperate countries, while hive bees do not.

The zenith of social life has been attained by the ants. The word that fits everything to do with ants is 'ruthlessness', though this is a human term, not properly applicable to unfeeling creatures like ants. What seems ruthless about ants is the cold efficiency of their social organization. One ant is a small, wingless, helpless creature easily crushed with a thumb, but even a few ants together becomes a formidable op-

Above right
Honey Bee (*Apis
mellifera*) feeding
at a flower.

Right
Leaf-cutter ant
carrying a piece of
leaf it has cut back
to its nest.

ponent. If they find a source of food they scurry back and forth between it and their underground nest, carrying away anything edible in individual loads which are sometimes incredibly bulky, and presumably heavy in comparison with the weight of the ant itself. If an ants' nest is broken open by a predator, some ants immediately start to carry away the pupae and larvae and hide them, while others swarm all over the intruder, biting as well as stinging. What can be a trivial irritation from one ant becomes serious, even dangerous when dozens or hundreds of ants attack at the same time.

The most primitive ants are the carnivorous driver ants and legionary ants. To support a huge population of carnivorous ants, all suitable prey within a convenient range is soon eaten, and this is apparently why these ants make no permanent nests, but 'march' in huge columns, devouring every living thing in their path, even large mammals if they cannot get away. Such a destructive way of life reminds one of a recurrent piratical stage in human societies, such as that of the Viking raids. Like them, it cannot lead to any settled colonization until it is replaced, or at least supplemented by an agricultural phase. Ants achieved this when they began to eat vegetable as well as animal food. We have seen that insects, like other animals, cannot get enough nourishment from vegetable food unless they can take in great quantities, and so they need a large storage capacity. For individual storage they have to use the abdomen, as in grasshoppers or caterpillars, but social life solves this problem with a communal store.

Ants store food in their untidy underground nests. They do not construct neat hexagonal cells like bees or wasps, and their nest is not even divided very clearly into areas for different purposes. Instead, they frequently move its contents about, including their brood, larvae and pupae. Much of their vegetable food is in the form of seeds or spores, which may germinate, and so the ants are often credited with being able to practise deliberate cultivation, thereby having reached the level of Neolithic man. Like much of their behaviour, this appearance of conscious purpose is possibly illusory, though the fungus-gardens of the parasol ants (*Atta*) seem to be an integral part of the nest where fungus grows on a compost of chewed leaves.

The immense success of ants stems mainly from two things: their versatility of diet and their flexibility of behaviour. The first could not be fully exploited without the second, and the key to the second is *trophallaxis*, a technical term for the practice of exchanging food, often partly predigested, between different individuals. It includes mouth-to-mouth exchanges, as well as one ant licking up substances passed out through the anus, or exuded from glands anywhere in the body. The most familiar example is ants soliciting food from aphids, stroking them with the antennae to make them discharge more honeydew.

Wood Ants (*Formica rufa*) on their nest.

With their usual versatility, ants, although among the fiercest of insects in the normal way, will tolerate within their nests a wide variety of species of other insects, which they attack only if these behave in some way abnormally, and so are not instinctively recognized. For instance, the larva of a hover-fly, *Microdon*, lives in the nests of the Wood Ant, and is normally tolerated, if not actively fed by the ants, in return for which it acts as a scavenger in the nest. It looks like a slug, in its normal position, but if it becomes turned over on its back the ants at once fail to recognize it, and attack. Such 'guests' of ants are called *inquilines*. Their exact relations with the ants are not always easy to discover, but attempts have been made to classify them into mere scavengers, endlessly dodging the ants; those which, like *Microdon* are tolerated; and those which enter into a reciprocal relationship with the ants, exchanging food in a trophallaxis. This last group are the true guests.

Ants have the same mechanism of sex determination as wasps and bees, so that fertilized eggs produce females and unfertilized eggs males. They differ in producing many more fertile males and females, which emerge from the nest for their mating flights on certain days in the summer. Millions may come out on the same afternoon, over a wide area. No one really knows what triggers them off, or how the different nests synchronize their flights. Those which are not snapped up by predators break off their wings on the ground, and the females either return to the old nest or find a crevice in which to start a new one. The female lays eggs, and rears her first brood on the food reserve in her own body, regurgitating for the purpose. After that the new workers take over, and the queen lives only to lay eggs.

There is a wide variation within the worker caste, greater in some species than others. Ants do not normally develop a true soldier caste like that of the termites (see below), and the variation in workers is mainly in size and proportions, and even more in behaviour. Some of this is due to differential feeding, but it must be realized that this reflects differences in *behaviour* of the workers during the feeding of the larvae. So polymorphism has its origins in differences of behaviour.

Unlike wasps or bees, ants normally tolerate more than one queen in a nest, but the overwhelming majority of individuals are workers. These are the only ants seen wandering about. They have a keen sense of smell, and establish scent trails between the nest and sources of food. Sometimes one of these trails leads into a house or store. When foraging ants catch an insect they

Above
Yellow Field Ants (*Lasius flavus*) with young stages.

Above right
Winged ants (*Lasius* spp) emerging for mating flight.

Right
Garden ant 'milking' aphids.

178

pull it about in an effort to break it into pieces small enough to be carried. Their efforts are not well coordinated, and do not result in moving the corpse in the right direction unless that happens to be downhill. Yet some ants can cooperate in a productive manner. Extreme examples, often quoted, include the weaver ants (*Oecophylla*), which draw leaves together, and then use the silk-spinning larvae of their own species to 'stitch' the leaves together. There are also reports of 'ant-bridges', where a string of ants hold one another head to tail, and swing across a gap, forming a bridge across which others can walk.

The ultimate development of trophallaxis and the mixed society in a nest is slave making. Ants belonging to two different species may sometimes share a nest, perhaps more often than we realize. Often one species takes over the nest by killing the queens of the other species, and absorbing the workers into its own colony. A further step is when ants of one colony make 'slave raids' into the nests of others, stealing the pupae and carrying them back to their own colony. When the adults emerge they become slave workers in an alien colony.

The life of ants is so complex that no short summary is possible, other than to say that it is difficult to set any limit to what they could do if the environmental pressure were strong enough. So ants are some of the most efficient of all insects, yet even they have their limitations. They are not aquatic, nor do they seem to have perfected any sophisticated method of communication rivalling the 'Dance of the Bees'.

This is the place to mention the only fully social insects outside the Hymenoptera. These are the termites, members of the order Isoptera. Although they are often called 'white ants', and their mounds are called 'ant hills', termites have only the most remote relationship with ants. They are insects with a gradual metamorphosis, closely allied to the cockroaches; indeed they have been called 'social cockroaches'. Since they are so often confused with ants, it may be helpful to list the resemblances and differences.

Resemblances. Both groups: live in huge colonies, with indefinite life; have a reproductive caste of winged males and females, which emerge on a mating flight, after which they shed their wings; most individuals are wingless workers, which share all the duties of the nest except reproduction.

Differences. Termites: have no larval stage, but hatch from the egg into nymphs which are not as helpless as the larvae of ants; there is no pupal stage; worker termites are not aggressive like ants, and do not seek animal prey; on the other hand termites have a soldier caste, big-headed, aggressive to insect intruders, some of them with powerful jaws; the workers are immature (juvenile) individuals of either sex, not just females as in Hymenoptera.

There are about 1700 species of termites, mostly in warm countries, but with a growing tendency to spread into cooler countries as a result of the importation of infested timber, and its use in heated buildings. Their nesting habits are highly diverse, but fall broadly into two types: drywood termites and subterranean termites. The former tunnel in dry wood, digesting the cellulose as well as the sugary cell contents, with the aid of a colony of intestinal protozoa. 'Subterranean termites' is something of a misnomer for the others, because although they do nest underground, they are well known for the huge mounds that they erect above ground level.

These termitaria are elaborate constructions with a very hard, concrete-like outer covering, and a softer interior of chewed, woody material, shaped into a system of complex galleries and chambers. Access for the termites is by underground passages. The function of the above-ground mound, apart from adding enormously to storage and living space, is to ensure a stable atmosphere, with almost saturated air and a uniform temperature. With this the termites can guard themselves against extreme variations in temperature and humidity which occur in the countries in which termites live. Within the mound breeding can go on continuously at maximum rate.

In general, termites do not store food as ants do. The workers mostly feed themselves as they forage, on wood, grass, or fungus. Some go out at night to collect lichens, and some termites cultivate 'fungus gardens' inside their nest. Trophallaxis is a major feature of the feeding habits of termites, and that is how they obtain their intestinal protozoa, from an older member of the colony. Saliva, regurgitated, partly digested food, and undigested food from the anus, are all fed to the queen and her attendant males, as well as to the young nymphs which need richer food than the fully grown workers.

Perhaps the most striking feature of termite life is what happens to the queen in the nest. Instead of leading an active life, like the ant queens, she remains in one place. She has to, because her abdomen grows to a grotesque size, up to 7 or 8 cm long. She becomes a helpless egg-laying machine, and depends entirely on the workers to feed her, and to take away the eggs as they emerge, and on the attendant males to fertilize her periodically. Unlike members of Hymenoptera, she is not able to store enough sperm from one mating.

When we consider the remote relationship between termites and social Hymenoptera, the similarities between their social life are more significant than the differences. In all social groups, the essentials are caring for the offspring communally, instead of by individual mothers; division of labour, with a worker caste to perform all the routine duties of the colony; and an elaborate system of trophallaxis, with food passed to and fro until every morsel of nourishment has been extracted from it. It is this mutual behaviour that binds the members of the colony together, and makes the whole colony into a sort of 'super individual'.

One order of insects has been left till last: the beetles (Coleoptera). Beetles stand apart from other insects in some respects. They are the

most diverse: it is said that 40 per cent of all insect species, and about one-third of all animals, are beetles. They are found everywhere, at all latitudes, all altitudes, and in all climates. They live on land or in water, eat every kind of food, animal or vegetable, and range in length from 0·6 to 160 mm. If these measurements are cubed the relative volumes are 1 : 18 962 962.

Since beetles are abundant as well as diverse, they must take first place as the most successful of all insects. While not the oldest surviving insects, they are known as fossils from Permian deposits, when they were just about the same as they are today. In fact, looking at beetles, one wonders what evolution was all about. Are all the other insects necessary? Yet even beetles have their limitations, mainly through their innate conservatism. They have stuck to the primitive biting mouthparts, and although they have exploited this equipment more fully than any other insects, they have not developed any true sucking forms, like those of Diptera, Lepidoptera and Hymenoptera, or the several other orders that we have discussed earlier.

Nor have beetles made great use of wings. Most beetles can, and do, fly, but with the hind-wings only, and not particularly well, nor readily (Fig. 40). Most of the time their wings are kept folded under the forewings, which are hardened into wing-cases (elytra). Even the biggest beetles, such as the Stag Beetles (*Lucanus cervus*) can take to the air, but in a heavy, rather bumbling way. In fact one most often notices and recognizes a flying beetle by its loud noise and heavy flight, with the elytra held up in the air.

The feeding habits of beetles can only be described as 'diverse'. They eat so many things

that it is probably easiest to say what they do *not* eat! They do not pierce to suck blood of either vertebrates or invertebrates. The nearest they get to this is the carnivorous larvae of the water beetle *Dytiscus*, where deep grooves in the mandibles are used to inject saliva into a victim, and then to suck up the liquefied tissues. Although there is a special term (canthariasis) for the invasion of the human body by beetles, this is scarcely ever a normal part of a beetle's life cycle. Larder beetles (*Dermestes*), and others that breed in stored products, are sometimes accidentally swallowed, and others may crawl into the anus, attracted by faecal matter. The most common cause of complaint is irritation, or even blistering, of the skin after accidental contact with a beetle or its larva. Many beetles have chemical irritants in their body fluids, and can expel droplets of these as a defence mechanism against predators: for example blister beetles (Cantharidae). If touched, they may react in this way as a defensive reflex.

Only one family of beetles is parasitic. Rhipidophoridae members are parasites of the larvae of aculeate Hymenoptera, and show that

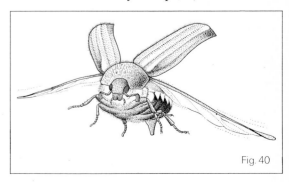

Fig. 40

this is no chance association by having the common parasitic adaptation of hypermetamorphosis. The first stage larva is an active planidium, which seeks out the host larva, whereas the later instar larvae are legless grubs. Apart from this one family, only a few isolated species of Coleoptera can be said to be parasitic, mainly externally, in the fur of mammals.

Although water beetles are sufficiently numerous to be a study in themselves, none of them is truly aquatic. They are air-breathing insects that hunt for food under water, but need to take their oxygen in gaseous form. There are two ways of doing this: either breathing through spiracles at the tip of the abdomen, which can be applied to the water surface, perhaps assisted by a respiratory siphon; or taking down a bubble of air for underwater consumption. Beetles of both groups need to come to the surface periodically to renew their supply of air, and at that time they are conspicuous when they are motionless at the surface. One subfamily of beetles, Donaciinae, avoids this risk by piercing the stems of underwater plants, and have the siphon specially stiffened and pointed for this purpose. These stems often contain bubbles of oxygen generated by photosynthesis.

Even allowing for their successful incursion into water, beetles are still characteristically terrestrial insects, and ground living at that. They always give the impression that their flights are temporary expedients to get them from one place to another, and that they fold their wings again with relief! This may be linked with the difficulty of folding the wings to pack them away under the elytra. The more perfectly the elytra close over the abdomen and convert the beetle into a sort of insect tank, the less the beetle seems to fly. It may be that beetles have sacrificed some of the advantages of ready flight for the protective value of the elytra. Many beetles have become flightless, even though wings are still present, and others have lost the wings entirely, and even locked the two elytra together.

The larvae of beetles have chewing mouthparts like the adults (with the exception of the larvae of Dytiscidae, as noted earlier), and their bodies reflect the activity or otherwise of the larva. Active larvae like those of tiger beetles (Cicindelidae) have three pairs of well-developed thoracic legs, and move about readily; the less active the larvae, the more their legs and other external features are reduced, leading to the C-shaped grubs of stag beetles, which have a well-developed head and thoracic legs, attached to a soft, baggy white abdomen; and in the extreme, to completely legless larvae of weevils (Curculionidae), which live hidden away inside plant tissues, seeds or grain.

The story of the beetles is one of a basically simple plan, subjected to almost infinite modification in detail. If the bodily structure of an insect is looked upon as a tool for living, there is a parallel in the tools man uses. He can either choose simple, all-purpose tools, such as hammers and pliers, with many varieties of each; or he can have special tools for the tasks concerned, which will be useless or at least inefficient for other purposes. The evolution of insects must have seen many of the latter, which served their possessors well until conditions changed, but then led them to extinction.

The long survival, and continued success, of the beetles is a testimony to the advantages of the simple approach.

The future of insects

Having spent some time trying to assess the relative success of the insects of the present day, and to look for underlying causes, it is tempting to speculate what may happen to insects in future. Evolution is the story of adaptation, the ability to meet the demands of the contemporary environment, and to adjust to its changes as time goes on. It is now possible to alter the physical environment much more quickly than man has ever been able to do before, to make changes in a few years, months or even weeks, that in the past needed long aeons of time. We can now make a dust bowl in a fraction of the time that it took for increasing aridity to destroy the grasslands of the Near East.

Consequently, insects and all other forms of life are under evolutionary pressures as a result of changes in land use brought about by man. In the past, his small efforts in cultivation have tended to increase the diversity of insect life, by breaking up large areas of forest, marsh or heath, and creating a mosaic of varied vegetation. The scale of present developments in agriculture and in urbanization is already wiping out much of this mosaic, replacing it with large areas of one crop, and changing the climatic pattern over large areas, or at least making the vegetational cover more vulnerable to climatic fluctuation. The pace of possible change increases all the time.

A more immediate effect of human activities is that wherever man goes he creates new, artificial environments in which insects may breed. These include 'container habitats' (a polite name for old cans, bottles, plastic containers), as well as the many derelict areas left when buildings are pulled down, or agricultural land taken over for roads. These habitats are soon colonized by weeds, and after them come the insects. The number of insects we eliminate by medical and hygienic methods is tiny compared with those we shall encourage by providing them with new habitats.

So the future, however uncertain for men, is bright for insects. Nothing short of total destruction of the planet will kill all the insects, and the survivors will evolve as successfully as ever. There may, however, be a shift of balance, from structural evolution, which takes a long time under a steady evolutionary pressure, to functional, physiological evolution, which is more rapid. We have seen this already in the way in which insects quickly become immune to new insecticides. The susceptible individuals are killed off, leaving the few immune survivors with a clear field, and soon there is a new popu-

Seven-spot Lady-bird (*Coccinella septem-punctatum*) emerging from the pupal case.

lation that is nearly all immune. Insects are particularly well equipped to profit from this sort of natural selection, because they lay so many eggs, and so few individuals survive to reproduce anyway. A change of environmental conditions merely means that a different set of more suit-able individuals are the ones to survive.

Future evolution in insects is most likely to come from those that breed most rapidly, and make the maximum use of both young and adult stages: aphids, beetles, flies. These are the insects that will need watching.

183

Insects and Man

Introduction

To the majority of people the insect world is associated with fields, flowers, trees and the countryside in general. While this conception is true for the vast majority of insects, there are many species which affect man directly and indirectly by invading his home, crops, barns and food stores and even attacking him personally.

Insects are the chief competitors of man for the domination of this planet. But it is only in the last one hundred years that man has developed a conscious realization of insect diversity. Linnaeus, in the mid-eighteenth century developed a system of classifying animals and plants but it was not until over one hundred years later, after the publication of Darwin's *Origin of Species,* that the importance of insects to health and economy began to be realized.

In the late nineteenth century Manson showed that filaria worms which cause elephantiasis are carried by mosquitoes, and the insect's association with malaria and yellow fever came about at the turn of the century.

Insects destroy man's growing crops and defoliate his forests. They are the vectors of micro-organisms which cause nearly all the major fevers of the tropics and the infection of man's livestock with fatal diseases. The timbers of man's buildings are attacked by insects, his stored grain and food are consumed and his household goods are invaded.

An insect pest is one that has become too numerous for man's comfort or has become a threat to his interests. Under ordinary circumstances insects, like other animals and plants, are kept in a state of balance or equilibrium by natural controlling factors, which include food

Food spoilage by insects: Common Wasps (*Vespula vulgaris*) eating a pear.

Large White (*Pieris brassicae*) larvae on a cabbage. This is one of the most destructive of all butterflies.

supply, disease, parasites, predators and weather conditions. Man is probably the greatest disturber of this balance, often providing conditions for a species to multiply, when it would not have done so on its own. Sometimes, like in an agricultural monoculture, alien insects may be introduced without their full range of enemies, for example, the Colorado Beetle.

Having brought about a state of affairs prejudicial to his own activities, man then has to control the situation. This he does by chemical or biological means. The overzealous use of insecticides has proved that total warfare endangers not only the insect pests but beneficial insects and thereby man himself. Biological methods of control are slower to show results but can be practised at low cost. The biologist aims to restore and maintain the natural balance among insect populations based on scientific study of the insect and the crop. An example of biological control was the introduction of the Australian ladybird into California to control the cottony cushion scale insect. However, perhaps the best hope lies in further research into the relative merits of control methods.

These same insects can live independently in the wild but because man creates ideal environments in which they can feed and reproduce, obviously they find these conditions preferable and breed rapidly. It is then that we think of these same insects as pests because they are in competition with man for his food supply.

Each year thousands of tonnes of food grown for man and his animals are destroyed by insects. In a world with an ever increasing population, the economics of this problem are very serious. It is not surprising therefore that vast amounts of money are spent on research into ways and means of combating pests. In a book published in 1967 entitled *Plant Protection and World Crop Protection*, the author, H. H. Cramer, estimated that the world expenditure on pesticides at that time was in excess of $1 000 million a year.

Fortunately for us less than 1 per cent of the nearly one million known species of insects are pests and these fall into two groups, those whose life cycle is completed on a crop used either directly by man or fed to domesticated animals and those species which attack man or his animals directly. In a great many instances the latter are responsible for the transmission of disease organisms such as those which cause malaria and sleeping sickness in man. Within this group can also be included insects which, although they are not actual carriers of disease, nevertheless are troublesome by making living and working conditions unpleasant, for example, the biting midges occurring in some northern areas of Canada, Britain and Scandinavia. Although they are present for only a brief period of a month or two each year, they can be a serious problem to those living and working in these regions.

185

Pests of stored products

The complete cycle of the agricultural year from seed sowing to the harvest when the crop is, to all intents and purposes, safely in the store, is very much in favour of the insects. In these days of intensive agriculture it is not very easy to establish the origins of the pests now able to plague the farmer by invading barns, silos, etc. Food storage areas, however large or small, have had their quota of uninvited guests for a very long time. Stone Age man in his attempts to conserve the results of his efforts at food gathering in times of plenty, established caches which could be resorted to in times of stress. Insects also found these food stores to their advantage. Whereas only a few seeds or grains might be found in a bird's or mammal's nest – the result of food gathering by the animal – here in the man-made store was food in relative abundance. As man became more and more involved in agricultural practice and grew larger amounts of harvestable crops, so the need to store large amounts became inevitable. The result was an increase in both the numbers and species of insects taking advantage of this situation.

The evidence for these attacks on food stored by man in the distant past is to be found in the votive offerings placed in the burial chambers of the kings and warriors, from time to time unearthed in archaeological 'digs'. The departments of antiquities in various museums throughout the world contain examples of such offerings damaged by grain weevils and similar insects together with the identifiable remains of the invaders.

From the natural habitat which the insects occupied many centuries ago, there has developed a vast population of some 150 species now infesting man's food. The crop is attacked either at harvest or immediately afterwards and this results in about one-quarter of the world's food supply being destroyed, estimated at a figure in excess of $25 000 million. During the years of this century alone man has increased the problem by developing rapid means of transportation from one country to another and thereby inadvertently introducing the pest species to new areas.

The problem of damage from storage insects is always more serious in tropical climates owing to the conditions favouring continuous breeding. Grain in some form – wheat, barley, rice, maize or sorghum – forms the staple diet of the world's population and all of these are attacked by species of grain weevil (*Sitophilus* spp). In tropical regions the adult weevil lays her eggs in the ripening grain in the field. To do this she bores into a grain with her proboscis. Having made a hole of the right proportion, she lays an egg in it, which is then covered with a gelatinous substance, sealing the hole. On hatching the legless larva bores into the kernel and completes its growth inside the grain (Fig. 41) where it pupates and eventually emerges as an adult weevil in the stored grain. In the warm conditions of, for example, South-East Asia, this whole cycle from egg-laying to adult emergence

Grain Weevil (*Sitophilus granarius*) a common pest of stored whole grain.

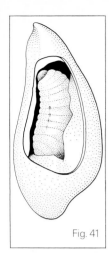

Fig. 41

Fig. 41 Cut away section of grain to show grain weevil larva inside.

Bruchid eggs – seen as white dots on peas.

could be as short as twenty-six days. The adult weevil can live as long as four to five months and during that period lay between 300 and 400 eggs within the harvested grain. We can see from this the seriousness of the problem, for under these conditions the destruction of the stored grains is a very rapid and continuous process. It has been demonstrated that Kaffir Corn (*Sorghum vulgare*) remains palatable for only three months after it has been harvested under tropical conditions due to taint from insect infestation.

Some of the insects found in association with man's food such as flour beetles and flour moths are more at home with the processed products. As their common name suggests they are usually to be found in a flour mill or food manufacturing plant. The Mediterranean Flour Moth (*Ephestia kühniella*) has been known as a serious pest of flour mills since 1877 when it was first reported from Germany. It appeared for the first time in the United States in 1892. Now it has spread to all parts of the world. Normally we associate the term 'moth' with a large spectacular night-flying insect possibly coming in through an open window on a warm summer night, attracted to the light. The species infesting stored foods are all small and of a dull fawn or grey colour. The adult has a wingspan of slightly less than 2 cm. Eggs are laid in accumulations of flour, such as occur around the base of machinery. These hatch in a few days and the larvae feed in the flour debris, crawling into ducting and milling machinery. Wherever they crawl, the larvae spin

silken threads and these in time mat together causing the clogging of machines and blockages in ducts and flour chutes, seriously disrupting the efficient working of the mill. The larvae are about 1 cm long when fully grown and pinkish white. The total developmental time from egg to adult during summer conditions is about eight weeks.

In addition to cereals, seeds of legumes (beans, peas, etc.) are an important item of diet. In Africa the cowpea is grown widely by local farmers as a cash crop. Among the most important pests attacking it both before and after harvest are the seed beetles (Bruchidae). Their eggs are laid attached either to the ripened pod or the harvested seed. The egg is an ovoid structure which the female attaches to the seed with a sticky secretion. This hardens to a covering resistant to damage. When ready to hatch, the young larva bites its way through the seed-coat and into the cotyledons arching its back against the top of the eggshell to obtain a grip with its mandibles.

The commonest species *Callosobruchus maculatus* is a rather square chestnut brown beetle 3–4 mm long with two black spots, one on each side of the elytra. These beetles are characterized by having very broad hindlegs. Each adult lays sixty to seventy eggs, sometimes depositing several on one seed. In store, the succeeding generations continue to breed until all the food reserves are used up. This species originated in the Old World continents of Africa and Asia and through the agency of man has spread through-

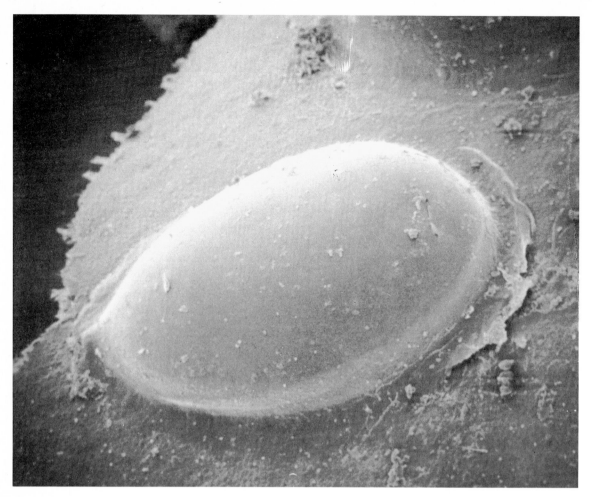

out all tropical and subtropical regions. Losses from insects of this type can be considerable. In Nigeria alone estimates of some 250 000 tonnes of cowpeas lost each year through damage by bruchid beetles are recorded.

So far we have only looked at the attackers of food but pests also invade valuable products found in warehouses. Possibly the most notorious of the non-food pests is the Tobacco or Cigarette Beetle (*Lasioderma serricorne*). This insect is found throughout the world wherever tobacco is grown and processed. The adult, a small oval yellowish red beetle about 1 mm long, lays its eggs in dried tobacco leaves from the time they are packed together into bales after curing. For those people concerned with the manufacture of cigars and cigarettes, the most troublesome period is after the finished product is put into store. One adult female lays as many as 100 eggs and each of these hatches into a small cream-coloured larva. The damage each insect does in the period from hatching to pupation can be quite considerable and in the warm conditions of an artificially heated store, the complete cycle takes only about six weeks.

Similar in size and appearance is the Drug-Store Beetle (*Stegobium paniceum*). Although not considered to be of such economic importance it is nevertheless interesting because of its curious feeding habits. It has been recorded as breeding on a variety of highly toxic drugs such as the dried roots of the plant from which strychnine is extracted and the root of *Loncho-*

carpus nicou var. utilis which, when ground up, gives the very useful insecticide 'derris'. As this beetle and its larvae are capable of eating any dried plant material, it can be a serious pest in the herbarium collections of botanical gardens and museums throughout the world.

With so many insects capable of causing loss to food and other products in store, man has attempted many methods of control. Going back to classical times we find numerous methods used to try to prevent pest attack. Before there was any conception of the life cycle of insects and their behaviour, pest attack was attributed to the work of displeased gods. Consequently it was imagined that rituals involving suitable sacrifices, prayers and incantations would prevent an attack or at least rid the owner of the crop or produce of the pest. Magic and witchcraft also played their part and still do in some remote areas of the world. Toads have formed part of magic ritual: just before harvest a toad was secured by one hindleg in the empty barn to keep the weevil away from the grain.

The methods used to prevent attack were not all so futile. The archaeologist has brought to light evidence of pit storage of grain and other foods in the very early days of civilization. Varro in the first century said that wheat stored in a pit, known as siri, from which we derive our word silo, would last fifty years and millet as long as a hundred years. There is a record of beans stored in what was presumed to be a pit in the first and second centuries BC for 220 years.

This technique of storage in underground pits was practised widely and these ancient pits can still be seen in the Middle East, parts of Africa and South America today. In the Mediterranean region some of them are still used in the same way by villagers. While this method of storage had the obvious advantage of keeping food stored safely out of sight of thieves and enemies, the quality of the product was greatly improved providing the siting of the pit was suitable.

The principle of pit storage is to prevent the ingress of oxygen so that insects and other pests such as vermin die by the increase of the products of their own respiration, i.e. the production of carbon dioxide. The effectiveness of the pits in achieving this varied enormously. If a pit was dug in hard impervious rock and with a small entrance, then the possibilities were high. In soft rock, such as sandstone, it would be well nigh impossible to exclude air from permeating the walls and any inherent infestation would continue to breed unhindered.

Trial and error must have entered into the early methods of control and many different techniques are recorded as pest preventatives which were the forerunners of our modern methods. Dressing of seeds with a mixture of soda and the black lees of olive oil supposedly gave protection against the bruchid beetles. Also the admixing of laurel leaves with seed was used as a protectant. Laurel gives off small amounts of hydrocyanic acid which would have some short-term effect on the insects.

The advent of really effective pest control had to await the advancement of other sciences namely chemistry and physics. In the early 1700s Italian and French researchers devised means whereby grain could be protected by heating after harvest to destroy any insects already there. It was by now realized that the factor of moisture content played an important role in either maintaining or preventing the development of the insect pest. Most control however still concentrated on field pests and it was not until the Second World War that the United Kingdom became seriously involved in the stored products' pest problems. Since that time great strides have been made.

It was found then that the foodstuffs stored in warehouses, at ports, etc., were infested to a fairly high degree. Coupled with this and contributing extensively to the spread of infestation, were the poor hygiene principles adopted by the owners. The need in wartime to conserve food is paramount and consequently a great campaign was launched to try to improve the situation. At this time it was fortuitous that a new and powerful insecticide was found and put to very effective use. This came to be known as DDT due to its long chemical name. At the time nothing was known about insect resistance to chemicals which developed as a result of vast quantities being sprayed and dusted in warehouses, stores, mills and farms. Since that time the problem of resistance has increased although initially these chemicals were very effective.

Further new chemicals in the armoury against pests were developed, first of all based on the same group, the hydrocarbons, to be followed later by the organo-phosphorus group. Without these insecticides man would undoubtedly have been considerably worse off in his battle to conserve his harvested crops.

Unfortunately, although the numbers of insects killed in pest eradication programmes were considerable, a nucleus of resistant insects survived each year to continue the population, building up a resistant stock. The alternative was to use another insecticide but in some instances the resistance built up against DDT was effective against other chemicals also.

Another technique developed and still employed today to great effect is fumigation. Produce stored in bulk, either after harvest or as a result of transhipment, may consist of several thousand tonnes of one commodity. To fumigate such a huge consignment a sheet or series of sheets made of a material impervious to gas are thrown over the stacks and sealed with heavy weights. Gas is introduced at the top of the stack or pile which sinks slowly down throughout the stack. The gas most commonly employed is methyl bromide although in certain circumstances a newer and more convenient material, phosphine, is used. Phosphine can be applied in tablet form to the stack after it is built or distributed within the bulk of grain as it is piled up. The material from which the tablet is made absorbs atmospheric moisture and combines to give off the gas which is lethal to insects.

The advantage of fumigation is that it does not leave residues of chemicals in the food that have to be removed before the food can be processed.

All of these methods of control add to the cost of the food by the time it reaches the consumer. The most effective answer is to start with a clean crop at harvest, put into a clean store, thus reducing the potential losses.

Domestic insects

By the utilization of materials around him for his personal needs, man has created the domestic pest problem. The wood from the forest used to construct his dwelling, the skins, furs and feathers of animals which he utilizes, all have their natural complement of insect scavengers. These have, over time, become more and more linked with man so that it is difficult now to find some of them in their natural habitat. Their function is to assist in the natural breakdown and decay of animal and plant material. Because we have chosen to use these products we must expect the normal processes to continue.

Man has used animal fibres as the basis of his clothing ever since he learnt to spin and weave. The natural food of the larvae of both the carpet beetle and the clothes moth is animal fur and feathers from birds, and they can be found in most regions of the world in the nests of birds and mammals, particularly those constructed in a sheltered situation and which invariably have a lining of furs or feathers. In some instances they can also be found feeding on the fur or feathers of a dead animal or bird. Their association with man has been due to an adaptation to his way of life. Before there were convenient eaves and holes in the walls of buildings for nesting, birds, such as the sparrow and starling, nested in holes in trees and crevices in rocks, indeed some still do.

In a domestic dwelling the larvae of the Varied Carpet Beetle (*Anthrenus verbasci*) in particular, wander from nests under the eaves where the beetle lays her eggs, and find their way into the home, usually via the airing cupboard, because it has holes to the loft through which water pipes pass. Airing cupboards usually contain some garments or bed coverings made from animal fibre, a food the growing larvae find very edible! Should they crawl beyond this area (and they crawl a long way for such small insects which when fully grown measure only 2 mm long), then carpets and rugs with wool fibres are attacked. The first thing the householder usually knows about this is when a small round hole appears in a garment or the pile of the carpet comes out where it has been eaten off from below. Fortunately, nowadays, the majority of the wool fibres used in clothing and more particularly those used for carpets, are treated with insecticides during the manufacturing process. Any insect feeding on such treated material will soon ingest enough to kill it. Problems arise however with the protection of valuable old carpets and furniture coverings to be found in museums and stately homes open to the public.

Carpet Beetle (*An-threnus verbasci*) larval damage to a museum specimen. Note long pupae in the centre of the picture.

Although such items can be treated there is always the danger of damage to the delicate colours, to say nothing of the cost.

Wood has always figured largely in the construction of dwellings and other buildings until recent years. It is the least durable of all building materials and is subject to attack by insects and fungi, sometimes a combination of both. Insect attack on wood in buildings, and also furniture, has only come to be recognized as an important factor in the deterioration of timbers within the last fifty or so years, whereas the decay of wood, due to fungi, has been recognized since earliest times.

One of the first insects to be drawn to the public attention was the Death Watch Beetle (*Xestobium ruffovilosum*), due mainly to the fact that it attacks large baulks of timber such as that used in main supporting structures of large historic buildings and churches. The beetle, 6–9 mm long, is the largest of the British Anobiidae, the group responsible for the bulk of damage to timbers and furniture.

The name 'death watch' has been used because of the tapping sound produced by the beetles of both sexes in the tunnels during the mating season from March to June and has nothing to do with the coincidental association of these insects with churches.

The natural habitat of the Death Watch Beetle is the decaying branches or parts of the trunks of a number of hardwood trees, the most commonly infested species being oak and willow although it has been recorded in, among others, ash, beech and hornbeam. In buildings the damage is found frequently in oak mainly because this was the favourite timber of the builders in earlier centuries.

The distribution and dispersion of this insect is fascinating because it very rarely, if ever, flies although it has well developed wings. On emergence from the wood and after mating, it is inconceivable that the female beetle would walk to another building with suitable timber in the right condition in order to lay its eggs. Such buildings are usually well scattered, certainly at a greater distance than the beetle would normally be expected to travel. It is therefore reasonable to suppose that all buildings infested by this insect have had the infestation since the time of construction which may be several centuries. In this connection it is interesting to record that some of the roof timbers of Westminster Hall, erected in 1394, when examined in 1913 were found to be nothing more than hollow shells. It is presumed that the infestation had been present in some timbers when the roof was erected some 500 years previously.

Dr R. C. Fisher working at what was then called The Forest Products Research Laboratory, found that the life cycle of the beetle was dependent on the scale of decay in the wood, caused by fungi, coupled with temperature and humidity. The higher the temperature and humidity, the more rapid the growth of the fungi and the shorter the life cycle of the beetle. Therefore under the cold dry conditions found in the roof spaces of some of the historic buildings in Britain, the life cycle could be very prolonged and this would account for the great period of time which has elapsed before any collapse of the roof timbers.

The Death Watch Beetle is not seen very often by the public and is usually only brought to their attention by appeals for funds to restore the damage caused by its larvae! It is however much more common than is realized. In a survey carried out by one of the leading control companies between 1960 and 1965, 6 000 infestations were recorded and this number almost equals the number of historic buildings and churches examined. The highest distribution is in south-west and central-southern England with a general decline as one goes northwards.

Apart from man who attempts to control it by removing infested timbers and spraying with insecticides, the Death Watch Beetle has two natural enemies, both beetles, *Opilo mollis* and *Korynetes caeruleus*. The larvae of these beetles are predacious on the larvae of the Death Watch Beetle. From evidence at present available, these insects do not appear to exert any real influence on the latter's control.

Another, equally destructive, common species in this group of wood borers is the Common Furniture Beetle (*Anobium punctatum*). It is much smaller than the Death Watch Beetle being only 2·5–4·5 mm long and widely distributed throughout the British Isles and the whole of northern, central and eastern Europe. As the name suggests, it attacks furniture as well as timber in buildings. Since 1945 it has increased to become a pest of major importance in the

UK. This fact is reflected in the large number of servicing companies carrying out treatments against it – the cause of about 80 per cent of their infestation problems.

The Common Furniture Beetle has now been recorded from all temperate parts of the world and it is suggested that it reached South Africa, Australia and New Zealand by the importation into those countries of infested articles of furniture, packing cases, etc.

The adult insect emerges in May or June and lives about four weeks during which period the female can lay up to eighty eggs, either singly or in rows of two, three or four. The eggs, described as lemon-shaped, are deposited in cracks, crevices and the rough end grain of timber; in fact almost any fissure big enough to receive an egg.

Most of the infestations found in buildings have a life cycle of three years or more depending on temperature, the nature of the wood and its moisture content. The Common Furniture Beetle is not, like the Death Watch Beetle, entirely dependent on the presence of some fungal agent decaying the wood. All of the softwoods in common use, together with most of the traditional hardwoods of Europe, are attacked. This insect is also particularly attracted to the older plywoods which utilized animal glue. The modern forms of ply, together with resin-bonded chipboard, are, it appears, immune to attack.

In connection with the Common Furniture Beetle it is worth quoting again from the published records of surveys carried out in the UK for the five-and-a-half years ending December 1965. These showed that about 75 per cent of all the 142 270 buildings surveyed had infestations by this insect with the greatest percentage concentrated south of a line from the Severn to the Wash.

There are many other species of minor importance which can infest timber. Concern is aroused by the appearance of a large oval hole, some 8–10 mm long in what otherwise appears to be sound, perhaps fairly old, furniture. One such species is on record as having emerged from a table thirty-two years after it had been manufactured. Fortunately these occurrences are rare and are mostly associated with hardwood imported from abroad. The long life cycle does emphasize the poor nutritional quality of some woods.

In order to assist in the breakdown of cellulose, the gut of some of these insects contains a symbiotic organism. The true gain to the insect from the presence of this is however not wholly understood.

Another group notorious for their destruction of wood are the termites (see also 'The Lives of Insects', page 118 and 'The Orders of Insects', page 206) of which some 1 800 species have been described. The majority of these are found only in tropical regions. Of the two or three European species, all are found in the Mediterranean region. The destruction of timber by these insects has brought them into very close contact with man who uses wood extensively.

The termites have a remarkable social system (see 'The Lives of Insects', page 118 and 'The Orders of Insects', page 206). The young termites on hatching are smaller additions of their older relatives. These are termed 'juveniles' and make up the larger part of a colony.

Termites, in common with a number of other insects, pass through a series of moults as they grow. How the young termite will develop is not a foregone conclusion fixed by hereditary genes, as in most insects, but is dependent on the type of food it eats coupled with the treatment received from other members of the colony. This combination determines the forms that arise in the community known as 'castes'.

The most easily recognizable of these are the 'soldiers' because of their excessively large heads and jaws. Soldiers have either very small eyes or none at all. As the name suggests, they function as guards in the colony, mainly at the entrance. The 'workers' who make up the bulk of the population and into which group most of the juveniles grow, have wing pads – the points from which wings could arise although they do not normally develop. The workers build the nest and repair it as necessary, gather eggs from the royal chamber and distribute them throughout the nest, bring food to the queen and king, and feed those young too small to fend for themselves.

The wood-feeding species have difficulty in obtaining sufficient nutrition, as the cells from which the timber is composed are very resistant to breakdown and it is in these cell walls that the nutriment of the wood lies. To overcome this the workers continuously reingest faecal pellets of other termites and with the help of special protozoa in the gut, the maximum amount of nutrition is derived from the wood. The dry wood infesting species *Kalotermes flavicollis* continue feeding in timber and reingesting until all that is left is a crumbling mass of dust.

The sexually mature 'reproductives' make up the remaining caste. These arise from time to time as winged forms which leave the original colony on a nuptial flight to found their own colony elsewhere. If either of the 'royal pair' should die, substitutes arise from within the colony by a worker or workers becoming sexually mature and taking over the duty of the dead member of the pair.

How these castes develop within a colony is still not clear but recent experiments have shown that the control of development of the 'reproductive' substitutes is governed by an inhibitory substance called a pheromone, produced by the 'royal pair'. Artificial exclusion of the 'royal pair' from the colony or even isolation from the remainder (by a barrier), providing they do not have physical contact, will enable substitutes to take over. Immediately any barrier is removed or the 'royal pair' reinstated, any substitutes would be killed and eaten. From this it can be established that a suppression of the development of any reproductive caste, except for the purpose of dispersal from the colony to found new ones elsewhere, is determined by the production of this inhibitory pheromone. As ter-mites are known to feed on the faeces of others, including those produced by the 'royal pair', the pheromone produced by them is passed from one to another with sufficient absorption by the individual to be effective.

The other castes have their numbers made up by a transformation process as yet not understood. Whatever the process, the colony somehow regulates its numbers of individuals in each caste according to its needs.

Although termites have been considered in the same context as wood-boring insects, this has no bearing on their zoological relationship. Their nearest relatives are the cockroaches, largely inhabitants of warm climates where numerous species are found throughout the world. In their natural habitats they live as secretive insects under stones, fallen trees and leaf litter on the forest floor, emerging after dark to feed on a wide variety of animal and vegetable matter. This could be dead insects, animal excrements, seeds and fruits from forest trees.

Man has been instrumental in transporting several species throughout the world to regions where they are not indigenous. The most frequently found species is the American or Ship's Cockroach (*Periplaneta americana*), an insect of about 4 cm in length and the Oriental Cockroach (*Blatta orientalis*) 2·5 cm long. They have been imported into Europe in sacks of food, packing cases, in fact anything providing shelter. Having arrived they became established in bakeries, kitchens and indeed any warm sheltered situation which would also provide food.

The adult female lays her eggs in a small case called an ootheca which she carries about attached to the body for some time. This protects the eggs from physical damage and also excessive heat and dryness. The young cockroach on emerging from the egg looks like a miniature version of its parents except that it has no wings.

It is not the amount of food these insects eat, even though they are comparatively large, but the fouling they cause wherever they go, which is the problem. Cockroaches emit a very unpleasant odour detectable long after they have departed, so that they have become detested wherever they occur. Modern hygienic methods of cleaning together with improved construction techniques have gone a long way to alleviate the problem. But modern building complexes of offices and hospitals with interconnecting underground ducting carrying services from a central point, have proved to be an ideal hiding and breeding place of the 'roaches' where control is well nigh impossible.

In these unnatural environments they will turn to almost anything for food. There are records of cockroaches attacking the leather bindings of valuable books in order to get at the paste used to stick them. One botanic garden had a problem when blooms of orchids disappeared mysteriously overnight from their display house. This was eventually tracked down to a population of cockroaches which emerged after dark to enjoy the feast. Sometimes their feeding habits can cause serious concern

when, for instance, they gnaw at the plastic covering of electric and telephone cables in buildings.

Another insect very much associated with houses is the cricket, immortalized in the phrase 'The cricket on the hearth'. Nowadays it is very rare to hear this sound so familiar earlier this century.

The cricket (*Acheta domesticus*) is a pale straw-coloured insect with a body about 1 cm long. The insect is always associated, like the cockroach, with warm places, hence the hearth and the region surrounding the oven of the old bakehouses. The chirping sound made by the male is produced by rubbing the wings together.

Some twenty years ago crickets were also to be found in very large numbers swarming over rubbish tips surrounding large towns, the warmth of the fermenting waste material being an ideal breeding ground. A change in the methods of treating the rubbish, i.e. either by the application of insecticides and rapid coverage with soil, or by incineration, has destroyed this habitat.

Now that the kitchen range and the old style bakeries have given way to modern methods of baking, the familiar sound of 'The cricket on the hearth' is a thing of the past.

While we may lament the disappearance of the cricket, no one would regret the reduction in numbers of that major nuisance in the home — the Common House-fly (*Musca domestica*). In all parts of the world house-flies live and breed in close association with man. In these days of enlightened thinking and knowledge of disease caused by bacteria, etc., the word house-fly has come to be regarded as synonymous with disease.

The larva is a smooth creamy-white maggot up to 1 cm long when fully grown. The female fly lays her eggs in any mass of decomposing organic matter and the heat generated by the bacteria in their action of decomposition is sufficient to enable the larvae to develop, usually taking six to seven days to become fully grown. They will breed in dung, rotting vegetable matter or the body of a dead bird or mammal, the only proviso being that it must remain moist. When fully grown the larva turns into a brown barrel-shaped pupa. The pupal state is achieved by the shrinkage and hardening of the last larval skin. In a few days the adult fly emerges. After mating, the female will lay up to 2 000 eggs and the whole cycle is completed again in seventeen to eighteen days. During cold periods of the year, the flies or their puparia become dormant and only emerge when warm conditions return.

Adult flies can feed only on liquid therefore they break down solid matter by saliva which flows down their extended tube-like mouthparts. These mouthparts have splayed out ends for increased efficiency. It matters not whether the fly is feeding on a heap of dung, a dead animal or uncovered food in the kitchen, the same principle applies. It is important to realize that by the very nature of their feeding habits, flies carry bacteria responsible for a number of diseases in man — typhoid fever, cholera and infantile diarrhoea to name but a few. These disease-causing organisms, apart from lodging on the feet of the fly, also adhere to hairs distributed over the whole body. When indulging in periodic bouts of cleaning, the fly brushes off any particles adhering to the body and as this toilet operation may take place on food which is intended for human consumption, the prospect is not very pleasant. From this it can be seen that it is not so much the larvae which are the

194

Blow-flies of the family Calliphoridae seen here on dead fish.

problem (they do perform a useful function in nature in the breakdown of waste material) but the continuous movement of the flies between their filthy breeding sites and places where food is kept and prepared.

The great distance a house-fly can travel contributes considerably to the spread of disease organisms. Experiments conducted in America have shown that flies can travel up to five miles within twenty-four hours from their place of origin and given time they may reach up to twenty miles. They are also known to follow refuse-collecting vehicles for considerable distances. This constant movement means that, having controlled a population of flies in a given place, there is always a fresh population ready to move in and take its place.

The house-fly was one of the first insects in which resistance to DDT was noted after the Second World War. This presented a serious problem to the people concerned with the control of public health insects. Nowadays the chemical armoury is more varied and current insecticides include BHC (benzenehexachloride) and pyrethrins. A high proportion of the household insecticides contain the latter. Pyrethrin is based on an extract from the flowers of pyrethrum (*Chrysanthemum cinerariifolium*). It has no residual action and therefore the spray must hit the insect to be effective.

In the home and places where food is prepared or sold it is essential that any chemical used for insect control must not be toxic to humans. Pyrethrins fulfilled that role. They were however expensive to extract and produce. The flowers can only be grown successfully in an area of high light intensity and sufficiently high temperature. The chemical manufacturers having analysed the pyrethrins, made a synthetic version that acted in basically the same way, but more efficiently. In addition, it is easier to produce in larger quantities. In spite of this, the battle against the house-fly continues.

Insects of medical importance to man

The use of the description 'medical importance' in connection with insects immediately brings to mind the thoughts of disease. The causative agents of disease were unknown to man until comparatively recent times. The perfection of the microscope enabled the scientist Sir Ronald Ross, at the turn of the century, to discover the members of the Haemosporidia which invaded the bloodstream of men and women and caused the condition known as malaria. Although it was a great step forward to find the causative agent, what had to follow was the knowledge of how the disease was transmitted from one person to another.

Gradually it became apparent that insects of various types were involved in the transmission of disease. All insects which act as vectors of disease have one thing in common – their method of feeding. In order to infect man, the bacteria, virus or protozoa must enter the bloodstream. The insects with which they are associated feed on blood and to do this they have mouthparts to pierce the skin.

Anyone who has felt the needle-like stylets of a mosquito on the bare skin will know the effect only too well. We refer to this as having been 'bitten'. This is not strictly true because the insect has not used teeth to inflict the wound but pierced the skin with the specially modified mouthparts called 'stylets'. At the same time it injects saliva into the wound causing the irritation we experience. The reaction of the skin and blood vessels below it to this injection varies from person to person, some having a strong reaction in which the area around the 'bite' swells and the irritation lasts a long time. Temperate zones are fortunate in not having problems of disease transmission by the mosquito. In certain parts of the tropics it is a very different picture.

Entomologists refer to mosquitoes as belonging to one of two groups, anopheline or culicine (Fig. 42). The difference refers specifically to the adults although there are well marked distinctions in the larvae. The anopheline female has very long legs so that when 'biting' her victim she has to adopt an almost vertical stance, her head being virtually at right angles to the surface on which she is standing. It is the anopheline group which is particularly responsible for the transmission of the malaria parasite. The

Fig. 42

female of the culicine type can be distinguished by her much shorter legs and consequently her body is parallel to the surface while feeding.

The mosquitoes entering buildings or flying around the outside are invariably females as the male does not 'bite' and is rarely seen.

The life cycle of the mosquito in any part of the world is inextricably bound up with the presence of water. The female mosquito deposits her eggs either singly or in small clusters upon the surface of a pool or on an object very close to the water. The larvae are commonly known as 'wrigglers' from their method of swimming by jerking their bodies through the water. At frequent intervals the larva floats to the

197

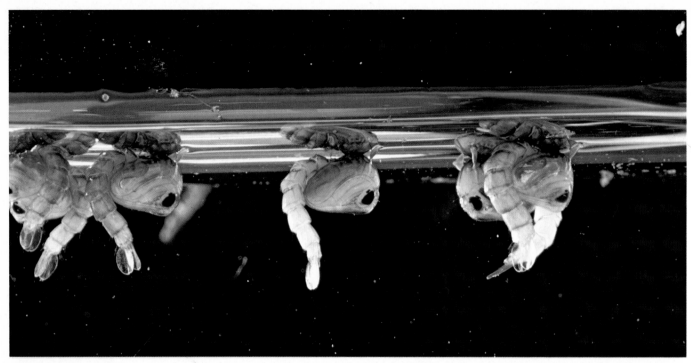

Left
Mosquito (*Culex* spp) pupae at the breeding site.

Right
Tsetse-fly (*Glossina austeni*) emerging from the puparium.

surface and pushes a slender tube through the surface film. It then draws in a supply of oxygen and after a brief period, returns to the lower waters of the pool. When fully grown the larva enters the pupal stage while still in the water and then rests, floating just below the surface. These 'comma' shaped individuals swim freely and very actively when alarmed. The adult emerges from a split in the back of the pupal skin while it is at the surface. Being very light it can stand on the surface of the water until its wings are fully dried and it can fly away.

In tropical regions other biting flies can be serious transmitters of disease. So severe can their effects be that man is forced to abandon attempts to live in some areas altogether. One of the most serious biting flies is the tsetse (*Glossina* spp). Over large areas of Africa they are responsible for transmitting the trypanosome causing 'sleeping sickness' in humans and another trypanosome causing 'nagana' in cattle.

The female tsetse, which looks like an overgrown house-fly with wings folded back over the body, gives birth to a fully grown larva which is dropped in a dry place and immediately enters the soil to pupate. After a relatively long period of thirty days, a new adult emerges and continues the cycle.

Other members of the true flies, black-flies (*Simulium* spp), are also serious vectors of disease over large areas of the tropics. They are particularly prevalent in riverine regions because their larval stage is spent in water. The adults 'bite' humans freely and so transmit the parasitic worm *Onchocera* which causes tumours, skin eruptions and sometimes blindness.

Another well-known insect which has troubled man for thousands of years is the flea of which in excess of 1 000 species are now known. Fleas which 'bite' man are not always the Human Flea (*Pulex irritans*) – dog, cat and bird fleas will also bite occasionally.

We have all read or heard of the effects of plague transmitted to man by the tropical rat flea living on black rats (and occasionally other species). Flea larvae of all species live in accumulations of debris and filth in dwellings, farm buildings, bird and mammal nests to name some of the situations, and feed on food particles, faeces from adult fleas, etc.

In these enlightened days, now that the need for hygiene is understood, it is becoming increasingly rare to encounter an occurrence of what was, in earlier times, an everyday accompaniment to living, the Human Louse (*Pediculus humanus*). These 'pearls of poverty' as they were called, were taken, not as one would have expected, as an indication of the low standards of the times but rather the reverse, as a mark of saintliness! Much has been written on the history of this insect and it has influenced, in some respects, the whole course of history, particularly in Western civilization, by wiping out vast numbers of the populations through the transmission of disease.

In the twelfth century when the body of Thomas à Becket was prepared for burial after it had lain all night in the cathedral following his murder, the garments of coarse wool he was wearing at his death 'boiled over' with lice that were leaving the now cold and lifeless body. Such a quantity of lice undoubtedly contributed to his speedy canonization for here, according to the tradition of the times, was obviously a man of great saintliness. Coming nearer to our own times Robert Burns, some 200 years ago, in one of his poems, comments on observing a louse on a lady's bonnet in church. By this time attitudes had changed and lice were less welcome.

The louse, of which there are two varieties, the Head Louse (*Pediculus humanus capitis*) and the Body Louse (*Pediculus humanus humanus*), are considered to belong to a small order of

Left
Mosquito emerging from the pupa.

199

degenerate insects with piercing mouthparts and legs adapted for gripping hair on the host's body. The Body Louse is from 10–20 per cent larger than the type found on the head although they will interbreed, suggesting little basic difference between them.

The Head Louse, possibly the better known of the two, lays its eggs on the head hairs of its host. Nymphs moult three times in their growth stage and then become adult, when they vary in colour from a dirty white to greyish black. The colour depends on their background during the nymphal stage. That is, a louse from a person with light skin and blond hair will produce a light-coloured adult louse, while one from a dark-haired person will produce a dark-coloured adult. Both varieties require about the same temperature (30 °C) to achieve steady growth and in experimental animals they both complete their life cycle from eggs to adults in approximately eighteen days.

Although hygiene has been the main reducer in the populations of lice in the civilized parts of the world, even here the vagrant and the transitory lodging house inhabitant still causes concern. The transference of head lice is by close contact and body lice can be picked up from bedding and infested furniture. Even in the very poorest conditions in underdeveloped countries, it is unusual today to find more than twelve lice on a person – high numbers on the body are extremely rare.

The louse is known to transmit typhus and trench fever and these diseases are particularly liable to flare up in time of war or civil disturbance when attention to hygiene is impracticable. Under normal conditions lice cause irritation and the resultant scratching allows the ingress of the staphylococci and other organisms.

With the arrival of DDT the problems with lice in the Second World War were drastically reduced. The treatment of large numbers of refugees and prisoners of war by dusting clothing with insecticide is now an accepted control method.

With the spread of education and better standards of living, personal protection against insect-borne infections will extend further afield and the incidence of such infections will decline. These improvements will follow the use of control against the parasite, the vertebrate host and the insect vector.

Here we are concerned with methods directed against the insect vector. These are twofold: (a) methods to prevent the insect coming into contact with the human host; and (b) methods to destroy the insect vector. In the first category biological methods have the widest application: for example, siting human habitations well away from the mosquito breeding sites or clearing an area of land between the human population and the tsetse-fly resting places.

In the second category, destruction of the insect vector is generally carried out by spraying insecticides. This method has been very successful in the control of mosquitoes and adult tsetse flies. Unfortunately, use of this method runs the risk of destroying beneficial insects and also may result in the insect vector developing and transmitting to future generations a resistance to the insecticides deployed for its destruction.

Some significant crop pests

Monocultures of plants, resulting in intensive agriculture, inevitably bring numerous pest problems. In Britain, the Wheat-bulb-fly is a serious pest of winter wheat. The potato crop, covering some 223 000 hectares in the UK is subject to attack by four common aphid species. All of these are vectors of a number of viruses such as leaf roll and potato mosaic. Plants treated with insecticide to control aphids can give increased yields in excess of 2·5 tonnes per hectare. One of these insects, the Peach Potato Aphid (*Myzus persicae*), also attacks sugar beet in Britain, transmitting yellows virus. It has a reputation throughout the whole of its worldwide range for transmitting over 100 different virus diseases in about thirty different families of plants.

Yields of brassicas, particularly cabbage, are affected by the Cabbage-root-fly. The maggots attack the main root system and kill off young plants. Older plants are stunted and fail to mature.

In the tropics, particularly Africa, stem borers of sorghum and maize are significant pests. The larvae of the Maize Stalk Borer Moth (*Busseola fusca*) burrow in the stems of maize and sorghum resulting in a considerable reduction in yield. Some of the present varieties of sorghum grown in Northern Nigeria have been bred to make plants resistant to the pest but older varieties can support as many as five larvae per stem given improved cultural practice, and still show a reasonable yield. Naturally occurring thick-stemmed grasses can act as reservoirs for this pest and have to be eliminated.

Also feeding on the leaves and stems of young maize and sorghum in East Africa is the African Armyworm (*Spodoptera exempta*). As its common name suggests, it appears as a descending army on crops, with the larvae devouring the young plants.

Outbreaks occur in fields just at the commencement of the rains, eggs having been laid a week or so previously. This moth engages in long migratory flights keeping ahead of the rains and moving in successive waves northwards from Tanzania in mid-March, the final wave reaching Ethiopia, the Sudan and the Red Sea three or four months later.

In recent research programmes, these migratory flights were monitored with light traps using ultraviolet lamps and one trap recorded 42 000 moths of this species in one night. When each wave of insects lands, having completed its particular contribution to the flight, each female lays 400 or more eggs, and so the sheer magnitude of the problem can be seen.

Citrus fruits, originating in South-East Asia, have been transported to almost all tropical and subtropical regions, where the climate is suitable.

Cottony Cushion Scale (*Icerya purchasi*) adults and juveniles.

Mediterranean Fruit-fly (*Ceratitis capitata*).

200

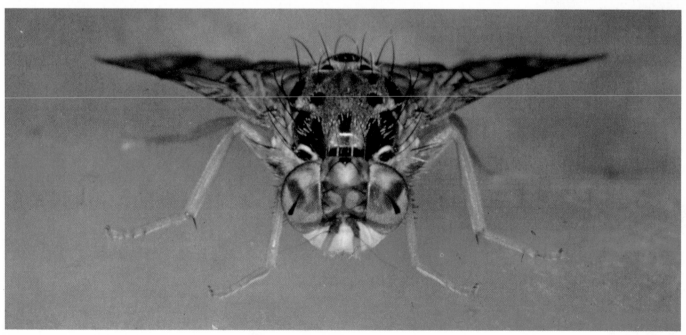

They are affected by the Cottony Cushion Scale or Fluted Scale (*Icerya purchasi*) originating in Australia. This insect, introduced accidentally into California in 1868, caused tremendous havoc in the citrus orchards, threatening the growers with total ruin. The scale insect was brought under control by the introduction of one of its predators, a small ladybird (see 'Beneficial Insects', page 203). Cottony Cushion Scale has spread to the other citrus growing areas and has been controlled in the same way.

Scale insects spend a sedentary life on the stem or underside of a leaf of a citrus tree. On hatching the insect crawls a few centimetres until it finds a suitable site to feed and complete its growth. During this period a small scale forms over its back and eventually envelops it completely. This protective scale is enlarged as the insect grows. When fully grown it produces a batch of eggs parthenogenetically under the scale. The eggs are deposited in a mass of waxy fibres looking like cotton wool, hence the common name. Owing to the large size of the egg

mass, one side of the scale is lifted up. Trees affected by this insect are also covered with honeydew, the excreta of the insects, on which sooty moulds grow, affecting the vitality of the trees.

Attacking citrus and also affecting peach, coffee, cocoa, fig, mango, to name a few, is the Mediterranean Fruit-fly (*Ceratitis capitata*). It is widespread in many parts of the world but particularly concentrated in the Mediterranean, Africa and South America. The larvae of this fly, similar in shape to those of the house-fly, emerge from eggs which have been laid below the skin of the fruit. Punctures caused by the ovipositor allow fungi and bacteria to enter and so the fruit rots and drops prematurely.

Three species of locust constitute sporadic pest problems for countries bordering deserts in the Old World. The Desert Locust (*Schistocerca gregaria*) is the most widespread, breeding in the Arabian and Sahara regions and developing into swarms spreading from the west of Africa to the eastern borders of India. The

Colorado Beetle
(*Leptinotarsa
decemlineata*).

settling of a swarm usually ends in complete, indiscriminate defoliation of any crops in the region.

Another serious pest is the Colorado Beetle, a native of Colorado. It became a pest when the potato reached North America from South America via Europe. Colorado Beetle is not specific to potato as it lived originally on Buffalo Burr (*Solanum rostratum*) and will now eat various Solanaceae. The seriousness of the problem to the economy of the United Kingdom is reflected in the control order passed by Parliament in 1933 and 1950 (The Colorado Beetle Order), requiring occupiers of land to notify the appropriate authorities of any suspect insect.

Beneficial insects

The pollination of flowers is possibly one of the greatest benefits afforded to mankind by insects. Thirteen orders have been recorded as pollinators and of these Hymenoptera, Lepidoptera, Diptera and Coleoptera form the most import-

ant groups. The insect is lured to the flower by either its colour or scent or a combination of both. It visits the flowers to obtain nectar and pollen for food and in so doing, carries pollen from one flower to another on its body, inducing fertilization.

The honey bee (*Apis mellifera*) is one of the first of the pollinators to be seen in the spring visiting fruit blossom and other flowers with apparently little discrimination. Honey bees have reasonably long tongues enabling them to reach the nectaries of most blossoms but in flowers where the nectaries are deeply seated, and cannot be reached by honey bees, the longer tongued bumble bees (*Bombus* spp) have the advantage. The tubular bells of the bluebell cannot be entered by the honey bee or the bumble bee but the latter has a long enough tongue to reach the nectaries by pushing its head just inside the bell's mouth.

In a great many plants the nectaries are exposed for all insects interested in the highly prized nectar. It is on this type of flower head

Above
Seven-spot Ladybirds (*Coccinella septem-punctatum*) hibernating in a crack.

Left
Bumble Bee (*Bombus terrestris*) visiting a tubular flower.

an injurious insect has been inadvertently introduced to another country away from any of its natural enemies. The Cottony Cushion Scale on citrus already mentioned, is a case in point. In Australia, where it is indigenous, there is a ladybird predator (*Rhodalia cardinalis*). This was imported into California, bred in large numbers and then released in the citrus orchards. Within a short while, the scale insect was brought under control. Another group of predators are the lacewings, Neuroptera. Equipped with large pincer-like jaws the larvae attack any small creature they may find in trees and shrubs, the skins of their victims often being carried around on the backs of the lacewing larvae.

The parasites, the other major division, are equally effective in exercising control over other insects but in a more subtle way – by attacking the host internally. The *Sirex* wood wasp of Europe has become established in Australia and the natural parasites of this, numbering six or more species, have been introduced experimentally to control the pest which causes large numbers of trees to die through the introduction of a fungus by its borings in the timber.

The Glasshouse Whitefly (*Trialeurodes vaporariorum*), an introduced pest in the UK, is familiar to most owners of greenhouses through its infestation of tomatoes, cucumbers and ornamental plants. The young stage is a sedentary scale-like nymph feeding on the underside of the leaves. Gardeners are able to control this pest by obtaining the scales which also contain parasitic larvae of a minute chalcid wasp *Encarsia formosa*. Emerging wasps lay eggs in the unattacked scales and so reduce the population. Being a pest of warmer climes, this insect and its parasites thrive at temperatures in excess of 21 °C.

In the mid-1920s fruit trees covered with patches of what appeared to be cotton wool were a common sight in Britain. These patches were colonies of American blight or Woolly Aphid (*Eriosoma lanigerum*). Another chalcid parasite (*Aphelinus mali*) was imported from New Zealand in an attempt to effect biological control of this pest. It took a number of reintroductions and about twenty years before it became acclimatized. Today American blight is very rarely seen in any quantity, being controlled naturally by the parasite.

Burying beetles (*Necrophorus* spp), one of nature's scavengers, bury the carcases of small birds and mammals, by scraping the soil from under them. The larvae of the burying beetles feed on the carcases and so break them down. In a similar way the dung beetles (*Geotrupes* spp and their relatives) perform a very useful function in the conversion of animal excreta into humus.

Insects in their natural habitats, like the rest of the animal world, are kept in balance by natural enemies, climatic factors and, possibly most important of all, the abundance or lack of food. This balance has been upset by the advancement of civilization because man, in his attempts to satisfy his everyday needs, interferes with the ecosystem.

or inflorescence that flies and beetles are most often seen.

In addition to the obvious benefits conferred by honey bees as pollinators, they are the producers of the original sweetening substance. Long before sugar was cultivated, man regularly raided the nests of wild bees to obtain honey for sweetening.

The rhyme 'Little fleas have smaller fleas upon their backs to bite 'em' is very true in the living world of insects, and it is very much to our advantage that this is so. There are two major divisions in the beneficial insects engaged in biological control – predators and parasites.

The association of ladybirds with colonies of aphids is a good example of a predator. Both the larvae and the adult ladybirds are carnivorous on the aphids. This specialized feeding habit has been put to good use by entomologists when

The Orders of Insects

With about one million insects known and more described each year, several methods of classification have been used to understand, study and to retrieve the information currently known.

The classification of the major groups of arthropods is still in dispute. 'Evolution and Distribution' puts forward a widely accepted view of four major divisions.

The Thysanura and Pterygota can be considered as Hexapoda. Manton's theory proposes a polyphyletic origin (i.e. convergent evolution) of the four separate phyla. Clearly, while this is possible, the alternative views are not yet ruled out and monophyly (single evolutionary origins) of the Hexapoda is also possible. This system proposes a sister-group relation between the Entognatha (Collembola, Diplura and Protura) and the Insecta (all the remaining insect groups). The classification which follows is a rather middle-of-the-road one in that the major groupings, Thysanura, Coleoptera etc., are recognized but their phylogenetic relationships are not stressed.

The insects are divided into orders (e.g. beetles, Coleoptera; flies, Diptera) of similar-looking and probably related groups. The orders are further subdivided into smaller groups and the system forms the basis of our information retrieval method for insects.

Although the first three groups (Collembola, Protura, Diplura) are not strictly insects in the modern classification, they have been considered so for many years and are included here.

The Cabbage White butterfly has its scientific name made up of two words which are always used together to refer to that insect. The first name, which always starts with a capital letter, is the genus, the second is the species name. For this butterfly it is *Pieris brassicae*. This is used internationally and overcomes the language problem. Whatever language the text is in, *Pieris brassicae* is always used for the Cabbage White butterfly (although of course, the popular name differs in every language). Similarly *Pieris rapae* is the Small White butterfly. Related species are placed in the same genus.

Cabbage White butterfly (*Pieris brassicae*) is classified as follows;

Genus	*Pieris*, contains a group of related species.
Family	Pieridae, a group of related genera.
Superfamily	Papilionoidea, a group of related families.
Suborder	Ditrysia, a group of related superfamilies.
Order	Lepidoptera, butterflies and moths, a group of related suborders.

Family names always end in -dae, superfamily names in -oidea. In the following text the related groups are arranged together. Species and genera have the scientific names in italics.

The orders are arranged starting with the more primitive, without a complete metamorphosis, to the more specialized insects which have a complete metamorphosis in their life cycle and include a pupal stage.

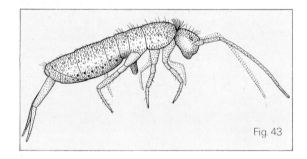
Fig. 43

Fig. 43 Order Collembola – springtail.

Order Collembola

Springtails are wingless arthropods which really do have a spring in the tail. Not a coiled one but a forked process (furcula) which goes under the body and, when they want to spring, is forced downwards, flinging the springtail upwards. Not all of them have a spring but those that do can use it even on the surface of water.

Lift up any flowerpot in the garden, turn over dead leaves even in mid-winter and you will see tiny creatures jump away. These will almost certainly be the ubiquitous springtails.

They are present in huge numbers in the soil, in litter, in birds nests and even on glaciers and snowfields where their appearance in thousands on fresh snow has given them the name snow-worms.

Springtails are believed to be the most abundant group for their sheer total numbers, although there are only about 4000 different species. Springtails vary in size from less than 1 mm up to 5 mm. Most have biting mouthparts which they use to feed on plant debris and other organic sources in the soil. Some of them are among the most widespread insects with species from the same genus in the Arctic and Antarctic.

A few species live on the shoreline and may be submerged by high tides. The Lucerne Flea (*Sminthurus viridis*) is a bright green, globular springtail which can appear in millions and do a lot of damage to the crops. Other springtails feed on pollen. During courtship, the male springtail deposits the sperm on the ground to be collected by the female, but in some species direct transfer of sperm from males to females occurs.

The globose Symphypleona, and the more elongate Arthropleona are the two main divisions.

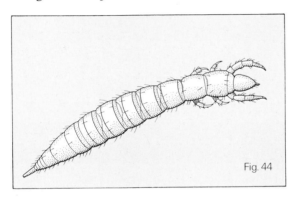

Fig. 44

Order Protura

This group of arthropods has not been given a popular name. They are minute (up to 2 mm long), colourless or white, soil-dwelling creatures, without eyes or antennae. Their front legs are held forward and probably act as antennae. They have eleven segments in the abdomen which is more than in true insects. The mouthparts are sunk into the head and are adapted for sucking. The proturans feed by extracting liquid from fungal hyphae. They are a worldwide group but are so small and inconspicuous that they have been studied very little.

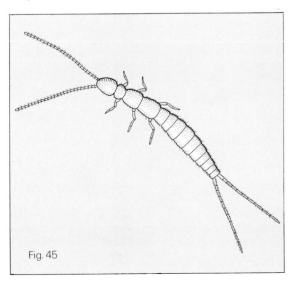

Fig. 45

Order Diplura

These two-pronged bristle-tails are similar to Thysanura (q.v.), getting their name from the two long processes at the tip of the abdomen. There are about 400 species known, many are worm-like, blind, soil dwellers. They live in the humus where they feed on Collembola and small insect larvae. While Diplura are generally small, one species is 50 mm long. There are three families, Campodeidae, without processes on the first abdominal segment, the Projapygidae, with a process on the first abdominal segment and the Japygidae, which also have a process but have the bristle-tails on the abdomen modified into pincers.

All the remaining orders constitute the true insects.

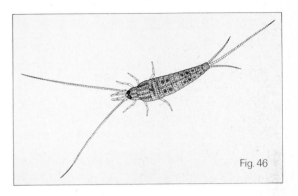

Fig. 46

Order Archaeognatha

These are the jumping bristle-tails, related to the Thysanura. They are slender, wingless insects usually small and generally less than a few centimetres long. About 250 species are known, mostly with three cerci (tails), large ocelli and eyes. Most species are nocturnal but on the coasts the shore bristle-tail may be seen in daylight on rocks above the sprayline. The Machilidae live in leaf litter and under stones, feeding on lichen and dead leaves.

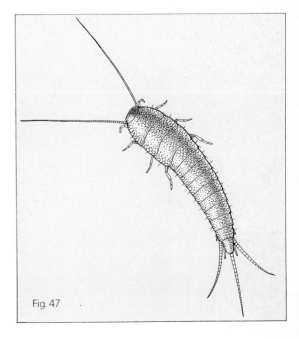

Fig. 47

Fig. 44 Order Protura – protura.

Fig. 45 Order Diplura – two pronged bristletail.

Fig. 46 Order Archaeognatha – bristle-tail.

Fig. 47 Order Thysanura – silver-fish.

Order Thysanura

The Thysanura contains a small group of wingless, primitive insects of which about 330 species are known. They are active insects, up to a maximum length of a few centimetres but most are very small. They have long antennae and small compound eyes. Thysanurans have three long filaments at the tip of the abdomen which give them their popular name of bristle-tails. Silverfish (*Lepisma*) are common household pests. These small nocturnal insects, also known as sugar mites, are common in houses in Europe and America. They can be destructive to paper and bookbindings and even to the backing of pictures hung on walls. Silverfish are covered by fine scales which give them their shiny appearance. A related species, the firebrat, is common in bakehouses and similar warm places. The mating behaviour of silverfish is complicated. The male deposits a packet of sperm on the ground and in the mating dance manoeuvres the female over this for her to take the sperm packet into her genital opening.

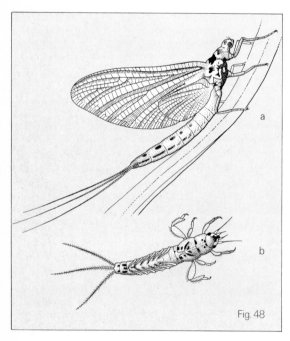

Fig. 48

Order Ephemeroptera

Although their name implies that they are insects with brief lives, it is only the adult which is ephemeral, living for a few hours or at the most a few days. By contrast their nymphal stage may last several months or even years. Ephemeroptera or mayflies are delicate insects with large gauzy, net-veined forewings, smaller hindwings and usually with two or three long processes on the abdomen. The nymphs have a gradual metamorphosis and are aquatic, they usually have gills along the sides of the body. They are common in streams where they dart about with their three long tails trailing behind them. They feed on plants and may browse on algae on submerged rocks.

Some of the nymphs burrow into the mud while others crawl over it looking for food. At the last nymphal moult when the wings appear, the subimago is produced. This stage is peculiar to mayflies and may last a few hours or a day. It is generally rather a sombre colour, called the dun by fisherman. Finally the dun moults again and the more iridescent adult insect emerges.

Mayflies emerge in swarms from the water and collect together, dancing over the surface in their brief aerial life. In all stages they are important for fish which eat them in large numbers.

About 1 500 species are known, which are divided into three superfamilies, the Ephemeroidea, the Baetoidea, and the Heptageneoidea each of which contains a number of families. Most mayflies are rather small insects but a few reach 6 cm in length. Once they have emerged their sole purpose is reproduction, they do not feed in their adult stage.

Order Odonata

What better name than dragonfly for this terror of flying insects. Dragonflies are commonly seen near water, although some species may migrate over land and sea. Dragonflies have large compound eyes and catch their prey in flight. Their antennae are short, and they have mandibles and long, but relatively slender, legs. They have a powerful flight, hunting in bright sunshine at speeds, in the larger species, estimated up to 40–50 km per hour. Their prey is seized in flight by the long legs and then transferred to the mouth. Dragonflies can hover in flight but at rest are less agile, their legs are not well adapted for walking. They have aquatic nymphs and their metamorphosis is gradual. The nymphs are elongate insects which stalk their prey under water, shooting out a special structure from under the head, the mask, with which they seize their prey. The victim is then transferred to the mouth where the powerful jaws make short work of it. They feed on other insects, tadpoles and even small fish.

One species of dragonfly which lives in Hawaii has a nymph which lives on land. Between 5,000 and 6,000 species of dragonflies are known.

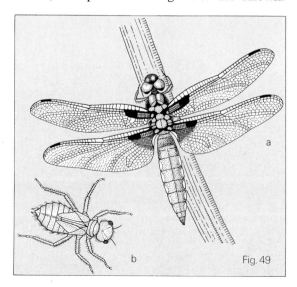

Fig. 49

Fig. 48 Order Ephemeroptera – (a) mayfly (b) mayfly nymph.

Fig. 49 Order Odonata (Anisoptera) – (a) dragonfly (b) dragonfly nymph.

There are three suborders, the Anisoptera, or true dragonflies (Fig. 49), the Zygoptera (damselflies; Fig. 50) and the Anisozygoptera, the latter is known only from fossils and a few living species in South-East Asia and Japan.

The dragonflies, Anisoptera, are the large species which rest with the wings at right angles to the body. The nymph has three small processes at the end of the body and is rather stout.

The damselflies, Zygoptera, usually fold the wings backward above the body at rest and are more delicately built than the Anisoptera. The nymphs have three long plate-like gills at the tip of the abdomen. Dragonflies and damselflies

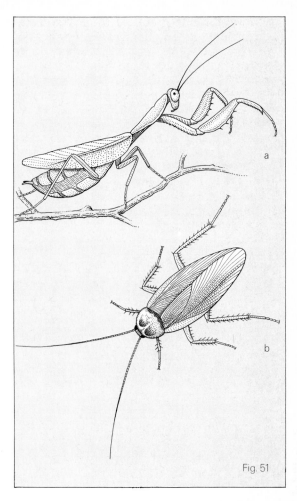

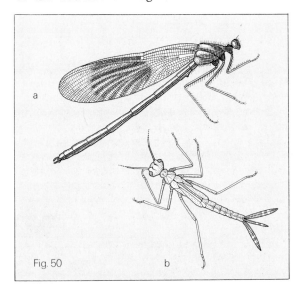

Fig. 50

Fig. 51

are great destroyers of insects and are very beneficial to man. In spite of this, their appearance and the very speed of the larger dragonflies have inspired fear. This is seen in some of the country names, horse-stinger, devil's darning needles, the latter from the superstition that they could sew up the mouths of children.

In mating the male dragonfly grasps the female behind her head while in flight. The two fly in tandem with the male above the female. The female bends her body round to reach the sperm pocket of the male and the two form a 'mating wheel'. The females lay their eggs in water, sometimes inserting them into water plants.

Order Dictyoptera

Cockroaches and mantids are both sinister in different ways. The sight of a cockroach scurrying across the kitchen can produce a shudder while a praying mantis, sitting in an attitude of supplication is just waiting for its prey to come near before seizing it in its outstretched arms! The concern about the cockroach (or black beetle as they are sometimes called, although they are not beetles) is not without foundation as their search for food takes them from rubbish, contaminated food to human food and they are known to transmit a number of unpleasant bacterial diseases, including typhus, dysentery and anthrax.

Some 3 500 species of cockroaches are known.

They are found all over the world although only a few species are closely associated with man.

Cockroaches, Blattodea, have long antennae, strong mandibles and a rather flattened oval shape. Their forewings are hardened, although not as strongly as beetles, into tegmina but the hindwings are membranous and used for flight. A few species have reduced wings and cannot fly. All have a pair of short processes (cerci) on the last segment of the abdomen. Young cockroaches (nymphs) are like the adults but lack the wings, showing more and more wing-pads after each moult until the adult stage is reached after the gradual metamorphosis.

Cockroaches, often shortened to 'roaches, are rapid movers and can hide in small cracks. These household pests are generally nocturnal, shunning the light.

The females lay their eggs in purse-like oothecae. The commoner cockroaches, which are common household pests, have been introduced to many countries by ships.

The second division of the Dictyoptera is the suborder Mantodea, or praying mantids which range in size from 1–16 cm in length. Some 1 300 species are known, living mainly in the tropics and subtropics.

They are well camouflaged insects, sitting still on branches with the long forelegs, which are specially modified for catching their prey, sticking out in front like two grasping pincers. They feed mostly on other insects and are useful predators, the larger mantids catch lizards and

even
capab
reduc
elong
slend
into s
insect
to 7·
Amer
nibali
often
with l
like t
have
editio

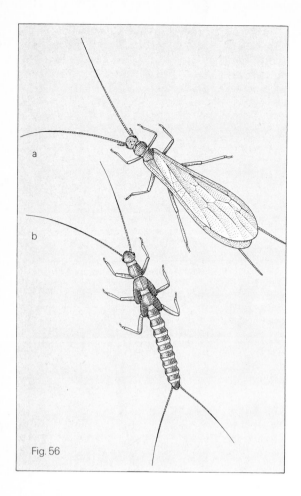

Fig. 56

Ord

Whit
for m
but li
have
speci
feedi
6-20
are l
mm.
white
when
head,
large
from
live i
fed b
varie
speci
are t
quee
the c
with
also 1
main
jority
caste
forag
soldi
(See
'Inse
Te
and s
up to

Order Plecoptera

Stoneflies are rarely found far from water where their nymphs live. The adults have net-veined wings which they hold flat over the body when at rest. They have long antennae and in many species two long tail filaments.

They are rather dull-coloured insects, whose hindwings are generally larger than the forewings. Their flight tends to be rather slow and fluttery. About 1 600 species are known.

The nymphs, which feed on plants and water animals, have two tails like the adults. Those which live in fast-flowing mountain streams can develop in water only slightly above freezing, many species are actually dependent on cold water.

Stoneflies are divided into two suborders. The Setipalpia which has carnivorous nymphs and the Filipalpia whose nymphs are mainly vegetarians. In both groups nymphs may spend several years in the water before becoming adult after a gradual metamorphosis. The adults themselves live only for a short time.

Adult Filipalpia have been known to damage fruitbuds but mostly Plecoptera are only important in the ecology of the stream. They become rarer as levels of pollution in streams increase.

Order Orthoptera

This order formerly included the Phasmida (or Phasmatodea) and Dictyoptera (q.v.). Orthoptera contains grasshoppers, locusts and crickets. Most of the Orthoptera are active, stoutly built insects. Depending on the species, the legs may be used for running, jumping or burrowing. These insects have large compound eyes and two pairs of wings, the front pair generally being more slender but slightly thickened; there are many wingless species. The abdomen of the female bush cricket usually has a stout sword-like ovipositor.

Many Orthoptera are active only in warm sunlight but some, particularly the crickets, are nocturnal. Some species are very well known for the sound they produce, the buzz of the grasshopper, for example, although the chirp of the cricket on the hearth is less often heard today. Orthoptera also includes the locusts, one of the plagues of man which bring destruction and famine in their wake. Orthoptera have biting mouthparts and are primarily plant feeders. Their sound is well known but it is less well known that each of the singing species has a distinctive song, as recognizable to the expert as different bird songs. The sounds, produced in different ways, are used to attract their mate.

Their eggs are laid in the ground or in plants and metamorphosis is gradual from the nymphs to the adult. Order Orthoptera is divided into two main suborders, the Ensifera, which includes crickets and long-horned bush crickets (sometimes called long-horned grasshoppers),

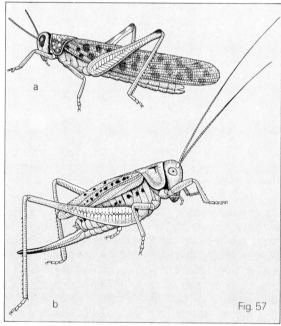

Fig. 57

and the Caelifera, the short-horned grasshoppers (usually just grasshoppers), locusts and grouse locusts.

The Ensifera, crickets, camel crickets and bush crickets are worldwide but commonest in the tropics. Some are phytophagous, but they are mainly hunters and feed on other insects. The Ensifera suborder is divided into several families.

The house and field crickets (Gryllidae) are black or brown insects with two long cerci (tail processes) and the wings, which are flat over the

Fig. 56 Order Plecoptera – (a) stonefly (b) stonefly nymph.

Fig. 57 Order Orthoptera – (a) locust (b) bush-cricket.

back at rest, are bent down slightly along the sides. They have long antennae. Sound is produced by rubbing the two forewings together. A row of pegs on one wing rubbing on a strengthened vein on the other. This sound is amplified by the stiffness of part of the wing membrane which acts like a drum. Generally it is only the males that chirp, but in some species both sexes chirp, the noise is primarily to help the sexes find one another. In crickets the auditory organs to receive the sound are on the front legs where the sound resonates, receptors in the leg act like directional microphones.

Crickets feed on plants but also on the remains of animals. Their chirping is mainly at night although they may be active in the day.

The bush crickets or katydids (Tettigoniidae) are widespread insect predators, usually living in trees or bushes. They are generally green or brown with very long thin antennae. A few species are plant feeders and at times can be pests. Their song is very loud (hence the name 'katydid'). The Great Green Bush Cricket of Europe, also found in England, is a large insect, 5 cm long. One species, the Wart-biter, as its name implies, has been used in country medicine. The bite, and the drop of liquid it puts on as it bites, are supposed to cure warts.

The Myrmecophilinae members have taken to living in ants' nests, where they feed on the ant larvae.

The mole cricket (Gryllotalpinae) has strongly modified forelegs for digging and spends most of its time tunnelling through the soil, biting through roots and being rather destructive on agricultural land.

The second division of the Orthoptera, the Caelifera, grasshoppers and locusts, is well known. The method of sound production differs from that of the Ensifera. In grasshoppers there are a series of pegs on the hindlegs which are rubbed against the slightly horny forewings. Some species produce sound by rubbing the hindlegs against the abdomen. The auditory organs are on each side of the base of the abdomen. Grasshoppers have short antennae and the majority are plant feeders. Most grasshoppers seen or heard on summer days are short-horned grasshoppers and they can sometimes be sufficiently abundant to cause damage to crops. These are nothing like as bad as the problem caused by other short-horned grasshoppers, better known as locusts.

Out of some 5000 species of short-horned grasshoppers, there are only about nine species of grasshoppers which swarm and earn the name locust. Their effect on man has been known since agriculture began. Plagues of locusts are short-horned grasshoppers moving in millions on migration. Most grasshoppers are solitary insects, including those grasshoppers which have the potential to increase rapidly and reach plague proportions some years, when we call them locusts.

Under certain conditions, shortage of food, local floods, the solitary grasshoppers congregate, and from their eggs the nymphs hatch and, because of their proximity to one another, stay together and tend to move actively in groups, foraging for food. These meet up with other groups and so the swarm of hoppers is formed which eats everything in their path. After a gradual metamorphosis the winged stage is produced and the swarm takes flight. The gregarious phase hoppers and adults are darker and have other differences from the solitary phase. They may fly long or short distances but when they land they devastate the vegetation. Until the swarm breaks up, they continue to move about. When eventually they get separated, by for example a storm, the isolated females will lay eggs and from these the solitary phase will be produced. Swarms are not produced every year and many generations of the solitary phase may occur before the next outbreak.

Desert Locusts and Red Locusts of Africa are potential plague species while Australia and South America have species which can reach plague proportions. Fortunately the majority of grasshoppers live solitary lives and are not serious pests.

Many grasshoppers are quite brightly coloured and often have very brightly coloured hindwings.

Grouse locusts (Tetrigidae) are distinguished from the grasshoppers by the elongation of the pronotum which is produced back over the body and in some tropical species the pronotum may be highly decorative.

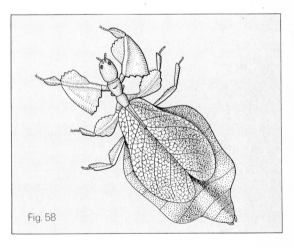

Fig. 58

Order Phasmida

Stick insects and leaf insects, as their names imply, resemble plants. When sitting on plants they are well camouflaged to avoid capture, especially since they are slow-moving insects. Most of them are tropical or subtropical and some are able to change colour. They tend to be rather angular, elongate insects, in fact stick insects may be 35 cm long, quite the longest, but not the bulkiest, of insects.

Many species are parthenogenetic, males are quite rare. Nymphs of stick insects can even lose a leg, regenerating it at the next moult.

The leaf insects have broad, expanded bodies and are usually green in colour with three pairs of rather similar legs. Many have very bizarre

Fig. 58 Order Phasmida – leaf insect.

appearances and they are protected by their close resemblance to the surrounding vegetation, sitting still during the day and moving mainly at night. There are some 2000 species of phasmids, usually females are larger than the males. They are all vegetarians, feeding on the plants around them. The common stick insect, often kept in laboratories or as a pet, is a parthenogenetic species of *Carausius*, originally introduced from the Orient. It is wingless like many species of phasmids.

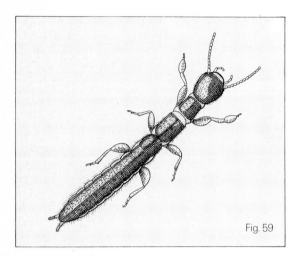

Fig. 59

Order Embioptera

A strange and little-known order of about 150 species called web-spinners because of their habit of living in silken tunnels.

The males have two pairs of similar wings, the females are usually wingless. They are small insects, some 15–20 mm long and have dusky coloured wings. They spin the webbing in which they live from glands in the first tarsal segment of the foreleg. The young live in these silken tunnels, under stones or bark. They are found in the warmer parts of southern Europe and throughout the tropics. Web-spinners have large heads with compound eyes and antennae like strings of beads. They are believed to be plant feeders but their biology is scarcely known.

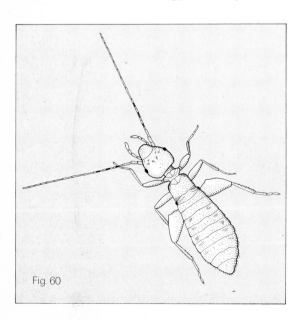

Fig. 60

Order Psocoptera

Booklice or barklice as they are sometimes called, are small (1–10 mm), rather delicate insects, with two pairs of membranous wings, although some species are wingless.

Over 1000 species are known and they are common on trees, in old books or musty papers, but they may occur in new rooms when the walls are scarcely dry. Their presence indicates dampness and by drying the atmosphere they will soon disappear. Most species have a rather large bulbous head and long thin antennae. Some species feed on the debris in bee hives. Booklice are usually reluctant to fly but sometimes occur in swarms. Although small, they are very active insects.

Fig. 61

Order Siphunculata

All lice were formerly classified under one order, Phthiraptera. Now there are two orders recognized, the Siphunculata and Mallophaga. Lice are wingless ectoparasites on birds and mammals. Lice of any sort sound revolting and the Siphunculata members have the added unpleasantness of transmitting diseases. The names 'lice' and 'lousy' have become words of abuse and their derivation from the insect is not surprising since lice tend to occur where standards of hygiene are low. All lice are wingless and are transmitted from one host to another when in contact. Lice are dorsoventrally flattened insects, with small eyes and mouthparts specialized for sucking.

Some 300 species of Siphunculata are known, all are bloodsuckers and this is why they transmit diseases. Lice occur on man, domestic animals and even on seals. They vary in size from 0·3–6 mm and are highly adapted for clinging onto the skin. The Human Louse (*Pediculus humanus*) is about 1–1·5 mm long and will bite humans, as does the more compact Crab Louse. The Human Louse has two forms, the Head Louse which feeds on the head, their eggs (nits) are glued onto the hair. The Body Louse feeds anywhere on the body, living in the clothing and only moving onto the body to feed.

Apart from the irritation of the bite, lice can transmit diseases like typhus and relapsing fever. The latter may be transmitted by the bite but more often gets into the body when the louse is squashed and the skin scratched, it is also widely transmitted in the excreta of the louse. Outbreaks of fever occur under conditions of crowding without good washing facilities; in the 1914–1918 war it was called trench fever. The Crab Louse generally lives in the pubic or perianal region and although unpleasant does not transmit diseases.

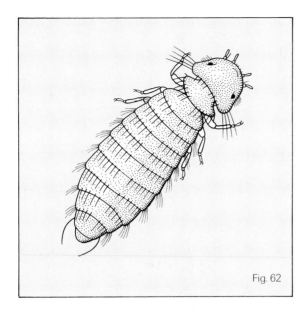

Fig. 62

Order Mallophaga

Mallophaga contains wingless ectoparasites of birds and mammals. They are the bird or biting lice, mostly small species, 0·6–6mm, and are flat bodied insects. They have claw-like tips to the legs to grip the feathers or hair, feeding on fragments of feathers and epidermis which they bite with their strong mandibles. They cause considerable irritation to their host, for example chickens with a heavy infestation scratch more and more and become listless, they may stop feeding and even die as a result of the infestation. Birds often give themselves dust baths to reduce their lice infestations.

There are some 2700 species of biting lice which are mostly host specific, the lice from one bird will not go onto another species. Lice die very quickly if the host bird is killed, transferring from one bird to another only when the birds are in contact, for example at roosts or nests.

The eggs of lice are stuck to the feathers and the young lice cling to these. Their metamorphosis is gradual with several moults before they become adult. A few species of Mallophaga feed on mammals but the majority are bird lice. The dog louse can endanger the health of its host, apart from the irritation causing them to scratch, the louse is the intermediate host of the dog tapeworm.

There are three main divisions of the Mallophaga. The Amblycera contains mainly bird lice. They have clubbed antennae which they hold in a recess in the head capsule. The Ischnocera members, which have rounded heads without recessed or clubbed antennae, feed on birds and mammals.

The third group of the Mallophaga is the Rhynchophthirina which have their head drawn out into a point. The group includes the elephant lice which feed on the Indian and African elephants. Their legs have very strong claws to help dig into the elephant's hide.

The older order **Hemiptera** is now considered to consist of two separate orders: Heteroptera and Homoptera. Popularly called the plant bugs, these two orders include a variety of insects, from 0·5mm–10·0cm in size. They have specialized mouthparts used for piercing and sucking. Most have two pairs of wings, well-developed compound eyes and are usually very active insects.

Many are important pests of crops, others, which suck blood, are involved in disease transmission. On the credit side many of them are predators, feeding on insects which may be crop pests, while the strange lac insects and cochineal insects are used directly by man.

The mouthparts of plant bugs consist of a rostrum in which are the fine stylets used to pierce the plant or the skin of an animal. Some of the bloodsucking bugs have enzymes which stop the blood clotting as they suck it up.

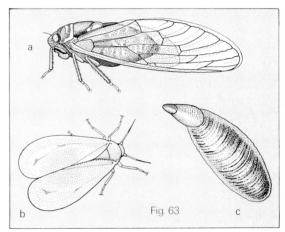

Fig. 63

Order Homoptera

The Homoptera have membranous wings which are usually held sloping over the body at rest. They are a very diverse group and are divided into three series, Auchenorrhyncha, Sternorrhyncha and Coleorrhyncha.

Auchenorrhyncha includes cicadas, leafhoppers and lantern flies. The auchenorrhynchs are themselves subdivided into two main groups, the Cicadelloidea and the Fulgoroidea.

Cicadelloidea, which includes leafhoppers, froghoppers and cicadas, are usually rather large insects with two pairs of membranous wings. The males produce the high-pitched buzzing sound so characteristic of warmer climates. The sound is produced from an organ on the base of the abdomen which oscillates a small membrane. Development of cicadas from egg to adult is through a series of nymphal stages and generally takes several years, metamorphosis is gradual. The nymphs develop underground, feeding on roots. The seventeen-year cicada, sometimes called the periodic locust, has a life cycle which actually last seventeen years.

215

Adult cicadas are plant feeders, frequently found on trees in warmer climates.

Mounds of froth on a plant stem hide the nymph of the froghopper, cuckoo spit or spittle-bug insect (Cercopidae). They are common, although the associated adults are less well known since they do not produce froth. The adult froghoppers are active jumpers and some are of economic importance on food crops. Buffalo treehoppers (Membracidae) derive their name from the remarkable processes growing out of the thorax. Some look very like thorns and the insects become almost invisible at rest on thorn trees. Leafhoppers (Jassidae) are usually small, the largest is 18mm, most are a few millimetres long.

They fly and jump readily and are common on most vegetation. All feed on the plant sap and many transmit plant diseases in this way. They are mostly slender insects.

In the Fulgoroidea some of the leafhoppers are of economic importance. Many of this group are rather bizarre in shape. Lantern flies, in spite of their name, are not luminous. Flatids are rather moth-like bugs whose gregarious nymphs are covered by long wax filaments.

The second division of the Homoptera is the Sternorrhyncha, including the psyllids or jumping plant lice (Psyllidae). They are small insects feeding on fruit trees and other plants, often causing gall formation. They may produce a sweet honeydew which attracts ants.

Whiteflies (Aleyrodidae) are tiny white, powdery looking insects found on the underside of leaves, they can be seen on cabbages even in winter. Greenfly, blackfly, plant lice or aphids (Aphididae) are very abundant pests on many plants. They are relatively uniform in appearance but many have complicated life cycles. Aphids have winged and wingless forms, the former have two pairs of transparent wings which rest roof-like over the abdomen. They are usually small insects, crowding together on the leaf or growing point of the plant.

On the abdomen they have two processes, cornicles, which secrete wax and juice and are used for defence, while the honeydew that particularly attracts ants is produced from the anus. Aphids are serious pests and transmit diseases to the plants, others cause gall formation while some which produce copious honeydew attract ants and bees. Aphid life cycles are complicated by the need in many species for two different host plants to complete their development. They are very prolific and may reproduce partheno-genetically (asexual reproduction), produce living young (vivipary), or lay eggs.

Enormous populations of aphids can rapidly be built up in a relatively short time. The feeding of large numbers of aphids on plants often causes distortion of the normal growth.

Related to aphids are the *Adelges*, or woolly aphids which, as their name implies, look like small tufts of white wool on the trees.

The vine phylloxera is a serious pest in vineyards and can destroy the crops.

The scale insects (Coccoidea) often look like small immobile marks on the plant of characteristic shape, like the mussel scale. These are the female scales, the males are winged, Many species are pests but the cochineal scale which lives on cactus is used as a source of the red dye.

The Coleorrhyncha has only one family, Peloridiidae, whose members live on mosses in rainforests in South America, Australia and New Zealand.

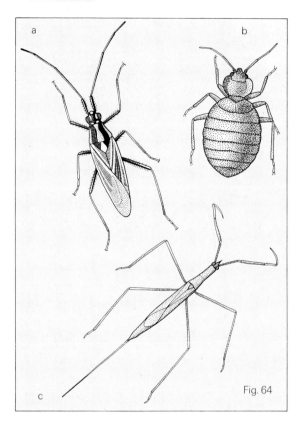

Fig. 64   Order Heteroptera – (a) plant bug (b) bed bug (c) water stick insect.

Order Heteroptera

Heteroptera is a large and varied group of species which feed on plants but also contains predatory and bloodsucking species. Their wings are generally held flat over the body and their forewings are partially thickened over the basal two-thirds. The two major divisions of the Heteroptera are the Gymnocerata and the Cryptocerata.

Gymnocerata includes bed bugs (Cimicidae) wingless, flattened insects common in warmer climates in unsanitary surroundings. They suck blood causing intense irritation, both on man and birds. Shield bugs (Pentatomidae) also known as stink bugs from the smell they produce, include many colourful species, some of which are crop pests. Assassin bugs or cone-nosed bugs (Reduviidae) are predatory insects, some of which feed on other insects while some are bloodsuckers of man and other animals. Several assassin bugs are disease carriers in the tropics and their bite alone is painful, especially the larger species. *Triatoma* in South America, carries Chaga's disease, the bug is sometimes called Darwin's bug since the famous naturalist was infected by the bite of *Triatoma*. One species of reduviid covers its forelegs with sticky plant resin and then sits with these extended, catching its prey on its own fly-paper! Plant bugs (Miridae) are common pests of many crops. In Africa they are particularly a problem for the cotton growers. Many other families of Heteroptera feed on plants and can be agricultural pests, others, like the pirate bugs (Anthocoridae) include species which can inflict painful bites on man. Many of the predatory bugs are particularly useful in destroying other insect crop pests. Pond skaters are common on the surface of freshwater where they skate over the surface on their long legs, catching small insects. *Halobates* is a marine bug, living far out to sea feeding on dead marine organisms and is one of the few marine insects.

Members of the second group of the Heteroptera, the Cryptocerata, are all associated with fresh or slightly brackish water. The giant water bugs which may be over 100 mm long feed on young fish, tadpoles and insects. Their eggs are gathered in masses in South-East Asia and are eaten as a sort of poor man's caviare. Water scorpions are predators which catch their prey in their modified forelegs. They have a long breathing tube from the tip of the abdomen. Water boatmen or backswimmers are common in lakes and ponds where many species use an enlarged pair of legs to row themselves through the water on their backs. They feed on small water animals, using their proboscis to suck out the body contents of their victims.

Fig. 65

Order Thysanoptera

Sometimes, during thundery weather, masses of tiny insects, less than 1 mm long fly about, not infrequently getting into one's eyes. These are thunderflies, stormflies or thrips, minute insects which are common in every flower head. They have sucking mouthparts and, when present, the wings are strap-like, fringed with long hairs. Thrips are usually yellow-brown or black insects and range in size from 0·5 mm to the largest thrip, 13 mm long, from New Guinea, but most species are small. Some thrips are predatory on aphids and mites while others are plant pests. Many are quite active and a few species can

jump. On the plants their damage shows as small silver spots where the thrips have sucked the contents out of a plant cell, some thrips transmit virus diseases. In pasture grasses they may be so numerous in the flower heads that seed production is prevented or reduced.

There are two suborders, Terebrantia and Tubulifera. Terebrantia females have a saw-like ovipositor which is used for egg-laying in plants. They usually have at least one vein in the forewing. The Onion Thrips (*Thrips tabaci*) is an important pest which transmits a wilt disease to tomatoes. Many thrips are greenhouse pests and can rapidly become numerous. Males in some species are rare, reproduction is by parthenogenesis.

The second suborder, the Tubulifera, includes the world's largest thrips; these are fungus feeders. The females lack an ovipositor and there are virtually no veins in the forewing.

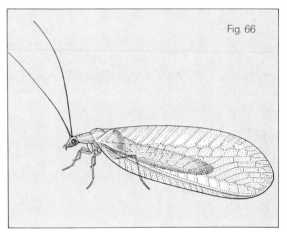

Fig. 66

Order Neuroptera

The Neuroptera are delicate-looking, gauzy-winged insects, well deserving their popular name, lacewing. They have four net-veined wings, often bright green bodies and golden eyes. Their flight always seems full of effort to keep on the wing, unlike the powerful flight of a fly. None of the order, of which there are less than 5 000 species, is harmful to man and many (if not all) are positively beneficial. They are all predators, both in the adult and larval stages, on greenfly, scale insects, thrips, caterpillars and many other harmful insects. Lacewings are now reared artificially in large numbers as a means of pest control. They are reared and released to help reduce insect pests such as the *Heliothis* caterpillar which damages cotton.

Formerly the Neuroptera was divided into the Planipennia and the Megaloptera. The latter is now considered a separate order.

The Neuroptera includes many rather dissimilar insects. The most widely-known family, the green lacewings (Chrysopidae) are frequently attracted to light and probably are the most familiar insects in the order. They are generally a beautiful green colour with translucent net-veined wings and golden eyes. They often hibernate in houses, sheds or warehouses in the winter

217

and as a result attract popular attention. Lacewings are also known as golden eyes, an equally descriptive name. They are totally harmless; in fact they should be zealously protected as friends-of-man, they are great destroyers of greenflies (aphids) which are so harmful to our cultivated plants. Lacewings are attractive insects, not inspiring the dislike or distaste that one feels for cockroaches or flies. Brown lacewings (Hemerobiidae) as their name implies, are more soberly coloured, but are no less useful to man. They have the fore and hindwings linked by a few bristles, rather similar to the frenulum of moths (q.v.). Some of the chrysopid lacewings have eggs on long stalks. These are attached to the plant in groups on slender threads, each thread has a minute egg at the end (stalked eggs are also found in the mantispids and berothids).

Lacewing larvae are very different from the adults, rather caterpillar-like but without as many legs. The larvae of some of the green lacewings cover themselves with debris to camouflage themselves as they move around.

Other families of lacewings are less familiar and there is scope for observations on their life history and behaviour.

The osmylids (Osmylidae) are large lacewing-like insects, looking rather like slow-flying dragonflies. Their larvae are all aquatic, feeding on other insects in the water.

The sisyrids (Sisyridae) also have aquatic larvae, but theirs are always associated with freshwater sponge and will not develop without these.

Psychopsids (Psychopsidae) are rather broad-winged lacewings with transparent, delicately patterned wings. They are rather rare, mainly nocturnal insects found only in Australia, South Africa and South-East Asia.

Even among the many strange insects in the Neuroptera, the nemopterids (Nemopteridae) stand out. They are lacewings whose hindwings are modified into long thin streamers. These trail out behind them when they fly, seeming to make them dance through the air.

Looking rather like ponderous dragonflies, the ant-lions (Myrmeleontidae) are not as strange in appearance as some of the other lacewings but have remarkable life histories.

Very similar to the myrmeleontids are the ascalaphids (Ascalaphidae). Their larvae do not dig pits as do the myrmeleontids, instead they hunt their prey over the ground. Ascalaphids are among the more powerful fliers in the Neuroptera, hawking for flies rather like the dragonflies. They broadly resemble these too and can be distinguished from them by the shape of their antennae. In dragonflies these are very short whereas in ascalaphids they are conspicuous, projecting in front of the head. In myrmeleontids, which are also rather similar, the antennae end in a prominent club.

Mantispidae is a small family of Neuroptera whose members can be recognized by their raptorial (grasping) forelegs which they use to seize other insects. In this they are rather similar to the praying mantids. Mantispids have a strange life history, their larvae feed on young spiders.

Dilaridae is a small family of lacewings recognizable from the others by the pectinate (feathery) antennae in the males.

The smallest of the Neuroptera are the Coniopterygidae or powder-wings. These insects whose wingspan may only be a few millimetres, are covered over with a white waxy secretion and can easily be confused with whiteflies (Homoptera, page 215). They differ in their mouthparts and wing venation. There are several other families in the Neuroptera, broadly similar to lacewings but whose biology and life history are even less well known.

All the lacewings have a complete metamorphosis with a pupal stage. This is the first of the insect groups so far considered which have this stage.

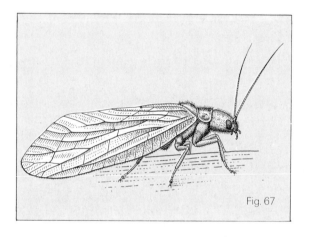

Fig. 67

Fig. 67 Order Megaloptera – alder fly.

Order Megaloptera

This was formerly considered a suborder of the Neuroptera and has many similar characters. Metamorphosis is complete and the adults have two pairs of net-veined wings.

The insects in this group are less familiar than even the lacewings. There are two main super-families, the Sialoidea and the Raphidioidea.

The Sialoidea or alder flies have aquatic larvae. The adult sialids are generally found in vegetation at the edge of streams and ponds. They have two pairs of wings and are rather more stoutly built than the neuropterous lacewings. They are generally dull-coloured but among them are some striking-looking insects. The genus Corydalis has very large insects with wingspans up to 160 mm and two huge sickle-like mandibles in the male which project out beyond the head, fearsome-looking but harmless insects.

The Raphidioidea or snake flies are a specialized group of terrestrial insects found everywhere except Australia. They have a long prothorax which means that the head projects a long way in front of the wings. Their larvae live under the bark of trees and they are voracious predators of insects and other small invertebrates.

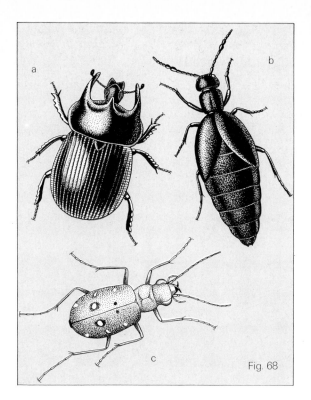

Fig. 68 Order Coleoptera – (a) geotrupid beetle (b) meloid beetle (c) cicindelid beetle.

Fig. 68

Order Coleoptera

Beetles are probably the most successful form of all animal life. Some 290 000 species are known and many more new species are described every year. Beetles have a long fossil history and in the present day beetles are found everywhere, except for the one place few insects have conquered, the seas, although many inhabit the tide line. Beetles do well in spite of man, and many have become adapted to make use of man's food and dwellings.

Many beetles are serious pests, many are valuable allies of man, and countless thousands of species live their complicated lives with little apparent impact on man but with considerable effect on his environment.

What is a beetle? Not cockroaches, which are often called black beetles. Beetles usually have shorter antennae, lack the cerci (tail processes) of cockroaches and the hardened forewings of beetles, the elytra meet in a straight line down the back, where in cockroaches they overlap.

Beetles are built like a strengthened box, they are the tanks of the insect world and this must be part of their success. They have a strong, thickened head and thorax and the elytra are thickened, protecting the hindwings and softer abdomen. In some families the elytra are short (Staphylinidae, Lampyridae) but the hindwings, when not in use are folded up underneath.

Beetles are so diverse with many shapes and colours that it is difficult to generalize. They have biting mouthparts, often strongly developed for tearing and biting, they may be huge as in stag beetles and in *Chiagsognathus* the mandibles may be longer than the whole body. Most have prominent antennae, with many segments and often these are many times the length of the body. In *Batocera* from the Solomon Islands the

antennae are 23 cm long. At the other extreme, ladybirds (Coccinellidae) have very short antennae. The shape of the antennae is often important in identifying beetles. The antennae may be slender or they may have many side branches, sometimes a tuft of branches at the tip. The weevils (Curculionidae) have a very elongate head with their mandibles at the tip of this elongate snout. The head and thorax may have large, branched processes giving a very bizarre appearance to the insect, the horns are conspicuous on the rhinoceros beetle. The hindwings, which are used by those that can fly, are folded up under the elytra.

Beetle flight is usually slow, the wings may be strap-like with hair fringes as in the feather-winged beetles, or they may be quite large and membranous. The legs are often modified for the particular way of life. They assist, for example, in jumping as in the flea beetles (Chrysomelidae) or they may be used for digging or swimming or just for rapid walking when they may be very long (*Acrocinus*).

Beetles are not all black or brown, in fact many are very colourful, some can even change their colour. Tortoise beetles (Cassidae) do this and the gold beetle or gold bug (*Metriona*) turns from a dull yellow to a shiny gold colour like the decoration on a Christmas tree.

The range of beetle colours goes right across the spectrum, common examples being ladybirds, cardinal beetles and the metallic green buprestids. Apart from being well armoured and often having strong jaws beetles have developed many other means of protection. In the bombardier beetles (Carabidae) there are two glands in the apex of the abdomen which produce different secretions. One has hydroquinone compounds, the other hydrogen peroxide. When the beetle is alarmed, these two chemicals are released into a special thick-walled chamber which acts as a reaction unit. The two chemicals react with an enzyme catalyst which decomposes the hydrogen peroxide, the oxygen given off supplies the gas pressure which forces out the hydroquinone solution. This produces a fine spray over the potential attacker. It deters birds and lizards which drop the beetle when the corrosive substance touches their mouth. Ladybirds (Coccinellidae), leaf beetles (Chrysomelidae) and blister beetles (Meloidae) are able to squirt out fluid from joints between the tibia and femur. These are usually distasteful or corrosive liquids and keep most predators away. Man is more severely affected by the blister beetles which include the Spanish Fly (a beetle not a fly). It is the chemical cantharidin in the beetle, which if taken internally even in small doses, is fatal for humans.

Beetles have larval stages which are quite different from the adult in appearances. A complete metamorphosis is present with the larva pupating, frequently in the ground, before emerging as the adult insect. Many have strange life histories. Blister beetles or oil beetles have a triungulin larva which is the first stage out of the egg. These try to attach themselves to bees, and, if successful, get into the bees' nest where they feed on the honey. Later the larva changes into a fat maggot which is then followed by a rather dormant stage. After this it moults to another maggot-like stage before pupating. One species (*Micromalthus debilis*) has a type of alternation of generations. The winter is spent as legless larvae, afterwards some pupate and from these adult females emerge. The larvae which did not pupate give rise to more larvae or to an egg. The larvae actually multiply by paedogenesis, producing more larvae without an adult stage in between. The eggs produced hatch and the larvae from them grow up rapidly, pupating to emerge subsequently as male beetles. The larvae which were produced from the mother larva spend the winter in that stage and then in spring this whole remarkable life cycle begins again. Life cycles in the beetles vary in length from a few weeks to seven or eight years in some species of wood borers while there are many records of wood borers emerging after the wood has been made into furniture! While many beetles pupate in the ground a few pupate in the trees and some, like some ladybirds and leaf beetles can be found hanging head down from plants.

Beetles can be found in virtually every habitat on land or in freshwater, proof of their success is their abundance and adaptations. Some species live with ants or termites, others are found only in bee hives while yet others are associated with dead animals or dry grain. Those living under bark of trees make galleries and live in relative safety but their effect on the tree may be dramatic. Some of them transmit diseases and the Dutch elm disease which devastated elms in Europe was carried by a scolytid beetle. Weevils (Curculionidae) are particularly adept at leaf-rolling. In the curled up leaf they place their eggs and the subsequent larva has a relatively safe retreat to live in. While many beetles are serious pests, many are helpful, keeping our environment clean by eating up all the dead animals and decaying plants, generally acting as scavengers. They can be described as the dustmen of the countryside.

The classification of beetles is complicated and is by no means entirely agreed by coleopterists. Beetles are divided into three suborders, the **Archostemata, Adephaga** and **Polyphaga.**

The **Archostemata** contains only a few primitive species, they were formerly more common as shown by their abundance in the fossil record.

The **Adephaga** includes mostly the carnivorous species.

Ground beetles (Carabidae) are active predators measuring from 1 mm–10 cm long. A few species are vegetarians. Some 24 000 species are known and while many carabids are black or dark coloured others are brightly coloured. Tiger beetles (Cicindelidae) are fierce predators as larvae and adults. They are often brightly coloured, fly readily and have prominent eyes for hunting.

The water beetles (Dytiscidae) are aquatic predators with predatory larvae, feeding on tad-poles and small fish. Whirligig beetles (Gyrinidae), whose activities on the surface of ponds and streams are well known, are also predators. They detect the sounds made by the prey on the water surface. Their zigzag movements are rapid but they avoid collisions with one another by their sound detection ability.

The family Paussidae contains small brown beetles, often associated with ants and the Rhysodidae is another small family, called the wrinkled-bark beetles, whose larvae and adults live in rotting wood.

The suborder **Polyphaga** contains the largest number of species in the enormously successful Coleoptera. In the classification used here it is divided into eighteen superfamilies, many of which are further subdivided.

The Hydrophiloidea are not all water beetles in spite of their name, many feed on decomposing plants. There are some 2 000 species.

The Histeroidea contains shiny black beetles which are predatory. They have angled and clubbed antennae, and some have been used in biological control against the banana weevil.

The Staphylinoidea is a huge group with many thousands of species. The Ptiliidae comprises the smallest beetles, 0·25 mm long with fringed wings under their elytra. Silphidae contains large carrion beetles, some of which are predacious on snails and caterpillars. Pselaphidae members are rather similar in appearance to ants and most species live in ants' nests where they feed on food intended for the ant larvae. The ants in return get a substance which diffuses from the base of the beetles' abdomen. The Scaphididae is a small group of fungus-feeding beetles. Staphylinidae or rove beetles are typical of the suborder, having rather short elytra under which the wings are carefully folded. Staphylinids curl up the end of the abdomen if threatened, giving a sinister appearance. One of the larger species, *Ocypus olens*, is 28 mm long and is known as the Devil's Coach Horse Beetle. There are about 20 000 species of staphylinid beetles, most of which feed on organic refuse, dung and generally rotting vegetation, while some are predatory and others live in association with termites. In the main they are great cleaners of the countryside.

The superfamily Scarabaeoidea contains beetles whose antennae have a group of plates or lamellae at the apex. They are often called lamellicorn beetles from the shape of their antennae. The Passalidae range in size from 1–8 cm, and live in rotting wood both as adults and larvae. Some of them are known to stridulate. The Lucanidae contains the stag beetles. This large (up to 10 cm) and ferocious looking insect is capable of giving a good bite with the large mandibles which stick out in front of the head – the females have much smaller, less conspicuous mandibles. Their larvae live in rotting wood and take several years to become fully grown. Dor beetles (Geotrupidae) are also known as clock beetles. They are large, rather rounded beetles which mostly feed on dung, taking it to tunnels to serve as food for their larvae. They have a slow bumbling flight and when at rest can often be seen to be crawling with tiny red mites, which run all over them, hence another of their names, 'lousy watchman'. The Scarabaeidae, scarabs or sacred beetles are a large group of some 19 000 species. Many of the species roll dung into a ball. This ball of dung is then rolled to the brood chamber, dug in the ground, and an egg laid on it. Other balls of dung are brought in and left as food for the developing larva. The Scarabaeidae is divided into several subfamilies. The Cetoniinae members are brilliantly coloured scarabs, usually with a metallic sheen. In the tropics they feed by day on mainly soft or liquid food while their larvae feed in decaying plant refuse. The Rose Chafer (*Cetonia aurata*) feeds destructively on rose leaves. The Dynastiinae or unicorn beetles are black, crepuscular insects with extreme sexual dimorphism. Many have horny processes on the head and thorax, for example the rhinoceros beetle which is a serious pest of coconuts. Melolonthinae, the cockchafers, whose larvae do great damage in grasslands and crops, feeding on the roots, are large beetles which are often attracted to light when they blunder noisily about. The Rutelinae members are chafer beetles which feed on the leaves and blossoms of roses and fruit trees. The Aphodiinae and Scarabaeinae are two smaller subfamilies of scarabs which feed on dung and are general scavengers. In the latter subfamily is the ancient Egyptians' sacred scarab beetle.

The superfamily Dascilloidea has species with thin or slightly serrate antennae. Many species of Dascillidae feed on grass roots. The Helodidae has larvae which live in freshwater, some adult helodids are good jumpers. The Eucinetidae is a small family of dascillids which live in rotting wood.

Byrrhoidea is a small superfamily whose species are capable of drawing their legs close to their bodies and lying motionless, hence their name, pill beetles.

The Dryopoidea members mostly live in or near the water. Psephenidae contains dryopids which have oval, flattened larvae, which live in fast-flowing streams in the Himalayas. The Dryopidae members have long claws on their legs which they use for holding onto vegetation in running water. There are several other families in the Dryopoidea.

The Rhipiceroidea members have a rather nose-like projection on the front of the head.

Buprestoidea contains mainly tropical beetles. The Buprestidae has about 15 000 species including some with the most beautiful metallic colours, often used in jewellery. The buprestids generally live in hot moist forests, flying freely. Their larvae bore into trees and are characteristic in shape with a very broad prothorax.

Elateroidea contains the click beetles, so-called from the noise made when they turn themselves over to get off their backs, flicking themselves over with an audible click. About 10 000 species are known and their larvae are often serious agricultural pests, popularly known as wireworms. The fireflies (*Pyrophorus*) are elaterid beetles which produce light which is much brighter than the common glow-worm (Lampyridae).

The Cantharoidea contains a number of small families, including the glow-worms which have luminescent spots on the abdomen. The males generally glow more brightly than the females, which are wingless rather like woodlice. The adult of the common European glow-worm does not feed but the larvae are active predators on snails and slugs. The Drylidae is a small family with strong sexual dimorphism, the wingless female being much larger than the male. Soldier beetles, Cantharidae, are predatory and commonly found in flower heads where their colourful, often red, elytra are conspicuous. Lycidae contains net-winged beetles with some 3 000 species which are mainly tropical and often have yellow and black elytra.

The Dermestoidea has many species which are pests, attacking fur, hides and wool. Popularly known as skin beetles or woolly bears, they have hairy larvae, often with brush-like tufts. Species of *Anthrenus* are often serious pests both of museum specimens and household carpets, but most dermestids are important scavengers of dead animals. The Anobiidae includes the notorious Death Watch Beetle which damages wood in old buildings. Its eerie tapping sound is made by striking the head on the wood and is nothing more sinister than display calls to its mate. Many anobiids are serious pests of stored food and include the Cigarette Beetle which, with related species, feeds on a wide variety of substances from flour to opium and tobacco. The Ptinidae or spider beetles are stored food pests, feeding on dried organic substances. Bostrychidae includes many wood-boring species which make tunnels in felled timber and dry wood, some may damage bamboo, coffee bushes, and sometimes are found in stored grain. Lyctidae contains the powder post beetles which can be serious pests in timber in houses.

The Cleroidea also includes species which attack grain. Other species are wasp-like in appearance and are predators on other small beetles. The clerids include *Necrophorus* the burying beetle which digs holes under the carcass of small animals, pulling the carcass into the hole and then laying an egg in it. The larva feeds on the decaying, but buried corpse.

Lymexyloidea is a strange group of elongate beetles which bore in wood and are called ship-timber beetles.

The Cucujoidea is a huge group divided into the Clavicornia and the Heteromera.

The Clavicornia includes the fungus feeders and stored product pests but also the ladybirds (Coccinellidae). These well-known beetles of which there are many species, are mostly predatory in the adult and larval stages, feeding on greenfly. The second group of the cucujoids is the Heteromera which includes the Tenebrionidae. This has some 10 000 species and include the mealworms, serious pests in meal and flour. The Meloidae or blister beetles have strange life histories. Some have short elytra, others full length ones covering the abdomen. The Spanish Fly (*Lytta vesicatoria*) from which cantharidin is obtained is a meloid beetle. The Oedemeridae is a family, many of whose members are shore-dwelling insects which scavenge on the tide line.

The Chrysomeloidea or leaf beetles are mainly plant feeders and wood borers. The Cerambycidae are borers in trees and a problem for the forester. They are usually large beetles with long antennae, hence the name longhorn. Bruchidae are mostly legume pests, living in the seeds, and can cause serious losses to the crops. The Chrysomelidae, leaf beetles, are one of the largest families of beetles with some 26 000 species. They include the infamous Colorado Beetle, a serious pest of potatoes, and many other pests like the Turnip Flea Beetle. The colourful tortoise beetles, Cassidae, have the edges of the body expanded making them rather shield-shaped. Their brilliant colours fade rapidly after death.

The largest superfamily of beetles is the Curculionoidea, weevils or snout beetles. They have the head extended into a beak (rostrum) and clubbed, angled antennae. Estimates of their numbers vary but some 50 000 species of weevils are known. Some are serious pests of crops, these include the banana weevil and the sweet potato weevil. The Curculionidae alone has some 35 000 species. Many of them are specialized leaf-rollers. Rice weevils, granary weevils have names which explain their habits. Cotton boll weevil is responsible for the annual loss of millions of dollars worth of cotton. Ambrosia beetles tunnel in trees and feed on fungi which develop on the walls of their tunnels.

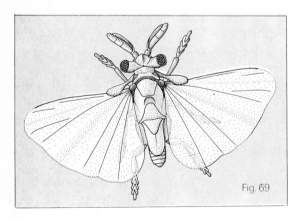

Fig. 69

Order Strepsiptera

Almost all the Strepsiptera, twisted-wings or stylops, are parasites. They are considered as related to beetles, but highly specialized in their own field. They undergo their development inside other insects. Males have wings and eyes which are slightly raised from the head and are from 1–7.5 mm long. The most striking features are the single pair of wings, rather round and fan-shaped from the metathorax, these are in fact comparable to the hindwings of other insects. The forewings of stylops are reduced to short club-like structures. This arrangement is the reverse of the Diptera (page 223). The females are usually internal parasites of other insects, remaining inside the last larval skin and with only a small bit actually protruding from the body of the host insect. Most of the structures, mouth, limbs, have disappeared in the sac-like female.

When they occur they cause the host to become infertile, it is said to be stylopized. The host suffers various changes in the body and can be distinguished from the unstylopized insect.

There are nine subfamilies of Strepsiptera, these include the Mengenillinae which are parasites of Thysanura (q.v.) and have free-living wingless females. The Halictophaginae develop in cicadas and other Homoptera as well as in Diptera and Dictyoptera (q.v.). Bees are attacked by the Hylecthrinae while the Stylopinae attack other Hymenoptera. The adult male stylops has a short life, often only a few hours. The male, on finding the female uses his aedeagus to penetrate any part of the female that is sticking out of the host insect. Sperm is transferred through the aedeagus into the body of the female and onto the eggs which are free in her abdomen. The young larvae leave the host when it is on a flower, the stylops larvae waiting there for a new host, e.g. a bee, to come near when they catch hold and hitch a lift to the bee's nest. There they attach to the bee's larvae, penetrating their skin and developing inside it. The female stylops will stay in the host, even after it is adult, but the male come out and flies to find the females.

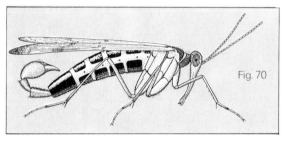

Fig. 70

Fig. 69 Order Strepsiptera – stylops.

Fig. 70 Order Mecoptera – scorpionfly.

Order Mecoptera

These insects are called scorpion flies from the way the tip of the abdomen of the male curls up over the body, looking very like the sting of a scorpion, but scorpion flies do not sting. About 300 species are known, most have two pairs of membranous wings which are held horizontally over the body. Their heads are produced into a long beak-like shape. They have long thin antennae and some species have very long legs. Scorpion flies are terrestrial insects, their larvae, which are caterpillar-like but usually do not have abdominal legs, feed on insects, generally in the moss or vegetation near the ground. The larvae live in short burrows in the soil coming to the surface to feed and pupating in the burrow. They have a complete metamorphosis.

Scorpion flies are useful predators, most feeding on insects in woods and hedgerows.

The Panorpidae includes the commoner

species in the more temperate parts. They frequently have wings speckled with brown, and feed on animal or vegetable material. They digest some of the food outside the body, vomiting up some of the digestive juices onto the food and lapping up the predigested result.

Bittacidae members are the hanging scorpion flies. They are hunters and look rather like daddy-long-legs. They cling with their forelegs at rest using the outstretched middle and hindlegs to catch their prey. Their head is elongate and they have a dagger-like beak which they use to suck the contents out of their prey.

Snowflies (sometimes called snowfleas), Boreidae, are usually wingless but can be recognized as mecopterans by the elongate, beak-like head. They jump readily and appear in large numbers in winter, their dark bronze-green colour showing up against the snow, even though they are only a few millimetres long. Snowflies emerge at the time of year when most other insects are hibernating.

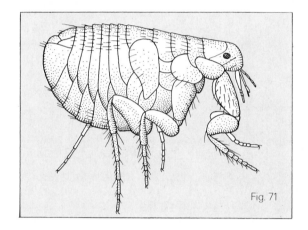

Fig. 71 Order Siphonaptera – flea.

Fig. 72 Order Diptera – (a) calliphoridae (b) calliphoridae larva (c) chironomidae (d) chironomidae larva.

Order Siphonaptera

Fleas are pests of man and domestic animals, not only because of the itching they cause but because they can transmit deadly diseases. The Black Death which killed millions of people in the Middle Ages was transmitted by flea bites. Few people would actually recognize a flea. If found they are squashed (with difficulty) but many harmless insects accidentally landing on us get squashed as 'fleas'.

Fleas are wingless insects, with a complete metamorphosis. There are about 1400–1500 species known. Their larvae are legless maggots which feed on organic debris which may collect, for example, between floorboards in houses. They pupate and hatch out after a complete metamorphosis, when the pupa is disturbed by a potential host. The adults are active ectoparasites which suck blood. Their mouthparts are modified for piercing and sucking.

Fleas are laterally flattened (from side to side) insects, contrasting with lice which are dorsoventrally flattened. This flattening helps them to move through fur and hair. They are covered with backward projecting spines which also help them to hang on to the body hair. They

are difficult to catch and even harder to kill, having a very tough exoskeleton. Their hindlegs are well developed for jumping. The Human Flea (*Pulex irritans*) which is 2–3 mm long can jump over 30 cm, and up to 20 cm high. Fleas are usually host specific but when hungry will bite anything while some species normally have a very wide range of hosts. Some seventeen families of fleas are now recognized, divided into two suborders, Pulicida and Apulicida.

Pulicida includes the Pulicidae and Tungidae. The latter is the jigger flea of Africa and America. The female burrows into the skin, frequently between the toes. These, if scratched, may become infected and gangrenous in the tropics. Dog fleas and cat fleas are different species of *Ctenocephalus* and can bite humans but the plague flea, *Xenopsylla*, which comes to humans from rats may transmit bubonic plague. The Human Flea (*Pulex*) is liable to transmit bacteria which can cause pneumonic plague.

Apulicida includes species which are ectoparasites of bats.

Thus a flea bite, small though it may be, can result in sickness or even death to man through the infections transmitted.

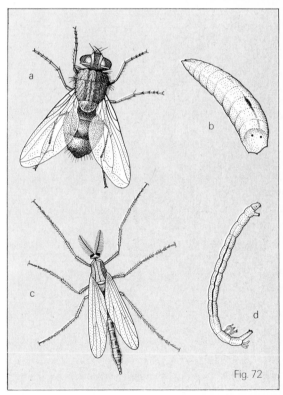

Order Diptera

There are about 85000 species of flies, characterized by the single pair of membranous wings. The hindwings are reduced to small knobs (haltères) which are important as stabilizers assisting with flight. Most flies have a proboscis which may be used for sucking or for piercing and sucking. The legless larvae (or maggots as they are commonly known) pupate in various ways, often in a hardened, barrel-shaped puparium to emerge after a complete metamorphosis. Dipterous larvae live in a wide variety of habitats and are frequently associated with decaying vegetation or dead animals. The adult flies are mostly sun-loving with a few notable exceptions such as the mosquitoes.

The head generally has large compound eyes, typical of active insects, but the antennae vary from fine plumose (feathery) ones in gnats to short, inconspicuous ones in house-flies. Certain flies have a special structure on the head, the ptilinum, which helps them to hatch from the puparium. The ptilinum is a sac which inflates, forcing the end off the puparium and enabling the fly to crawl out. The remains of this can be seen as the ptilinal suture on the front of the head. In the house-fly the structure of the proboscis is complicated. It can be used for sucking liquids which the fly produces by putting some saliva onto its food and then sucking up the partly digested juice produced. The labella lobes at the tip of the proboscis can be spread out, enabling small teeth to scrape the food and small particles of food can be ingested in this way.

The mouthparts of biting flies are modified in various ways. In the female mosquito (and only the female bites) the long proboscis has a series of grooves in which there are the slender stylets formed from the maxillae and the mandibles which actually penetrate the skin. The sheath does not penetrate but bends as the stylets penetrate. The saliva passes down another duct, the hypopharynx, into the wound and carries an enzyme which prevents the blood clotting, allowing a free flow up the proboscis. The mouthparts of tabanid flies (horse-flies) are similar, the mandibles and maxillae have serrate tips but the whole proboscis is shorter and stouter than that of the mosquito.

While most species have wings, in some they are reduced or absent. Reproduction in Diptera takes many forms from simple egg-laying to larvipary (larvae born alive). In some species paedogenesis occurs with one larva producing more daughter larvae without an intervening adult stage. The larvae occur in many habitats and, while they are usually legless maggots (as used for bait by fishermen) others, like mosquito larvae, are active swimmers. Some larvae are internal parasites while others are vegetarians. Both in their larval and adult stages flies have a tremendous effect on man and his environment. They may be useful, as for example in cleaning the environment of dead animals or decaying vegetation, but their impact is often damaging with disease transmission such as malaria and sleeping sickness, or crops may be destroyed by stem-boring fly larvae. Some larvae affect man directly, developing in his skin. In the tumbu-fly of Africa the larvae burrow and produce boil-like swellings on the skin. The names of many flies evoke some idea of their habit or habitat, flesh-flies, coffin-flies, dung-flies and house-flies. All were given their names from some aspect of their biology.

Several classifications have been suggested for the Diptera, the one followed here has been widely used. Three main divisions of the Diptera are recognized, suborders Nematocera, Brachycera and Cyclorrhapha.

The Nematocera are the mosquitoes, midges and gnats, generally the smaller and more delicate species, with very hairy wings. Their antennae are usually very long with many segments, often plumose in the male and the larvae have a recognizable head (in many others the head segments of the larvae are not so distinct). Most of the Nematocera have sucking mouthparts and many, especially the females, are bloodsucking.

The Tipulidae, crane-flies or daddy-long-legs, is a family with over 11 000 species which mostly have very long legs. Their larvae, popularly called leather-jackets, can cause serious injury to grassland and cereal crops where they feed just below ground in the spring. Other species breed in rotting wood or in water. There are several subfamilies of crane-flies.

The Trichoceridae or winter crane-flies have ocelli on the head (these are absent in Tipulidae) and occur in swarms on cold but sunny days in winter.

The Dixiidae or meniscus flies are a small group of non-biting flies with aquatic larvae whose adults are less hairy than many mosquitoes, but otherwise they are rather similar to mosquitoes. The larvae live suspended from the surface of slow-moving water, usually against an emergent piece of vegetation, at the meniscus.

The wood gnats, Anisopodidae, do not bite and are common in houses in spring and summer, their larvae feed in rotting wood.

Bibionidae includes St Mark's flies whose larvae feed in rotting vegetation. The adults are stouter than most nematocerans. They are rather hairy insects and fly slowly with their legs hanging down.

The Simuliidae are medically important flies known as black-flies or buffalo gnats. They are small with hairy wings and, although both sexes have piercing mouthparts, only the females bite man and other animals. They are persistent bloodsuckers, sometimes appearing in large numbers and their bites can lead to a fever which causes death. Their larvae live in fast-flowing streams where they sieve particles of food from the water. These tiny flies are a particular nuisance in the more temperate regions and in the summer months are a problem in the Arctic.

The Psychodidae, moth-flies, or sand-flies, are often common in houses, particularly round drains and sinks where they can breed. They are tiny, very hairy flies which hold their wings roof-like over the body when at rest. Moth-flies do not bite but sand-flies can cause serious problems when they appear in large numbers, transmitting a bacillary disease, known as sand-fly fever.

The importance of the Culicidae, mosquitoes or gnats, is well known. Some of them are the intermediate hosts of a number of diseases, for example malaria is transmitted through the bite of an infected *Anopheles* mosquito. Mosquitoes are usually rather slender, slow-flying insects with a long proboscis and, in the males, plumose antennae. Generally they have scales as well as hairs on the wings. About 1500 species are known, their larvae and pupae are aquatic. The species of *Culex* are bloodsuckers which are common in houses in more temperate areas. They sit with the hindlegs raised high and the body held level, thus distinguishing themselves from the anopheline mosquitoes whose hind end points upwards when at rest. The mosquito lays its eggs in water and often it is important for the egg production that the female has a blood meal before laying the eggs.

The larvae swim actively and may be seen in most standing pools or water-butts. They come to the surface for their respiratory siphon to take up air, moving up and down at will. They pupate in the water to emerge a few days later after a complete metamorphosis. The whine of the wing-beat of the mosquito is a familiar sound in the still of the night. Many different species of mosquitoes are found near water where they can make life unbearable with their biting. The anopheline mosquitoes which transmit malaria are responsible for tremendous suffering and mortality in man. Yellow fever and guinea worm are two other mosquito-borne diseases.

The lake-flies, Corethrinae, are related to mosquitoes but do not bite. Their aquatic larvae, called phantom larvae, which are almost completely transparent, have two air-sacs which help them to float. Swarms of lake-flies can be enormous and in parts of Africa their larvae are pressed together to form an edible sticky cake.

Cecidomyiidae, gall midges are tiny, only a few millimetres long but their activity can often be seen on plants where the bizarre gall growths they induce reveal their presence. Many are serious agricultural pests. The hessian-fly, introduced accidentally into the United States, is very destructive to grass. Gall midges have whorls of hairs on each antennal segment, and rather simplified venation.

Mycetophilidae or fungus gnats feed in decaying vegetation or rotting wood. They do not bite and are very small delicate insects. Sometimes their black headed larvae are common in mushrooms and present problems for the growers. Some 2000 species are known.

The related Sciaridae whose members are mostly fungus feeders are so abundant at times that their larvae, moving in millions in dense columns across the forest floor, are called snake worms and were looked on in former times with awe, foretelling some impending disaster.

The Chironomidae have mostly aquatic larvae. They are non-biting midges (or gnats), often abundant round lakes. They are delicate flies with very plumose antennae in the males. They lack the scales on the wings found in Culicidae.

The suborder Brachycera includes a heterogeneous collection of families, in recent classifications they have been divided up between the other major divisions and the name Brachycera not used. Basically the venation differs from the

two other major groups, usually with a discal cell in the forewing. Soldier-flies, Stratiomyidae, are large bristleless flies usually with white, yellow or green markings. The adult flies do not bite but are nectar feeders. Many of the larvae are aquatic and are carnivorous but others feed on decaying vegetation.

Snipe-flies, Rhagionidae, are slender, harmless flies with sucking mouthparts used in feeding on other insects. Their larvae are predatory too. One species, *Vermileo*, builds a funnel-shaped trap in the ground, rather similar to that of ant-lion larvae, into which small insects fall.

The Tabanidae family includes bloodsuckers, horse-flies and clegs. Many more names are applied to these vicious flies when they bite! They arrive silently with gleaming coloured eyes and when they bite cause intense irritation and swellings. They bite cattle but readily turn to humans if they are near. About 3000 species are known and some of the big horse-flies, *Tabanus*, are among the largest Diptera. Horse-flies have a stout proboscis, but only the females bite, the males feed on nectar.

Empididae or dance-flies, are small hairy flies mostly active predators of other Diptera.

The Nemestrinidae contains large flies with many extra veins near the apex of the wings. They generally live in hot dry places.

The Asilidae contains large bristly flies with large eyes and a tuft of hair forming a 'mouth beard', the robber-flies. They are active predators eating wasps, dragonflies and many other powerful insects which are apparently well protected.

Bombylidae or bee-flies, as their name implies, look like bees but only have one pair of wings. They are commonly seen hovering over spring flowers. Their larvae are mostly parasites of other insects.

Dolichopodidae are frequently metallic green and are long legged flies which feed on other insects.

The Cyclorrhapha suborder is divided into three sections, Aschiza, Schizophora and Pupipara. Cyclorrhaphous flies have small, three-jointed antennae with a small arista (bristle) on or near the tip. Most have the ptilinum to help emerge from the puparium.

The Aschiza differ from the others in lacking the ptilinum.

The Phoridae members are small, active flies with a humped back. Their larvae live in decaying vegetation but some are also found in termite and ant nests. The family includes the coffin-fly (*Conicera*) which can maintain many generations of flies on bodies in coffins, although how the fly gets into the coffin in the first place is a mystery.

Pipunculidae consists of a group of small flies with very large eyes whose larvae are parasites in leafhoppers and cicadas.

Hover-flies, Syrphidae, are conspicuous, often large flies (up to 20 mm), frequently patterned yellow and black resembling wasps. They are strong flyers and, as their name implies, hover well. The larvae of some species feed on aphids, others are aquatic and include the rat-tailed maggot whose snorkel breathing tube enables it to live in stagnant water. The adult of one species, *Eristalis*, is very like a bee in appearance and is often mistaken for one. Other species of hover- or drone-flies have larvae which feed on food as varied as plant sap and cow pats. The narcissus bulb-fly is a hover-fly whose larvae attack the bulbs and which can be a problem for horticulturalists.

The Conopidae members are rather wasp-like flies with big heads, they feed on nectar in flowers. Their larvae feed as internal parasites of other insects, including bees and wasps. Their taxonomic position is in dispute, they are close to the Syrphidae but have characters of the Aschiza and Schizophora.

In the section Schizophora the species have a ptilinum and the Schizophora is divided into two subdivisions, the Acalypterae and the Calypterae.

Acalypterae members have small or vestigial squamae, small lobes on the base of the wing margin. Most acalyptrates are small flies.

The Tephritidae contains the large fruit-flies which are common and include the Mediterranean fruit-fly (*Ceratitis*) whose larvae are serious pests in warmer countries, destroying peaches, apricots, tangerines and other fruit. Other tephritids have larvae which live in leaf litter while yet others are gall makers or leaf miners.

Members of the Agromyzidae are small flies, mostly with leaf-mining larvae. These larvae develop between the upper and lower surface of a single leaf. Their damage can be seen as serpentine trails or blotches on the leaf.

Piophilidae includes the Cheese-skipper (*Piophila casei*) whose larvae live on cheese but will also feed on bacon and rotting carrion. These larvae hop over the food as they jerk their body, hence their name.

Members of Diopsidae have their eyes conspicuously out on stalks. Their larvae tunnel in stems and can be pests of cereals in the tropics. Also a serious pest, the carrot root fly, *Psila*, can cause heavy crop loss. This fly is in the Psilidae.

Coelopidae includes the seaweed or kelp fly, *Coelopa*, whose larvae feed in rotting seaweed on the shore, the adult flies appearing in huge numbers causing discomfort to the seaside holiday-makers.

Drosophilidae contains the small fruit flies, common among over-ripe fruit and near vinegar or wine. One species of *Drosophila*, a tiny fly a few millimetres long, has been of inestimable value in genetic research.

Members of Ephydridae are shore-flies, related to drosophilids, whose larvae can live in salt pools. The brine-fly lives safely in salt pools where little else can survive. *Psilopa* is the remarkable petrol fly whose larvae live in crude petroleum pools. Their respiratory tube takes air from the surface and they feed on other insects which fall into the petroleum and die.

Braulidae contains the bee louse (a fly not a louse) which is a small (1–1·5 mm) wingless fly that lives in bee hives, the fly larva feeds on pollen in the honeycombs. The adults live mainly on queen bees, sucking the food from the queen's tongue.

The larvae of the Chloropidae, frit-flies, live in cereals. They include the frit-fly, *Oscinella*, some 3 mm long, which is a serious pest of grain crops. The larvae burrow into the stem, preventing grain formation.

The Gasterophilidae members are known as bot-flies, stout flies, 11–13 mm long and rather bee-like, which lay their eggs in the hair of horses. The young larvae hatch and are then swallowed by the horse as it licks itself. The larva passes to the horse's stomach where it attaches itself to the stomach wall, feeding on the food in the horse's stomach. When fully grown the larva releases its hold and is voided with the faeces, pupating in the ground.

The second superfamily of the Schizophora is the Calypterae. These flies have conspicuous squamae at the base of the wings and include the familiar house-fly and bluebottle.

The Oestridae contains the warble-flies which are similar to the bot-flies. Their larvae live in the nasal cavities or skin of mammals. The larvae of *Hypoderma* damage the skin of cattle making large swellings, called warbles.

Calliphoridae, the blow-flies, bluebottles and greenbottles are common household pests as well as pests of stock. Their larvae are carrion feeders and in the case of *Lucilia sericata*, a greenbottle, the larvae feed on the flesh in wounds or sores on sheep burrowing into the skin and causing death if there are many fly maggots.

Tachinidae members are large hairy flies whose larvae are parasitic in other insects. Many are useful to man and parasitize various caterpillars which are pests. The cluster-fly, *Pollenia*, has larvae which live parasitically in earthworms.

The Muscidae includes the common house-fly (*Musca*) and the stable-fly, *Stomoxys*. Many of their larvae feed on rotting vegetation or meat, others are pests of crops. Although the name house-fly is used, there are several different species which are grouped under this name. Many are liable, because of their feeding habits, to transmit diseases. The adult fly moves indiscriminately from dung and carrion to the food on our table. They carry organisms causing diarrhoea and typhoid. The stable-fly is a blood-sucker with a painful bite but the 'common house-fly. does not bite man. The bite of the tsetse-fly, *Glossinia*, transmits the trypanosomes which cause sleeping sickness disease in Africa. The disease is fatal for man and his stock if bitten by an infected fly. The female tsetse-fly keeps her eggs in her body until they hatch. The fly retains the larva inside the body, which grows gradually. When it is ready to pupate it is 'laid' by the female, pupating almost immediately.

The final division of the Cyclorrhapha is the Pupipara which contains highly modified flies.

They are ectoparasites of birds and mammals. Their wings are often reduced in size, many are flightless.

In Hippoboscidae, louse-flies, the adults are very flattened and tough. They include the sheep-ked fly, *Melophagus*, which attacks sheep, cattle and horses. Both this and the forest-fly, *Hippobosca*, produce living larvae which pupate as soon as they are laid. Hippoboscids are common on birds where they can be found crawling over the feathers. The Nycteribidae family contains blind, wingless flies which are ectoparasites of bats. The Streblidae members are also ectoparasites of bats but they have wings, which, in some species, are shed once they are safely on their host.

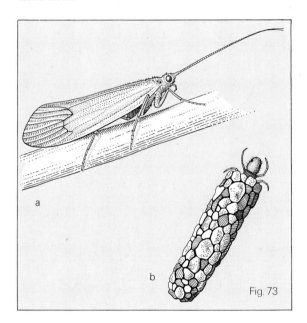

Fig. 73 Order Trichoptera – (a) caddis fly (b) caddis fly larva and case.

Fig. 74 Order Lepidoptera – (a) butterfly (b) moth.

Order Trichoptera

Caddis flies, or to use some of the more attractive names given to them by fishermen, sedge flies, silverhorns or welsh buttons, are aquatic insects which spend most of their life as larvae in the water, and their adult life near it. They are hairy, rather moth-like insects, dull coloured with long slender antennae and two pairs of wings. Most of them do not feed in the adult stage. The adults appear in large swarms over lakes and rivers and they and their larvae are important items in the diet of fish.

Some of the artificial flies used by fishermen are modelled on caddis flies. Caddises are attracted to light but, except when they appear in large numbers by lakes or rivers, are little known to the public.

Their larvae are probably better known. Most people fishing in freshwater or idly turning over stones in streams will have seen the strange cases that the caddis makes out of twigs or sandgrains. Generally the case shape and texture is characteristic of the species. Some larvae are free living, while others spin webs which act as nets to catch the minute particles of food in the streams.

The larvae are rather caterpillar-like but lack the abdominal legs. They pupate in the water, usually fixed to the stones or plants in shelters constructed by the larvae. The pupae swim up to the surface and the adult emerges on the water surface.

Adult caddis flies hold their wings roof-like, sloping over the body when at rest. Not all species have aquatic larvae, at least one European species has a larva which lives in damp moss on land.

About 7000 species are known which are divided into two main divisions based primarily on characters of the adult palps.

The Annulipalpia whose larvae are elongate with the head protruding in line with the body (prognathous) and include both free-living and case-bearing species. The last segment of the palp is ringed or annulated.

The Integripalpia have the head of the larvae directed downwards, almost at right angles to the body. The last segment of the palp is undivided.

Caddises are found in most water which is free from pollution, some being specialized to live in fast-flowing streams while others prefer still water.

Fig. 74

Order Lepidoptera

There are about 165000 species of butterflies and moths, many more new species are discovered every year. Of this total 15000 are butterflies the rest are all moths. The name Lepidoptera is derived from two Greek words meaning scale-wing. The scales, which come off as a fine powder when the wing is touched, are finely sculptured and of several different shapes

227

when seen under a microscope. Each scale is arranged in a small socket on the wings and over the body and forms a complete, overlapping cover. Lepidoptera members have two pairs of wings which are covered with scales and are usually patterned, although a few species lose most of the wing scales. The patterns and colours are produced either by pigments in the scales or by the reflection from the surface of the scale of light of different wavelengths.

Pigments are responsible for the white, brown and red scales which combine in different proportions to make different colours. The reflections give the metallic and iridescent colours. The pattern is made by the arrangement of these scales. Colour and pattern may be used for different purposes in different species. They may attract mates or they may be sombre colours to camouflage the insects at rest. They may also be bright colours, warning that the insect is distasteful, and, in some species, the warning colours may be mimetic. In this case the insect may not be distasteful but it is imitating one that is, to mislead potential predators.

The wings have thickened ribs on the membrane called veins and although serving to support the wing membrane, blood may also circulate in them. Differences in the venation are used to classify the Lepidoptera, most families having their own characteristic type of venation.

There is an immense amount of variety in the colours, patterns and wing shape in the Lepidoptera. The wing margin may be relatively smooth as in the Cabbage White butterfly or they may have ragged margins as in the Comma butterfly (Papilionoidea) or leaf moths (Pyraloidea). The hindwings may have tails as Swallowtail butterflies or these tails may be enlarged to make the entire hindwing into one long streamer as in *Himantopterus* (Zygaenoidea). The wings may be dissected into lobes as in the manyplume moths (Alucitoidea) where the fore and hindwings are each divided into six lobes. The wings may be lost altogether in some species, particularly in the females, although the males are winged.

Size as well as shape varies in the Lepidoptera. The moth, *Thysania*, (Noctuoidea) has a wingspan of 300 mm while some nepticulid moths (Nepticuloidea) have only a 3 mm wingspan.

There are few fundamental differences between butterflies and moths, the division is popular rather than scientific. Butterflies are generally day-flyers and have small knobs at the tips of their antennae. Their method of linking the fore and hindwings is different from moths. Moths sometimes have a pectinate antenna, butterflies never do. Butterflies usually fold their wings upright above the body, wings in moths are folded flat over the body. However there are many exceptions to this and the other 'differences'.

Most Lepidoptera have a proboscis (haustellum or tongue). This is a tube under the head which is coiled up when not in use and extended when the insect is feeding. In the hawk moth, *Xanthopan*, (Sphingoidea) the proboscis fully uncoiled is 300 mm long and is used to feed on the nectar in tubular flowered orchids.

In the life history of the Lepidoptera there are four stages, egg, caterpillar, pupa (or chrysalis) and imago (adult insect; Fig. 72). The eggs are usually laid on or in plants but some species scatter their eggs in flight.

The caterpillar, which is also called a larva, grub, maggot or even a worm, hatches out from the egg and feeds voraciously. This is the stage that does the damage, the term 'moth-eaten' should really be 'caterpillar-eaten'. Caterpillars feed on many different parts of plants from flowers to the roots. They tunnel into the stems of trees, the caterpillar of the goat moth (Cossoidea) bores tunnels 15 mm or more in diameter in willow or ash, and others, living there for three or four years. Some caterpillars are predatory, feeding on other insects. These are usually aphids or scale insects (Homoptera) but one caterpillar, recently discovered, catches and eats flies. Caterpillars usually moult five times, growing larger after each moult. When fully grown the caterpillar looks for somewhere to pupate. If it is the caterpillar of a butterfly it forms a chrysalis without making a silken cocoon but most moths pupate inside a cocoon. Finally the pupa or chrysalis splits open and metamorphosis is complete with the emergence of the imago. When it first emerges it is a rather scruffy insect and has to rest while its wings expand and dry out.

There are four major divisions of the Lepidoptera, the Zeugloptera, Dacnonypha, Monotrysia and Ditrysia. These divisions contain a number of superfamilies into which the 130 families of Lepidoptera are grouped. The first families are often called microlepidoptera to contrast them with the (usually) larger macrolepidoptera. This division is often used for convenience but is not a good one.

The Zeugloptera has only one family, Micropterigidae. These are mostly small, dayflying moths (wingspan about 10 mm). They differ from all other Lepidoptera in having functional mandibles in the adult moth which they use to chew pollen from flowers. They do not have a proboscis. They have even been considered as belonging to a separate order from Lepidoptera but currently they are still considered as moths.

The Dacnonypha has one superfamily, Eriocranioidea, with three families. These are small moths and include the Eriocraniidae whose species are found in Europe and North America and which have legless leaf-mining caterpillars.

There are three superfamilies in the Monotrysia.

The Hepialoidea or swift moths have similar fore and hindwing venation. They are worldwide with large species in Africa and Australia, some with wingspans of 180 mm. Their caterpillars feed mostly on roots and at times can be pests.

The Nepticuloidea has two included families. These are some of the smallest Lepidoptera with wingspans of 3 mm. Their caterpillars are leaf miners, spending their lives between the upper and lower surface of one leaf.

The Incurvarioidea has four families. One of the incurvariids is the yucca moth (*Tegaticula*). The female gathers pollen from the yucca flower with special processes on her mouthparts. This pollen is pressed by the female moth onto the stigma of the flower, pollinating it. Then the moth lays her eggs in the ovary of the yucca where the seeds will grow. When the young caterpillars hatch they feed on the developing seeds, some of which are left untouched. In this way the caterpillars get their food and the plant is assured that some seeds will ripen.

The last division, Ditrysia, includes the vast majority of the moths and all the butterflies.

The Cossoidea superfamily, the goat moths, includes many species which are large, wingspan 240 mm. Their caterpillars are often wood borers.

There are many species in the Tortricoidea, bell or tortrix moths. These are divided between two families. The apple codlin moth (Tortricidae) is a common species whose caterpillar is the maggot commonly found in apples. Jumping beans at first sight appear to have nothing to do with moths but inside each bean is a caterpillar whose movements actually cause the bean to jump. When the caterpillar pupates the bean will no longer jump. Eventually the moth that emerges from the bean is rather similar to the related apple codlin moth.

Superfamily Tineoidea is a huge group of generally rather soberly coloured moths, some of them have caterpillars that feed on fur, skin and wool. These include the notorious clothes moths, of which there are several species. The caterpillars of bagworms, Psychidae, make cases of small pieces of stick round themselves. The wingless female psychid stays in this case, the males are winged and emerge from the cases to search for the females.

The Yponomeutoidea is another large superfamily of diverse species divided into six families. The clearwing moths, Sesiidae, lose most of the scales from the wings after emerging from the pupal case. This transparent wing, together with their yellow and black coloration complete the mimicry of wasps. Caterpillars of some yponomeutids (Yponomeutidae) are common in hedgerows where they form extensive and prominent silken webbing inside which they feed.

The Gelechioidea superfamily also contains large numbers of species, including the cotton boll worm, Gelechiidae, whose caterpillars damage cotton causing losses amounting to millions of dollars.

The Alucitoidea has three rather distinct families and includes the many-plumed moths, Alucitidae, whose fore and hindwings are each divided into six segments, or plumes.

The Castnioidea has only one family of large and colourful day-flying moths which are common in Central and South America with a few species elsewhere.

The Zygaenoidea is a strange group of seven families of moths. These include *Himantopterus* and the burnet moths (Zygaenidae). The latter are red and black moths commonly seen flying in meadows of Europe and North Africa in the daytime. Many zygaenids are brightly coloured, iridescent, day-flying moths. The Limacodidae and Megalopygidae are moths with slug-like caterpillars whose hairs can sting severely if touched.

There are five families of moths in the superfamily Pyraloidea. In the family Pyralidae there are many species which are important pests of field crops and stored food. Species of flour moths, *Ephestia*, are common pests of flour in mills, shops and warehouses. The corn borer, *Ostrinia*, is a problem in maize growing areas. One pyralid moth, *Acentria*, not only has aquatic caterpillars but the wingless female moth swims under water to lay her eggs.

The Pterophoroidea superfamily contains the plume moths, delicate, long-legged moths which hold their rolled wings at right angles to the body when at rest and look like the letter T. Caterpillars of plume moths are small spiny creatures. The caterpillar of one plume moth, *Buckleria*, feeds on the leaves of the insect-eating plant, sundew (*Drosera*).

The next two superfamilies (Papilionoidea, Hesperioidea) contain all the butterflies. Most butterflies are insects of warm summer days, flying in the sunshine, but a few species fly in the evening and into the night.

The Hesperioidea is made up of two families of butterflies. The Hesperiidae contains the skippers, awls or cloudy wings. Compared with other butterflies they are rather soberly coloured. They also differ from other butterflies in the shape of the antennae which are angled at the tip and, although thickened like all butterflies at the tip, taper to a point. Flight in the skippers is rapid and dashing, hence their name. Related to skippers are the giant skippers, Megathymidae, of America. Their caterpillars burrow into the stems of cacti, unlike most butterfly caterpillars which feed exposed on the plant.

The Papilionoidea contains all the remaining butterfly families. The Swallowtail, Papilionidae, is one of the well-known families. Many of the exotic papilionids are used in decorative wall plaques. Not all papilionids have tails on the hindwings. The birdwing butterflies, *Ornithoptera*, include some of the large, beautiful, and for the dealers, most valuable, butterflies. Although they are now protected by law, they still appear in dealers' catalogues. Among the white, sulphurs and yellows, Pieridae, are some of the few species of butterflies that are actually pests. The Small White butterfly is a widespread pest of cabbages and has been introduced accidentally into many countries. While most pierid butterflies are white or yellow an exception is the almost uniformly orange-red Albatross butterfly (*Appias*). The Clouded Yellow butterfly is one of the many migrant pierids. The yellow coloured Brimstone butterfly of Europe, appearing in early spring, was called a butter-coloured fly, later contracted to butterfly. The Nymphalidae or brush-footed butterflies are common and generally large, powerful flying, butterflies. Their name comes from the brush of scales on the reduced forelegs of the adult. Some of the species are well known like the Painted Lady, Red Admiral and tortoiseshell butterflies.

The *Morpho* butterflies of South America are large, brilliantly iridescent blue butterflies which are frequently used in jewellery or sold for decorative purposes. The Owl butterfly (*Caligo*) gets its name from the huge eyes on the underside of the hindwings. Many nymphalids are well known migrants. The Painted Lady (*Cynthia*) moves north as spring progresses northwards in Europe. The Monarch butterfly of North America flies from Central America across the United States to Canada in spectacular numbers, a few even reaching Europe. The satyrid butterflies, the browns, include a number of dusk-flying species like the widespread Twilight Brown, common from Africa through India to Australia. The Lycaenidae, blues, hairstreaks and copper butterflies have mostly iridescent colours on the upper surface with complicated patterns on the underside of the wing. They include the Large Blue butterfly whose caterpillars live in ants' nests. The Nemeobiidae or metalmark butterflies are related to the blues and most have fantastic iridescent colours. They occur mostly in America.

All the remaining superfamilies are moths. The Geometroidea is divided into seven large families. Their caterpillars usually lack the four middle pairs of abdominal legs and move by arching their backs, alternately extending and looping the body as they progress. Their odd movement has given them many names among which looper, earth measurers and inchworms are the commonest. While most species are nocturnal there are a few colourful day-flying species. Geometrids are common moths, often seen fluttering round lighted windows and even in mid-winter on milder evenings the aptly named winter moth may be seen.

There are two families in the Calliduloidea which are related to the geometrids. They include colourful day-flying species which, when at rest, hold their wings above the body like butterflies.

The superfamily Bombycoidea is a complex group of thirteen families of moths. These include the Saturnidae which are mostly large, well-patterned species like the Atlas Moth (*Attacus*) which is one of the largest Lepidoptera. *Bombyx mori*, Bombycidae, is the silk moth of commerce. Their caterpillars, better known as silkworms, feed on mulberry and spin their silk for their cocoon. Unravelling this silk and spinning several strands together produces the commercial silk thread.

The Sphingoidea superfamily contains hawk moths or hornworms, mostly large species with rapid flight. Their large caterpillars have a horn on the tip of the abdomen, but, although they look fierce, they are harmless. The migratory Hummingbird Hawk Moth, which hovers in front of flowers like the humming birds themselves, and the Death's Head Hawk Moth, are two of the better known species.

The Notodontoidea has three families of moths. They include the prominents and puss moths. The caterpillars of the puss moth have two tails and a remarkable pattern and look quite alarming when disturbed, but are harmless. The caterpillars of the Processionary Moth (*Thaumetopoea processionea*) move in long columns, head to tail, of thousands of caterpillars moving from one area to another. These columns of marching caterpillars can devastate plantations, ruining acres of trees.

The Noctuoidea superfamily includes seven families as diverse as the colourful tiger moths, Arctiidae, and the rather dull, but economically important owlet or noctuid moths, Noctuidae. The tiger moths are mostly day-flying and their hairy caterpillars, rapidly moving in rather a sinuous way, are called woolly bears. The underwing moths, Noctuidae, are readily attracted to light and are the rather fat-bodied, fast-flying species. When they settle they frequently hold their wings roof-like over their backs. Noctuids are common moths and many are serious pests of crops. These include the turnip and cabbage moths and many species whose caterpillars bore into stems, damaging cereal crops. Noctuid caterpillars often attack plants at ground level and from the damage they cause are called cutworms. Although most noctuids have rather drab-coloured forewings some have brightly coloured hindwings. Many noctuids are migratory, in Australia the Bogong Moth may appear in millions in Canberra on its annual migration.

Order Hymenoptera

This is a huge group of insects with over 70 000 species. These include the smallest insects, fairy flies (Mymaridae) only 0.25 mm long but some Hymenoptera are up to 5 cm long. Hymenoptera have two pairs of transparent wings with relatively few veins on them. They include some well-known insects like bees, wasps and ants but also many less familiar species like the tiny parasitic wasps. The size of these small wasps belies the effect they may have on the environment of man. These minute insects pass their whole life cycle inside the larva or egg of another insect. Their importance in destroying many insect pests is immense.

The mouthparts of Hymenoptera are generally for biting but are often modified for sucking. The fore and hindwings are usually linked together by a row of hooks and their flight in the larger species is powerful and noisy.

The female abdomen has an ovipositor for egg-laying and in many species this is modified for piercing and sawing or stinging. The larvae are generally legless (except sawflies) and they have a pupal stage, emerging after a complete metamorphosis. Many live in colonies like ants and bees. Many Hymenoptera use their sting to paralyse their prey in which they then lay their eggs. Their larvae can thus develop in a living but totally immobilized host.

Fig. 75 Order
Hymenoptera – (a)
ichneumon wasp
(b) bumble bee
(c) ant

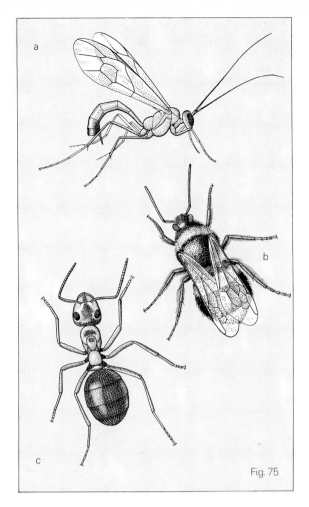

Fig. 75

In many smaller species males are unknown and eggs are produced parthenogenetically. One characteristic of most Hymenoptera is the constriction of the body, the wasp-waist. This is between the first abdominal segment (which is fused to the back of the thorax) and the rest of the abdomen. This narrow waist probably enables the rest of the abdomen to be flexed in any direction, helping oviposition or stinging.

The mouthparts of bees are modified to form a proboscis while in wasps, although the jaws are powerful, the adult feeds more by lapping up its food. The wasp jaws are used for biting and tearing food which the wasp collects for its larvae.

Classification of the Hymenoptera is complex but two major divisions are made, the suborders Symphyta and the Apocrita.

The Symphyta or sawflies are Hymenoptera which lack the wasp-waist. Their larvae are plant feeders and have legs on the abdominal segments, looking rather like caterpillars of Lepidoptera, but sawfly caterpillars generally have legs on each abdominal segment whereas caterpillars usually have four or fewer pairs (not including the last pair or claspers). There are five superfamilies of the Symphyta.

The Xyeloidea members vary in size up to 25 mm long. In the Xyelidae the females have a long ovipositor and the caterpillars, which feed on pine cones, have legs on all the abdominal segments. The Pamphilidae lack abdominal feet in the larvae and include *Neurotema*, a common web-spinning sawfly which is a pest of fruit trees in Europe.

The Siricoidea contains wood wasps or horntails which are large yellow and black insects, 40 mm long and look like giant wasps, but without the waist. Their larvae burrow into wood. Although rather alarming and wasp-like they cannot sting.

The Orussoidea has species whose larvae are ectoparasites on wood-boring beetles.

The Cephoidea includes a number of agricultural pests, including the wheat stem sawfly whose larvae tunnel in the stem.

Tenthredinoidea is the largest sawfly superfamily and includes both agricultural, horticultural and forestry pests. The pine sawfly (*Diprion*) is a serious pest in Europe. Some sawflies cause gall formation on the plants they attack. Currant bushes are often damaged by a leaf-eating sawfly (*Nematus*).

Suborder Apocrita is a vast group, all wasp-waisted. Thirteen superfamilies are considered here, the majority of the first ones are parasitic wasps, often known collectively as Parasitica. The larvae of these minute insects live internally in eggs or larvae of other insects.

The Trigonaloidea includes species whose larvae parasitize sawflies. Many species are polyembryonic, producing many larvae from one egg.

The Ichneumonoidea contains the ichneumon flies which are parasites. Some 1600 species are known and many are parasitic or hyperparasitic on Lepidoptera. The family Aphiidae has species which are parasites on aphids. The larvae develop in the body of the aphid which they eventually kill. Braconidae contains usually small species with parasitic larvae although a few are large and colourful, up to 190 mm long, but of this, 175 mm is the long slender ovipositor. *Apanteles* is a small braconid often seen when its bright yellow cocoons are found arranged round the dead body of a caterpillar. The larvae develop in the caterpillar, emerging to pupate. The Ichneumonidae includes *Rhyssa*, which parasitizes the wood wasp, *Sirex*. The female has a long ovipositor and drills down through the wood to lay her egg on the hidden *Sirex* larva. Ichneumons even swim under water to parasitize the aquatic larvae of caddis flies.

The Evanioidea superfamily of ensign wasps, are mostly parasites of cockroaches but a few species parasitize solitary bees. The abdomen of the ensign wasp appears to rise high out of the back of the thorax.

The Cynipoidea members are mostly very small, inconspicuously coloured insects. They lack the black patch, pterostigma, near the apex of the forewing. Cynipids are often gall makers and one species forms the spangle gall on the leaves of oak, a flattened, roundish structure on the underside in autumn. This species, like many other cynipids, has an alternation of generations. The adults emerging from these flat galls after the winter are all females which lay their eggs on the young oak shoots. The galls produced here are round and soft and from these

231

the summer generation emerges, looking different from the spring brood. Gall wasps produce the familiar oak-apples on oak trees and another small wasp, *Diplolepis*, produces the galls on roses which appear as a mass of straggly red fibres, the robins' pincushion gall. The Figitidae has species which are parasitic on dipterous larvae. The Ibaliidae has brightly coloured species which have an ovipositor about 22 mm long, this they conceal coiled up in an abdomen only 8 mm long.

The Chalcidoidea superfamily has many species which are parasitic or hyperparasitic on other insects and very few are more than 1–2 mm in length although there are a few larger species. They are of great economic importance destroying many insect pests. Most chalcids have only one vein visible in the forewing and all have short geniculate (elbowed) antennae and most lack the pterostigma. A few species have larvae which are plant feeders but the vast majority are parasitic. They include the Agaontidae or fig wasps which have a close association with the pollination of figs. Other families include the Torymidae, parasitic in the larval stages of other insects or gall makers and the Chalcidae, parasites on the larvae and pupae of the Lepidoptera. The Eurytomidae members are very diverse and include gall makers and pests of cereals, e.g. *Harmolita*, the wheat straw-worm. Perilampidae is a small group of wasps with a curious high arched thorax and small triangular abdomens. They are often hyperparasites of Lepidoptera. The Pteromalidae is the largest family of chalcid wasps, parasitizing insects. Some are hyperparasites of Lepidopterous larvae. Encyrtidae parasitize the eggs, larvae and pupae of various insects. They have antennae which are frequently thick at the base and apex, giving a slightly dumb-bell shape. The Eulophidae family contains very small species, some parasitizing scale insects. Among the numerous Tetrastichinae one species parasitizes the eggs of leafhoppers. When its parasitic larva has consumed the contents of the host egg it breaks out, burrowing through the stem to search for other eggs, thus it begins life as a parasite while ending up as a predator before pupating in the stem. The minute members of Trichogrammatidae are all egg parasites, their whole life cycle takes place inside the egg of another insect. The Mymaridae, fairy flies, have their wings reduced to thin straps which are fringed with long hairs. They include the smallest known insects.

The Proctotrupoidea superfamily has a slightly protruding ovipositor, most species parasitize the larvae of Diptera or Coleoptera. Pelecinidae is an American family which has very long ovipositors, making the whole insect some 50–60 mm long.

The Bethyloidea members often have wingless females and most have parasitic larvae. They are small black wasps, useful parasites on crop pests. The Dryiinidae family contains peculiar wasps, parasitic on Homoptera. The female has the forelegs modified to form pincers which are used to hold her prey while the eggs are laid. Their developing larvae, which are inside the host insect, form a bubble on the side of their host which gets larger and becomes very conspicuous. The insect parasitized by a dryiinid cannot reproduce.

The Chrysididae or cuckoo wasps are beautifully coloured, often with a metallic sheen. They lay their eggs in the nests of bees and other Hymenoptera where their larvae develop parasitically. They are well adapted to protect themselves against the surprise return of the bee to its nest. The cuckoo wasp rolls itself into a tight ball and feigns death. The limbs of the wasp fit into grooves in the body and the whole insect becomes an armoured ball. Frequently the bee will push this out of the nest, when the wasp quickly unrolls and flies away.

The Scolioidea are mainly tropical. The female locates beetle larvae in their underground burrows, stings them and then lays her egg in the living, but immobilized beetle larva. The Typhiidae family also attacks beetle larvae but go for even the larvae of tiger beetles, which are fierce predators in their own rights. The wasp circles the tiger beetle larva, moving in quickly to sting it before laying her egg. The Mutillidae are yellow and black or red and black wasps with fine hairs on their bodies from which they get their name, velvet ants. The wingless female is particularly ant-like as she runs about. They have a vicious sting if handled incautiously.

The ants, superfamily Formicoidea, contain only one family, the Formicidae. Ants range in size from 1 mm–4 cm. They have one or two anterior segments of the abdomen constricted into a stalk, the pedicel. Some have a sting but the more specialized ants have developed other chemical means of defence. All ants are social insects and most have different castes with workers, soldiers and reproductive castes. They have angled antennae and their social life and habits are very well developed. They form colonies which range in size from a few individuals to over a million inhabitants. The division of labour may be extreme but the highly organized social behaviour keeps the colony running. Many other insects have taken to living in ants' nests, some actually feed on the ant larvae, others just scavenge, cleaning up the nest. Ants are able to navigate using the direction of the sun and also by following chemical trails. Many ants are useful in keeping down the numbers of other insects and in parts of Europe the nests of the red wood ant (*Formica*) are protected by law.

There are about 14 000 species of ants, they are divided into several subfamilies. Some ants are predatory, some use the workers of another species as slaves to feed their larvae while others even grow their own food. Their biology is one of the most amazing in the insect world. Ponerinae contain the more primitive species with one-segmented pedicels and they retain a sting. They make fairly simple nests and include the bulldog ants which may be 25 mm long and have a vicious sting. The Dorylinae subfamily, army or driver ants are predominantly tropical. These ants move in vast columns. All living things move when the column of driver ants approaches, or risk being torn to pieces. Sometimes they are useful in clearing insect pests out of houses as they march through, but the humans have to move out until the ants leave. In many army ants the workers are blind while the soldiers have good eyesight, defending the column with their powerful jaws, which easily penetrate human skin. The flying males of the army ants are large with fat brown bodies. They are common in the tropics where they are known by the descriptive name of sausage flies. There are several other subfamilies of migratory ants. The Myrmycinae members have a two-segmented pedicel and often retain a sting. Many are tree dwellers, building their nests there and, if you are unlucky enough to shake some onto you, you quickly understand one of the Swahili names – 'maji moto', hot water! The harvester ants gather seeds or fungal spores and plant the latter in specially prepared beds. Dolichoderinae are stingless ants that defend themselves by producing an evil-smelling chemical. They have a one-segmented pedicel and include the argentine ant, *Iridomyrmex*, which has become a pest in many countries. The Formicinae includes the red or wood ants (*Formica rufa*). The slave-making ants, *Polyergus*, of the Amazon, whose jaws are useless for feeding and are only used for fighting, capture the pupae of other species, killing off their parents. These pupae, when they hatch then forage for their new masters. The genus *Lasius* includes species which collect the honeydew produced by aphids. The Oecophyllini includes ants which sew leaves together to make nests, using their larvae, which produce silk, for the purpose. Honeypot ants, such as *Myrmecocystus*, live in the desert, feeding a few workers in the colony until their abdomens become distorted with the food. These swollen ants then act as a living food-store for the rest of the colony, regurgitating the food when needed. Studies of ant colonies have revealed some amazing stories and have given rise to a whole new branch of biology, sociobiology.

Leaving the ants, the superfamily Pompiloidea contains wasps which are predators of spiders. The female catches and stings the spider to immobilize it. She lays her egg in the paralysed, but living spider which is then literally eaten alive by the larva. Most pompilid wasps have long legs and prey on even the dreaded Tarantula spider.

The Sphecoidea or digger wasps are solitary wasps and include *Ammophila*, the sand wasp, which is predatory on other insects. Sand wasps seek out caterpillars which they sting and then bring back to their nest where the wasp egg is laid on the paralysed caterpillar. There are several groups of solitary wasps, all with strange life histories.

The Vespoidea superfamily includes the true wasps and hornets and are some of the best-known insects. Some species are social, others solitary in habit. Potter wasps make small clay urns which act as nurseries for the young. The subfamily Vespinae contains the common wasps and hornets, so characteristically coloured black and yellow. The Hornet (*Vespa crabo*) has a powerful sting and causes severe pain to the unfortunate victim but is only rarely fatal. Wasps make their nests with wood which they chew, mixing it with their saliva. This forms a papery but strong nest. Generally they make hexagonal-shaped cells in which they rear their young. Their social life is an annual affair and they do not swarm like the honey bees. The queen wasp is larger than the workers who feed their young on insects or bits of dead animals. Wasps do a lot of good in killing off insect pests but they are themselves problems for fruit growers.

The Apoidea superfamily contains the bees, of which some 2000 species are known. Their heads have a well-developed tongue which is used to feed on nectar and the young are fed on a similar diet. The bee has been used by man as a source of honey from the earliest times. The special characters of the Apoidea, other than typical hymenopterous characters, are the broad, flattened, first tarsal segment of the hindleg. This is covered with a dense coat of hairs which scrape off the pollen into the pollen basket on the tibia. The pollen basket is used for carrying the pollen, collected at flowers, to the nest. There are solitary as well as social bees. The Halictidae is a family with both social and solitary species. The Megachilidae family contains leaf-cutter bees also known as mason bees. They cut neat pieces out of leaves which are then carried to their nests. There are also species in this family which live parasitically in the nests of other leaf-cutter bees. Carpenter bees, Xylocopidae, are large bees which tunnel into wood. They lay their eggs in these tunnels, which may be up to 30 cm long. The larvae feed on pollen which the bee has stored for them in the tunnel. Mining bees, Andrenidae, dig short tunnels in the ground where they store pollen and honey for their larvae. The family Apidae includes the honey bees, bumble bees and stingless bees, which make brood cells for the young of wax (the honeycombs) and rear the young in these cells. They are important, apart from the honey they make, because together with many other insects they act as pollinators of flowers and are vital in the fruit orchards. Honey bees include a number of species but the common or Hive Bee (*Apis mellifera*) has been taken all over the world. The life of the hive is a marvel of social organization. Many bees have developed parasitic habits, using other bees' nests as shelter and their workers to rear the young of the parasitic bee. The African Honey Bee (*Apis mellifera adansoni*) has a severe sting which can cause death to livestock and humans. Since being introduced into South America it has spread and caused several deaths. Although stingless, some *Melipona* bees can bite while others have corrosive secretions which can burn the skin. In spite of this the Hymenoptera on balance is one of the groups of insects most useful to man.

AIDS TO INSECT CLASSIFICATION

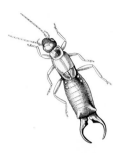

There is still controversy over the classification of the major groups of arthropods, but the scheme below is now widely followed. Since nomenclature is so complex, a specimen order (Coleoptera – Beetles) is classified to assist the reader to identify names mentioned in the book. The suffixes common to superfamily, family and subfamily names are italicized in this table. The system of naming in universal use is known as the binomial system, that is, each kind of animal is referred to by two names. The first, always spelled with an initial capital, is the name of the genus – generic name. The second is the name of the species – specific name. These names are printed in italics.

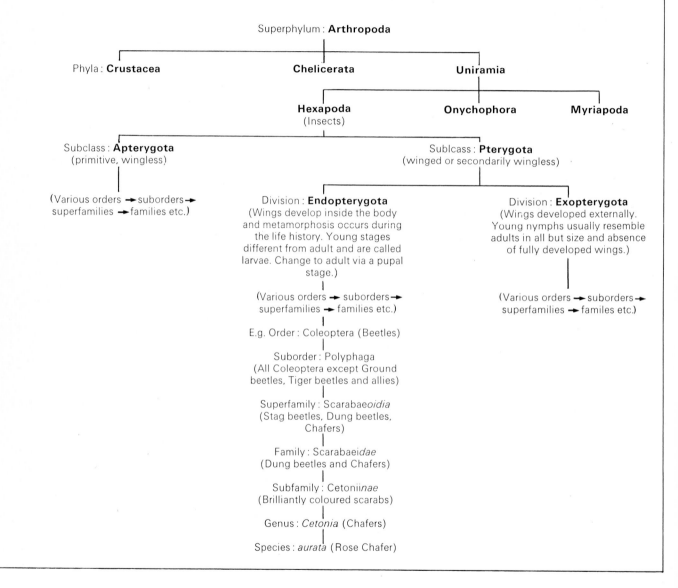

Superphylum: **Arthropoda**

Phyla: **Crustacea**   **Chelicerata**   **Uniramia**

Hexapoda
(Insects)   **Onychophora**   **Myriapoda**

Subclass: **Apterygota**
(primitive, wingless)

Sublcass: **Pterygota**
(winged or secondarily wingless)

(Various orders → suborders →
superfamilies → families etc.)

Division: **Endopterygota**
(Wings develop inside the body
and metamorphosis occurs during
the life history. Young stages
different from adult and are called
larvae. Change to adult via a pupal
stage.)

Division: **Exopterygota**
(Wings developed externally.
Young nymphs usually resemble
adults in all but size and absence
of fully developed wings.)

(Various orders → suborders →
superfamilies → families etc.)

(Various orders → suborders →
superfamilies → familes etc.)

E.g. Order: Coleoptera (Beetles)

Suborder: Polyphaga
(All Coleoptera except Ground
beetles, Tiger beetles and allies)

Superfamily: Scarabaeo*idia*
(Stag beetles, Dung beetles,
Chafers)

Family: Scarabae*idae*
(Dung beetles and Chafers)

Subfamily: Cetoni*inae*
(Brilliantly coloured scarabs)

Genus: *Cetonia* (Chafers)

Species: *aurata* (Rose Chafer)

Bibliography

Blaney, W. M *How Insects Live* 1976, Elsevier-Phaidon, Oxford

Brohmer, P. (ed.) *Fauna von Deutschland* 1971, Quelle and Meyer, Heidelberg

Busvine, J. R. *Insects and Hygiene* 1966 (2nd ed.), Methuen and Co. Ltd., London

Cain, R. F. *Animal Species and their Evolution* 1971 (3rd ed.), Hutchinson, London

Callahan, P. S. *The Evolution of Insects* 1972, Holliday House, New York

Chapman, R. F. *The Insects : structure and function* 1969, English Universities Press, London

Chauvin, R. *The World of an Insect* (translated by Oldroyd, H.) 1962, Weidenfield and Nicholson, London

Chinery, M. *A Field Guide to the Insects of Britain and Europe* 1973, Collins, London

C.S.I.R.O. *The Insects of Australia* 1970, Melbourne University Press

Dobzhansky, T. *Genetics and the Origin of Species* 1951 (3rd ed.), Columbia University Press

Evans, H. E. *Life on a Little-known Planet* 1968, Dutton and Co., New York

Farb, P. *The Insects* 1975 (U.K. ed.), Time-Life Books, Virginia

Fogden, M. and Fogden, P. *Animals and their Colours* 1974, Peter Lowe, London

Free, J. B. and Butler, C. G. *Bumblebees* 1959, (New Naturalist), Collins, London

Friese, G. *Insekten* 1970, Veb. Bibliographisches Institut, Leipzig

Graf, J. *Animal Life of Europe* 1968, Warne, London

Gilmour, D. *The Metabolism of Insects* 1965, Oliver and Boyd, Edinburgh

Grzimek, B. (ed.) *Animal Encyclopedia* Vol. 2. *Insects* 1975, van Nostrand Reinhold, Berks.

Hickin, N. E. *Household Insect Pests* 1974, Associated Business Programmes, London

Imms, A. D. *A General Textbook of Entomology* 1957, (9th ed. revised Richards, O. W. and Davies, R. G.), Methuen, London

—— *Insect Natural History* (3rd ed.) 1971, Collins, London

Klots, A. B. and Klots, E. B. *Living Insects of the World* 1959, Hamish Hamilton, London

Lyneborg, L. *Beetles in Colour* 1976, Blandford, London

Mayr, E. *Animal Species and Evolution* 1963, Harvard University Press

—— *Populations, Species and Evolution* 1970, Harvard University Press

Oldroyd, H. *The Natural History of Flies* 1964, Weidenfield and Nicholson, London

—— *Elements of Entomology* 1968, Weidenfield and Nicholson, London

Proctor, M. and Yeo, P. *The Pollination of Flowers* 1973, Collins, London

von Frisch, K. *Animal Architecture* 1975, Hutchinson, London

Watson, A. and Whalley, P. *The Dictionary of Butterflies and Moths in Color* 1975, McGraw-Hill, Berks.

Whalley, P. *Hamlyn Nature Guide : Butterflies* 1979, Hamlyn, London

Wickler, W. *Mimicry in Plants and Animals* (translated by Martin, R. D.) 1968, Weidenfield and Nicholson, London

Wigglesworth, V. B *The Life of Insects* 1964, Weidenfield and Nicholson, London

—— *The Principles of Insect Physiology* (10th ed.) 1977, Methuen, London

Acknowledgements

Photographs
Aquilla–Duncan I. McEwan 54, 55, 122, 124 bottom; Aquila–G. W. Ward 29 top, 98, 158 top, 183; Aquila –A. Wharton 155; A. Beaumont, Lowestoft 95, 102, 104–105, 179 bottom, 202; Sdeuard Bisseröt, Bournemouth 29 bottom, 31, 32; The British Museum (Natural History), London 17; Colin G. Butler, St. Austell 195; Kevin Carlson, Wroxham 116–117; Michael Chinery, Sudbury 158 bottom; James Cross, Weybridge 22, 108 bottom, 111; Adrian Davies, Wallington 25, 26 top, 53 top, 176–177; John B. Free, Harpenden 21, 23, 99 bottom, 113, 175 bottom, 196; Hamlyn Group Picture Library 16; Howard Lacey, Croydon 181, 205; Audley Money-Kyrle, London 22 bottom, 134, 166, 179 top: Gill Montalverne, Lisbon 79, 201 bottom; The Natural History Photographic Agency– A. Bannister front endpaper, title spread, 8, 26 bottom, 27, 30, 65, 86, 109, 112, 191, 201, front jacket; The Natural History Photographic Agency– Ivan Polunin 106–107; The Natural History Photographic Agency–N. A. Callow 68, 175 top; The Natural History Photographic Agency–J. H.

Carmichael Jr. 47 bottom, 76; The Natural History Photographic Agency–S. Dalton 24, 49 top, 49 bottom, 50–51, 53 bottom, 59, 60–61, 63, 70, 115, 120, 136, 138–139, 143, 162–163, 174, 186, 194, 204, back jacket; The Natural History Photographic Agency–F. Greenaway 71; The Natural History Photographic Agency–Brian Hawkes 185; The Natural History Photographic Agency–G. E. Hyde 34–35, 36–37, 88–89, 90 bottom, 99 top, 145, 149, 159, 160, 186–187, 203; The Natural History Photographic Agency–Ken Preston-Mafham 28, 33, 62, 69, 90 top, 97 top, 97 bottom, 101, 110, 124 top, 125, 126, 127, 128, 135, 140, 146, 151, 154, 164, 165, 173 top; The Natural History Photographic Agency–M. W. F. Tweedie 13, 19 top, 19 bottom, 42; Oxford Scientific Films, Long Hanborough 18, 47 top, 56, 57, 77, 83, 84–85, 85, 91, 93, 96, 103, 108, 114, 129, 133, 148, 153, 167, 168, 170–171, 173, 178, 188–189, 197, 198 top, 198 bottom, 199; Brian Selman, Newcastle-upon-Tyne 48; Ben Southgate, Ascot 187, 188 top; Peter Stiles, London 184; Gunter Ziesler, Munich back end paper, jacket front flap, jacket back flap.

Index